★

"Fever?" Skidmore stared down at the corpse. "What the hell is it?"

"That's not the guy." I took a step away.

"Not the guy?"

"Those are his clothes—I mean, that coat is what the man was wearing last night, and those construction boots, too. This guy even looks a little like him, but this is not the man who was in my kitchen last night."

Skid blinked.

"Maybe it's the light," Melissa offered. "Plus, a man looks a lot different when he's dead."

I was staring down at the body, trying to make my eyes change their mind, to admit that the dead man on the cold ground was the same thing as the live man in my warm kitchen. I was almost swayed, when the second deputy, a kid named Crawdad Pritchett—champion fiddler at age seven, deputy by age nineteen—called out.

"Yonder comes Ms. Jackson."

☆

PHILLIP DePOY

THE
DRIFTER'S
WHEEL

WORLDWIDE®

TORONTO • NEW YORK • LONDON
AMSTERDAM • PARIS • SYDNEY • HAMBURG
STOCKHOLM • ATHENS • TOKYO • MILAN
MADRID • WARSAW • BUDAPEST • AUCKLAND

Recycling programs
for this product may
not exist in your area.

THE DRIFTER'S WHEEL

A Worldwide Mystery/June 2009

First published by St. Martin's Press, LLC.

ISBN-13: 978-0-373-26674-6

I am a traveling creature/traveling through this land,
today I am a warning/to woman and to man.
—Sacred Harp hymn, nineteenth century

History is an angel being blown backward
into the future.
—Laurie Anderson

ONE

"THE GUN EXPLODED, blood erupted, and Jacob lay dying on the brothel floor." My visitor coughed. "There's the way to start a story. None of this 'hair was flaxen by candlelight' or 'night as black as an empty grave.' Start with the murder. Let the rest of it unfold, like history. Sometimes history turns on that little: a single moment, a single bullet."

"Go on." I glanced at my Wollensak tape recorder, made certain that it was running smoothly—I'd just turned it on, though he'd been talking for a while. I didn't want to let anything else go unrecorded. His story was too strange to miss another second.

"It happened in the autumn of the year, when murder feels at home, because so many other things are dying." More coughing. "The murderer spat as they led him away from the body. I'll tell you who he was in a minute, the murderer. The victim, Jacob, was nearly sixty, and would not see the coming morning. He had just made love with a prostitute from Buenos Aires. As a result of that union, quite unexpectedly, a baby would be born. Jacob and the woman had slept in bed for an hour or so, and then come downstairs to practice a new dance the prostitute had brought from Buenos Aires: the Tango. It was late, the house was quiet, they had no music."

His coat was army surplus, double breasted, olive green, button epaulets at the shoulder. At least a size too large, it grazed the floor when he walked. He'd most likely purchased it for next to nothing—or maybe it had been donated to a shelter where he'd found it. Aside from the coat, there was nothing to tell me who or what he was except the remarkable face. Not a wrinkle or a pore, it could have been a boy's face, except for the eyes, which belonged to a man who was at least two hundred years old.

I had no idea what he was doing in my house. I'd come home in the early evening from Eden Cemetery. It was mid-October and the leaves were blazing; the maple and oak trees around the graveyard looked like fire from a distance. If you sat under them, in that fine and private place, you could hear the burning away of the old year, smell the smoke of smoldering leaves. It had been a useful occupation for me. I was all too ready to set flame to the old year, anticipating the clean white snow that might come in a month or two. Some others in my little town seemed to find it odd that I would go to a cemetery for repose, but I spent so much of my time among the dead, it didn't seem the least bit out of place to me.

When I'd arrived home, there he had been: a tattered rag on a stick, black hair covering his eyes, asleep on my front porch. If he had been anyone from Blue Mountain he would have known the front door wasn't locked, and he might have been asleep on the sofa. I always kept the front room perfectly cleaned, in the great Southern tradition, for unexpected company.

He'd come awake when my truck pulled up to the house, and sat rubbing his eyes until I put my foot on the steps. Then, without a word of introduction or explanation, he'd simply started talking. He'd followed me in through the living room and into the kitchen. All the rooms downstairs were, in fact, one big room. Bronzed oak beams framed the place. A larger than normal galley kitchen lay to the right as you came in the front door. A cast-iron stove had been set into the stone hearth to the left by a large picture window. Quilts on the walls suggested church windows; the blond wooden staircase in the far corner led up to the bedrooms.

Obviously someone had told the man that I collected stories—maybe he even thought he could get money or a meal out of me. He could have used both.

"Where was this again?" I was taking notes while I listened. It's never enough just to tape-record a folk informant. I wanted to describe his demeanor as he was telling me his rambling tale.

"Madam Briscoe's House in Chicago, long after the Civil War. Damn, Fever, keep up! Is that what you said your name was? Fever? Odd name for a man."

In fact I had not told him my name. I only nodded.

He mumbled something incoherent, then, "Where was I?"

"Dancing the Tango."

"That night the city slept under the merest sliver of moon." He picked up the story as if he'd never faltered. "It was a splinter of light stuck in the black sky. The house was clean, the floors softened by Persian rugs, thick pillows strewn casually in the corners. The front door was red, but the rest of the edifice was dove white. Aside from the parlor and a modest kitchen, the downstairs was occupied primarily by the madam. Her rooms and office took up most of the ground floor. On the second, third, and fourth floors were only bedrooms. Each had been painted a slightly different color; other than that they were exactly the same: a frame bed, a thick rug, clean sheets, dark curtains, a large mirror, a table with a basin and pitcher, a small chifforobe, and a photograph of Lincoln."

His eyes were darting everywhere, as if he were sizing up the house. It made me nervous. Maybe he had plans to try something like a robbery. He wouldn't have been much of a match for a man my size. In fact, he was in more danger than I was. When I'm nervous, and a little frightened, I'm liable to strike first.

The kitchen itself remained calm, as it always did. The exposed rafters were hung with spices recently pulled from the garden: bundles of rosemary and tarragon; braids of bay. The light was buttery; the air was pleasantly warm, touched with a hint of cinnamon. The old chrome and Formica table where we sat was mirror clean, and the counters were clear of clutter. Nothing in that room suggested a visitor that was dangerous, but I felt a bit—a trickle—of adrenaline pumping at the back of my neck.

"Could you describe the house more?" I could hear that my voice sounded tense.

"The front porch was imposing; the door was always locked.

Any lucky entrant immediately faced a gliding dark-wood staircase daring the visitor to ascend. To the left was the parlor, draped in burgundy, lit by a single twelve-candle chandelier which the madam said was made of French crystal. To the right was a more businesslike office where appointments were made. No one was admitted to the house without advance notice, prior recommendation, and a fee. Or a gun."

He paused, looking around my kitchen. It was probably two in the morning by then. He seemed, for a moment, not to know where he was.

"Do you want some more espresso?" I blinked at his empty cup.

"Oh, yes," he said instantly, "I'd imagine I would. Great stuff. Great taste—considering we're not in Paris, and this isn't the right century."

I stood, refusing once again to take the bait. Twice before he'd made odd references to the current century, obviously expecting me to ask for an explanation. But I knew from dozens of experiences with men like this one—and a lifetime of collecting folk information—that some comments are tests. A good way to stop the flow of strange stories or interesting facts would have been to address any one of his pointed references to time. So: "Think I'll have a bit more myself." I scooped up my own cup and turned to the espresso machine on the counter.

Outside, the night birds filled up the dark, wood doves made the air kinder, and a nearly full moon silvered every leaf and pine needle.

When I turned back around, there was a gun on my kitchen table.

The stranger was sitting exactly as he had been, eyes a bit unfocused, head to one side. The only thing different was the pistol in his hand—a dandy antique or a replica, I couldn't tell which. His right hand was on top of the handle, but the gun was flat on the table. He seemed not to notice it.

It was the only thing I could see.

"The Tango, you may know, was a scandal because it was so lascivious." His tone had shifted again to a somewhat more scholarly diction. "Two people danced too closely. Public opinion declared it a disgrace to tempt the baser self with such an open display. The Tango, we were told, would be the ruination of Western civilization. Nevertheless, at the beginning of the twentieth century, the Tango swept Europe off its big…European feet. In Paris this public passion was exhibited at the Palais des Glaces in 1913, where some couple danced sixty-two straight Tangos and won first prize. But even in that most liberal of cities the dance was seen to be a nearly criminal act, lewd and perilous. Discépolo's famous quote in *Les Temps Modernes* attempted to explain this in terms of a philosophy. 'The twentieth century is a trash heap. No one can deny it. We are living in a brothel.' Do you know Discépolo? He was called the Tango philosopher. And he was an idiot. Anyone with a more historical eye could have seen the Tango was simply the newest assertion of the ancient movements which engendered our species. The activity of copulation. In the beginning the world was without form, and a vast silence lay upon the deep. All was one. That ended when the *One* became *Two*. From two came many, through a popular combination of carnal begetting and cellular mitosis. The Tango was an echo of the begetting. Mitosis, where a single cell spontaneously divides, is harder to understand and involves the theory of biogenesis."

He paused just long enough to give me the eye—again daring me to call him insane, which, I assumed, many before me had done. The gun appeared to have been well used.

I have no idea why my choice of action consisted primarily of academic one-upsmanship. Maybe I thought that if he realized I was a man of letters, he would resist the urge to do something rash. In truth, it had been a long time since I'd talked to anyone with his kind of brain and native intelligence. Even when I was at the university I'd rarely met anyone with his breadth of knowledge. I suppose I thought of the university exactly *because* his arch diction was more scholarly than conversational. That might have been what prompted me to rise to the occasion with words, at first, rather than actions.

"Perhaps mitosis is only a biological metaphor," I responded, heading back to the table with his espresso. "Greek mythology tells us we were all once one sex in the beginning. We were split in two by angels or gods envious of our bliss. Those gods are dead, but we're still split, looking for our other half. When the two halves find one another at last, they're united. They dance the Great Tango."

Hearing myself talk, I realized why I had chosen to respond in that manner. I wanted him to know that he was dealing with a formidable opponent in the Crazy Game. I knew my comments were partly to engage him intellectually and partly to keep him at bay in case his intention was to shoot at me with his pistol.

He stared at me, a vague grin attached to his face, and then offered me a single nod. Without warning he stood up, scraping his chair backward on my kitchen floor. The pistol was in his hand, lowered, barely visible in the folds of his oversized coat.

"Greek thinking." He reached down and finished his espresso in one sip. "I am reminded of the poet Ovid—a quote that is both pertinent to me and beautiful to hear: 'The spirit wanders, comes now here, now there, and occupies whatever frame it pleases—and so the whole round of motion is gone through again.'"

"'Only the bodies,'" I continued the quote, "'of which this eternal, imperishable, incomprehensible Self is the indweller, are said to have an end.' It's from *Metamorphoses*."

"It is indeed," he said softly, "and truer words were never spoken."

"Why do you mention it—the quote from Ovid?" I couldn't resist the question.

"Why do I mention it?" He seemed to have come to the conclusion that I was an idiot. "It's only the point of the story. The whole point. *The spirit wanders!*"

I looked him straight in the eye, a direct confrontation. Either he would calm down or he would shoot me—anything was better than worrying about that gun.

"Sit down." I fixed him with an overwhelming gaze. "Finish your story."

He took a deep breath. I sat. He did not.

"Yes." He was confused again; he set the gun down on the table. "Where was I? What haven't I told you?"

"Who killed the man? You were going to tell me that."

He began pacing in the kitchen, the barrel of the pistol disappearing into the coat's long sleeve.

"When the Tango music started," he went on, as if answering my question, "the two dancers crushed together, laughing and stumbling—a sad and funny parody of the dance that would soon sweep Europe. The killer stepped up close beside them. Anyone would have thought he was about to cut in. He tapped Jacob on the back. Jacob turned around, unable to focus his eyes because of the enormous amount of whiskey he'd consumed. There is no way to tell if Jacob recognized the man or not, but the man said, 'Let us go out to the field.' Do you recognize it?"

I nodded. "It's what Cain said before he killed his brother, Abel."

You can't grow up on my mountain, partially raised by rabid Pentecostal preacher Hezekiah Cotage, and not know your Bible. I was momentarily afraid that he was working himself up to fire his gun, but instead my response seemed to calm him a bit. His response, on the other hand, did nothing to soothe me.

"That's when the gun exploded." He closed his eyes, tired. "The woman, who was called La Gauchina, looked down at the body, then at the man who had fired bullets into it. 'What did he do to you?' she said. 'Who was he?' The man spat: 'I'll tell you what he did: He left his family in time of need. I'll tell you who he was: He was my older brother, and should have done better.' The killer had fought for the Confederacy, you understand, and the dead man had taken a Union uniform."

"I see." I tried my best to be steady—the man was looking increasingly unbalanced.

"The woman, La Gauchina, had no idea she was pregnant at that moment, but she was. At the sight of Jacob's dead body, La Gauchina renounced her life in the brothels and worked, instead, for the rest of her life, as a guitarist in an all-girl orchestra. Her babe was fed each day on the milk of song."

His hands were trembling, and his eyes seemed to focus on moments long past. It was obvious that nothing in the present seemed real to him. All I could see was the black muzzle of his pistol quivering like a divining rod.

"Her baby was born in 1901, the same year President McKinley was assassinated by an anarchist and Queen Victoria died all on her own."

"An era *will* end," I ventured cautiously, "one way or another."

"The twentieth century had begun," he agreed. "I find it significant that in that same year the hormone adrenaline was first isolated—a defining discovery in my mind. It was the end of the Victorian Age and the beginning of the Age of Adrenaline."

Once again I had the sense that he was goading me, or somehow trying to intimidate me with his knowledge, the way some men in academia would have done. I sensed that I could not let it pass.

"Yes." I did my best to sound impatient rather than frightened. "Also in that year Marconi transmitted his first telegraph radio messages, so we might just as certainly refer to it as the Age of Irritatingly Instant Communication. I feel I can match you senseless fact for meaningless statistic all night long in the historical trivia category."

It could have agitated him further. Luckily for me, it only egged him on instead.

"And against such a background," he drawled, "that baby came into this world. All life, in my opinion, is built on such shaky emotional scaffolding. It's a wonder that any of us is ever born at all."

"But *born* is just exactly what it was," I said, deliberately trying to lighten the mood, steer things away from the factoidal challenge, and the violence it might provoke.

"Nine pounds, seven ounces," he nodded. "The mother called him Truck."

"That was his *name*?"

"The mother was in some pain when she made her final push. She said, 'What is that down there, a baby or a *truck*?' and the doctor winked. 'He's a big one!'"

The night had pushed on with no help from either of us, and stars were winking through the trees, white beaded bells whose only sound was light. I had a distinct ringing in my ears and realized I was clenching my teeth so hard it was making my jaw hurt.

"All right." He sat down at the table once again. "Time to finish the story—and get to the punch line, the great *reveal*. Ready?"

"I don't know." I started to say more, but he interrupted.

"The pivotal year is 1914, when Archduke Ferdinand was assassinated in Sarajevo. This acted as an excuse, of course, to engender World War I, which History began, at first, to call the War to End All Wars. The boy, Truck, decided to enlist. He was only thirteen years old. His mother was quite clear about her opinion. 'You're not going,' she said. 'It's not our fight. What do I care if a bunch of foreigners kill each other. I only care they don't kill you. You're important.' God's sense of humor is so strange that it is often difficult to fathom. On the night He invented human nature, He laughed from midnight until sunup. He laughed so hard He could barely breathe, and refrained from creating anything else new in human beings for the next ten thousand years."

"But Truck went to war?" I prompted, a bit confused by his digressions.

"Yes, and his mother went with him."

"What?"

"She wanted to go to Paris to teach Tango lessons. Truck told her that the only popular dance in Europe was the dance of death. Can you believe it?"

"He was a teenaged boy. You're allowed to give out such dramatic pronouncements at that age, don't you think?"

Without warning, the gun appeared again. I froze. The visitor used it to crack a knuckle on his other hand.

"You don't understand," he whispered with gripping reverence. "Ignorance had made the boy holy, the way innocence makes a newborn holy. He was an ignoramus, but he was St. Ignoramus of Chicago—the patron saint of all underage boys who enlist in an army to fight in a war. And now for the punch line. Ready?"

"I suppose." I had my hands on the underside of the table, ready to flip it toward him if he pointed his pistol at me and tried to shoot. It would knock him flat.

"Here it is." He smiled. It radiated across his face and into an aura several inches thick around his body. "That was me. That was I. That was the author of this story. I am Truck."

"So—you fought in World War I."

"*Yes*," my visitor insisted, on the brink of exploding. "I fought in *every* war. The spirit wanders—only the body comes to have an end!"

"I'm not certain what you mean when you say you fought in every war," I began, ready to stand and fling the table.

"You're probably wondering why I visit you today, Dr. Devilin." He seemed drowsy, ignoring my implicit question. His gaze was wilder than ever, and the smile had become a grimace. "You probably wonder how I know you. I do know you. You've recorded conversations like this with other people. My relatives. My brothers and such."

"I have?" I asked before I could think.

"Yes. God. Are you deliberately dense?" His eyes were nearly rolled back in his head.

He seemed on the verge of firing his gun.

"Listen," I said steadily, about to cave in on him, "you're going to have to calm down, here—"

Without warning, he twitched once, then slumped in his chair. "Damn—that coffee. It makes me tired. I have to sleep now."

Before another syllable passed his lips, he put his head down on the kitchen table and immediately began snoring.

For a second I sat there, afraid to move. After a moment I looked under the table. The gun was in his lap. I moved my chair carefully so that I could stand up, afraid to wake him, but he was dead to the world.

I thought I remembered something about a version of narcolepsy in certain schizophrenics; the memory came from a long-faded graduate psychology class.

Then I realized I had to use his nap as an opportunity to call the sheriff.

I stood as silently as I could, stopped the tape recorder with a click that should have disturbed him but didn't, and stepped silently to the phone on the kitchen wall.

The cord on the receiver stretched enough for me to tiptoe around a corner into the living room after I'd dialed.

It rang seven times before a voice said, "Police."

"Skid?" I whispered.

"Fever?"

"Listen, there's a guy in my house. I found him passed out on my front porch. He's asleep in the kitchen now, but I think he might need some kind of help. He's got a gun."

"In his late twenties, army surplus trench coat, boyish face? Antique-looking pistol?"

"You've gotten other calls," I assumed. "He's been to other places on the mountain tonight."

"He has. Can you keep him in your kitchen until I get there?"

I stepped farther around the corner away from the kitchen so as not to wake the man in question.

"Pretty sure I can at this point. He's asleep. But could you come right away? Let me just say again: He's got a *gun*. He's making me nervous."

"He should."

"Really? Who is he? Where else has he been?"

"He might be dangerous, Fever. Don't mess with him."

"*Mess* with him? I'm tape-recording him."

"I might have guessed." I could hear a bit of a smile in the words. "Well, keep it up, if it makes him stay."

"No kidding, Skid, what's going on with this guy?"

"I'll be right up." He hung up.

I stared at the phone, listening to the dial tone.

Apparently Sheriff Skidmore Needle, in his official capacity, was a bit short on the niceties of conversation—or phone etiquette. If I hadn't known him for most of my life, I might have been at least surprised. As it was, it was just one more example of the many ways in which Skid's personality had changed since he'd become sheriff.

When he was a deputy, he seemed to revel in the long, slow

unwinding of a conversation. Something that could have been said in several words took long, colorful paragraphs. I missed that. In his elevated office he'd become something of a spendthrift with words. In the old days, he would have spent at least another moment telling me why I had to keep a stranger in my house, what the stranger had done.

It was one more sad indication of the modern age, my visitor's so-called Age of Adrenaline, I concluded. Ours was a time when speed seemed more important than depth or breadth or anything else. Damn the modern age, I was thinking, if you couldn't even say good-bye before you hung up a phone.

I was aware that my mind was rambling to keep from thinking about the man with a gun in my kitchen.

Unfortunately, when I went to hang up my own phone I saw that speed might have been of the essence in this particular instance.

The kitchen was empty. The man was gone.

TWO

THE PHONE WOKE me at six in the morning. I didn't even have a chance to say hello.

"Fever, damn it," Skidmore growled, as if we were already in the middle of a conversation, "can you come over to the back road behind the Jackson place? Right away?"

His voice was primarily static and ambient noise. He was calling from his squad car.

"Good morning, Skidmore." My voice, on the other hand, sounded like a rock being sawed in half.

"That man who was in your kitchen last night? The one you let get away? I believe I'm looking at him dead right here."

"What?" I sat up.

"He's wearing an overcoat two sizes too big, he's got black hair, and he's in his late twenties."

"Sounds like the man." I squeezed my eyes shut for a moment, trying to wake up. "What's going on?"

"Well, after he disappeared from your house last night, I didn't go home. I sort of prowled around looking for him. And about ten minutes ago, I found him."

"No." I sat up. "I mean, who was he, do you know?"

"No idea. Look, can you get over here right away? It'll be light in a little while, and I think the school bus comes this way."

"Oh." I saw his point. "Let me—what? Get some pants on, swallow one cup of espresso, and I'm there. Right behind the Jacksons'?"

"You can't miss us," he sighed into the phone. "We'll be where all the flashing lights and police cars are."

Fine, if that's the way he wanted it.

"Didn't this man visit other people before me? Did you call any of them?"

"I'm not waking people up at this time of the morning to look at a dead body."

"You just woke *me* up."

"Are you going to put your pants on," he hissed, "or do I have to come up there with my nightstick?"

"I don't know why it's always me," I complained, stirring in the bed. "People around here are starting to get the idea that I'm the kiss of death or something. Every time there's a dead body in Blue Mountain, I'm around it."

"Is it my fault that you're best friends with the sheriff?"

"Yes! It's your fault exactly! You're the only person in town I like, and you turned into a sheriff. What the hell is *that*?"

"You like Hek and June."

"The only person my own age. Look—"

"Could we continue this argument in person, Fever?" Skid lowered his voice. "You really want the school kids to see a dead body?"

"It is coming up on Halloween."

"Fever, damn it—"

"I'm on my way."

Less than half an hour later I was standing on a dirt road looking down at a corpse. I'd thrown on a charcoal T-shirt and black jeans, a thin rust-colored sweater, and black hiking boots. My hair, supernaturally white for no reason I could understand, was so unkempt that it felt like an albino squirrel perched on my head. It was cold in the shadows, so I tried to stay in the morning sun.

Skid had called only two deputies, and no one else was around.

The Jackson place was off in the distance, and lights were still on in the house. They'd probably seen the flashing police cars. It wouldn't be long before someone from the family ambled down our way.

If we'd been down in the town, dawn might have been further away, but up on the mountain the night was almost gone. Everything was in shades of gray. The three policemen were dark shadows. Their cars were black and white. The body on the ground could have been a pile of dead leaves.

I'd parked my old green pickup truck a little away from the police cars so that an ambulance could get past it. I assumed that Skid had called for one.

"How did you even see this in the dark?" I was staring down at the body. "I'm standing right here and I can't make out anything about it."

"Headlights caught it." He shrugged.

This was one of the things that made Skidmore Needle my best friend in the mountains. He had absolutely no ego. Everything was luck or happy fate or, though he would never put it to me in so many words, God. He hadn't found a dead body, his headlights had.

"It looks like the guy, and who else would it be? Those are his clothes." I had my arms folded in front of me.

"Then why do you sound like that?" Skid asked plainly.

"Like what?"

"Like you're not sure."

"Because I can't see his face," I complained, a little more petulantly than I had intended.

"Melissa!" he hollered.

Deputy Melissa Mathews appeared out of nowhere.

"Yup?" Her voice was lively; her face was bright.

"Would you shine a light on the face of the deceased, please, ma'am? I lost mine, and Dr. Devilin can't see in this light. I believe he may need glasses. Could you help him out?"

"Sure can!" Melissa instantly produced an oversized flashlight and snapped it on.

I was momentarily blinded.

"Enough light?" Skidmore asked calmly.

Melissa was holding a lighthouse.

"It's enough for a small country." I squinted, shielding my eyes from the eerie white blaze.

"He complains when he can't see," Skidmore told Melissa, "and he complains when he can."

"He's not awake yet," Melissa said sympathetically.

But she didn't turn off her torch.

Almost as if it were a movie scene, fading from white into a gray, dappled pattern, the face of the dead man slowly appeared and came clearer.

I took a step closer.

"Did you get his gun?" I asked Skidmore.

"No. Haven't found it yet. But that gunshot wound in his chest has powder burns all around it. He may have shot himself in the heart, which isn't that easy to do, really. And he may have flung the gun somewhere as he was dying. We'll get hold of it directly."

"Maybe."

"What?" He came to stand beside me. "What do you see?"

"Not sure." I held out my hand. "Melissa, could I have that flashlight?"

"Sure." She handed it over.

I knelt by the body, shined the light a little off to the right of the face, and let the halo illuminate him. That light was more like the light in my kitchen, and I could see what I wanted to see.

"Okay." I stood and offered Melissa her flashlight back. "Damn."

"Fever?" Skidmore stared down at the corpse. "What the hell is it?"

"That's not the guy." I took a step away.

"Not the guy?"

"Those are his clothes—I mean, that coat is what the man was wearing last night, and those construction boots, too. This guy even looks a little like him, but this is not the man who was in my kitchen last night."

Skid blinked.

"Maybe it's the light," Melissa offered. "Plus, a man looks a lot different when he's dead."

"What would—" Skid began, then faltered.

"I admit it doesn't make sense." I rubbed my eyes and stared at the dead man again. "What possible explanation could there be for a look-alike, dressed in the same clothes as the man I saw, lying dead on a back road this close to my house? Maybe I'm just not awake."

The eastern sky was bleeding red at the rim of the horizon. The mountain peaks did their best to hold back the onslaught of day, but rocks are earthbound, and light is made of angels. Light always wins the battle, even though it isn't always the right thing. That morning could have used a few more moments of darkness, only there it was: red sky at morning.

I was staring down at the body, trying to make my eyes change their mind, to admit that the dead man on the cold ground was the same thing as the live man in my warm kitchen. I was almost swayed, when the second deputy, a kid named Crawdad Pritchett—champion fiddler at age seven, deputy by age nineteen—called out.

"Yonder comes Ms. Jackson."

We all looked up toward the Jackson place. She was still a long way off, but Mrs. Jackson was indeed making good time, old as she was.

The back road where we were standing was little more than dirt and weeds. A ramshackle fence, made primarily of graying wood and rusted nails, ran along it that might have kept something in at one time, but only really served as a guide to help drivers know how the road ran.

Up the hill behind that fence lay an array of golden grass, wild ageratum, and blackberry brambles. Beyond that, at the top of the rise, sat the Jackson home, a white two-story place built just after the turn of the last century and well taken care of, enough to make it last until the turn of the next, except for an act of God. A covered porch littered with a dozen rocking chairs surrounded the entire home. Though I couldn't see it from where I was standing, I knew there was a garden at the front of the house, mostly annuals. There would probably be pumpkin-colored mums there, so late in October.

Mrs. Jackson, who claimed to be over a hundred years old, wrapped in a thick brown sweater, was motoring in a very determined fashion right for the dead body.

"Melissa!" Skid called. "Get something over the body. You got a blanket in your trunk?"

She nodded and moved quickly.

At that exact moment we all heard an ungodly rumbling at the western end of the road. It sounded like a tow truck was dragging an old battleship up the mountain. A second later, headlights on despite the break of day, a banana-colored school bus appeared, rising from the darkness and shadows at the far end of the road, coming our way.

"Damn." Skid moved toward the body.

The school bus had plenty of room to get past my truck and could easily have maneuvered around the police cars as well, but the driver slowed, uncertain how to proceed. A child's face appeared in every window.

Melissa had the blanket out of her trunk and was rushing toward the corpse. Mrs. Jackson, in a preternatural burst of energy, was nearing the fence; children were clamoring in the bus.

Skid stopped where he was, looked around, then turned back to me.

"Ever have one of those mornings?" There was a hint of a smile in his voice, if not on his face.

That was another reason Skidmore was a man everyone liked. He had a sense of humor even in the most hectic of moments.

The bus came to a standstill just shy of the first police car. Mrs. Jackson steadied herself on one of the fence posts and peered in the direction of Melissa Mathews. Melissa smoothed the blanket over the body and stood.

"Crawdad," Skid said calmly, "would you go over and help that bus driver get around our cars and on his way?"

"Her way," Crawdad corrected. "It's Ms. Henley driving today."

"Crawdad," Skid began, only a bit exasperated.

"Yes, sir," the deputy interrupted, moving quickly toward the bus.

"Hey, Ms. Jackson," Skid called.

"What is all this?" she wanted to know.

Skidmore ambled her way, moving deliberately slowly to belie the chaos of the moment.

"Not much." He smiled.

"Is it somebody dead under that blanket?" She stared at Melissa.

Skid arrived at the fence where Mrs. Jackson stood.

"Yes," he told her. "Yes, ma'am, I believe it is."

"It's a vagrant," Melissa offered. "Nobody we know, I mean."

Behind me I could hear Crawdad trying to talk the school bus driver into moving along. He had to shout. Mrs. Henley had opened the doors to better see the hubbub and the kids on the bus were louder than the old engine. Combined they made a righteous noise.

"We're in the middle of an investigation," Crawdad hollered as politely as he could manage. "That's all I can say."

Mrs. Henley was loath to leave it at that. Several children began to catch on to the situation, and a wildfire of speculation rampaged through the bus. The words "dead body" were flying about with a good deal of vigor.

Without turning to look at the bus, Skidmore bellowed, "Ms. Henley, if you don't move that bus *right* now, today will be the last day in your life where you drive a school bus."

The sound of Skid's voice was piercing. The children fell silent. Even the bus seemed to quiet down.

"Please, ma'am," Crawdad added.

Without further ado, Mrs. Henley sniffed, closed the bus doors, and edged her mammoth vehicle around the police cars, slowly, staring at Skidmore the entire time. The children inside were frantic, filled with glee: it was coming up on Halloween, and they'd seen a dead body. Life was wonderful.

Mrs. Jackson was more difficult.

"Who you say it was?" She craned her neck trying to see underneath the blanket.

"Vagrant," Skid sighed heavily, "like Melissa said, ma'am."

"Then what's *he* doing here?" She lifted her head in my direction.

"I *told* you," I muttered to Skidmore, "people are starting to worry when they see me because there's always a dead body around."

"Ask around if you want," Skid told Mrs. Jackson, his

patience straining. "Last night there was a vagrant wandering around up here bothering folks. The final house he came in was Fever's, and so I called him to see was this man here the same one that was in his house. That's all."

"Well, is it?" She folded her arms and leveled a defiant look at me.

I was momentarily saved by the sudden, grating siren of an ambulance. The driver had turned it on only half a mile away to let us know he was coming.

Skid moved closer to Mrs. Jackson.

"I'm afraid I'll have to ask you to go on up to your house now, ma'am." His voice was granite. "We've got to get the body over to the Deveroe boys."

The Deveroes were our funeral parlor owners, previously wild boys from the back woods whose chief occupation was hunting feral swine. Everyone knew them. They had undergone a miraculous transformation when their sister had gone temporarily missing—it had changed their way of living. They had gone to mortuarial school. Their funeral parlor had in it a lab that the county coroner used.

"He didn't answer my question," Mrs. Jackson said firmly. "Is that the man who came to your house last night?"

I looked at Skid.

The ambulance clattered up the dirt road, siren swelling.

The sun began to burn off its red color, working its way toward daylight. Light comes up in the morning in the mountains almost as quickly as it disappears at night.

Skidmore only glanced at Melissa for a second, but she sprang into action. With little more than a lift and a leap, she was over the fence and headed toward Mrs. Jackson.

"Let me help you back to your house, ma'am, would you mind?" Melissa's voice was honey.

"I don't need any help to get to my own house," Mrs. Jackson complained.

"You don't need any," Melissa shot back sweetly, "but isn't it nice to have some?"

She sounded like a good daughter; even I was calmed by her

voice. Mrs. Jackson took one more look at the body, then acquiesced, pulling her sweater around her and taking Melissa's arm. In truth, it was a bit of an incline up the hill back to the Jackson house, and Melissa really was a help.

As the ambulance came to a stop, siren silenced, Skid motioned for me to come have one more look at the body. He pulled back the blanket.

I leaned over and stared. The sky was at least half blue. I could see the man's face clearly. The hair was different, the nose, the mouth—and the coat fit better. The dead man was bigger than my visitor. Still, the resemblance was uncanny.

I straightened up.

"Sorry." I shook my head. "This is not the guy."

The ambulance men appeared behind us. They stood for a moment before one sniffed.

"Okay, Sheriff, what've we got here?" His voice was a parody of authority.

Skidmore was watching Melissa help Mrs. Jackson back up to the house at the top of the meadow's rise.

"I have no idea," Skid said finally, rousing himself from an odd reverie. "Let's get him over to the Deveroes and see."

THREE

SKIDMORE AND I stood outside the Deveroe Brothers' Funeral Parlor in the autumn air. The sky had turned a cloudless, steel-hard blue. The breeze was filled with smoke from burning leaves, and the Deveroes had set several pumpkins on the front porch of their place of business.

The parlor itself was a Victorian-era mansion, once the finest home in the county. It had long since been converted to an Addams Family establishment, but the boys weren't stuffy about their occupation. At Christmas there were always twinkle lights on the porch, at Easter the railings were hung with baskets of eggs, and in October there were pumpkins—never carved into jack-o'-lanterns—decorating the steps. The only vehicle in the parking lot was a relatively new motorcycle, an incongruous invader. I assumed it belonged to one of the brothers.

"It's not a suicide." Skidmore stared off into space.

"I didn't say it was." I stared at his profile. "You mentioned—"

"The angle of the bullet when it went in," he continued, as if he hadn't heard me, "means that somebody held a pistol to his chest and shot him through the heart."

"It does?"

"My conclusion is that the man who was in your kitchen last night killed the man who is in the funeral parlor this morning."

"What are you talking about?" I took my hands out of my pockets. "Why would you come to that—"

"The dead man is dressed in the same clothes as your visitor. How else could he have gotten those clothes? The simple answer is that the man you saw changed clothes with the dead one, don't you think?"

"No, I don't think." I scowled at him. "Did he kill the man and then change clothes? Did he talk the victim into trading coats and *then* shoot him?"

"*After* the change of clothing, the man in there was shot through the heart with a pistol." Skid twitched his head in the direction of the funeral parlor, and the dead body that lay within.

"I see." I did my best to make it obvious that I was humoring him.

"And the man in your kitchen threatened you with a pistol."

"It wasn't so much a threat as a display, as it turned out," I corrected, "but I understand your point, I think."

"So you see that your visitor killed the man we found this morning."

"I see that as one possible scenario, yes." I shrugged. "I don't know how good it is."

"You tape-recorded the man?"

"I did."

"I'll want to hear those tapes pretty soon." Skid turned to me, caught my eye. "What was he talking about?"

"It was a little spooky, actually. He seemed to think he'd been born before World War I. He talked about the murder of his father by his uncle. Like Hamlet. And he referred to himself as a wandering spirit."

"He was crazy."

"Yes. But he was also one of the more intelligent people I've ever met."

"Up here, you mean." Skid looked down.

"I mean anywhere."

Skid was impressed. "Why do you think that?"

"A lot of things. He was kind of a history buff, knew a lot of meaningless academic minutiae. We also talked about Greek philosophy and the introduction of the Tango in Chicago."

"Damn." Skid shook his head, the hint of a smile on his lips.

"Of course, as I was saying, he also seemed to think he was this transmigrating soul who didn't pertain to any one particular time."

Before Skid could comment on that, the front door of the

funeral parlor scraped open and we both turned. The sour county coroner, Millroy, appeared in the doorway. He was a Jack Webb look-alike: cheap cotton suit; tight crew cut; gaunt, tired face.

I didn't care for Millroy, and Skidmore liked him less. He'd come to town from Rockford, Illinois, and took every opportunity he could to demean people in Blue Mountain because he considered himself something of an urban sophisticate. He'd been a coroner in Chicago for about twenty minutes before they'd dismissed him for, it was rumored, taking liberties with one of the dead bodies in his charge. I was certain that the stories were unfounded, but the fact that they were still circulating around town was evidence of the general disdain most people felt for the man.

"Well, it was suicide," Millroy announced, not really looking at anything. "Gun was pressed right up on the victim's chest. One shot was fired. No evidence of a struggle. I need to see the gun, of course."

Skidmore shot me a glance before he responded. "No gun at the scene. I looked for a good while, and Deputy Mathews combed the area for two hours after I left. No gun."

"Deputy Mathews." Millroy sighed.

It was impossible for me to tell whether the sigh was a result of his longing for Melissa Mathews, which was oft-repeated gossip in town, or the fact that he didn't really trust a woman to do a deputy's job, which was certainly an element of his other-century attitudes in general.

"Also—and I'm certain you took this into consideration," Skid said slowly, "but it looked to me like the bullet went straight in."

"It did," Millroy confirmed.

He stepped off the porch and joined us in the sunlight, pulled a pack of Camel cigarettes from his inside suit coat pocket, and fished for a smoke. It was just one more image of a man out of time.

"Make a gun," Skid said to me.

"What?" I had no idea what he meant.

"Make a gun." He held up his thumb and index finger, the way we had when we were kids playing soldiers or cowboys in the woods.

I smiled, remembering hundreds of long summer days when Skid and I had killed a thousand imaginary villains—with a gun like the one I'd just made.

"Point it right at your heart," he instructed.

I did.

"Look here." He motioned for Millroy to stand next to me.

Millroy lit his cigarette and moved my way, making a show of his reluctance.

"Don't take too long," I told him, straight-faced. "I don't like this thing pointed right at me."

"What is it?" Millroy's tone was a full-voiced demonstration of weary indulgence.

"See how the gun barrel's at an angle?" Skid offered. "You've got to extend a bit of conscious effort to make the gun point straight in. It's not a natural position."

I looked down. My gun was a little angled. In order to make it perfectly straight I would have had to contort my wrist and my shoulder.

"I don't care," Millroy objected. "What kind of person is going to just stand there and let someone else press a gun on his chest without any struggle at all?"

"Somebody really scared?" I ventured.

"Somebody who didn't take the gunman seriously?" Skid added. "Maybe because he *knew* the gunman?"

"It was a suicide!" Millroy insisted, louder.

"It was not a suicide." Skidmore's volume matched Millroy's. "*Damn.*"

"Who is the coroner in this hick town?" Millroy exploded.

"Where's the actual gun?" Skid fired back. "If he killed himself, why wasn't the gun in his hand, or right nearby? *And* I didn't notice any powder or discoloration on either of the victim's hands. I mean, damn, Millroy, you don't think I thought about this at the scene? You don't think I checked everything?"

"I don't know what you checked and what you didn't," Millroy snaped. "I don't know why you're getting worked up at me. And now I wonder if I want to go up to the scene and have a look around for that gun myself. You and Deputy Mathews seem to be pretty good at distracting one another. Maybe you missed something."

"Swing and a miss," Skidmore said, smiling a little too broadly. "If you mean to insult me, you'll have to use something a little more current. Gossip about me and Deputy Mathews died down about two years ago. You might try talking to me about the music my oldest girl is listening to on the radio. That gets me pretty mad sometimes."

"All I said—" Millroy sighed.

"If you call it a suicide, you moron," Skid snapped, "I can't go out and find the murderer. That will keep me up at night, and I'll get mean. I don't like to be mean. I take it out on people around me. It can get really bad."

"I've seen it," I volunteered.

"Watch that 'moron' talk, you dumb-ass cracker, I'll put a hurt all over you."

"Boys, boys," I intervened, mostly kidding, "name calling will get us nowhere. I'm going to have to ask you to go to your respective corners."

"Did you already make out the report?" Skidmore asked, obviously unwilling to let it go.

"Yes, I did." Millroy threw his cigarette on the ground, blew out a gray steam, and squinted.

"If you file it as a suicide—" Skidmore hissed.

"When," Millroy declared.

Skidmore sucked in a deep breath, held it for a second, and closed his eyes.

"If you file it as a suicide," Skidmore began calmly, "I say again: It makes it harder for me to go out and catch the murderer. I have to go about it unofficially—in secret—and I don't like secrets. So I'll tell you what I'd like you to do. I'd like you to wait a bit, just a little bit, before you file officially."

"I understand there's been some sort of computer virus going around that's wreaking havoc with the county system," I im-provised. "Maybe it would be best to wait, say, forty-eight hours before you trusted the system with your report?"

"If I'm right," Skid added, "it'll keep you from *looking* like a moron, which I'm sorry I called you. And if I'm wrong, it'll give you a really good opportunity to lord it over me."

"Win-win," I told Millroy, smiling.

Millroy stared down at his cigarette. It was still glowing orange in his shadow on the ground.

"I guess I'd hate for that virus to screw me up," he said fi-nally, crushing out his smoke. "What's today? Tuesday? How about if I do a few more tests. But if you don't bring me some-thing to stop me by the end of business on Thursday, I'm filing as I see it now."

Skid nodded once.

Though we had barely more than forty-eight hours, that didn't seem too short a time. The man we would be looking for was almost certain to be hiding on the mountain where Skid and I grew up, a place we could walk in our sleep. No one would hide him; he'd be on his own, easy to find.

We'll most likely get him tomorrow, I thought.

"And I'm sorry I called you a dumb-ass cracker." Millroy was staring at the ground. "'Cracker' has implications of racism, and I know you're not remotely a racist, not anything like it. You're a perfectly *ordinary* dumb-ass. That man in there killed himself."

"Long as I know where I stand." Skid blinked once at me and headed for his police car, parked beside my truck.

I followed Skidmore; Millroy went back inside the funeral home.

"I'm not sure I completely grasp—" I began.

"If he files his report with the county," Skidmore explained, opening his car door, "and it says suicide, I have a whole lot of explaining to do when I log in hours and fill out reports about an ongoing murder investigation concerning the same dead body. And don't even begin to suggest that I could do the work and not file the paper. I *have* to file the paper."

"There's that much paperwork in your job?"

"It's all paperwork," he sighed. "There's no *job* to it."

"Jesus, really?" I stood beside my truck. "Your work's almost as bad as a college professor's."

"I don't see the point of insulting me." He started the car.

"So we have a little more than forty-eight hours." I leaned back on the passenger door of my truck. "So let's get started. Where do I go?"

"You could have a talk with the other two people the stranger visited. I mean, he bothered about ten people one way or another, but he only talked to two." His eyes were glued to the ground. "I believe you're really going to want to talk to them."

"Why is that?" I could tell he was uncomfortable.

"Well, one of the people is Hovis Daniels, that old man you used to interview so much before he started getting put away all the time. He's out again, living on the Jackson property as usual—about five hundred yards from where we found the body. I still don't think he pays any rent. Mrs. Jackson's just—"

"Doing her Christian duty."

"Something like that," he agreed. "I went up to question him when I first found the body, but he wasn't there. It's a pretty good coincidence that a dead body was found so close to his shack, though."

"Yes. I'll talk to him almost immediately. Who's the other person?"

"That's the thing." He shifted in his seat. "The guy visited your—well, your fiancée, Lucinda, last night, too. She's the one that called me first. That's how I knew the guy had been—"

"What?" I snapped. "You're just now telling me this? What's the matter with you?"

"I didn't want you to get upset."

"Well, of course I'm upset!"

"Because you're concerned about Lucinda," he began, looking down, barely holding back a grin, "or because I used the word 'fiancée'?"

"Damn it, Skidmore, is she—"

"She's fine. Don't you think I would have told you before

now if there was a problem? The guy left; she locked her door; then the guy came to your place. That's the story."

"That's part of the story," I corrected. "A more significant element of the plot is that he came to my place with a loaded gun, and then he used that gun later to kill another man. That's worth mentioning."

Of course I wanted to visit Lucinda first—right away, in fact—but Skidmore talked me out of it. I knew better, anyway. She was at the hospital, and nothing was ever serious enough to keep her from going to work. I knew not to bother her there until it was time for the lunch break. So when Skidmore took off, I walked around, got into my truck, and headed back to the dirt road behind the Jackson place.

FOUR

HOVIS DANIELS HAD lived in the little shack down the mountain from the Jackson home on and off for fifty years. It had no electricity or running water, only a wood-burning stove for heating and cooking. Hovis was a memory more than a man—something collectively recollected in our community. He was the last existing emblem, as far as I knew, of the way things used to be. He was also, as I had often said in articles about him, a living time machine. His stories were so vivid, so perfectly remembered, so clearly visualized, that he could take you with him when he went into the past. Alas, that perfect ability would occasionally overwhelm Hovis, and he'd forget which decade was supposed to be his home. When that happened, he'd be put away, as Skidmore'd said, in the county facility for the mentally disabled. Hovis had spent the last few years there. Skidmore warned me three times that Hovis was more unbalanced than he had been when I'd interviewed him before, that he was getting senile and gun crazy—obviously a bad combination.

The day was warming nicely, approaching sixty degrees. The clear light across the meadows on that part of the Jackson property seemed to illuminate everything and bend around solid objects, leaving no shadows anywhere. My old green truck clattered up the road, bouncing in trenches and thumping over rocks until I saw the gray wood shack come into view. I pulled off the road as best I could, scraping paint from my passenger door on the wire of the fence. The shack was a quick jump over the fence and fewer than thirty steps across the field, but I moved slowly. Hovis was of the old school where visitors were concerned. Until he knew who was headed his way, he'd have his hunting rifle out, cocked, and pointed at the door. If he didn't like the sound of his guest, he was liable to take a shot. He'd never actually killed anyone, that I knew of, but when he once wounded a teenager who was selling chocolate bars for his high school band trip, Sheriff Maddox, Skidmore's late predecessor, had locked Hovis up and thrown away the key.

So I headed toward the shack very slowly.

In years long gone by, the custom was to "hello" the house, calling out from a good distance. That way you could let your host know who was headed for the front door. Hovis still appreciated the gesture. Feeling that a bullet in my arm or my leg might impede the progress of my work, and considering that we only had a short amount of time before Millroy filed his erroneous report, I thought it best to indulge in the tradition.

"Hovis! It's Fever Devilin coming up to your house. Okay?"

"Saw you drive up." His voice was muffled from within the hovel. There was only one door, and the lone window was on the other side of the place, but the spaces in between the wall boards were wide enough to see through. "Come on in the house."

It wasn't a warm invitation, but I hadn't expected congeniality from Hovis. He was absolutely unconcerned with the niceties of the world. His home attested to that, and the experience of his life had confirmed a less than sunny disposition.

As I drew nearer to the front door, I heard a click. I stopped for a second, fearing he might have cocked his rifle, but decided he'd only unlocked his door and forged bravely ahead.

"You're not pointing your hunting rifle at the door, are you, Hovis?" Better safe than sorry.

There was a long moment of silence followed by a gentle clatter.

"Not anymore," he answered, finally.

I came to the front of his place and waited. After another heartbeat or two, the door swung open and he appeared.

Hovis looked much older than the last time I'd seen him. He was in his nineties as it was, but he looked like he was made of papier-mâché. He had, perhaps, seven hairs on his head, all white wires. His skin was nearly the color of his cabin, the same as a pale rain cloud. His eyes were runny and rimmed in red, his hands were more vein and bone than anything else, and he hadn't shaved in a while. He was dressed as I had always seen him, in a white cotton dress shirt and denim overalls, well worn but clean. His boots were old, and I imagined that there were holes in them. The part of the picture that made me take a breath was the fact that the clothes and the boots were the same as they had always been, but Hovis was smaller, so they looked huge on him.

"You ain't bring your tape machine." It was an observation, not a question.

"No." *Never give out more information than you need to*, I reminded myself; *let him do the talking.*

"I expect you come about that boy."

He stepped aside so that I might follow him into his cave. It was dark and Spartan, swept clean and remarkably fresh-smelling.

The inside of the cabin was just as I remembered it. The wood-stove on the wall opposite the door was warm, and something was simmering in a pot on top. To the right of it there was a cot piled high with quilts, perhaps ten. To the left of the stove there was a table and two chairs; on the table, a place setting for one and a huge coffee mug beside an ancient tin percolator. The room was illuminated by two oil lamps, not daylight—the window's curtains were pulled tight. On the floor at the entrance lay a rug someone had given him long ago, a scene of quails nesting in the middle of it. The rafters of the shack were hung with dried rosemary and eucalyptus, which accounted for the pleasant smell. I wondered if anyone had watched out for the place while Hovis had been away. It appeared to be in fair shape for a place so often abandoned.

"What boy do you mean?" That was all I was willing to say.

Hovis motioned for me to take the lone chair, and he collapsed backward into his bed, right next to his hunting rifle.

"I saw you all out there this morning." He wheezed a bit. "Old, but I ain't stupid. Sheriff found a dead body. I saw it."

"Before the sheriff got to it?" It was a risky question that I regretted asking the second it escaped my lips. It was liable to put him on the defensive, build a wall between us that I wouldn't be able to break through.

"No." He sat back against the wall, his arms falling limply at his sides, hand on his gun. "The car woke me up—police car. Looked outside. Saw Skidmore Needle. I always liked him. Forgot he was the sheriff until I could think about it better. I hated that Maddox. He was a mean'n."

"He was that," I agreed, taking a seat.

Sheriff Maddox had probably mistreated Hovis in ways that would have been legally actionable, but a fat sheriff in a small town can do just about anything he wants to a crazy old man. When Maddox died, no one in town went to his funeral. Skidmore, a longtime deputy, had been unanimously elected to the vacated post.

"Wait." I tried to think of how to ask my question. "The sheriff told me he came up here to talk to you when he first found the body, but you weren't here."

"Maybe I was," he rumbled, "and maybe I wasn't."

"You saw him coming," I assumed, "and hid."

He nodded once, but I looked around his single small room. There was no place to hide.

"Hate to see that boy dead." Hovis tapped his index finger on the barrel of his rifle.

"You mean the one out on the road this morning."

"Who else is dead?" he shot back, irritated. "Course I mean that boy. He was confused, but he was all right. Being confused don't make you wrong *all* the time."

"You knew him?"

"I did not." Hovis closed his eyes. "And I did."

"How's that?"

He sat in silence for a moment; then the wrinkles around his mouth seemed to crack upward.

"You ain't bring you tape machine," he said softly, "but you talk like you did. Your friend the sheriff send you?"

Old, not stupid.

"Sort of," I admitted. "You and I have talked about a lot of things over the years, so he thought you'd talk to me about this.

He wants to know what the boy said to you. That boy visited me last night, too, you know."

Hovis's eyes snapped open.

"He had a pistol," I continued, looking at the floor.

"That's right." Hovis leaned forward, and his hand clutched the rifle's stock. "Nice gun."

"Really?"

"Antique, I guess they'd call it now. Like the one I had in the big war."

"You had a pistol like that when you fought in World War II?"

"Not certain what happened to it." Hovis managed to stand. "I made some coffee. It's still hot."

He ambled his way, shuffling more than walking, toward the percolator on the table. I knew he was offering me his hospitality, and it would have been rude of me not to take some, but I didn't care for the way he looked, and he was using his rifle as a cane. It dragged along the floor of the cabin, then thumped down hard as he took another sliding step. His hand trembled a bit on the barrel.

"All right, Hovis," I sighed.

He stopped in his tracks, turned, and locked eyes with me.

The shadows in the room shifted as a flock of starlings shot by, headed south. The frantic activity of wings produced an unnerving contrast to the stillness inside the shack.

"All right *what*?" Hovis pronounced each word with absolute clarity.

"All right *this*. I won't treat you like a crazy old man if you just quit acting like one." It was another risky gambit, calling his bluff, but I was beginning to remember the way Hovis liked to treat anyone he didn't trust.

I had an instant image of my first encounter with him, in that very cabin. I couldn't have been more than eleven years old. Skidmore and I had stolen some tomatoes from Mrs. Jackson's kitchen garden, and nearly gotten caught. We'd run into what we supposed was an abandoned outbuilding, only to come face-to-face with Hovis Daniels and his rifle, which he had aimed right for Skidmore's head.

He seemed to have some vague notion that he was the care-taker of the Jackson property, though he certainly was not, and wanted to know what we thought we were doing stealing from the kindest woman on the mountain.

Skidmore started apologizing, but I had the idea it would be best to tell Hovis my dark motivation. I explained to him that I wanted tomatoes to throw at the car that was parked outside my house—a car that belonged to a man who was seeing my mother while my father was out of town. Hovis nodded once, lowered his rifle, and offered to help carry the tomatoes.

I'd made a great show, later that same week, of making certain Hovis saw me when I'd gone to confess to Mrs. Jackson and offer to work in her garden for as long as she thought would suffice as punishment.

The point was that if I just told Hovis what I really wanted to know, he would stop playing with his gun and pretending to be senile.

"Okay," he said finally, voice steady. He stood halfway between his bed and the table where I sat waiting.

"The man who was in my house last night talked about Chicago and World War I." I sat back. "He thought he was from another time."

Hovis smiled. He tossed the rifle backward, and it landed neatly on the bed. He stood up straight and walked slowly but firmly to the table and sat down.

"He told me he killed his brother during World War II," Hovis offered, smiling bigger. "He's crazier than me—and I'd admit that's going a far piece."

"He said he killed his brother?" I turned my chair to face him. He was pouring coffee. "When he was at my place he talked about fratricide, but he said his uncle killed his father. Like Hamlet."

"Sometimes you have to tell a story a few times before it comes out right," Hovis observed.

There was a perfect truth.

"Do you remember what time of day it was when he visited you?" I asked.

"Late afternoon." He narrowed his eyelids, concentrating. "He just come down from Ms. Jackson's place. She run him off. I believe she called the sheriff on him."

"So he had this pistol, the visitor—you saw that," I went on, trying to get him to the point, "and he told you about—what? His exploits—"

"Said he was a spy in the Big War." Hovis set the pot back on the table. "It was June 14, 1940, that German troops marched into the city of Paris."

I glared at Hovis, unable to decide if he was beginning a story or having some sort of breakdown.

"Why do you mention that?" I thought it best to ask.

"I don't mention it at all," Hovis countered. "*He* did. That boy last night. Do you know much about the Great War, Fever? Man your age, in my experience, has two general ideas about history. One is his own lifetime, and the other is anything that came before it. That's the problem with you young people, the main one."

I could almost see the gears in Hovis's head beginning to turn faster, the thoughts warming, the words coming unstuck from hidden places in his brain, places that hadn't been used much during his...incarcerations.

The primary reason I had always collected information from Hovis, and he had never disappointed, was that he was a near perfect authority on local genealogy. That ability, however, had also produced in him a rolling and expansive vision of history. If he got revved up—and he didn't always—he could paint astonishing portraits of dozens of historical periods. That's why I sometimes referred to him as a time machine.

"Did you know," Hovis continued, "that one of the big songs on the radio that year was called 'The Last Time I Saw Paris'?"

It wasn't a real question, it was a challenge. Hovis wanted to make certain I was going to be able to keep up with him, was able to understand the irony of that title.

"You can see why it would be a hit," I said quickly, taking up the gauntlet. "The last time most people in the world had seen Paris, it had been the City of Lights. But on June 14, 1940, it was plunged into darkness."

Hovis nodded.

"And did you know," I went on, perhaps a bit too immodestly, "that Ernest Hemingway had just published his book *For Whom the Bell Tolls*?"

"'Any man's death diminishes me,'" Hovis quoted perfectly. "'Never send to know for whom the bell tolls; it tolls for thee.'"

He seemed to be doing a bit of gauntlet gathering himself.

"John Donne wrote that." I nodded. "Hemingway took his title from it."

"If you say so." He picked up his coffee cup.

It was coming back to me, the thing that I'd always found disconcerting about Hovis: When he wanted you to think he was a pathetic old man, his accent and diction—even posture—were one way, but when he rose to his storytelling self, his entire demeanor was better, and his vocabulary improved to a frightening degree. There was no way to tell which one was the real Hovis Daniels, especially since one of the times he'd been at the county mental facility he'd been diagnosed—erroneously, in my opinion—with multiple personality disorder.

"At the same time," Hovis said softly, "in 1940, the caves at Lascaux were discovered—in a different part of France. You know what those are?"

"They contain prehistoric wall paintings that, I believe, are over twenty thousand years old."

"The caves were discovered accidentally by two boys playing ball." Hovis slurped a loud sip of coffee. "Their dog ran after the ball and disappeared into a cave. The boys followed. To see better, they lit matches, and suddenly, brilliantly, before their eyes, painted on the cave walls, they saw the most outstanding examples of prehistoric art ever discovered."

"Yes." I knew he was coming to a point.

"Some boys were playing ball and exploring caves," he continued. "The boy that visited me last night? He told me that he spent his younger days in Paris, sticking rocks the size of his fist into the runners of Nazi tanks so that the tanks would malfunction. So that the Nazis would have a harder time destroying the city he loved. He also said he was packing the artillery on those tanks with silt from the Seine. The silt would dry in the heat of the day, and then when some Nazi bastard tried to fire the artillery at the citizens of Paris, the gun would explode and do more harm to the tank and its occupants than to the citizens of the city."

"But Hovis," I interrupted, trying to get past the boys story.

"On the very same day the boys in Lascaux were discovering caves," Hovis continued, as if he hadn't heard me, "the boy we both talked to last night was crawling through the sewers of Paris. He was trying to find an underground route to a certain Nazi headquarters. When he lit a match to see where he was, suddenly what exploded before his eyes, painted on the sewer walls, was the most outstanding example of a swastika he'd ever seen. Two seconds later, he was standing, as best he could, in the glare of Nazi flashlights, with seven guns pointed at his head."

"But you could see that the man who visited you last night," I insisted, "was probably not even born in 1940."

"I could see that," Hovis agreed, however hesitantly. "Still. When you were talking to him in your house, didn't you get the idea that he was describing things that had actually happened to him?"

"Yes."

With a shock that snapped my neck I realized that the man in my kitchen last night had talked to me exactly the way Hovis always had—same flowing, oddly connected view of history and its seemingly random facts. The man had done an almost perfect imitation of Hovis, in fact.

The question that unbalanced me at that moment was something like: Had the man copied Hovis, or had Hovis instructed the man?

"Hovis," I began slowly, "did you know this person, the one who visited us last night?"

"I did." He finished his coffee.

"You know who he was?"

"I do."

Hovis stood, coffee mug in hand, and shuffled toward a

basin beside the stove near a worn lead water pump. He was moving like an ancient man again, and I sat back in my chair, afraid that he was through talking to me about anything.

Without warning he darted toward the bed as if he were twenty years old, scooped up his rifle, clicked the safety, and pointed the muzzle right at my head.

"I know who he is," Hovis said steadily. "But I'm not sure about you."

I knew better than to rile him in any way. This wasn't the first time he'd had a sudden mood shift in my presence; in fact, it had happened many times. Twice he had shot at me. But he'd never pointed a gun at my head. It was disconcerting.

"Why aren't you sure about me, Hovis?" I asked as calmly as I could manage. "I've come to this place dozens of times to talk with you."

"You don't bring the tape machine," he snapped, "you come from the police, and you don't understand the visitor. That ain't like the Fever Devilin I ever knew."

With very little reflection, I realized he was correct. Any other time I'd come to visit him, I'd brought my old Wollensak, whether I'd needed it or not. And I'd never been to visit him before with any agenda other than collecting odd stories and checking on mountain genealogy. I'd approached the entire interview like a stranger. What had made me do it?

"I see your point," I admitted. "I'm not behaving the way I usually do."

"That's right." The barrel of the gun didn't move.

"I'll tell you why I think that is. Besides you and me, the stranger visited Lucinda Foxe last night. You know that she and I are engaged."

"What?" The gun lowered and a huge grin appeared. "You and that nurse woman? Spoke for?"

"Yes," I said, trying not to show my relief at the change in his demeanor. "I've declared for her."

"I'll swan." He sat back on his bed, gun still in hand, grin still on face. "That's a good match, that is. She's always been very kind to me. And so have you. The boy visited her last night, too?"

"Yes, he did. And I'm worried about it."

"Damn." His eyes seemed to clear a bit. "What am I doing pointing a gun at you? I tell you what: Being in that nuthouse, the county house? I believe it makes me worse, not better."

He was probably right. I'd been to the place only once, but it was sufficient to tell me that the prevailing philosophy there came more under the heading of incarceration than of aid. Most of the patients were given double doses of their medication every day—something I'd heard referred to as chemical lobotomies. Which, of course, made it easier to handle the inmates on the inside and made it much harder for the inmates to adjust on the outside. That was government psychiatry at its best. A bit of compassion colored my irritation at having a gun aimed at me.

"That's all right," I assured him, my pulse slowing. "I haven't had enough coffee this morning. I probably needed a little excitement."

"I wouldn't have shot you *much*," he offered.

"Look, Hovis," I said, rallying. "I *am* here because Skidmore asked me to come, but I'm also here because I'm involved, and so is Lucinda. I want to know what's going on. And you know something about all this. Something you're not telling me— even though I'm pretty sure I know what it is."

It was a good gambit, guessing there might be a secret and then pretending to know what it was. It worked very well in Blue Mountain, where everyone had deeply hidden secrets, and everyone's greatest fear was that those secrets would be discovered.

"Okay." He let go a heavy sigh, and the smile left his face. "I'll tell you. But you got to keep it in your heart. This ain't for Skidmore Needle. You got to promise me that. This is for you and your intended, so you'll know what's what. Promise me."

I clasped my hands, stalling. What to do?

"See, Hovis, if it has to do with the murder—"

"What I want to tell you don't have a thing to do with the killing." Hovis leaned toward me and lowered his voice. "And we both know that the boy who visited us last night ain't dead.

I can't say I'm *exactly* sure who that was on the road this morning. But you know it weren't the boy."

I stared back at him, unwilling to give anything away.

"So promise me you don't tell nobody else what I say to you," he concluded.

"If it has nothing to do with the murder," I said haltingly, "I suppose I could keep it to myself."

"Is that a promise?" he snapped.

"Yes." My eyes were steady, aimed right back at his.

He nodded once, accepting my solidarity.

"The one that visited us last night," Hovis whispered, "is not of our time here on this earth. He wanders in and out of a river. Sometimes he's here, sometimes he's not."

I hadn't meant to roll my head backward, it just happened.

"I know!" Hovis insisted at a stage whisper. "I know it seems impossible. But that one travels. And when he does, he always finds his brother, and kills him."

"What?" I blinked.

"That body on the road out there this morning," Hovis said so softly I could barely hear him, "was his brother. He's chased him down the hallways of time, Fever. The one we talked to last night? That was *Cain!*"

FIVE

EVEN OUT IN the sunlight around the shack, I couldn't shake the eerie mood Hovis had woven into the fabric of our conversation. Once he'd told me that our visitor was a man who ignored the confines of linear time, I'd begun making my way out the door. Not because his insistence made me nervous, but because I knew there was nothing coherent that could come from his belief. He had spilled over into the boundless regions of his own subconscious, and would be of little further help to my inquiries.

He did, however, prompt me to want to speak to Lucinda right away. As I made my way across the meadow toward the fence, I devised a sort of surprise luncheon scenario, the kind people in love sometimes enacted, as I understood it.

"You come back when you talk to your intended," Hovis called out from behind me. "You tell me what she said, hear?"

I waved in his direction without looking back. In seven more steps I was over the fence and grabbing the chrome on the door of my truck.

Lucinda was the head nurse at the county hospital. If she had been born a hundred years earlier, she would have been the midwife of our town—two hundred years earlier and she might have been its witch. Long out of high school and college, she somehow had managed to maintain not only a student's looks but also an enthusiasm for learning new things I found absolutely fascinating. Her desire to gather new ideas was the perfect complement to my passion for discovering old ones. There seemed no end to the things we could find in common, or the joy we found in sharing those things. And while this perfectly balanced friendship assured our relationship of solidity, there were always new horizons to be explored in other aspects of our mutuality—aspects of a more physical nature. Oddly, those explorations were the one subject we never discussed. It was as if talking about them would take them out of the astral plane on which they existed, and make them merely ecstatic, instead of transcendent. Perhaps it had been the mention of John Donne in Hovis's shack that created the psycho-sexual metaphysics in my mind as I parked my truck in the visitors' parking lot of the county hospital. Whatever had prompted those thoughts, they were the perfect fuel; they propelled me through the revolving doors, down the isopropyl-alcohol-scented hallways, all the way to the central nursing station.

"Well." Lucinda's face seemed to glow a more healthy amber than the fluorescent lights would ordinarily have allowed. "This is a surprise."

Her dark auburn hair was nearly hidden by the white cap; black eyes flashed and made her perfect porcelain face seem even more pale.

"I'm a little surprised myself," I admitted, gliding up to the counter.

"I love that pumpkin sweater on you," she said, setting down the file she had in her hand.

"And I think you know how I feel about your nurse's uniform." She blushed. Several other nurses did, too.

"My plan is to spirit you away for a spot of luncheon," I said quickly, "and you can't say no because if you do you'll have to stay behind when I leave and answer a few dozen questions about my penchant for starchy white dresses."

She shook her head.

The nurse beside her laughed, looked up at me, then said to Lucinda, "You know we can cover things while you're gone. And it is nearly lunchtime at that. Go on ahead."

I beamed at said nurse, whose name tag said Stacy Chambers.

"Nurse Chambers," I announced, "I'm going to see to it that there's a little something extra in your Christmas stocking this year."

Nurse Chambers lowered her face but raised her eyes to meet mine.

"Well, Dr. Devilin, I don't usually wear stockings, but I'd make an exception in your case."

The other nurses gave forth appropriately scandalized nonwords, mostly along the lines of *ooh.*

I nodded. "Serves me right," I told Nurse Chambers. "I should never attempt the idle flirtation. I only invite such mockery."

"What makes you think I was mocking?" Nurse Chambers jutted her chin in my direction.

"Because he knows if you were serious," Lucinda answered, "I'd have to place-kick you into the middle of next week."

"Might be worth it," Nurse Chambers said, blinking at least three times.

"Fine," Lucinda said breezily, rounding the counter of the nurses' station, pocketbook in hand. "Remind me about that when I get back from lunch."

"'Bye," Nurse Chambers oozed.

A few of the other nurses made the same noise.

"Perfectly grown, adult nurses," I said, falling in beside Lucinda, heading back down the hall for the exit, "behaving like high school girls."

"It's your own fault," she accused, taking my arm.

"I disagree. It has nothing to do with me. People who work in hospitals have enlarged libidos. Ask anyone. Why else would there be so many doctor shows on television?"

"And I suppose it's catching? Your libido seems to provoke you to speak differently to my nurses than you do to anybody else in town."

"Yes, because it *is* catching."

"God." She went first through the revolving door.

Once we were out in the autumn air, her face lost a bit of its ebullience, and she fell silent.

"Okay, so you know why I'm here," I admitted.

"About last night." She didn't look at me. It seemed obvious that she didn't want to talk about her experience with the visitor.

"Did you know that the person who visited you also came to my house, and also spoke with Hovis Daniels?"

She stopped in her tracks.

"And did you know," I continued, standing beside her, hoping she would look at me, "that Skidmore called me at six this morning because he'd found that man dead on the dirt road behind the Jackson place?"

Her eyes shot to mine.

"And did you know—"

"Stop." She held up her hand. "That man is dead?"

"No, as it turns out, I don't think he is." I motioned for her to come along to the truck. I didn't want to have the conversation in a parking lot. "Skid thought it was the man, but I went to look at him, and it wasn't the same person. It was, however, a very similar face, and the dead man was dressed in our visitor's clothing. So."

"Let's go," she murmured, heading for my truck. "I have to tell you what he said to me last night—even though you won't believe it."

Miss Etta's diner was crowded, as usual. Lucinda and I waited for a table by ourselves, even though several customers invited us to sit with them. I made half-hearted excuses about wanting to sit alone with my fiancée that were taken for embarrassment.

When a table finally came available, Lucinda set her purse down on it, and I took off my sweater to leave it on my chair. The room was stiflingly hot, though Miss Etta, asleep behind the cash register, had on a thick cardigan and was covered with an old, well-used quilt.

We made our way through the noisy tables to the kitchen, where there were plates piled beside the stove. The service was simple: Take a plate, dish up anything on the stove—or in it—and take it to your table. Eat heartily; pay six dollars as you left. The price had only recently gone up. And the food was a healing prayer.

The fried chicken that soaked for twenty-four hours in cold buttermilk before being turned into golden clouds was the local favorite, but I always preferred the game birds—Miss Etta's euphemism for any bird her great-great-nephew Boomer had caught or shot the morning before. Quail, partridge, dove, pheasant, wild turkey—usually a combination of all—were in the dish. The birds were boiled, and the meat was pulled from the bone, dredged in flour, lightly sautéed in olive oil, then placed in a casserole dish with turnips dug that same morning, greens intact, and fresh purple-hull peas. Everything was covered in chicken broth and cloves of garlic and cooked in an oven whose temperature gauge had long since been lost. But the dish had slow-cooked overnight, and it was hidden in the oven under tinfoil. I always fancied that not everyone knew to look in the oven, there were so many earthly delights on the stovetop. My delusions were shattered nearly every time, of course; the dish was always at least half empty when I went to put some on my plate.

Lucinda, inexplicably, put only steamed spinach, whole honeyed baby carrots, and a single piece of *Miss Etta's Special Sourdough Bread* on her plate.

The sourdough bread was a bit legendary, in that many claimed Miss Etta's starter came, in part, from the same sour mash that her moonshining neighbors used to make distilled spirits. These distilled spirits, however illegal they may have been, would have gotten any ten sinners into heaven. I knew because I had tasted it. Offer a bit of it to St. Peter and anything else would be forgiven, any other transgression washed clean; the great gate would swing wide. That same ecstasy could be found in Miss Etta's bread. You could taste the corn ripening in the field, the woodsmoke from the still, and the cold breeze as it washed through the maple trees, dropping jagged red leaves all around you. Every bite was a scandal.

Armed with such manna, we wound our way through the crowd, back to our table, and I began to eat. Lucinda began, instead, to talk.

"Wait until you hear this, Fever," she whispered, though it was hardly necessary in the noise of the room. "That man last night? He told me all about his wife, the woman he loved—that he was married to right after the Civil War."

I stopped chewing for a moment, but that was all.

"He told me," I said calmly, "something about going to fight in World War I—and he regaled Hovis Daniels with tales of espionage in occupied France twenty years later."

"How is Hovis?" she asked, her voice warming.

"Crazy as he can possibly be and still be out of custody." I breathed in the steam from the game birds, eyes half closed. "He held a gun on me and then told me that our visitor was Cain."

"Was *Cain?* From the Bible?"

I nodded, unwilling to waste a word when chewing was a much more delightful occupation.

"Well, he means no harm, bless his heart," she sighed, staring down at her spinach.

"So about the guy, the visitor," I prompted.

"Yes." She settled into her seat, picked up her fork very primly, and held it over her plate. "Here's what he said, as far as I can remember. It was so strange. He said he'd suffered a trauma. He said the first thing he could remember in life was the sound of someone singing. He woke up in a field hospital and heard it. He saw that he lay in bed, delirious, one among hundreds. Most of the other men had had their hands or feet or arms or legs hacked off. He had been dragged from the battlefield at Gettysburg. The singing he heard came from a group called the Hutchinson Family. They'd been at the field hospital for a month."

She stared at me.

I never ceased to marvel at Lucinda's ability to talk about the goriest subjects over a meal. Working in a hospital had inured her to the horrors of failed or flawed human flesh.

"What are you thinking?" she demanded after a moment.

"Sorry." I swallowed and stabbed my fork at the game bird. "This is really good. Look. He was talking about the Hutchinsons, a fairly famous singing group. Sometimes they're called America's first protest singers. They went around Civil War camps—"

"That's what he said!" She couldn't hold back. "The group he heard had moved from camp to camp entertaining Union troops for several years. They were renowned performers, especially in the person of the black-haired soloist Polly."

"I don't know her, but they were all deeply committed abolitionists and advocates of equal rights for women." I leaned forward. "These ideas, new as they were at the time, were a feature of all their performances. Most of the songs they sang protested war. All war. General McClellan, in fact, made the decision to cancel all their performances. He said their music was a disgrace, and their ideas were too radical. McClellan halted their tour in Gettysburg and ordered them to disperse, but they did not. Instead they wrote to the president. And when Lincoln heard about the singers' plight, he countermanded Mc-Clellan's decision. He told the general to reinstate the tour, at the general's own expense. And do you know what Lincoln said? He told McClellan, 'Theirs is the music I *want* my soldiers to hear. In times like these, art is the only thing that keeps us alive.' Isn't that great? Of course, the irony there is that shortly thereafter, President Lincoln went to see a play and lost his life in the theatre."

Lucinda set down her fork. "Do you want to hear what he told me, or do you want to do all the talking?"

"Sorry." I immediately put more food in my mouth. Best way to shut myself up.

"In the field hospital at Gettysburg," Lucinda continued after a brief moment of head-shaking, "Polly apparently took to wandering amongst the soldiers, offering what solace she could. It helped to pass the time *while they were waiting to hear from the president*—see, he told me that part."

"Sorry," I managed to say around a bite of turnip.

"So this Polly, she stood next to the man's cot and sang Mozart while the doctor prepared to saw off his right leg."

"Mozart?"

"One of the parlor songs," Lucinda said breezily. "But he said he'd been given so much whiskey he had no idea what was going on around him. All he knew was that a woman was singing somewhere. But she stopped singing to speak to the doctor, and do you know what she said? She said, 'I'm no expert, of course, but that leg looks dislocated. I saw something like it when my brother fell from a horse. Why couldn't you shove it back into place the way we did then—and not saw off this man's leg? Aren't you tired of sawing off men's legs?' And the doctor exhaled; the hand that held the saw relaxed. He hated his job. He just wandered away, and this Polly person twisted the leg, then snapped it back into its socket. The man said he had never known such pain, and he passed out completely."

Lucinda picked up her fork and stabbed a baby carrot.

I swallowed. "Yes. The thing is, when he talked to me he seemed to have in his head the kind of personal details that you could only have if you were remembering an experience."

She nodded. "Or if you had studied up on them, like for a test."

"That was your impression?"

"Well, his breadth of knowledge concerning the Hutchinson Family, which I had never heard of, was impressive. I'm sorry to say it this way, but he sounded a little like you do when you get off on one of your intellectual tangents."

I sat up straight. "If I occasionally explore a phenomenon that may be a few steps off the path, I'm only gathering berries, as it were, for the rest of the long journey."

"I know you *think* that your digressions will eventually contribute in some way to the larger picture, but they don't always." She was looking down, barely able to keep a smile from her lips.

"I know you *think* you're funny, teasing me about my intellectual tangents."

"Well," she said, shifting in her seat, "they *are* amusing."

"And they *always* have something to do with the point, my digressions."

"Well," she began, obviously in doubt.

"We were talking about our visitor," I insisted.

"Let's see." She set down her fork, apparently unable to eat and think at the same time. "He told me that the Hutchinsons' reinstated singing tour left Gettysburg while he was recuperating. When he awoke the doctor told him about the woman who saved his leg and maybe his life—and that she was gone. He vowed then that he would find her, follow her across the highest mountain, to the ends of the earth, to hell and back."

"As luck would have it," I interrupted, "he only had to pursue her as far as Atlanta."

"How did you know?"

"Because I am a man of mighty intellect," I sighed, "and

because as a sophomore at the university I studied the Hutchinson Family as part of a ballad and broadside course in the folklore department. They really were quite extraordinary in their day, very sociologically advanced. And some of them lived in Atlanta."

"I give," she acceded, teasing. "You actually *do* know everything."

"I don't know why I have to keep reminding you of that." I smiled back.

"Yes, he went to Atlanta," she said, continuing her recollection of the stranger's story. "They met early in 1865 at a church social, a dance. They were both Catholics. He came into the church during a sweetheart dance. Polly had no sweetheart."

"Hard to believe."

"Not really, especially in that day. I think it's likely that men were intimidated by her fame, her beauty, her intelligence."

"Well, you're probably right there," I agreed. "And the population of eligible bachelors in Atlanta had been severely reduced by the war."

"But here's the good part. He told me that when he talked to Polly the first time, she asked him how he was wounded, and he told her he hadn't been injured in the battle at Gettysburg. He said his leg had been dislocated when he was wrestling with an angel, and he told her his name was Jacob."

"There was a Jacob in my story—the one he told me." I nodded slowly. "But then he told me his name was Truck."

"No, I mean, that's a story from the Bible," Lucinda pressed. "Jacob wrestled with an angel all night long, and the angel dislocated Jacob's leg."

"That's right." My recollection of the story was hazy, but it was there.

"And apparently they were mad for each other after that." Lucinda blushed. "Before the older women at church could stop it, fire had seized them both. He told me he often ran from the field in the middle of the morning to be with Polly. He ran. They had six children, and the whole family could be seen planting roses, painting the farmhouse, singing in the kitchen while they all made dinner. There wasn't a man in the world who loved his own family more. That's why it must have been such a shock to Polly, to everyone, when he ran off one day and didn't come back."

"He left her?"

She nodded. "Never went back."

"Did he say why?"

"I think he was going to," she said, picking up her fork, "but the phone rang about then. It was Stacy, you know Stacy—the one you were just flirting with? She was calling about the—she couldn't read Dr. Mercer's handwriting, and she wanted to give this patient her medication; it was nothing. But when I came back to the porch, he was gone. Like he'd never even been there."

"Why do you say it that way?"

She leaned forward and lowered her voice. "We were sitting in those rockers on my front porch, you know, the ones with those nice blue cushions on the seats? And when I came back out, there wasn't an indentation in the pillow where he'd been sitting. I noticed that."

"What time was he there at your place, do you remember?"

"I came home from work and he was on the porch." She cocked her head. "I'd say it was about six o'clock."

"You were late."

"A little." She resumed her eating.

My food was gone.

"So that means," I mumbled, thinking to myself, "that he visited Hovis first, me last."

"Is that important?"

"Well," I said, taking in a big breath, "if I'm wrong, and the guy Skid found this morning is actually the guy who visited us last night, I'm the last one to see him alive."

"But you think the dead man is someone else." She kept eating.

"I do, however odd it may seem. I mean, the dead man looks a little like the man I spoke to last night—"

"Dressed in the same clothes." She continued my thought.

"You'll have a look at him when you're finished eating." I stared down at her plate. "If you ever do finish eating."

"You eat too fast."

"Fine." I sat back. "But do you mind having a look at the body?"

"Of course not." She scooped a bite of purple-hull peas on her fork with a crust of the manna bread. "Do we have to go get Skidmore?"

"He seems to be leaving this part of it to me while he does other things."

"Like what?"

"Paperwork." I grinned. "He has to sit in that stuffy old office while I get to have lunch with the prettiest girl in town."

She looked up instantly. "Is *she* having lunch with you? I better hurry up and finish my bread; she'll be mad if she sees me still sitting here when she walks in."

"You know very well—"

She smiled, and it shut me up instantly.

"You're very sweet to me, Fever," she murmured, "and there's no other boy in town who would take me out to lunch with the promise of a dead body for dessert." She blinked once.

"And how many other women in these parts," I countered, "could eat spinach and talk about corpses at the same time?"

"Made for each other," she sighed, mocking me.

"The point is," I insisted, "that our visitor was trying to tell us something. It made sense to him. I mean, he didn't ask me for money or a place to stay or anything like that."

"Same here." She popped the last bite of bread into her mouth.

"So why did he visit us," I continued, "and what was he trying to say?"

"Well," Lucinda said, staring at the tabletop, "he didn't seem to be trying to tell me anything but his story. I mean—he's just a wandering soul."

"Except for the fact that he probably couldn't have fought in the Civil War, World War I, *and* World War II."

"Maybe he was telling someone else's story." She shrugged. "We should hurry on over to the Deveroes'. I kind of have to get back to work—wish I didn't."

I reached for my wallet; she stood. A quick half an hour was the best I could have hoped for. Lucinda had worked too hard for most of her life. She was genetically incapable of slacking off. When it was time for her to go back to the hospital, there was no argument about it.

"I'll just speak with Miss Etta," I said, heading for the cash register.

Miss Etta, as usual, was asleep in a very uncomfortable chair close to the kitchen door. I knew she had been awake since four that morning, cooking and preparing the place for her customers. Her hair was white smoke, wreathed in a pale halo just above snowy eyebrows. Her face, ancient but barely wrinkled, was the very model of serenity. I lifted a twenty-dollar bill from my wallet as quietly as I could, but Miss Etta spoke to me, eyes closed, as she always did.

"That's too much, Fever. They was only two of you."

"But we enjoyed it as much as four people would have," I told her, placing the twenty in the cash register.

"You trying to figure out who it was they found behind the Jackson place this morning?"

I had long since given up wondering how she knew everything, and saw everything with her eyes closed. I just nodded.

"More power to you." She resettled in her chair and was silent. "Tell Lucinda she's right."

Lucinda was already at the door. I glanced at her and then back down at Miss Etta.

"I know she's usually right about most things," I said hesitantly, "but to what, in particular, do you refer?"

The whisper of a smile touched Miss Etta's lips. "You two are made for each other," she said softly. "Peas in a pod."

I took in a breath to respond, thought better of it, and followed Lucinda out the door.

The sun had warmed the pavement, and, in turn, the air had expanded. A cool, watery breeze against the sun-warmed skin: there was a sensation barely matched in heaven, in my opinion.

"So what are you going to do?" Lucinda was already climbing into my truck.

"I'm going to take you back to the Deveroe Brothers' place,"

I answered, opening the driver's door, "and then I'm going to take you back to the hospital."

"I mean after that."

"Depends on what you say about the body."

It was close to one o'clock when we pulled up to the parking area on the side of the yard at the Deveroes'. Donny Deveroe, most vocal of the family, appeared on the porch.

"Thought you'd be back," he called before I'd even turned off the engine. "Sheriff told me that you might have been the last man to see the deceased alive. Hey, Ms. Foxe."

"Hey, Donny," she said, sliding out of the truck. "How's that thumb?"

"Still hurts," he said shyly, "but it ain't all swole up like it was." He held it out for us to see.

"Casket slammed down on it last week," Lucinda confided to me as I came around the truck headed for the porch.

Donny was the size of a barn, but his face was scrubbed and blushing, his brown hair combed back, and he wore a fresh black suit.

"Hear anything from your sister?" I asked him.

"I believe she's expecting," he said hesitantly. "She and Able might finally have a baby."

Sister Truevine and her husband had moved to Athens, Georgia, so that she could attend the university.

"That's very nice," I told him. "I know they wanted to start a family."

"Come on in." He turned and held the front door for us. "I reckon you didn't come to talk to me about my kin."

"Right—the reason we're here," I said in a very deliberate voice, "is that the man you have back there might have visited Lucinda last night, right before he came to see me."

"Oh." Donny had learned, as a part of his mortuarial studies, how to offer the perfect noncommittal response. "Then won't you come in."

He stepped aside, and we entered the quiet of the funeral parlor itself. The hallway was spotless. To our left was a perfect Victorian sitting room. The staircase that led to the office upstairs had been given a recent lemon scrubbing. The banister was more mirror than wood.

"Back this way," Donny said, his voice lowered, "as you know."

He slid effortlessly past us and led the way. In a little room at the end of the hall sat a gleaming chromium table covered with a snow-white sheet. He folded back the sheet covering the body as if he were performing some sort of magic trick. His face was a solid mask of dignity, and his hands moved with the delicacy of a dancer.

Finished with his effort, he stood back, hands clasped in front of him.

Lucinda peered down at the face of the corpse. I was more interested in the dead man's hands.

"Donny?" I asked softly. "Why is he wearing those?"

The corpse was sporting some very large plaid cotton gloves.

"Sometimes," he whispered, as if he were in church, "when a person dies suddenly and it's a little cold where they got killed at, if it's a killing, then blood can rush to the extremities. His hands are all swole up and gross looking. We ain't had time to fix it yet—but we will."

Lucinda's concentration was more appropriate.

"Can you turn up the lights in here?" she asked, not looking at Donny.

"Of course." He took a single step to his left, touched a slider on the light switch, and doubled the illumination in the room.

Lucinda appeared not to be breathing. She didn't move. All her concentration was focused on that pale, blue-veined face.

With a sudden pulling back of her head, she sipped a loud breath.

"Nope." She bit on her lower lip. "This is not, in fact, the man I talked to last night. Looks a little like him. Dressed like him. Not the same."

"Well." I nodded.

"Then," Donny stammered, losing a bit of his professional composure, "who the hell is he?"

I glanced at my watch. I had roughly fifty-two hours to answer that question, and I had no idea where to begin.

SIX

ALL THE WAY back to my house, after I'd dropped Lucinda off at the hospital, I tried to convince myself that the time constraint placed on finding the murderer was artificial. Millroy's obstinate stupidity meant nothing. Even if he filed his report, I could still go on looking for the man who had been in my kitchen. Skidmore could work surreptitiously. He'd done it before.

But I knew the more urgent truth of it. If we didn't find the man in two days, that would almost certainly mean he'd escaped Blue Mountain, and once he was gone from our home, the odds of ever finding him were relatively hopeless—unless I could piece together some meaning from the man's fantastic stories.

As I pulled up into my front yard, I realized that I might be able to learn about the man if I could make sense of his fictions. He had been fairly specific in each of his tales, naming real places and people. I wondered if those bits of information might lead to a greater portrait of the stranger, and perhaps expand our possible time frame beyond the two-day prison set for us by Millroy. For that I needed a bit of assistance.

I climbed down out of the truck and all but ran into the house. I had the phone in my hand and was dialing before the door slammed behind me.

"Andrews?" I said into the phone. "If you don't put down whatever it is you're doing and help me, a killer will get away."

"Oh, hello, Fever," he said very casually. *"That* again?"

Winton Andrews was, as I had always said, the most unlikely Shakespeare scholar in America. A rugby player from Manchester, England, tall, blond, and bony, he was the sort of person who would bet he could drink you under the table in a neighborhood bar—and win the bet. He had, in fact, directed plays at the newly rebuilt Globe Theatre in London and had once unearthed a document that seemed to be from Christopher Marlowe to Thomas Kyd warning him that Shakespeare's *Hamlet* was better than Kyd's. It had yet to be authenticated to everyone's satisfaction—and probably never would be. See, a little thing like that could, apparently, roil the waters of Shakespeare scholarship to the boiling point. His reputation in the academic community was growing. He had been my best friend in Atlanta before I'd left the university, and we'd remained close enough that it was not the first time I'd called upon his aid. In fact, it might have been the fifth in fewer than that many years.

This time, however, after I'd spent nearly a quarter of an hour regaling him with the facts of the situation, his reaction was different from the usual one.

"No." He sounded as if he might be chewing something.

"What do you mean, *no?*"

"I mean I can't leave Atlanta at the moment. We're in the middle of homecoming week, and I have midterm exams to finish, and you know it's Tuesday, right? I just can't take off in—"

"But someone's been killed!"

"Be that as it may," he mumbled. He was definitely eating a sandwich or something—right into the phone. "Two other faculty are out with the flu, and I have to take over some twentieth-century lit course with absolutely no idea—hey, Vonnegut wrote *Slaughterhouse-Five*, right? And P.S.: why is it that you only call me when someone's dead?"

"Not always." I was quite deflated. He had never refused to help me before. "We went fishing that time—nothing happened then."

"That's right," he countered. "*Nothing*. I did not catch a single fish—not fish *one*."

"Well, which is it: There's too much going on when you visit me," I demanded, "or not enough? You can't have it both ways."

"I can't have it at all, is what I'm trying to tell you." He swallowed loudly. "It's *Tuesday*."

"But," I stammered, "I have to... Didn't you hear the part about my having to find the man by Thursday?"

"Fever," he said sternly, "I can't help you with your little mystery novel moment right now. I'm up to my armpits in students who can't *spell* Shakespeare."

"*Shakespeare* couldn't spell Shakespeare," I grumbled. "He signed his name differently on different documents. *You* showed me that."

"And I'm trying to get my tenure portfolio together this year, you know. I have to put it all in some new Web program called Sedona that takes forever to—"

"Andrews—"

"No! Final! I can't leave my office; I can't even go to my house. I'm too busy to *breathe*."

I stood for a moment in stunned silence.

"I could come up on Saturday," he ventured after a moment. "I'll need a break—"

"Saturday will be too late!" I insisted.

"Well, there it is." He sniffed. "If there's anything I can do for you from my lonely little office here on the second floor of the Arts and Sciences Building, then I'll try to squeeze it in between three and four in the morning. Otherwise, include me out."

"But..." I trailed off.

He took the phone away from his mouth and I heard him say, obviously to someone coming into his office, that he'd be right with them.

"Look, Dr. Devilin," he said into the phone, "on top of everything else, I have advisees. One of my students is here now for her advisement appointment, so I have to go."

"But." It was a complete sentence.

"Um," he said, completely distracted. "Okay. Well."

"I'll let you know how it comes out." I sighed.

In the moment of silence that transpired, I could hear the student in his office say that she wanted to graduate by Christmas.

"No weekend invitation?" Andrews said to me at last.

"Let me see how everything goes."

"Right, then," he said cheerfully, and hung up.

I stood holding the phone a second, staring at it, a bit stunned.

I barely heard the door creak behind me.

"Put that phone down, boy," the voice said, "and turn around, or I'll just shoot you in the back."

I stood frozen for another moment before my mind allowed me to recognize the voice.

"Hey, Hovis." I hung up the phone and turned slowly to face him.

He was pointing his hunting rifle directly at my heart.

"What'd you tell that sheriff?" His eyes were slits; his voice was a snarl.

"Since I talked to you? Nothing. I went and had lunch with Lucinda at Miss Etta's. The game birds were really good today."

"Then why'd he come to arrest me?" Hovis stood like a statue.

"Skidmore came to arrest you? After I left?"

"He did." His voice softened a bit. "You didn't know?"

"I did not." I held up one hand. "Would you mind lowering your rifle? If it goes off and messes up this kitchen, are you going to pay for it?"

"I don't have any money," he objected.

"So—" I motioned for him to lower the gun.

He would not.

"Why he to come and take me away? Again." Hovis stared out the window.

"How did you get here?" I knew he didn't have a car. "For that matter, how'd you get away from the sheriff?"

He grinned. "I got my ways."

"There's no place to hide in that shack."

"I *got* my ways," he insisted, grin gone.

"Right. So—what? You came to shoot me because you thought I'd told the sheriff—"

"I thought you told him I was crazy again." He sniffed. "I'm not. Just because I told you about that boy that visited us last night. What I said."

"Yes. Well. There was something strange about him, I'll give you that. I'm not as convinced as you are that he's a character from the Bible."

"He's a traveling creature," Hovis said softly. "He's not real.

He walks up and down the hallways of time, and he comes to visit now and again, as a warning to other men."

"All right." I nodded once.

"This is a nice kitchen," he said thoughtfully, looking around. "I really would hate to mess it up."

"Right." I stared at the barrel of the gun. "Then you ought to stop pointing that thing at me."

"I'll stop pointing this thing at you when you stop lying to me."

"I'm not lying to you, Hovis." I tried edging my way into the kitchen, but that made him nervous.

"Where you think you get to?" He lifted the barrel. "I don't want to shoot this thing, but you make me nervous. I don't like to be nervous. I shot up that man from the hospital when he jumped at me. You're not about to go jumping at me."

The expression on Hovis's face was one I'd seen before: a combination of fear and confusion. He wouldn't mean to shoot me, but if something startled him, he might pull the trigger. Skidmore had told me about the man from the county hospital who'd rushed into the little shack on the Jackson property and gotten a chest full of bird shot. His lungs still hadn't completely healed.

I didn't know what Hovis had in the rifle he was pointing at me, but I felt that I would be needing my lungs in top working order, so I stopped moving into my kitchen.

I noticed that his worn brown construction boots were covered in sticker burrs from a certain weed that grew on the eastern side of the mountain. That meant he had come along a fairly difficult slope to get to my house, but it was a straight shot and he could have scrambled quickly—under ten minutes—to my front door. It would take a car on back roads nearly twice that amount of time to travel from his shack to my house. How he'd escaped his shack if Skidmore had been standing at his front door was a tougher nut to crack.

"Listen, Hovis," I began slowly, "I'm just guessing, here, but don't you think it's possible that the sheriff considers you a suspect because the body was found fifty feet from your home? Not to mention the fact that the deceased visited you the night before."

"He visited you, too." The gun twitched.

"And if the body had been found in my front yard, the sheriff would have come to talk to me about it, don't you think?"

"First off," he said, his throat tightening, "sheriff didn't come to talk, he came to arrest. Said so. Second, he don't treat me same as you. A crazy old man don't have the same kind of legality as a good friend of the law does. You know I'm right."

Alas, I did know. Skidmore would be fair with Hovis, but the county would not, given his record, afford him the same consideration.

"All right." I folded my arms. "So what's your plan? If you shoot me, you *know* the law will put you away."

He looked away from me for an instant, then snapped back to his cold stare.

"I can't go back to that county nuthouse." He sniffed. "I ain't got that many more good years left, and I sure as hell don't want to spend them in that place."

"Then don't shoot me." Simple.

"Yeah." He took in a huge breath. "I guess not."

He lowered the gun, but only a little.

"You want some coffee now?" I offered.

"The thing is," he said, not hearing me, "I don't know *what* I did last night. I recall speaking with the boy. He told me his stories, I told him mine for a mite. We had a drop. I don't take that much anymore, but Ms. Jackson's cousin Red? He makes some fine private cider."

I didn't know Red Jackson, but I'd heard of him. I bought my illegally distilled apples elsewhere. Red's was made quick and priced to move. I preferred a better-crafted beverage, though mine did cost at least three times what Red charged.

"You drank with the stranger?" I moved cautiously toward my stove.

"One thing led to another." Hovis had still not set down his rifle. It remained primed; his finger was still on the trigger.

"And you're not certain how the evening ended."

"I know I didn't kill him!" The gun was right back where it had been, pointed directly at my chest.

"Not that I want to add any further confusion to the issue," I said slowly, freezing, "but you and I both know that the body Skidmore found this morning did not belong to the man we talked to last night. Remember?"

"I remember," he snarled resentfully.

"Well, don't you think that's strange?" I thought perhaps if I got him thinking about something else other than shooting me, I might have a chance of getting him to set down the gun. "I mean, you talk to some strange young man, and the very next morning a dead body is found on the road behind your place?"

"Wait." His mind was swimming, obviously, and his eyes were unfocused. "The dead one ain't the same as the one... Wait."

The gun went down again. Hovis closed his eyes. A single tear escaped from between the lids of his left eye.

"Hovis?" I ventured.

"I'm confused." He didn't open his eyes.

"Maybe you should sit down." I didn't move. I didn't want to startle him.

After a second his shoulders relaxed, and he set the gun against the door frame again. This time he opened his eyes and sailed straight for my kitchen table.

"I believe I will have a swallow of your coffee, if you're a mind to make some."

His hands were shaking, and his voice was suddenly hollow sounding. He sat at the table, staring straight ahead.

I knew better than to make my espresso and got out the French press instead. Hovis was used to watery, rust-colored brew. I started a kettle and pulled out the coffee grinder.

"What's that?" he asked, sounding very tired.

"Coffee grinder. I buy fresh beans and grind them myself. It tastes better."

"I know." He sat back. "Before the war, the Big War, I used to have a hand-crank coffee grinder. That's when I lived up top of Devil's Hearth, you know—that part of the mountain. Had a nice place."

He'd told me about his cabin several dozen times, but I thought it best to allow him to reminisce about better days.

"It's pretty this time of year, when all those old oak trees start to turn colors." I poured beans into the grinder.

"I still hike up there from time to time." He sighed. "Sit where the cabin used to be. If I close my eyes and hold my head just right, I can hear Barbrie's voice."

He rarely mentioned his wife, long dead. I didn't know if it made me feel safer or sadder.

"Little Barbrie." He was speaking to himself.

She had died when an epidemic of influenza had torn though the Appalachian Mountains in 1956. They'd been married for five years and had saved enough money to buy a larger farm. Barbrie, her name a diminutive of Barbara after the ballad "Barbara Allen," had miscarried twice owing primarily to bad nutrition and hard work. The new place would have meant an easier life and, in all probability, a family. But when she'd contracted the flu, Hovis stopped all his work to take care of her. He'd once told me that he had tended the body for three days after she had died, hoping she was only asleep. In the end he came down off the Devil's Hearth with the body in his arms. Mrs. Jackson, some vague kin of Barbrie's, had taken Hovis in, tended to him for a time, then put him to work on her farm. The old-timers in Blue Mountain who were inclined to kindness said that she did it from the dictates of her Christian heart. Those more inclined to a harsher view said that she did it to keep Hovis nearby so that she could chastise him for letting Barbrie die. She was often heard to say that the girl had most likely died because Hovis kept her apart from her family. Hovis was burdened, nearly daily, by the concept that he'd killed the woman he loved. A few of the worst gossips in town blamed that guilt for the collapse of Hovis's mind.

"Do you take sugar?" I asked him softly.

He opened his eyes. "I could use some."

The afternoon had turned golden. Autumn light burnished the clouds, and a chevron of geese arrowed its way through them, headed south. The wind picked up, and showers of red and brown leaves decorated my lawn, my porch. It seemed to me that the earth had joined me in a moment of relief:

Winter, like a gun, had been laid aside for a while, despite the fact that it was so obviously nearby. It just wasn't time for its blast—yet.

Alas, like most moments of such repose, that one was short-lived.

With no warning whatsoever, there was a thud on my porch as if a sack of apples had been dropped, and the front door flew open. Sheriff Skidmore Needle appeared, pistol in hand.

"Swear to God, Hovis," he growled between clenched teeth, "if you reach for that rifle, I'll put a bullet in your arm and take my time getting you to the hospital."

Hovis was twitching, but he did not reach for his gun.

Deputy Mathews appeared to Skidmore's left. She had come in the back door, pistol pointed toward Hovis and—because I was standing in the wrong place at the wrong time—also toward me.

I set down the coffee mug I had chosen for Hovis and took a step away from him.

"Don't you move, either, Fever." Skidmore's eyes were locked on Hovis. "I don't want to be distracted wondering which way you're going to move in case I have to shoot my gun."

Hovis turned slowly to face Skidmore, breathing with some difficulty.

"What in hell you want with me, Sheriff?" he asked. "What's so important you and your deputy have to point your guns at a crazy old man?"

"Well, Hovis," Skidmore answered, appearing absolutely at the end of his patience, "I tried coming up to your house over there and just talking with you, but you disappeared somehow, and when a man runs from me, I get to thinking he may have done something I won't like. So I'm bound to ask: Have you done something wrong recently—you crazy old man?"

"No."

"There's my point." Skidmore took a step toward Hovis. "If you haven't done anything wrong, why did you run?"

"From the police?" Hovis's face seemed to crack, and he was suddenly laughing. "Are you serious? Sheriff Maddox used to put me in his trunk and leave me there overnight. And every time

I see a uniform, I end up in the county nuthouse. I ain't had a good experience of your kind, and once burnt is twice shy."

It wasn't that hard to see his point.

"Well, then, let me tell you why I came to talk with you, and why I've got my firearm out." Skidmore took another step. "I found a dead body not fifty feet from your front door early this morning, and he was shot with a pistol like the one you used to have, a gun from the Big War."

Hovis looked over his shoulder at me. "You tell him about that?"

"I haven't seen—"

"Hovis!" Skidmore demanded. "You tell *everybody* about that gun. I don't believe there's a person in this county who doesn't know about your World War II pistol."

"And that's what killed the man you found—" I began.

"Fever, would you mind staying out of this?" Skidmore whined. "I'm kind of in the middle of something here."

"Sorry." I leaned back against the counter.

"So, see, Hovis," Skidmore continued, a bit more reasonably, "I wanted to ask you about that. But after you vanished from your house—which you'll have to tell me how you did that one day—I went through all your things. And I couldn't find that pistol anywhere. Unfortunately for you, a policeman's mind works this way: The murder weapon is missing, that means the killer got rid of it. You see it on the television shows all the time."

"Ain't got no television," Hovis grumbled.

"No, that's not the point," Skidmore sighed, lowering his gun half an inch. "What I'm saying is that you were a pretty good suspect in a murder investigation, and then you fled the scene—which makes you a great suspect."

"Suspect?" Hovis demanded.

"We found a man murdered—" Skidmore answered at double his previous volume.

"What possible motive could Hovis have had," I said, baffled, "for killing a stranger in the middle of the—"

"Fever, damn it!" Skidmore's gun was aimed right at Hovis's head, and he took another step forward.

It scared me almost as much as it did Hovis.

"They do talk a lot about *motive* in those television shows I was telling you about," he said softly to Hovis. "In this case I believe it has something to do with a bit of evidence Dr. Devilin is unaware of."

"What?" I couldn't help taking a step forward; it was practically involuntary.

It was also very unfortunate.

When I leaned toward Skidmore, he looked up at me. When he looked up at me, Hovis leapt up from his chair. When Hovis leapt up, he reached for his rifle. When his hand went to grab it, Deputy Mathews shot her gun. When she fired her gun, a bullet came out and went into Hovis Daniels's hand—the very hand that was on his rifle. The bullet went though the hand and right into my refrigerator, where it damaged, I was later to learn, my eggs. Not to mention the mess that Hovis made by bleeding onto my floor and my counters.

Skidmore turned in a motion too fast to see and had the muzzle of his gun right on Hovis's forehead. Without a word he motioned to Deputy Mathews and she moved, again faster than I could quite make out, to put handcuffs on Hovis while Skidmore kicked the hunting rifle to the floor and away from us, into the living room.

It all happened in less than three seconds, and Hovis was on the floor, in handcuffs, bleeding and moaning.

"God damn it, Hovis," Skidmore muttered.

"She shot me!" Hovis apparently couldn't believe that someone as nice as Melissa Mathews could have fired her pistol into his hand.

"Jesus." I blinked and leaned backward again.

From nowhere Melissa had produced a bottle of hydrogen peroxide and a roll of gauze. She was dabbing the wound she had made, cleaning it. In under a minute, it seemed, she had bandaged the hand and gotten Hovis to his feet.

"I guess we'll take you to the hospital after all," she sighed. "I'm sorry I had to shoot you, Hovis. But you were reaching for your rifle. I'm *supposed* to shoot you if you do that."

She said it as if she were explaining to a student why she'd handed out a bad report card.

Hovis seemed to accept it with a degree of resignation, however, nodding silently. Then he looked up at me.

"Sorry, Fever," he managed hoarsely. "I guess your kitchen got messed up after all."

"It's okay." I tried to smile at him.

"You know I didn't do this." His eyes burned into mine. "You know who did. You have to help me. How many times I told you a story that you used to make good for yourself? How many things I taught you about over the years? You got to do this one thing for me now, Fever. I need help and ain't nobody else on this earth to do it but you. I got no one and nothing. You're the onliest one can do it. I'm saying, you have to help me."

I rubbed my forehead.

"Seriously, Skidmore, what possible reason could you have… I mean, you *know* that the man you found this morning—"

"I'll tell you what I know," Skid shot back, tight as a drum. "I heard from Donny Deveroe that you took Lucinda to visit the deceased. Neither one of you believes that the dead man is the same as the one who visited you'uns last night, but I don't agree. Deputy Mathews is right: A man looks different dead—different enough to confuse you both. I also know that Hovis Daniels has or had the pistol that I believe killed the man I found this morning. And here's what I know that you don't, because, despite what you're always telling me, you actually *don't* know everything: Donny found a locket in the dead man's coat. It's a pretty little piece of jewelry that used to belong to Barbrie Daniels—but it now has her picture inside."

"That boy stole Barbrie's locket?" Hovis appeared about to explode. "Where is it? Give it to me!"

Hovis was suddenly wild. Absolutely ignoring his wounded hand, he grabbed Skidmore by the arm and shook him.

"Give me Barbrie's locket!"

Skidmore flailed his arm and Hovis fell backward; Melissa caught him.

"Take him out to the car," Skidmore snarled.

Melissa nodded and, with surprisingly little effort, dragged Hovis out of my house in a heartbeat, stopping only to scoop up his rifle off my living room floor. He was struggling and mumbling, but apparently no match for Melissa's youthful vigor.

"The locket is the motive, wouldn't you think?" Skidmore finally put away his pistol. "You see the way Hovis is about it."

"Look," I began, "that old man didn't kill anyone, and you know it."

"Once again," he said, more calmly than before, "I'm happy to tell you what I know. I have now arrested a suspect in the murder of a young man I found on the road in back of the Jackson place early this morning. *That* is the report I'm about to file with the county. And after I do I'm going to tell Millroy I have a man in the jailhouse and have filed said report."

"But—"

"What that buys us is a bit more breathing room," Skidmore said, turning to head out the door. "Millroy can't very well file a suicide if I've already put in a murder suspect. So you can go find the actual murderer—if you think it's different from Hovis Daniels."

I couldn't ever remember having heard the phrase "a twinkle in his voice" before, but Skidmore certainly had one.

"Do you mean—" I began.

"It's nice to leave you astonished at *my* work," he said over his shoulder, "for a change."

I followed him through the living room to the front door. I decided against berating him for using Hovis in such a manner—unless he actually did suspect Hovis. I opted instead for the academic choice: making fun of his diction.

"You know," I told him, gathering my wits, "you said 'you'uns' a minute ago, when you were excited."

"I did not."

"You can make a boy a sheriff," I insisted, "but you can't kick the country out of his mouth."

"Shut up." He clattered down the steps. "You got work to do."

I watched him move deliberately toward the police car. Hovis was settled in, and Deputy Mathews was climbing in up front. Skidmore didn't look back, but I knew he was smiling.

SEVEN

THE PHONE RANG for a long time before Andrews picked it up.

"Sorry," he began, "what?"

"It's me again," I said quickly, "and in fact I did figure out a way you could help me between three and four o'clock this coming morning."

"Hello, Fever," he sighed. "I'm really—"

"You have access to Galileo at the university," I fired back. "All I want you to do is look up Polly Hutchinson, around 1865, from the famous singing Hutchinson Family, and tell me who, if anyone, she married."

In the silence that followed my request, I had a moment to reflect on how odd a task it must have seemed to him. Meanwhile, I gathered up a handful of paper towels, dabbed a bit of water on them, and began wiping up Hovis's blood. A lot of things seemed normal to me in contrast to that.

"This will help you find out who killed somebody this morning in your little town?" he asked at last.

"It will set my mind at ease about something," I told him hesitantly, "so that I can pursue other more probable avenues."

"You're trying to entice me with your vague suggestions and your weird request," he accused, "but it won't work. I don't care what happened up there, I can't help. Look her up on the Web yourself."

"I've done a bit of research on the Hutchinsons over the years, and I barely remember Polly. Sister Abby was one of the important family members, but Polly? I think she might have been a granddaughter or a younger member. See, there ended up being two groups, and during the Civil War they popularized tunes like 'The Battle Cry of Freedom' and 'Tenting on the Old Camp Ground'—they were the precursors of the Weavers in the early 1960s."

"The Weavers?" He was growing irritated, I could tell.

"Protest singers," I told him. "Songwriters that influenced—"

"Stop!" he demanded.

"A normal Web search is two inches deep." I tried as hard as I could to sound angry about it. "I need heartier genealogical information."

"Damn it." Andrews countered my invented anger with the more genuine item of his own. The worst had happened: He was curious.

I could hear papers rustling, then scratching.

"Polly Hutchinson," he sighed, "1865."

"You're a wonderful person," I told him in only slightly mocking tones.

"I'm not spending more than ten minutes on this," he warned, "and I mean it when I say I won't get to it until after midnight."

"Wonderful person," I insisted.

He hung up.

The sun was low, hanging over the tops of the trees, but at that time of year night would come on quickly. I knew Lucinda wouldn't be coming home until later, but I thought we might have dinner together. I wanted to talk things over with her, say out loud all the puzzling things in my head where our visitor was concerned. A slant of dying light filled in places all over the oak trees where leaves had been only hours before. Red illumination seemed to set the limbs on fire—and seemed an echo of the blood on my floor.

I finished cleaning, trying not to think too much about the way Hovis had told me I had to help him. Even though he'd pointed his rifle at me, I decided he hadn't really intended to shoot me.

I sat in my living room, staring out the front window past the rockers on the porch at the beginnings of a sunset. I tried to make my mind connect the three stories the visitor had told, but I soon discovered that waking up at six in the morning and having your life threatened before sunset actually makes for a better nap than any kind of thinking.

The phone woke me. I had no idea what time it was; the night outside had fallen black and moonless because of the cloud cover. I swam upward from a deep pool of sleep, fighting my way to the surface. The phone kept ringing. I managed at last to turn on a light beside my chair and stagger into the kitchen to make the phone stop bothering me.

"Hello?" It didn't even sound like my voice.

"Fever?" Andrews even thought he might have dialed the wrong number.

"What time is it?" I mumbled.

"Two in the morning." He was impatient. "I *told* you."

"You're just doing this to prove a point," I sighed, waking up a little.

"Do you want to hear what I found out or not?"

I turned on the kitchen light, which proved a mistake. It blinded me. I had to feel my way to a kitchen chair—noisily.

"Okay," I said, clearing my throat, "shoot."

"So to the point of my investigation: Either you're screwing with me," he sneered, "or someone's screwing with you."

"Um." I couldn't think of anything better to say at that moment.

"There was a Polly Hutchinson, all right, in your famous singing Hutchinson Family, but she died when she was eleven, of influenza, on tour with the family during the Civil War. There was also, however, a Polly Hutchinson who was a young singer in 1945 in Atlanta. She was a descendant of the patriarch of the singing family, Jesse Hutchinson, and *she* was married to a man whose name, whose *given* name—believe it or not—was Truck."

That woke me.

"Truck?" I sat straight up.

"I know," he said, mistaking my response. "Even someone with a name like Fever can afford to make fun of the name Truck."

"What was his last name?" I held my breath, for some reason.

"Truck? Wait…here it is. Jackson. Truck Jackson."

It would be an exaggeration to say that my brain exploded,

but there were certainly all manner of facts and ideas colliding with enough force to give me a stirring headache.

"Jackson." I managed to repeat the name.

"Why?" Andrews asked. "Is that important?"

"Did you happen to find out anything more about that Polly Hutchinson?"

"Like what?"

"When she died?" I ventured.

"Wait." He shifted the phone to his other ear, and I heard papers rattling. "She's still alive. Living in a granny high-rise close to the university, in fact. All of eighty-two years old. She was a large contributor to the opera when the Met—"

"She's still alive? Polly Hutchinson?"

"Polly Hutchinson *Jackson*. Yes."

"I'll be down there in the morning," I said instantly. "I've got to get a few things straight in my mind, and make a few calls, but I'll be there by eight this morning at the latest."

Right then I couldn't have explained why I felt such great urgency, but I had to talk to this woman, ask her about Truck Jackson.

"Wait, you mean you're coming to my house?"

"Would you mind? You don't have to do anything more, except point me in the direction of the place where this woman lives."

"Do you want to *stay* here?"

"As many times as you've stayed in my house," I snapped, "you're going to begrudge me—"

"I'm not begrudging anything," he groused, "but you usually invite me to stay, I don't invite myself."

"You just did!" I insisted. "Earlier this very evening on the phone, you invited yourself up here."

"After—"

"Right! *After* you turned down my invitation."

"Sort of." He was losing steam. He hadn't had a nap the way I had.

"Look, I'm just saving us a few steps. Can I come stay with you or do I have to get a hotel room?"

"Damn, Fever, of course you can stay here. Damn."

"You're working too hard," I told him. "It's making you grouchy. You should go to bed."

"You know," he said weakly, "you're really..."

He couldn't quite seem to verbalize what I was, really, so he just hung up.

I stood there with the phone in my hand for, perhaps, a full two or three minutes, listening first to the dial tone, then to the siren-like noise it made to warn me that it was off the hook, and finally to a recorded message that insisted I hang up. I did not. I stood listening to the silence afterward, because I liked the metaphor: After a good conversation, like a good life, there is a calm moment of the dial tone, followed by the panic of the moment of death, the final words from some professional, and finally...silence.

I only took another three seconds after that to realize I was standing in my kitchen after two o'clock in the morning, thinking about how peaceful death must be.

I stood, touched the button, got a dial tone, and called Skidmore. Surely he would be used to people waking him up in the middle of the night.

The phone rang for a good while before he answered.

"Damn," the gravel-gargling voice muttered.

"Skidmore?" I whispered.

"Who is this?"

"It's Fever."

The night was so black that my kitchen window was a mirror. I couldn't see anything outside; I only watched myself talking on the telephone.

"What—" But he couldn't form any more words.

"I'm really sorry to call you at this hour, but I've just gotten some important news. I mean, news that might mean something to your current investigation."

"What time is it?" he managed.

I glanced at the kitchen clock.

"Two-fifteen in the morning."

"What?"

"Listen. Jesus. I had no idea you were such a sound sleeper. You might think that a person in your line of work—"

"Fever!" He seemed a bit more awake.

"The man who visited me last night said his name was Truck," I reminded Skidmore.

"He did?"

"I told you that. Anyway, here's the thing." But at that moment I couldn't quite figure out how to tell him I'd come to the conclusion manifested by my strange information.

A man from the Civil War married a woman who lived in 1945 who was married to the thirty-year-old man I'd spoken with the night before who was the man from the Civil War. Suddenly I wasn't certain I'd done the right thing in calling him.

"Fever?" he growled into the phone. "You said, 'Here's the thing.' So can you tell me 'the thing'? Please."

"Yeah," I grumbled, "the short of it is this: I believe that his last name was Jackson. Truck Jackson."

"Wait."

I could hear him sitting up in bed. I could even hear his wife, Girlinda, asking him what he was doing on the phone in the middle of the night.

"Jackson?" he asked. He was nearly awake.

"And while we do not have, I believe, that person at hand, we do have someone who looked an awful lot like him in the back room at the Deveroe Brothers' Funeral Parlor. And you might be able to at least find out if *he* was a Jackson. Wouldn't that seem to be an important—"

"I'll get Ms. Jackson first thing in the morning," he said, clearing his throat. "Have her to look at the body."

"Although if he was a relative," I ventured, "you'd have to wonder why she didn't report him missing."

"It hasn't even been twenty-four hours yet."

"Oh. Right."

"Some of these Jackson boys," he told me, "I mean some of her nephews that live up on the Bald? They can get on a pretty good drunk and be gone for a week, God knows where."

"Okay, but she would know if the dead man were a Jackson. And I'm going to Atlanta in a minute to follow up on something there, maybe somebody who knew the murderer."

"In Atlanta. You call Dr. Andrews?"

"I did. All right, then. Sorry, again, to wake you."

He sighed. "You did the right thing. I'll only be a little mad if Ms. Jackson says she don't know who the dead man is. And if she does know him, I guess it might make some things easier to figure out."

"Tell Girlinda I'm sorry, do you mind? Your being mad at me is one thing, but the last thing in this world I need is to have Girlinda Needle upset with me."

"That's the truth," he agreed, and I could hear the grin in his words.

We hung up, and I dialed Lucinda.

She answered crisply on the second ring: "Lucinda Foxe."

"You don't even sound like you were asleep," I told her, only a little surprised.

"Fever." Her voice relaxed a bit. "You know, I get calls in the middle of the night all the time. And I'm kind of a light sleeper, as you are well aware."

"Yes." I may have blushed a little. I thought I even sounded a little blushed. "So. I'm going to Atlanta in a second, I just wanted you to know."

"You found out something."

"Yes. I think it's possible that the man we talked to last night was named Truck Jackson."

"Jackson? Oh my. That would be important. But remember he told me his name was Jacob."

"Jesus."

"What?" she whispered.

"Jacob Jackson."

"Oh my God." She understood.

Someone named Jacob Jackson had been a young boy of sixteen in July 1863. At one o'clock on a hot afternoon, two Confederate signal guns fired to begin the worst artillery battle in the history of warfare—to that date. Jacob had come from a small town in Georgia called Blue Mountain, and was killed in Pickett's Charge on that battlefield near Gettysburg, Pennsylvania, but there was no mention of him anywhere in our town's history—no statue, no notice, not even a grave marker in the Eden Cemetery.

Jacob Jackson had fought for the Union Army.

It was often told that he had been killed in the battle by his own brother, a relative of Stonewall Jackson, and that his body had been left to rot in the sweltering aftermath of the campaign. Three of my favorite local ghost stories, collected years before, involved the wandering spirit of Jacob Jackson looking for a home that he would never find, asking in vain to speak with his brother.

EIGHT

THE DRIVE TO Atlanta was much stranger than usual. That mood gathered around my car like low fog that rose up from sheer cliffs off the side of the road and hissed from dark crevasses between gray rocks. My headlights accomplished little more than the illusion of light, offering a vague glow around my old, rusted green truck. It surely served more as a warning to others that I was coming than as a way to light the road before me.

A near constant rain of dead leaves, colorless in the night, pelted the windshield. Wipers caught half a dozen at a time and smeared the fog across the glass, making it impossible to see. If a deer—or a human being—had been in the road, I would have made quite a mess on the highway.

The tension of driving blind was exacerbated, of course, by the unshakable recollection of the ghost stories I had heard about nights like that, a lonely ride on a dark road after midnight—heard them since I was six or seven years old. No matter that I was a rational man in the twenty-first century, possessed of a doctoral degree and the keen perceptions of a person of letters—after midnight, tired and blind, the primal fears hold sway.

How many times had I awakened in my bed at three o'clock in the morning, knowing to my soul that the sound I'd heard on the stairs was nothing more than the creaking of an old house, but nevertheless breathing quickly, heart thumping in my chest like a badger in a trap, afraid of what was rising upward, coming toward my room?

And how much stronger was that feeling when the safety of home and bed was gone?

I had driven that road a hundred times, in the darkness and

in daylight. I could probably have gone safely down it with my eyes closed tight. But that night, all the turns were wrong; angles were strange; signs and markers were unfamiliar.

And who was to say what manner of spirit rode the same wind that drove dead leaves? Who could tell what shadow had just moved suddenly out of the corner of the eye?

I was two seconds away from actually becoming Ichabod Crane when a BMW roared out of the fog, over the rise, and blinded me with its high beams. I sniffed, and gathered my thoughts. As the car shot past, I fancied that I saw the same look of relief on the driver's face that he saw on mine: We were both, despite our fears, still among the living.

The mood did not entirely evaporate. Enough lingered to make the rest of the drive down the mountains a sort of autumn carnival, a delicious shiver in the remembrance of Octobers past. Orange pumpkins leaned through blood-red chrysanthemums in my mind, the way my father always found time to decorate our front porch when I was a child. And instead of the terror of the ancient ghost stories, I found comfort in their lessons.

The primary lesson of most ghost tales is that you ought to finish your life here on earth before moving on to the next. If you don't, you may have to stay here for a while, bereft of body, attempting to do in death what you did not accomplish in life. The morals that applied to me were simple: Tell Lucinda that you love her while you can; rid yourself of the ghosts of your parents once and for all, before it's too late; if you want to stay in Blue Mountain, stay—if you want to go, go. Don't wobble or you might be stuck there whether you want to be or not.

They were good lessons to learn.

I thought about stopping in Dahlonega, Georgia's momentary minor gold-rush town, to look for all-night coffee and to clear my head, but my truck wanted to keep driving, and I let it have its way.

Another few hours and I was on the outskirts of Atlanta. The sun wouldn't be long in rising. Atlanta's rain had passed in the night, and the sky was swept clean, waiting for a blue that only autumn or Maxfield Parrish could accomplish.

As usual, traffic was a bit heavy, though not what it would be in an hour. Coming from the north, heading into town, I would have been in stand-still, parking-lot traffic if I had left Blue Mountain an hour later. As it was, it took me almost an hour to get from my first distant sighting of the city skyline to the brighter vision of Andrews's brick home.

I pulled into his driveway, stretched, and turned off the engine, glancing at my watch. It wasn't seven o'clock yet. I wondered if he'd be awake. As if in answer, he appeared in the front window.

I got out of the truck, and his front door opened.

"You made good time." He yawned. "You didn't get caught in all that mess north of the perimeter?"

"I think it was just starting as I passed by." I made it to his front steps.

"Well, there's coffee on—not your standard of same, but it's chock-full of caffeine, which is all that's important to me." He stepped aside to let me in.

His living room looked exactly the same as it had the last time I'd been there. It was cozy, and offered a fine fireplace with built-in bookshelves on either side of the mantle and the dining room was large and filled with light in the morning.

The house technically boasted three bedrooms, but for Andrews there was one bedroom, one office, and one room where he kept everything that seemed to confuse him. The junk there was an assortment of old unwanted Christmas gifts, broken furniture, boxes yet unpacked from his move into the house, years before.

The living room, however, was relatively free of clutter. A vase of dried flowers—the only sort he could manage—helped to enliven the mantel, sitting between two cinnamon-colored candles. All in all the place said, "I'm a straight, academic bachelor. I have no idea what to do with a house, but I take myself too seriously to live in an apartment."

Whereas Andrews said, at that very moment, "I have an eight o'clock class. I can't chat."

"Of course not," I responded instantly. "Just tell me where Polly Hutchinson Jackson lives, and I'll be on my way."

"You think you're just going to drive over there and burst into her room?" He laughed. "They have security personnel for the likes of you."

"I have a plan," I confided. "I brought my Wollensak."

"Oh, well, then," he mocked. "Stand back. The man has a tape recorder."

"I also have a laminated card that identifies me as a certified field researcher for the American Folklore Society."

"Is there such a thing?"

"The society," I told him in what could only be described as a snooty tone, "is *the* national association for folklorists and publishes a quarterly, the *Journal of American Folklore,* for which I have written over fifty articles."

"Flip you," he responded in his most exaggerated English accent, "a very large fish."

"Be that as it may," I said, grinning, "I have invaded many a facility for the care of elderly Americans with no more than that card and my trusty tape recorder, and have saved hundreds of stories and facts from extinction. Do you mistake me for someone who does not know what he's about?"

"We'll see," Andrews said, obviously in doubt.

"So will you tell me where she stays," I asked, "or do I have to call a cop?"

"Mrs. Jackson lives at the Suncrest Retirement Village, corner of Ponce de Leon and Clairmont."

"It's not Ponce that far out," I corrected him, "it's Scott Boulevard."

"I don't care if it's the last act of *Aida,* you know where I'm talking about."

"That I do," I agreed. "And so I'm off."

"You don't want coffee?" he said, slowing down a bit.

"Your coffee?" I tried to make it sound as if we were talking about something from a sewer.

"Fine. You don't want to relax for a second after your drive?"

"I thought you had to get ready for your class."

"I do," he stammered, "but now I feel guilty for mistreating you."

"Then I have you where I want you," I answered him in mock triumph. "Look, I'll go see if I can talk to the woman. If I can, I'll be done by lunch and probably come back here for a nap, if that's all right with you. If I can't get in to see her, I'll be back sooner and rustle up some grub."

"Grub?" he sneered. "What, from my chuck wagon? You're a cowboy now? I thought you were from the American Society of Useless Academic Disciplines."

"You have eggs in the refrigerator?"

"I do," he sighed, giving up his argument. "You still have your key to this place, I assume."

I held up my key ring and showed it to him.

He turned away. "You're sure I can't get you anything?"

It was an idle threat. He had no intention of getting me anything, and would not have known what to do if I'd asked.

"Maybe I should have a bit of coffee," I ventured, still standing in the doorway. "The drive may have dulled me."

"You know where it is," he mumbled without looking back, heading toward his room.

I closed the front door and wandered hopelessly into the kitchen, dreading the very thought of the lukewarm, rust-colored water in his Mister Coffee machine.

When what to my wondering eyes should appear but a very fetching French press on his kitchen counter, filled to the rim with opaque obsidian, and a plate of golden croissants, steam actually rising off them. That white vapor seemed a happier version of the fog through which I had recently come, and an antidote for it.

"You tricked me," I called out.

"I *surprised* you," he corrected.

In truth, he had. I would never have suspected that he owned a French press, let alone that he would go to the trouble of using it for the likes of me. And how he had timed warm bread without knowing when I would arrive was a great mystery.

"You're speechless," he said, appearing in the doorway to the kitchen.

"I'm...touched." I looked between him and the coffee. "If

you're not careful, you may actually turn out to be an adult one day."

"God forbid," he said, and was gone once more.

By the time he returned to the kitchen his hair was combed, he was wearing a tie, and I had finished my coffee.

There was one croissant left, and he took it.

"Ready?" I said, taking my coffee cup to the sink.

"We're away."

I followed him out through the living room and onto the porch. He made one sideways nod to the front door, and I knew what he meant. I tried the key I had on my own key ring, and it worked, clicking the lock cleanly.

"All right, then," he said, heading toward his black BMW, "will you be here when I get home?"

"Possibly," I answered, climbing into my truck.

I sat for a moment, getting my bearings and trying to think of the best way to get to Ponce de Leon. Andrews waved and was gone.

NINE

THE SUNCREST RETIREMENT VILLAGE was, the large, prominent sign at its gate told me, specializing in the care of the memory impaired. Andrews hadn't told me that. Maybe he hadn't known, or maybe he'd found it amusing that I might have difficulty trying to mine memories from someone who didn't have them.

The very imposing front gate, which was closed, stood twenty feet tall and was made of iron spears. There was a pristine security station to one side, brand-new but designed to give what a second-rate architect must have thought of as a rustic appearance. Its exterior was covered with cedar shingles, and there was a faux chimney sticking foolishly out of the roof.

I pulled up to it and rolled down my window.

"Hi." I flashed a smile. "I'm Dr. Devilin, here to see Polly Hutchinson Jackson."

The man in the booth smiled back.

"Good morning, Doctor. Let me just see here." He surveyed a long list in front of him. "It's not on today's roster. Let me just give a quick call inside."

He picked up his phone before I could say anything.

"Bob," he said almost instantly, "I've got Dr. Deffling here at the front gate, and I don't see him on today's list."

He listened for a moment, then glanced up at me.

"What's it pertaining?"

"I'm collecting some stories from Mrs. Jackson," I said. "I've done the same thing with Dr. Bradley over at the DeKalb County Senior Center."

I was hoping I'd remembered the name correctly. It had been years since I'd done any collecting at that particular center.

The guard stared. "Collecting what, now?"

"I'm authorized by the Library of Congress," I told him, reaching for my wallet, "to interview Mrs. Jackson concerning her experiences as a singer during World War II. I'll record the interview, perhaps a song or two, and the tape will go into the archives. It's an effort to preserve the past, and to learn from it."

He kept staring at me but spoke into the phone. "You get all that, Bob?"

Apparently, Bob did.

"When was the last time you worked with Dr. Bradley, Bob wants to know."

"I don't remember, but I collected some stories from two of his day groups. There was a man named Fred something or other who used to be a minister in Columbus, and owned goats." That much was true.

The guard nodded. "Fred Pasley, Bob says. Bob used to work over there is how he knows Fred's name. It was a while back, but Bob says you're legit." He pushed a hidden button and the great iron gate began to swing inward. "He says let you in. Go to the main house and see Bob. You can't miss it."

Improvisation and luck are two of the most essential tools available to the field collector, and I was generally blessed with both.

The village inside was quite pleasant, if a bit of a Disney fantasy. The woods were sculpted within an inch of their lives, and the driveways to the larger houses off the main road appeared to be paved with cobblestones.

The main house loomed at the end of the road, five stories high and impressive despite the same treatment as had been given the security booth. It was painted in textbook examples of what were contemporarily considered soothing colors. Set, as it was, against a perfect autumn-blue, cloudless sky, the building looked more like an artist's rendering than an actual place.

As I neared the front door of the place, a man emerged. He was dressed in the same kind of uniform as the man in the security booth, and he had a clipboard in his hand. I assumed he must be the fabled Bob.

I pulled up to him and leaned out the window.

"You must be Bob," I said, offering my hand.

He took it, shook it once, and cleared his throat.

"Do you have a picture ID, sir?" He was all business.

I retrieved my wallet and produced my driver's license and my card from the American Folklore Society. He took his time looking at them both and then looking at me, studying my face. He walked around to the back of the truck, made a great show of taking my tag number, and then came back to the driver's side.

"She's not expecting you," he said at length.

"What would be the point of arranging anything like that with her?" I asked him, trying to sound confidential. "You know she wouldn't remember it the next day."

"I don't know Ms. Jackson personally, Dr. Devilin." He shrugged, handing me back my cards. "But you're right, most of them here don't know what time it is. She's in Villa 680, around to your right. If she won't let you in or she asks you to leave, you will have to vacate the premises through the front gate and tell the man up there what happened. Agreed?"

"Of course."

That was good enough for Bob. He turned without another word and went back inside the main building.

I wound my way through impossibly immaculate landscaping and found myself at Villa 680 in short order. The sun spilled recklessly through ruby leaves and made golden bars across the front door of the tiny faux townhouse.

There being no driveway, I parked in front, a little up on the curb, fearing I might block the road if I didn't. I hoisted my Wollensak from its spot on the front seat and headed for the doorbell.

Before I had taken two steps, the door flew open.

"Welcome, welcome, welcome." The woman was stunning. Her gray hair was lustrous and full, and perfectly cut in a simple wave. She wore a black pantsuit that only accentuated her hair, made it a silver crown. Her skin was supernaturally clean and clear, barely wrinkled and completely poreless. But her eyes were the most startling: bright green gems, burning with an inner strength and passion that one generally lost by age thirty.

"Mrs. Jackson?" I ventured. Surely not.

"Polly, please."

She said it with such easy charm that I was nearly at a loss for what to say.

"That little man from the main building called to say you were coming," she explained, stepping aside so that I might come into her home. "Isn't he just the funniest thing ever?"

"Well," I said hesitantly, "laughter was not *my* first impulse."

"Come on in." She beckoned, hurrying me. "We'll sort it all out."

"I'm Dr. Devilin," I began, holding out my free hand.

"Of course you are." She took my hand and squeezed it.

She backed into her living room, and I went in.

The place was astonishing. However irritatingly false the outside of her home might have been, the interior was absolutely that genuine. Perfectly cared-for antiques ruled the room—an overstuffed sofa, tables, two wing chairs, an ancient leather one, deco lamps—but they were accented by startlingly modern art on her walls. The combination was rich beyond belief. I was struck dumb.

"I see you like Duy Huynh," she told me, following my eyes to one of her paintings. "I just love his sense of whimsy. I've bought something of his from every show he's had at the Aliya Gallery. Do you know it?"

"I do not," I confessed, staring at the painting.

In the painting, a young woman in a full-length dress was walking across the surface of a lake under a full moon's light, and everywhere she had stepped a water lily, red and white, had appeared. The painting hung over the marble mantel of a modern fireplace.

"May I offer you some sort of beverage?" she asked briskly. "You don't appear to be a brandy-this-early sort of a person, but one never knows."

I tore my gaze from the painting and found her eyes equally disconcerting.

"What are you having?" I asked.

"I'm having just the tiniest bit of mimosa. The champagne is very crisp—though it's only Saint-Hilaire."

"What sort of a person would I be, indeed," I told her, rallying, "if I didn't keep you company."

"That's the spirit!" She moved toward the kitchen immediately.

The kitchen was a tiny galley affair, built for efficiency. Hers was stocked with gleaming chromium appliances and dazzling All-Clad cookware, which hung from a rack attached to the ceiling over a sort of breakfast bar.

"We'll talk in the living room, if you don't mind," she said as she poured a full glass from a pitcher on the counter. "You can set up your tape recorder in there."

I turned toward the sofa. There was a very nice burled coffee table upon which several fine magazines were displayed. I fanned out three copies of *Better Homes and Gardens* and set the Wollensak on them. One of her lamps was close by, and I plugged in next to it. The multidirectional microphone was placed at the other end of the table, atop a recent issue of *Gourmet,* and I was set.

She glided in with a glass in each hand, handed one to me, and planted herself just right of center on the sofa, legs crossed, arm out, ready for anything.

I took one of the wing chairs, sipped, smiled, and nodded my thanks.

"And they say Southern hospitality is dead." I saluted her with the glass.

"Who would say a thing like that?" Her eyes were blazing into mine.

"Mrs. Jack—"

"Polly," she insisted.

"Would you mind if I said that you're not remotely the person I expected to find?"

"I pride myself on making a career, Dr. Devilin, of confounding expectations. As you may well know, I sang with Benny Goodman after Peggy married Dave Barbour, the guitar player, and she left the band. By 1950 she was in *Mr. Music* at

Paramount, with Bing. My point is that no one believed I could hold a candle to my greatest rival. But I had the last laugh. Peggy had so many face-lifts toward the end there that her gob was stuck in a perpetual grimace. I suggested that she play the Grinch on television, but nobody would listen. I, on the other hand, remain to this day as God made me—well, God, collagen, and Botox, but let's not quibble. Whose countenance reigns supreme today, I ask you?"

"If by Peggy you mean Goodman's singer Peggy Lee," I said slowly, "you are the undisputed queen—though I risk being ungentlemanly if I am forced to point out that she is, in fact, dead."

"There you are!" Her hand gestured so wildly that I feared a mimosa shower, but not a drop escaped her glass. "Who's lasted and who hasn't, that's my point. Let her try to sing with anyone now. It's almost impossible to get a recording contract once you're dead. Whereas I will shortly release my newest CD, which I'm now, in your honor, going to call *I'm Alive and Peggy Lee Is Dead So Who Would You Rather Have Singing to You in Your Living Room?*"

"It's a long title." I sat back and sipped again.

"Well, that's what these kids today go for."

"I see."

"All right." She set her drink down on a side table and leaned forward. "I think I've charmed you enough, at least for the moment. What's this all about?"

"I am, believe it or not, a folklorist," I said evenly. "I collect and preserve all sorts of things—"

"No." She folded her hands. "You may be a folklorist or you may be a used car salesman, but neither occupation applies, exactly, to the reason you're here."

Her face was filled with light.

"Yes." I set down my drink as well, midway between tape recorder and microphone. "I've come to ask you about your husband."

"Really." It wasn't a question, it was more an accusation.

"Was his name Truck Jackson?"

"It was." She sighed. "And it wasn't."

"Sorry?"

"How much do you know about his exploits during World War II?" Her lips thinned. "Are you from the government?"

"God, no," I assured her, reaching for my wallet.

I produced my card from the society. She glanced at it, the soul of skepticism.

"When I was sixteen I acquired a cabaret license that said I was twenty-two." Her voice had grown cold. "You don't really expect me to believe this one, do you?"

I sat back. I wondered what secret she could be hiding that would make her so suspicious.

"I was on the faculty of the university that exists just five minutes from here." I put my card back. "If you like, you can call over there and ask them why they shut down their folklore department, and what ever happened to Dr. Devilin, that nice man who used to go around asking people all those quaint questions. Or you could call Dr. Winton Andrews, who still works there, and ask him to vouch for me. Or you could call the ex-governor and ask him how his mother is doing, the one whose stories are mentioned in Dr. Devilin's book *Ancient Wisdom for the Twenty-first Century.* His local number is 404-345—"

"I should call your bluff," she said, "but I don't have that many gentleman callers anymore, and I like a certain level of delusion with my mimosas or they don't taste as good. So let's say for the moment that you're fascinated by me, and you're trying to loosen me up by making me think the subject is my husband, Truck."

"You've found me out." I picked up my drink. "Why maintain the charade? I'm a fan, and will always be. I heard you once at the Rainbow Room in New York."

"There you go." She sat back, flashing a Buddha smile. "That's the kind of thing I'm looking for—ignoring the fact that I never sang at the Rainbow Room. I'm not quite ready for my close-up yet, Mr. DeMille."

"Let's take this tack, then," I countered. "You couldn't have been much more than sixteen years old when you met Truck Jackson, who had just returned from, I believe, Paris, where he fought for the resistance. He was fairly young himself."

Her eyes instantly acquired a haze, a bit of saltwater, and a faraway look. "He saw me at the Egyptian Ballroom at the Fox theatre on New Year's Eve, 1945."

Her cheek tinted ever-so-slightly red. After more than sixty years, the thought of that night made her blush. I had, once again, the same sensation I'd had when the man in my kitchen had been talking: that time was more malleable than I ordinarily thought; that a fond enough memory was only a yesterday away, no matter what the calendar said.

"He was a young soldier," I prompted.

"I didn't know that," she said, her eyes still lost in a vision of the past. "He was dressed in a blue double-breasted suit. He knew Dag, one of the trumpet players in the band, and after midnight he convinced Dag to let him sit in. He played beautifully, and I told him so. He told me he'd only done it to catch my eye."

She looked down at her mimosa as if she had no idea what it was.

"It worked, then," I said softly.

"You haven't turned on your tape recorder," she answered, looking up at me.

"I usually ask first." I cleared my throat. "Would you mind if I turned it on now?"

She nodded once. Before I had a chance to adjust the microphone, she started talking again.

"Do you know about his parents, Truck's parents?"

"His parents?" I glanced up at her.

"They lived in Paris; that's where Truck was born. When they heard that their son had been captured, they flew without a second's thought straight to the detention hall where the boy was held. His father told the Nazis, 'I'm an American citizen. This isn't our war. This boy is just a little simple. He was just exploring the sewers for fun. There's no need to keep him here.' That's where Truck was captured, in the sewers. He was trying to blow up a munitions dump. The Nazi lieutenant who was in charge of the boys-in-sewers division of Nazi headquarters disagreed. The Nazi lieutenant arrested them all—Truck and his parents. Truck tried to get his parents off by saying they were just protecting him, trying to shield him—that they didn't know anything about his activities. But in the end, they were all arrested. His mother, Truck's mother, made an unusual plea. She asked the Nazi to keep the family together. The lieutenant told her he would ask—but what happened wasn't up to him. He had his orders...like everyone else. That, of all things, made Truck's mother angry, but her voice was not defiant. It was kind—even sympathetic. 'I don't take orders from anyone,' she said. 'I'm fighting to keep my home and my family. *You're* fighting because someone orders you to. I'm fighting because I'm in love in Paris.' Isn't that wonderful? Don't you just love her?"

I nodded.

"The next few weeks were a nightmare," she continued, increasingly in a sort of trance. "The lieutenant had, in fact, seen to it that the Jackson family were not separated. But his higher-ups were convinced beyond any doubt that this was a famous saboteur family, and they must be publicly executed to curtail further instances of such nuisance. There was even a trial, of sorts. The Jacksons were not allowed to speak. The Nazi judge was clear on that subject. 'Paris is now a German city, and as such only allows *German* citizens the rights normally accorded in a court of law. As you three are not German citizens, you have no voice in my court.' The three were sentenced to be shot, along with about fifty or so other resistance fighters, on November first, La Toussaint, All Saints' Day. The prisoners were taken to the outskirts of the city at noon on November first. They were forced to dig trenches. They all knew what the trenches were for. When the digging was finished, the prisoners were lined up in a neat row with their backs to the trenches. Young Nazi soldier boys lined up opposite them—only a few feet away—and were given orders to fire their guns into the prisoners."

She took a long gulp of her drink, not looking my way, and continued.

"The second before the rifles exploded, at the last possible moment, like a dance, or a curtain call, Truck's parents both stepped in front of their son—simultaneously, gracefully. It was a final, sweeping Tango step. Bullets ripped their bodies and they were dead before they fell backward, on top of their son. Bulldozers moved in and shoved the bodies into the trenches, then covered them with a little dirt. But the Nazi in charge of the mass execution of the innocents had forgotten to bring the lime, so the burial activity was ordered to cease for the moment. They left the dirt loose and the grave shallow, deciding to come back the next day with the lime. By sunset the Nazi troops were gone."

She took another healthy drink and closed her eyes. This was obviously an often-told tale—the words were part of a script that had long since been set in her mind, but the emotion with which she was saying them was disturbingly immediate.

"Then—after it was certain that absolutely no one else was around—Truck began to move. He could barely breathe. The dirt choked his lungs. The tangle of dead limbs and bloody faces seemed to beg him to stay, almost tried to hold him in the grave. But he wrestled upward, into the light of the setting sun, red on the western horizon. He was not thinking. He was only moving. When he found himself free of his tomb, he noticed that a bullet had grazed his left thigh. The blood had already dried. He tried to stand, but found he could not. He tried *not* to cry, or to scream or to dig into the ground in the hope of finding his mother and his father also, somehow, miraculously alive. He knew better. All he could do was sit on their grave and watch the sun set. Some time after dark, he dragged himself into the woods nearby and fell asleep under a pile of leaves. When he woke up he looked all around, got his bearings, took a deep breath, and walked to Spain. I met him three months later in the Fox theatre in Atlanta, Georgia."

Tears were running down her cheeks. Both our drinks were gone.

"We were married the next May—May Day, in fact."

No note I could take, no description I could imagine, not even the tape recorder could hope to capture the absolute melancholy in her voice. During the course of her story she had turned from autumn's sunlight to winter's rain.

The gentle objectivity in which I'd been trained forced me to derail the mood in order to keep the information flowing.

"You don't have a picture of him, do you?" It was the first thing that came into my mind.

"Surely." She stood and moved quickly, hand outstretched, to the marble mantel, snatching a small wood-framed photograph.

She didn't look at it. She thrust it in my direction.

"That's him, holding his trumpet."

I flashed to my feet and reached for the picture. Maybe it was the mimosas, or the fact that I stood too quickly, but I lost my balance when I saw the face in the photograph and nearly came down onto the coffee table.

She reached her hand my way, absently, much more a gesture of help than an actual attempt to catch me. I steadied myself like a tightrope walker and looked down at the picture again.

There he was: the man who had been in my kitchen. His hair was different, and the look in his eye was…what? More innocent? Still, they were both obviously related—closely related.

"Would you mind if I borrowed this?" I managed to ask.

"I would mind." She shook her head. "You can't have it."

My head was swimming. To keep from appearing a complete idiot, I ran over the details of her story in my mind, looking for anything that might mean something to my current inquiry, something to hold on to. I found something quickly, even though it was absurd.

"You described the parents' final gesture," I said in tones as warm as I could manage, trying to clear my head, "as a Tango step."

"I did?" She returned to her seat.

"Why would you, I'm just curious, use such a description?" I was thinking about the way the stranger had talked to me about the invention of the Tango.

She shrugged, struggling to rally from the story.

"Didn't the Tango figure into the death of his father, Jacob?" I asked carefully.

"Jacob wasn't his father," she said quickly, hand flying in the air. "That was his brother."

The second she finished her sentence I could tell she regretted saying it. She opted for the perfect hostess response.

"Another mimosa?" She stood.

"I'm fine, thanks. The story you told me is one you've told hundreds of times, I can tell that. Sometimes you use a certain phrase and it's just a part of the rhythm and you hardly think about the origin of the phrase, but I'm wondering about it, since I know that Truck's mother was quite the Tango expert."

It was a gamble. Even though the things the stranger told me in my kitchen could not have been completely accurate, I had decided to use them as a factual basis out of which to ask questions. The risk was that things the strange young man had told me were not at all related to the things that Polly Jackson knew.

"Truck never talked about his mother." She'd clamped down. Her voice was iron, and she moved with great deliberation into the kitchen to renew her drink.

"So when you said Tango—"

"Tango, Charleston, Peppermint Twist. Damn, I could have said anything! It was a story, a touching story from long ago. Why are you harping on the details?"

"Professional hazard." I tried to make it sound like an apology. "Unfortunately the gold, for me, is often in the details. Sometimes my interest in them can be taken for rudeness. Please believe me when I say that I'm fascinated, even if I *seem* obnoxious. I want to hear everything."

She stopped her movements in the kitchen, set down her glass, leaned on the breakfast bar, and glared out at me.

"Well, I'm done. You're pretty good at this. Better than the others. I can usually drag out the old stories and turn on the tears and have them running for the hills. Nobody ever caught the Tango thing before."

I knew I had to be very careful with my response: I really didn't know what she was talking about, but I had to answer her as if I did, or the conversation would likely be over. I decided, inexplicably, to employ something very much like the truth.

"I had a visit from Truck on the night before last—Monday night, late."

She was a statue. She didn't even blink.

"He told me about his mother's interest in the Tango, and even discussed a man named Discépolo, sometimes referred to as the Tango Philosopher."

A Cheshire smile appeared on her face.

"Some of the others tried this," she said sweetly, "deliberately trying to confuse me. Truck's been dead for more than fifty years. And you were doing so well with your odd manners and your folklore disguise. Now I can dismiss you. Still, you got farther than most."

"A man who told me his name was Truck sat in my kitchen Monday night and talked to me about a murder in Chicago— the murder of his father."

She stayed where she was, preferring to keep the kitchen island in between us—and some heavy, skull-crushing pots close at hand, I imagined.

"Well, that's a different story." She had mustered a bit of dramatic irony, it seemed. "How old was he?"

"Perfect question," I answered. "Couldn't have been more than thirty."

She exploded in a coughing sort of laughter for a moment or two.

"You know, I don't look it," she managed after the laughter had subsided a bit, "but I may be a touch older than that. And Truck was older than me—not by much, but still."

"Well, believe it or not, that visitor is the reason I'm here." I folded my arms and sat back, expression serene.

She cocked her head in my direction.

"I don't know what it is about you," she said slowly, "but you've got a thing."

She sighed heavily, pushed herself away from the breakfast bar, and motored back into the living room, sans glass.

"So here's the short of it, Dr. Devilin." She crashed down into her place on the sofa. "Truck Jackson was, without a doubt, the love of my life. We were married for five years almost to the day—never an hour apart—when he got news that there was trouble at his home. He was from the North Georgia mountains, but he never talked about his relatives there, or his home."

"I thought you said his parents were from Paris." I instantly regretted interrupting her.

"He was only interested in me, and our life together!" she exploded. "I sang, he played trumpet; we did all right—and we wouldn't have cared if we didn't."

"So, he heard from his family in the mountains," I said as soothingly as I could muster.

"He got a telegram, believe it or not. There was no phone in his ancestral manse. Something about the fact that since his parents were dead—in Paris—there were questions about an inheritance from the older branch of the family. He told me he had to go, but he'd be back as quickly as he could. There was a train that went from Brookwood station here in Atlanta up to someplace called Pine City, the town next over from his. How he got from Pine City to his house in Blue Mountain—that's his hometown, not just a mountain—I have no idea. But he walked in the front door, called out to his great-grandmother, heard a noise on the porch, and before he could even turn around his brother shot him dead. Shot him with an army pistol he'd gotten in the war. Don't know why. Never found out. Wasn't invited to the funeral, if there was one. I'm not even certain that they knew we were married. That was in 1950. Since then I've been married four more times—even though, as you see, I kept the last name of my first and only real husband—and outlasted every one of them. When the last one died, I came to live here. It's my version of giving up."

She cast a disdainful eye about her place.

"I have so much to ask you." I turned off the tape recorder. "And I would like to talk to you about your singing, and your ancestry—I'm quite familiar with the Hutchinson Family and dying to know more about them. But at this moment I have to know who it was that sat in my kitchen who told me his name was Truck."

"Why?" It was a simple, obvious question.

"Because that man, I think, killed his brother Monday night."
She pasted me with a withering glance.

"Nice trick." She smiled. "Better than most. Not falling."

"You seem to think I'm one of a group of people who've visited you before." I smiled back. "The thing is, I'm telling you the truth, however ridiculous it may sound. It's my only weapon. So I am genuinely wondering who all these other people to whom you refer—"

"Government!" She spat the word. "Truck was involved in some top secret work after he almost died in Paris. Every couple of years since he *actually* died, someone like you comes to ask me questions. Once it was the pest control man, that was a good disguise. Once it was even a little girl trick-or-treating. Don't know how they got her to pester me. That was before I moved here, of course. We get no trick-or-treaters here."

Her demeanor had changed so radically from the time I'd walked in the door to that moment that I had to take stock. It gradually dawned on me, as she played with the starched creases in her pants, that she was revealing the true reason she was living at Suncrest Village.

"Why does Bob the security man keep letting them in?" I asked, fearing the answer.

"He's in on it!" She stared out the window. "He doesn't talk to me in person, but I get these calls from him every now and again. They seem innocuous, but I know the score. He called me just before you came."

"Now I've upset you," I told her, "and I hate that. I really just wanted to get some of your stories on tape."

"Oh, I know what you want." She stood, not looking at me. "Time for you to go."

"Mrs. Jackson—"

"Polly!" she shrieked. "How many God-damned times do I have to tell you?"

She was on the verge, it was clear, of a blistering hysteria. The last thing I needed was to spend the rest of the morning explaining what I'd done to upset poor Mrs. Jackson in Villa 680.

I managed to lift the photograph of her husband without her seeing, and stood, winding up the microphone cord.

"I'm very sorry that I disturbed your morning." I hurried as quickly as I could. "I had no intention of upsetting you, and I apologize from the bottom of my heart."

I pulled the tape recorder's plug out of the wall with a rude jerk. The cord flew my way, and I caught it.

Polly Jackson was breathing with great difficulty and staring at her carpeting.

I lifted the Wollensak and pocketed the microphone, holding out my free hand to shake hers.

She did not take it.

"Did I offer you a mimosa?" Her eyes lifted in my direction, but did not meet mine.

"I really ought to be going." I backed toward the door.

"I'm not certain…" Her gaze drifted out the window.

There was no telling what she was or was not certain about.

I opened the door. She followed a few steps behind. I stumbled toward my truck and knew she was standing in the doorway watching me leave.

"Do come again," she said, draping the words in the sprightly overgarment of Southern courtesy. "And next time be certain to ask me about my favorite subject: me!"

Her arms flared and one knee crooked, the parody of a showgirl.

"Indeed."

I laid the tape recorder on the passenger seat, and when I turned to wave good-bye, she was gone and the door was closed.

TEN

As I DROVE OUT through the gates of Suncrest Village, waving at the security men, I tried my best to piece together what had happened. I'd dealt with Alzheimer's patients before, and there were certainly hints of that in Polly Jackson's behavior: the strange confusion of facts, the immediacy of the past, the notion that trick-or-treating children might be government spies. But I found the more lucid moments particularly haunting. I felt compelled to discover just how much of what she had told me was true.

The trouble with my research in general is that it almost demands digression. I had a nearly overwhelming passion to find out more about the through line from the radical protest singers of the 1800s to this big-band singer who replaced Peggy Lee. What an article that would make. I also wanted to know more about Truck Jackson's exploits in Paris, how his parents came to be there, so far from Blue Mountain. And what happened to Truck when he left Polly. Did his brother actually kill him?

But as I pulled out onto Ponce de Leon, I realized how little sense any of it made. The man in my kitchen could not possibly have been Polly's husband, or even her son.

Damn, I thought, *I forgot to ask her if she had children. That's a pretty important fact of the matter. How could I have let her throw me off my game to such an extent? Damn.*

All the way back to Andrews's house I tried to untangle the knot of evidence and information, lay it out in straight lines, make sense of it.

I failed.

Andrews's house appeared before me just as I was deciding that everything Polly had told me was a lie, or at the very least a confused truth. I pulled into his driveway uncertain how to proceed. I'd been so sure I would get some kind of weird clarity out of talking to Polly Jackson, though I couldn't have said why, exactly.

I climbed out of my truck. The day had turned, quite nicely, into the dazzling sort of autumn morning: high clouds brushing a cobalt sky; rust-colored leaves dancing in the air; a warm moment in sunlight colliding constantly with a cold moment of shadow. I clutched the key ring, tried not to be distracted by the impossible beauty of the day, and made it to the door before it struck me that the question of inheritance had been, at least in Polly's troubled mind, the reason for her husband's death. As far as I knew, the Jackson clan scarcely had two roosters to rub together, let alone anything to pass on to progeny. What possible inheritance could have been worth murder?

But mostly I was wondering if I might be able to find photos of the Jackson family online, or would I have to wait until I got back home? The man in Polly's photograph was so much like the man who had visited me, I got a chill turning the key in Andrews's door.

The living room was comforting somehow, a bit warming. I went immediately into the kitchen to fix a bit more coffee for myself, clear away the mimosa. Unused as I was to drinking in the morning, I felt very disoriented, and the events in Polly's home had made that sensation much worse. I was just beginning to calm down when the telephone rang and jangled my nerves once again. It seemed to ring ten times before the machine answered.

After the audible mechanical answering message and the beep, I heard the voice of Andrews.

"Fever? If you're there, pick up."

I reached for the phone instantly. "You're calling me?"

"How did it go at the place? You didn't get in to see her, right?"

"Alas, as it happens," I sighed. "I did. And it was a very weird encounter."

"You did see on their sign that the primary group who live there are what they euphemistically refer to as memory impaired."

"Yes," I sneered, "and thank you so much for telling me that."

"I thought it would be more jolly for you if you discovered it for yourself."

"Right," I grumbled. "Thank you again."

"Still, you got in. All's well."

"But you won't believe the scene that ensued." I sniffed.

"Look," he said quickly, "if you can wait until I'm done today, I could go back to the mountains with you when I get home this afternoon. If you like."

"I thought you had—"

"I handed in my tenure portfolio, I've finished meeting with all my advisees, and my seminar class could use a day to discuss things among themselves. I never cease to be amazed at the discoveries they make when they talk to each other instead of listen to me."

"Yes, that is amazing." I failed to keep derision from invading the syllables.

"Okay, shut up. Do you want me to go with you to the mountains or not?"

"The fact is," I admitted, "I really could use—"

"All right, then, it's settled. I should be home by three-thirty."

"You don't mind if I use your computer here in the meantime, do you?"

"Of course not. See you in a bit."

He hung up.

I only paused a moment to consider that there must be some ulterior motive in Andrews's change of heart. That would come to light by and by. I had more important issues to investigate.

How, for example, could the same man have fought in the Civil War, World War I, *and* World War II—and then visited my house in the first decade of the twenty-first century? I was very excited to see if I could find photos of all these men, even more adrenalating to think that they might all be of the same face.

By the time Andrews got home, I'd spent a very frustrating five hours, on and off, going from one Web site to another without finding anything of use. It had only exacerbated my primary objection to Internet research: a million miles wide and half an inch deep.

I'd found plenty of gruesome photos of the battle at Gettysburg, many more than the Mathew Brady lot I'd expected. No familiar faces had appeared. I'd also found that the Jackson family had, indeed, seen family members in all three wars in question, including the anticipated bit of information that during the Civil War, Jacksons had fought on both sides of the conflict. After that I'd spent a relatively heartbreaking half an hour contemplating the brother-against-brother notion of that war, and another ten minutes wondering if wars had always been fought for a combination of lofty ideals and venal greed. It proved a very depressing exercise, so I turned to a bit of research concerning the singing Hutchinson Family.

Originally known as the Tribe of Jesse (after the founding sire), they split into two organizations just before the Civil War (Tribe of John and Tribe of Asa), both billing themselves as the Hutchinson Family and touring soldier encampments. Brother against brother again.

I tried to escape into more modern times, hoping to find Polly Hutchinson's picture with the Goodman band. Alas, according to all the research I could dig up, no one named Polly Hutchinson had ever sung for that organization. Peggy Lee replaced Helen Forrest, but that was the only information I could find. The sad business of searching for Polly Hutchinson yielded only private genealogical Web sites that had nothing to do with *my* Polly, pioneer women who had died in the 1800s, a swimming pool supply company. Of the woman I had met, the vast electronic ocean yielded nothing, and was silent.

So by the time Andrews arrived, I was lying on the sofa in his living room trying to sleep.

"Well, this is fine," he grumbled, coming in the door. "I'm out slaving over a hot stove all day while you're here sleeping in your nice cool sewer."

I opened my eyes.

"Are you actually trying to quote *The Honeymooners* to me? Have you completely lost your entire English sensibility?"

"It's a funny line." He closed the door behind him. "Catching a nap?"

"Keeping depression at bay," I corrected him.

"Ah, Internet research," he deduced immediately, "I know how you despise it. Fortunately for you, I am a proud citizen of the twenty-first century and have waded the waters for you. This so-called Truck Jackson whom you seek? His family was from your neck of the woods, as you people say up in, well, your neck of the woods."

"You know that I already knew that, right?"

"You did?" He stopped midmotion. "Did we talk about this? I'm telling you, this semester is so absolutley insane I barely remember what I've told one person before I'm making something up for the next. Damn it. You knew this? Of course you knew this. He was from Blue Mountain. I wasted hours of valuable time helping you find something you already—"

"Hours, Gracie?"

"All right, minutes, George," he admitted, "but I don't have any to spare."

"Not a minute to spare?"

"Are you mocking me?" He scowled.

"As much as I can in my present state. I'm depressed. Polly Jackson, the woman I met this morning, is…" What, exactly, was she?

"She's one of your famous reverse ghosts," Andrews answered my unspoken question. "She's a woman whose body is still here with us, but whose spirit, or most of it, has already gone. That's your theory I'm quoting."

"I know my theory." I sighed heavily, trying to sit up. "*That's* what I find so sad. I liked the woman I met when I first came into her home."

"But by the time you left," he responded in a very somber tone, "that woman had vanished."

"Yes."

"My grandmother had Alzheimer's, and lived with us toward the end. One moment I was little Winnie and she was telling me about the good old days of England, a time when the

Maypole had been the center of most towns, instead of the War Memorial. And the next moment she didn't know who the hell I was and accused me of stealing her diamond earrings—which, of course, she had never possessed. My parents dealt with it fairly well, but I was only seven years old. It scared the bejesus out of me."

I let a second of reflection pass before forcing the mood to move on.

"She called you *Winnie?*" I could not keep the glee from my voice.

"It's short for Winton, she only—"

"But *Winnie?* Really?"

"God, am I sorry I—"

"*The Adventures of Winnie and Fever,*" I intoned. "Brought to you by Bon Ami, the friendly kitchen cleaner!"

"I'll pay you twenty dollars to shut up."

"As it happens, I'm a bit strapped for cash." I shut up and held out my hand.

"I'm packing." He headed for his room. "I'm going with you up to the hills of Habersham, but I'm not talking to you for the next three days."

"There's a blessing," I fired back. "Where's my twenty?"

"Perhaps you should look for it in your hat."

He vanished into his room.

Half an hour later we were on the road. Alas, so was every other resident of the state of Georgia, and all seemed bent on killing me—me, *personally.* We achieved the downtown connector a little after five-thirty and spent the next hour in parking-lot traffic before we were past the perimeter.

"At this rate," Andrews yawned, glaring at the setting October sun, "we'll be in your house by midnight."

"Once we're past the—"

"At this time of day the traffic goes like this past Canton," he snapped.

"Um, okay," I responded, "then why didn't we wait at your place for a while?"

"It's like this until after seven!"

"Calm down. Christ. You'd think that *you* were the out-oftowner, not me." I started humming to myself, an old tune called "Johnny Has Gone for a Soldier."

"If you keep up that noise, I'll sing 'Henry the Eighth,' loud as a bastard, over and over again—the Herman's Hermits song. I can do it."

"You're testy."

He slumped. "I really need this vacation."

"It's not a vacation," I warned him. "It's a murder investigation."

"Pa-*tay*-toe, pa-*tah*-toe." He rolled the syllables around in his mouth with great exaggeration.

"All right." I sighed. "Here, very briefly, are the facts. A man came to my house Monday night, told me a weird story, disappeared, and then either ended up dead on a back road the next morning, or ended up killing a man who looked almost exactly like him by the next morning."

"And this man had the unlikely name of Truck Jackson."

"He said so. But the Truck Jackson that was married to the woman I met with this morning would have to be in his eighties, and the man in my kitchen was barely thirty. Not to mention that the Truck Jackson we're talking about—"

"As if there could be more than one…"

"Is really dead," I concluded. "Killed, or so Polly Jackson told me, by his own brother."

"This is eerie," he conceded. "It has great eeriosity."

"Even more so when you know that the man who visited me also visited a crazy old man and my friend Lucinda early that same night, each time claiming to be someone else."

"Some other person?" He sat forward, a bit more awake.

"Sort of. It's a little confused, but I think he was, each time, a variation of someone in the Jackson brood. Always killing his brother."

"And then a man who looks almost exactly like him ends up dead. Say, this is good."

"And when you talk to the person, the visitor," I said, tones hushed, "he's very convincing. I could believe that he might actually be someone from another time. Or a person who could visit people in other times as easily as I visit you in Atlanta."

Andrews looked around. "I hope he doesn't have to contend with this kind of traffic."

After another hour of just that sort of thing, the cars began to part bumpers, speeds eased up over ten miles per hour, and night fell over everything. I turned on the classical music radio station, and Andrews settled back watching the moon rise. By nine-thirty or so we'd made it to Dahlonega. I wanted coffee, and Andrews was hungry. Once he mentioned it, I was, too.

A very nice café was open in the more picturesque main part of downtown. We sat, ordered expensive coffee and overpriced sandwiches, and Andrews perused the festoonery on the walls.

"So this used to be a mining town, is that right?" he finally asked, staring at a flattened, burnished plate that had once been used to pan gold.

"Yes. You can still go sift though silt and find a bit of gold dust if you like. Tourists do it all the time. It's a large part of the town's revenue. That and the Smith House on Chestatee."

"We've eaten there," he said, voice reverent, obviously remembering the fried okra. "Why aren't we there now?"

"They don't stay open this late. They're a family restaurant. Families eat early. Strange single men eat dinner this late, not families."

"Well, we're certainly not the only ones here tonight." He looked around. The place was kind of crowded for a weeknight.

"We might be in the middle of Gold Rush Days," I told him.

"What?"

"The town has a sort of festival to commemorate the first discovery of gold here—1828, I think."

"Plus, it gives the rubes an excuse to gawk at the autumn colors while they're eating a ten-dollar tuna sandwich." Andrews was nothing if not a cynic. "Did anyone ever really find gold here?"

As I continued to look around, I had the strange sensation that the objects in the room were trying to tell me something; that I was seeing information there that was important, but that I couldn't quite bring to the front of my mind.

"Gold was found," I told Andrews, "but it really wasn't the sort of gold rush that, say, California experienced. Even today people will tell you that the really significant veins were never found. Old-timers will tell you that miners didn't go far enough, deep enough. It's all still out there somewhere, silently waiting to be discovered."

"What do you think?"

I focused on Andrews. "I think that the promise of gold is more alluring—and more dangerous—than actually finding it."

"The fantasy is more powerful than the fact."

"Yes." I nodded. "Reality is always doomed to disappoint, whereas the dream is always perfect."

"But the hope of finding something like that," he said, his eyes wandering back to the gold pan, "something that will change your life—it's a thing that keeps some people going when everything tells them to quit."

Thank God our sandwiches came at that moment and saved us both from any further such far-flung philosophies, before either of us started quoting from *The Treasure of the Sierra Madre*—or singing the theme song from *Fame*.

We were back on the road in under an hour. The drive from Dahlonega was much less strange with someone else in the truck.

The fog had lifted a bit from the night before, and instead of careening down a mountain, I was struggling up it. My old truck demanded to be set in lower gears about half the time. We were nearly another two hours getting to Blue Mountain.

Andrews had settled in his seat and was napping on and off, so I was left to worry that I'd spent a whole day in Atlanta with little more to show for it than a confused recollection of a lost woman and a Shakespeare scholar. Neither of which, upon even the most shallow reflection, was likely to help me a great deal in my current endeavor. In fact, Polly Hutchinson's ranting only confused matters; and I would most certainly have to discover why Andrews had changed his mind about coming with me before I could trust anything he said or did.

So by the time the truck pulled into my front yard and I turned off the engine, I was cold, tired, and no closer to any answers than I had been twenty-four hours before, with only one day left to find out anything that might help Skidmore. I had the distinct, sinking sensation that this time, for the first time, I would be of absolutely no use to him. And to make matters worse, my failure might lead to the conviction of an innocent old man. If Skidmore had no other suspect, he might keep Hovis Daniels. The real killer would get away.

Why had I gone to Atlanta? It had been a stunningly rash mistake. I could see that. And what good would Andrews be? Why had I thought he could help? And, seriously, what sort of person drags a good friend into a situation where a murderer, a man utterly unhinged, is on the loose? And on top of it all, I could see the deadline, Millroy's arbitrary deadline, coming at me like a cannonball.

"Are we going to sit in the truck all night," Andrews murmured, "or are you going to invite me in for a drink?"

I roused myself.

"Come on," I grumbled. "I've got your favorite apple brandy."

He sat up instantly and throttled the door handle, trying to get out of the truck as quickly as he could.

In point of fact, the term "apple brandy" was probably too genteel an appellation for the clear liquid lightning he liked. I had a dozen or so bottles in my pantry. When John Chapman, the real Johnny Appleseed, planted his legendary leafy legacy, the trees were welcomed not for the promise of bobbing apples, nor for Mother's apple pie. The primary reason early Americans wanted the red fruit was for the production of fermented or distilled potables: applejack, apple beer, apple brandy—even apple wine, if you can call such a noxious concoction wine at all. But the queen of these, in Blue Mountain, at least, was a sort of Kirschwasser-strength, finely distilled apple brandy, so clear that it was, in fact, transparent, invisible to the eye. In the first taste one could actually experience the very cooking fires of Johnny Appleseed himself; a morning in 1807; an autumn afternoon when sunlight stopped the motion of the falling leaves for a moment, and all the world was still because all the world knew peace; a perfect contentment. Of course, the second taste sometimes provoked unconsciousness in the uninitiated.

Andrews was, however, quite initiated, and beat me to my front door, enlivened by the mere promise of such elixir. He stood there, forgetting that I never locked my door.

"It's open," I mumbled.

"Oh, right." He stumbled in.

Before he was three steps past the threshold, he fell, collapsing into a rumpled mess on the floor.

I was wondering what he had tripped over when a black boulder flew out of the doorway and landed on top of me.

Wheezing and stinking, the man instantly had his hands around my throat. He was squeezing so hard that he shut off the blood going to my brain and my eyes rolled back in my head. I was seconds away from blacking out when I kicked out with both legs, pushed myself over onto my side. The man was surprised, lost a bit of his grip, and we ended up lying side by side on my front porch.

If the moon had been full I might have seen more clearly, but even as it was, I was almost certain that my attacker was Truck Jackson—easily fifty pounds lighter and a head shorter than I. Before he could get his bearings, I pushed myself away from him and scrambled to my feet.

He moved quickly as well, up on one elbow and producing a pistol out of nowhere.

"I don't want to shoot you."

His face was still mostly shadow, but the voice confirmed his identity. Who else, I thought foolishly, would be attacking me at this time of night?

Apparently unthreatened by the sight of a gun, I kicked at it and connected, knocking it out of his hand and into the yard. He flew up and off the porch, chasing it. I went after him.

He was breathing like a broken accordion, and staggering as much as searching for his gun.

I flung myself forward and grabbed his arm. It was mostly bone. He turned toward me and the next thing I knew there was a forehead in my face. A sickening crunch and a blazing pain told me that he might have broken my nose with a head-butt.

His problem was that pain made me angrier—maybe there

was a bit of panic in my blood as well. It seemed obvious that if he found his gun he would shoot me.

So I shook his arm violently and twisted, the way I'd seen dozens of people do when they were wringing a chicken's neck. Something snapped and he howled. I kicked the back of his right ankle and his foot flew upward. He lost his balance and landed hard on his back; I could hear the breath knocked out of him. He lay, groaning and cursing in a language all his own, on the ground.

I raged about for a moment, found the gun, and held it out for him to see.

"Did you drop this?" I said between heavy breaths.

"Give it to me," he managed weakly, "it's mine."

"Yes, I know it's yours. You just tried to shoot me with it, remember?"

"No, I didn't. And it's not loaded."

I pointed the gun at his knee, no more than five feet away.

"Really?" I pretended to squeeze the trigger.

"Stop!" He scrambled to sit up. "Stop it!"

"Look," I barked, "I'm going to shoot you in that knee in one second. You've caused me a great deal of distraction."

A low rumble from my doorway caused me to look that way. Andrews was dragging himself to a standing posture.

"What the hell?" he stammered, holding the side of his face and squinting in my direction.

Before I could say the first word of explanation, a tree limb cracked against the side of my skull and I wobbled sideways, dropping the pistol.

A furtive black shadow shot past me, retrieved the gun, and pointed it directly at Andrews.

"Move, Andrews!" I bellowed.

But the gun exploded, blood erupted, and Andrews crumpled onto my living room floor.

A second shot fizzed past my arm.

I dove toward the darker shadows at the side of the porch, hit the ground, and rolled insanely, tumbling down the slope of the yard.

I stopped myself and bolted to my feet, eyes wild. But the yard was vacant; the man had disappeared.

Andrews was as silent as the grave.

ELEVEN

THE NEXT HOUR or so was a blur. I barely remembered wandering inside my house to call for an ambulance. I remembered dialing Skidmore and Lucinda only a little better. Sometime after that Andrews sat up holding his bleeding head, growled like a bear, and told me he wanted to go back to Atlanta. He stopped when he saw all the blood on my face, panicked, and went inside to the phone before I could stop him. I tried to explain that I'd already called the emergency number, but he demanded another team. So by the time Lucinda arrived, there were three police cars and two ambulances in my yard. And neither Andrews nor I was willing to go to the hospital.

Lucinda, with a combination of great tenderness and a nurse's cruelty, snapped the cartilage in my nose back into place. I hollered so loud it chased a battery of bats from the trees in my backyard.

Paramedics were talking about how lucky Andrews had been. The bullet had barely grazed his temple and the side of his skull just above the ear. An inch to the left and he'd have been dead in seconds; half an inch lower and he'd be deaf on one side. As it was, he didn't really even need stitches. He was cleaned up and patched up while Lucinda was still dabbing my face with hydrogen peroxide.

My front door was the most seriously wounded. The bullet that all but missed Andrews had split the timbers in my thick oak door.

That door had endured several such assaults, and I was propelled, in my dizzy state, to see a metaphor. A door is an entrance. My entrance was constantly attacked, even though I never locked it. Why would that be, and what did it mean for my psyche?

As luck would have it, Lucinda called me back to the world of the relatively sane.

"There." She was putting away her kit. "Does it hurt?"

"Yes, it hurts. I broke my nose."

"I know, sweetheart." She said the words in such comforting tones I nearly cried.

"My houseguest will live?" I lifted my head in the direction of Dr. Andrews. He was holding court.

"When the bullet was coming my way," Andrews was telling paramedics and deputies, "I knew I had to be sharp. I pulled a bit this way, then dropped. The man with the gun went after Dr. Devilin then. But by the time I managed to rouse myself, he had vanished."

"Did you get a look at him?" Deputy Melissa Mathews was taking notes and, as usual, was less charmed by Andrews than he would have hoped for.

"He was a shadow." Andrews looked up into the sky. "There was only moonlight."

"He'll live," Lucinda assured me, a faint smile on her lips.

Deputy Crawdad Pritchett was busy digging in my front door, trying to dislodge the bullet there, I assumed.

Sheriff Skidmore Needle sat down beside me.

"You okay?"

"Define 'okay,'" I mumbled. "My nose is broken."

"Aw," he disallowed, examining my face, "it's all fixed now. Plus, I can't see what harm it could do—face like yours."

"Shut up and bite me, do you mind?" I glanced up at him.

"I'm a little busy for that right now," he said. "Let's just get the facts."

"It was the guy." I lowered my voice. I had no idea why. "It was Truck Jackson or Jacob or whatever his name is, the guy that visited us. The guy that killed the man who's lying over at the Deveroe Brothers' Funeral Parlor."

"You think."

"I *do* think," I insisted. "Look, not to be too frantic about it, but there's a maniac loose. He thinks he's immortal or that he can time travel or *something*—and he has a really big gun!"

Skidmore looked over at Andrews, then into my house past where Crawdad was working.

"Take me through this," Skid said slowly. "The last time I saw you I was hauling Hovis Daniels out of your kitchen. I come back the next night and Dr. Andrews is here, shot up, and your house is a mess."

"It is?" I stared at Crawdad.

I hadn't even noticed. I peered in. The living room had been ransacked, I could see that. I started to stand.

"Hold up," Skid insisted, his hand on my shoulder. "First things first."

"You mean about Andrews," I surmised. "I called him to ask for his help; he refused. But he did a bit of research for me, and it prompted me to run off—foolishly, as it turns out—to Atlanta. I did manage to bring him back with me, however, so that he could dodge a bullet on my front porch."

"What made you think you wanted to go to Atlanta?" He shook his head.

"I told you I was going when I called you."

"Really?" He squinted, trying to remember.

"A woman named Polly Hutchinson." I caught Lucinda's eye. "One of the descendants of the famous Hutchinson Family. She claims to have been a big-band singer in the late 1940s. She was married to Truck Jackson."

"Oh, my," Lucinda whispered. "No wonder you wanted to go."

"Didn't pan out?" Skid asked.

"I met with her. She's in her eighties, memory challenged, and—she said that her husband, whose name was, in fact, Truck Jackson, came up to Blue Mountain over a question of inheritance in the Jackson tribe."

"That doesn't sound foolish at all," Skid said, all attention. "You said your trip to Atlanta was foolish—"

"That Truck Jackson came up here in 1950 and was never seen again." I sighed. "And the woman who told me about it, this Polly Hutchinson Jackson, is just the littlest bit nuts."

"But—" Lucinda began.

"Where's my apple brandy!" Andrews roared. "Damn, what

do I have to do? Get shot? Wait. Already did it. And I still don't have my damned apple brandy."

"He may be verging on hysteria," I whispered to Skid.

"Verging?"

"Come on," I called to Andrews, standing, "it's in my pantry, unless someone took it in the raid."

"Raid?" Andrews looked around.

"Come in the house," I told him.

We danced past Crawdad and confronted my living room. It was a wreck. Chairs were shoved everywhere, pillows thrown asunder, books and records and CDs and tapes strewn everywhere—but my tapes had endured the worst wrath.

Tapes.

"Wait." I froze. "Hold on."

"What is it?" Skidmore was right behind me.

"I think the guy was looking for the tape I made of him. The tape recording of our conversation. Look."

The primary carnage in the room consisted of boxes of reel-to-reel tape. The really valuable ones I had locked up in my room upstairs. The more casual catalog had been alphabetized in rows on the bookshelves that had been built into both sides of the fireplace. Every tape was on the floor, many out of their boxes. I breathed a momentary prayer to the gods of compulsion who had forced me to label every tape as well as every box with catalog numbers, descriptions, exact dates, even times. Putting everything back in order would be relatively short work—unless something was missing.

"Why would he want that tape?" Skid actually scratched his head, the way a sheriff in a bad movie might.

"No idea." All I could do was survey the battlefield and worry about the losses.

Andrews appeared beside me. "Well, obviously he said something on the tape that he didn't want anyone to hear. Do I have to think of everything? And where the *hell* is my apple brandy?"

Before I could even turn to Lucinda for help, she was on her way to my pantry. Andrews caught on a second later and followed her, mute and, for some reason, limping.

"Can you remember—" Skid began.

"I'm trying, but it was all a jumble: the Tango, an Argentine mother, World War I. It was more on the order of telling a story he could only half remember than recalling things that actually happened to him. Or maybe I'm reading that into his words because I know that the things he told me couldn't, logically, have happened to him."

Skid cast his eye over the wreckage in my living room. "Well, he said *something* that was true enough to make him come back to your house, do this, and shoot a pistol at you two."

"The pistol." I held my breath for a second. "You realize it's probably the one that Hovis Daniels owned. This man obviously stole it from Hovis when he visited him."

"Along with the necklace," Skidmore added, "that had the picture of Barbrie in it."

"Right. And the problem for Hovis now is—"

"That a stolen picture of his dead wife and a pistol that belonged to him and everyone knew it," Skid said tersely, "combine to make Hovis the clear suspect in our murder investigation, even though we both know he didn't do it."

"So you do know that?" I asked him.

"Yes." He glanced over at Deputy Melissa Mathews, who was going through my tapes on the floor in a pair of latex hospital gloves. "I did that for Millroy. Turns out to be a problem."

"Because now Millroy will be convinced that the stranger's death was murder," I agreed, "but he'll be convinced that the murderer is Hovis."

"Growing up," Melissa said, not looking up from her work, "us kids used to hear stories about the Jacksons' caretaker, and how he killed a lots of people, mostly kids who went onto the Jackson property. We never stopped to think that no one we knew had ever actually lost a playmate or gone to a funeral. It was a Halloween story. But it adds to Hovis's troubles now."

Deputy Crawdad eased up behind me, standing next to Skidmore.

"We used to have a dare," he said softly, "me and my brothers. You had to wait till after dark, then you had to jump the Jacksons' fence, run touch the front door on that old shack where Hovis stayed, and get back to the road without, you know, getting shot. We did it all the time at the first of every school year growing up. After Christmas, not as much. I always felt bad about that when I got, you know, growed-up enough to realize we probably had a hand in driving Hovis crazy."

"The chances are good," Skidmore said to Crawdad without turning, "that he wasn't there. By the time you were a kid, he was put away."

Andrews wafted in from the kitchen, a tumbler full of clear fire in his hand, and stood to make his own observation of the scene.

"You have *really* let your housekeeping skills deteriorate." He took a healthy swig. "I remember when you used to file those tapes on a shelf instead of on the floor."

"How's the head?" I asked him.

"What head?" He grinned and lifted his glass to me.

"Perfect." I returned to the matter at hand, kneeling on the living room floor. "The tape would have Monday's date on it. It's the only one with that date."

"Are all the dates like this?" Melissa held up one tape for me to see. "I mean, like 02/07/97?"

"You have tapes from 1997 on the shelves in your living room?" Andrews marveled.

"I have some that are dated 1962," I told him proudly. "My Wollensak is the same model as Alan Lomax used to record his Library of Congress tapes. And I have copies of some of *his* tapes."

"Really?" Andrews moved further into the living room.

"Could we focus on the point at hand?" Skidmore interrupted impatiently. "Tomorrow is Thursday. We have to figure all this out by sundown tomorrow or things get a whole lot more complicated."

"At least we know the real killer hasn't escaped off the mountain," I offered.

"Hey!" Deputy Mathews held up a tape. "You don't really have tapes as far back as 1917, do you?"

"What?" I squinted in her direction.

"This one says 11/08/17. Now, Monday was the seventeenth, I believe, so is it possible you got the day and the year reversed?"

I stood and waded through the tapes on the floor. "Very possible. I was pretty tired—and, you know, the man had a gun."

I took the tape from Melissa.

"Play it," Skidmore insisted. "Where's your machine?"

"In my truck."

Less than three minutes later I'd retrieved the Wollensak from under the passenger's seat, lugged it into the kitchen, and was ready to play the tape. Everyone had gathered silently around the kitchen table.

"Here we go," I whispered.

The reel turned, and a voice cracked the silence.

"The gun exploded, blood erupted, and Jacob lay dying on the brothel floor."

TWELVE

I AWOKE BEFORE sunrise on Thursday morning, got ready to leave as silently as I could manage, and headed downstairs. I intended to put up the rest of the tapes, a task I had not finished the night before, and be gone early from the house.

To my great amazement, Andrews was already up, rummaging through the kitchen for something to eat. His hair looked like a frozen blond fountain. He had slept in his clothes, as he often did, and they made him a lively parody of absent-minded professor.

"Yes." He barely acknowledged my entrance into the kitchen. "Apple brandy: good. Morning after: bad."

I was already dressed for the day: black jeans, rust-colored flannel shirt, comfortably worn-down black work boots.

"You don't have to go with me, you know." I drifted toward the espresso machine.

Skidmore would be busy most of the day with some sort of forensic voodoo. Melissa had offered to listen more carefully to the visitor's tape enough times to find out why he had wanted so badly to steal it—we hadn't heard anything like that the night before. Crawdad had gathered some of his old school chums, and they were combing through the woods between my house and the Jackson place in an attempt to ferret out the ferret. I had volunteered to visit Mrs. Jackson and speak with her concerning the strange presence of someone calling himself Truck Jackson—not to mention hinting at Jacob Jackson, the family's black sheep—and the possibility that her in-law caretaker, Hovis Daniels, was a murderer.

The morning dawned quickly, and hard as a stone. Golden

light gave everything a layer of rich warmth, but it was fool's gold—only the appearance of heat. The air was more honest, made from little thorns of ice. In autumn the eye is often so deceived, but the skin always knows the truth. The illusion of warmth is autumn's seduction: Cranberry—and wine-colored leaves spiral through sunlight's fortresses of gold. But the year is old, and the unwary traveler, distracted by these swirling visions, may sometimes be unaware of the bone-white hand just behind him, a sudden dying of the light, and the silence of the coming snow.

"Why, exactly," Andrews said at last, "did you want me to come up here? I mean, why the urgency?"

He had found a box of Cheerios and was eating handfuls of the cereal, sans milk. Several of the tiny circles stuck to his face.

I started to explain that we had such a short amount of time to find out a great many things. I had in mind to tell him about Hovis Daniels, and his plea for my help, something no one else would give him. I was even preparing a short speech about keeping Lucinda safe from the roving maniac. Instead, I told the truth.

"I was afraid to do this by myself."

"Do what?" He stopped eating.

"I don't like what I'm thinking." I avoided looking at him and pretended to busy myself with the espresso machine. "I'm thinking that this man, Truck Jackson, might actually be all the things he says he is. I'm afraid of the turning wheels of Time, the way he rides them. And I know that's a little unbalanced; thinking that, I mean. So I'm worried that maybe I'm not completely stable. Given my upbringing and my life in general, it's not so hard to imagine that my mind would capsize eventually. Not that I'm feeling anywhere close to that, but I'm...not steady. I just needed, I don't know, someone to look at what I'm looking at and assure me that they see it, too."

He resumed his breakfast, digging his hand into the box with abandon.

"And that *someone*," he mumbled around a mouthful of cereal, "can't be Lucinda because you don't want to seem like a pansy to her; and it can't be Skidmore because he's getting

more and more like a real sheriff and less tolerant of your—
how shall we say?—eccentricities. So I'm your boy, because
for one thing I always think of you as a little off-kilter—so no
surprises there—and for another I razz you about everything
so it makes you take your whole gestalt a bit less seriously. I
get it. You'd do the same for me. Do you have any milk?"

That was it. That was Andrews. He tossed the empty cereal
box on the counter behind him and headed for the refrigerator.

"*Now* you want milk?"

"Didn't think of it before." He grabbed the handle of the
fridge with a touch of desperation. "Not awake yet."

"Look—if I'd known you were going to get shot in the
head—"

"You wouldn't have asked me to come. Clearly." He stood
with the refrigerator door open, grabbed a nearly full carton of
milk, and drained it. "But—"

"And I haven't told you everything. An innocent man may
be convicted of this murder, and the man who shot you might
get away, if we don't have some answers by this afternoon."

"But," he repeated, as if he hadn't heard what I'd said, "if
you had known that coming to my defense five years ago was
going to piss off the wrong people at the university and lead to
the demise of your department, would you have done *that?*"

"Yes." I said it instantly.

"There you have it." He flashed the merest moment of a
smile in my direction.

We never talked about the situation that nearly put Andrews
in jail and had, in fact, started a series of events that shut down
my folklore program at the university. It was old news.

Andrews stood there a moment, holding the empty milk
carton in his hand, staring at me.

"It doesn't even hurt," he said at length.

"What doesn't?"

"Where the bullet skinned my skull. I can't even feel it this
morning." He put the empty carton back in the refrigerator and
closed the door. "I'm hoping the hair turns white along the scar.
Think how cool that would look."

"Like the bride of Frankenstein."

"No," he groused. "Like—a racing stripe."

"So you can look fast standing still."

"Are we going?" He looked around the kitchen. "Or should I eat something else?"

"No, we're leaving," I assured him.

The espresso machine was ready. I made us each a triple to go, and we headed for the door.

The ride to the Jackson place took a bit longer than it needed to. I drove slowly under the pretense of not spilling my espresso, but, in fact, I used the extra minutes to fill Andrews in on all the details, all the things I was thinking about Truck Jackson, Millroy's imposing deadline.

By the time we pulled up to the Jacksons' front yard, we'd nearly finished our espresso and were both armed with a battery of questions.

The original Jackson home had been built in 1711, rebuilt from the ground up in 1906, and Edna had been born in it shortly after that—or so she always said. It had been whitewashed every spring since its completion, and glowed like a lantern in the morning sun. Set back from the road at the top of a rise, it offered a stunning view of the valley below where the town rested, if you were standing on the porch at the back of the house. Two stories were wrapped in that porch; it went entirely around the house. More than a dozen handmade rocking chairs were placed casually about. The roof was blazing silver tin, and that, too, was often refurbished or replaced. There were white lace curtains in every window, and a rich, buttery light always seemed to back them, as if a warm fire's glow emanated from every room in the house. Smoke, afraid to be any other color than white, curled into the sky from two of the four brick chimneys. Whitewashed stones lined the walkway to the front steps, and behind them that morning there were blood-red mums and deep purple ageratum. At every corner of the home there was a giant tea olive shrub, nearly as tall as the house—probably planted soon after the house was built. The flowers of the shrub there were negligible to the eye, but their scent ravished the air, and every breath filled the lungs with the beauty of a dying year's last memories.

I turned off the engine.

"Mrs. Jackson may be the oldest living resident of Blue Mountain." I stared at the front door. "She's set in her ways, militant concerning her religious beliefs, and meticulous about her home. If you spill anything, insult anyone, or let a curse word slip, we'll be shuttled out before you even begin to apologize."

"Right." Andrews tossed back his last swallow of espresso, eyes glued to the house. "Put me in, coach."

"Damn," I whispered, climbing out of the truck.

"Shh!" Andrews chided. "What did you *just* tell me?"

"But I forgot to ask Skidmore if he'd had a chance to bring Mrs. Jackson over to the Deveroes' to look at the body, see if she knew who it was."

"Can't you just ask her now?" Andrews whispered back.

"I guess." I would have preferred foreknowledge.

Before I could gather my thoughts any further, Edna Jackson appeared in the doorway.

Framed there, she looked more an old photo-portrait of a woman from another time than a flesh-and-blood human being alive in that morning air. Even the light refused to impart more than a sepia tone to her area of the front porch. She was dressed in a long chocolate-colored dress under a huge white Irish lamb's wool sweater. Her hair was perfectly coifed, the exact shade of the sweater. The hem of her garment covered her feet, but the toe of some sort of black slipper barely made itself known there.

She stood in the doorway with her arms folded in front of her, face set in her usual stern glare. Her wire-rimmed glasses reflected the morning light and made her eyes round bright diamonds, impossible to read.

I thought for a moment she was going to tell us to go away. Instead she raised her hand in the most commanding gesture I'd ever seen in real life; Andrews and I halted in our tracks.

"I'd expect you're here about that dead'un they found back of the house." Her voice crackled like breaking ice. "If you think you can convince me to go look at the body, get right back in that rusty old truck. Sheriff already tried. I see the dead at church."

"No, ma'am," I said slowly. "We're here to talk to you about Truck Jackson."

Another of the techniques gleaned from years of field research in the mountains—and often with characters as solid as Mrs. Jackson—was the *assumption of knowledge* rule. Never ask a question first. If you do, people might get the idea you want to find out something. That makes them wonder what you're after, and they spend all their time trying to outfox you instead of answering the questions you're eventually going to ask. The rule worked about 80 percent of the time.

In the case of Mrs. Jackson, asking her if she knew anything about Truck Jackson could have prompted a quick "no" and a hasty send-off. Assuming that she knew all about him and informing her that I did, too, was a much better opening gambit—but it could have gone either way.

She aimed her gleaming glasses right at me and took a deep breath. After one more moment of frozen glaring, she turned abruptly and vanished into the shadows past the door of the house.

Andrews shot a glance my way. I shook my head warning him not to move or speak. Another second clicked by.

"Parlor." That was all, but it was our invitation to cross the threshold.

I started in; Andrews failed to stop a momentary grin.

The foyer was a startling contrast to the exterior of the house. The moment we entered we were confronted by a stern staircase, with a banister that began and ended in a carved wooden lion's head, and turned finials that looked as if they'd been made from the wheel of a sailing ship that brought the Jacksons from Scotland to America.

It was dark, but we could see to our right a formal living room filled with centuries-old antiques and lace doilies. That room was not for the likes of us. If a minister or a politician were visiting, that room would be set for light refreshments and superficial conversation. Our room lay to the left, a less formal parlor where a fire blazed in the hearth and the curtains had been pulled aside to let in some of the day's light.

Mrs. Jackson was nowhere to be seen.

I nodded my head in the direction of the parlor, and Andrews followed me in. The room was only slightly brighter than the sepulcher of the hallway, despite tall windows in two of the four walls. The brown and ginger Persian rug that completely covered the floor seemed to absorb most of the light in the room. The fire popped occasionally, but seemed a bit afraid to make too much noise or illumination. The mantel was a single carved piece of ivory and looked like a sculpture of ice. Even in previous centuries the furniture would have been called quaint.

Neither of us felt comfortable sitting down before we were invited to. That parlor was the sort of room where one expected to see the heads of offending relatives mounted on the wall above the mantel—especially given the stern nature of Mrs. Jackson's brand of religion. No one could hope to meet her standards. She had once told me that Jesus was all good and well for the lesser Christians, but too kindly and coddling for her tastes. She preferred, she said, the Christianity of the Old Testament. When I made the mistake of pointing out to her that Christ had not yet been born in the Old Testament and that the volume was primarily a Jewish historical and educational text, she chased me from her house with a poker from the ornate fireplace set. That had been nearly seven years before, and she clearly still held a grudge. I was a bit surprised that she'd let me in at all, considering her vehemence that day.

"Sit down!"

Andrews and I both jumped. Mrs. Jackson had slipped in behind us, silent and sour.

"Your home is lovely as ever," I began, looking around for the right spot to sit.

"Introduce me to your companion," she insisted impatiently.

"Ah. Yes. This is Dr. Winton Andrews," I said quickly.

He held out his hand. She stared at it, then up at his face.

"You're a real doctor or one like him?" She twitched her head in my direction.

"Um." That was, apparently, all Andrews could think of to say.

"There." She pointed where he was to sit.

He sat immediately.

She stared at me. I stared back. That tableau could have lasted hours, but for the entrance of another Jackson. She was dressed in a floor-length Empire dress, her dyed red hair pulled back in a tight bun. I thought she was called Simple but I never knew if that was a name—a sort of Shaker homage—or a description. No one I knew had ever heard her speak, and she was easily in her sixties.

Simple brought in a tray upon which was perched an ancient teapot and four exceedingly breakable cups.

I chose the most masculine seat in the room, a leather wing chair that was certainly over a hundred years old. The leather was softer than a baby's cheek.

Mrs. Jackson glided to a Queen Anne love seat and settled herself in the exact middle of it—the way Polly Hutchinson Jackson had in her own home in Atlanta. I found that comparison heartbreaking, for some reason.

The woman called Simple began to pour tea, and Mrs. Jackson coughed for a full minute. Andrews kept glancing my way, obviously nervous beyond the dictates of the situation, for some reason.

"Truck Jackson," Mrs. Jackson began abruptly, her voice startling even Simple, who nearly spilled her final cup of tea, "was a war hero. I believe I have a photograph of him in an album somewhere."

Simple began handing out teacups.

"Truck Jackson visited me Monday night." I accepted a cup from Simple. "Drank coffee in my kitchen."

Andrews was so surprised by my blunt approach that I thought his head might begin to spin around.

"Not much," Mrs. Jackson responded, almost allowing herself to smile. "He's been dead for fifty years. Fifty years or more."

"Yes," I said instantly, resting my teacup on my right knee, "that's what I found so unusual about his visit."

Simple held a cup out in Mrs. Jackson's direction, but she waved it away with a flick of her bony wrist.

"Revenant," Simple said, not to anyone in particular.

"I agree." I took a single sip of tea.

"Not good. This time of year." Simple appeared deep in thought.

"He also paid his respects to Lucinda Foxe," I said, staring into my cup, "and to Hovis Daniels before he came to my house."

"Hovis?" Mrs. Jackson sat up even straighter—a feat I would not have thought possible—and focused her eyes on mine.

In the light of the parlor it was easier to see her eyes past her glasses. They were black coals where heat had once been—and could be again with the proper fuel, I thought.

"The man told Hovis he was a World War II hero, told me he was a veteran of World War I, and insisted to Lucinda that he'd fought in the Civil War. But he also told her that his name was Jacob."

Simple stopped moving. Mrs. Jackson stopped breathing. Talking about ghosts as if they had actually visited me was not enough to slow down our conversation, but the mention of Jacob Jackson brought everything to a halt.

"Simple, please sit down," Mrs. Jackson commanded after a moment.

Simple sat almost immediately, on an embroidered footstool, and leaned forward like a child. It couldn't have been a comfortable posture.

"We don't mention that name in this house, Dr. Devilin," Mrs. Jackson sniffed. "I expect you know that."

"I know that someone visited me and Lucinda Foxe on the same night, claiming to be a Jackson. He had a gun, and I believe he killed the man who was found behind your house Tuesday morning. The sheriff, for reasons of his own, has arrested Hovis Daniels for the murder. The strangest verifiable fact in this matter is that the dead man and our visitor look enough alike to be brothers. And since the one who's still alive claims to be at least two or three of your relatives, the sheriff wanted you to have a look at the dead body to see if you recognized him. Since you won't do that, I have questions of my own." I took a breath. "That, in a nutshell, is the situation."

"Ordinarily I'd ask you to leave after a bag of wind like that," Mrs. Jackson said, sitting back. "But I understand that you're a troubled boy, and I must have patience with the damaged souls of this earth. I suppose anyone raised by those trashy parents of yours would grow up bent and broken. So I forgive you, because it is my Christian duty. But keep your tongue civil. My patience is not boundless. Ask anyone."

She glanced, only for an instant, at Simple, and the woman on the footstool shivered, closing her eyes. I tried very hard not to think too much about that.

Mrs. Jackson had used a ploy that had certainly worked on most people around her, a combination of sanctimonious religiosity and stiletto attacks on the psyche. It hadn't worked on me because no one on earth could think or say worse things about my parents than I had, and I found her hypocrisy laughable.

So I smiled. It seemed to do the trick: She cocked her head at me like a spaniel trying to figure out what had happened.

"My theory," I announced, glancing at Andrews so that he might know it was time for him to join the conversation, "is that my visitor was one of two things. The first thing he could have been is, as you have suggested, a revenant, a wandering shadow—"

"A traveling creature," Simple piped up.

I was startled by the sound of her voice. It was melodic and very rich.

"'Today I am a warning,'" I quoted, "'to woman and to man.'"

"Simple is a great one to sing in our church," Mrs. Jackson said, without even a hint of pride—or approval.

"In Mrs. Jackson's church," I explained to Andrews, mostly to irritate Mrs. Jackson, "they do not believe in musical instruments, which they believe are primary tools of Satan. They do sing. I've told you many times about Sacred Harp music."

"Oh, right!" He sat up. "Those weird harmonies."

"Simple and I were sharing a moment of one song called 'I Am a Traveling Creature,' and it's a fairly frightening example of the genre. I believe in one verse a dying woman prays for some hope of relief, but the spirit of God says, 'Too late.'"

"That's enough!" Mrs. Jackson exploded.

"Mrs. Jackson believes in that sort of divinity," I went on, "one that has more punishment than forgiveness in its arsenal."

"I can see that," Andrews nodded, enjoying the fact that the old woman was getting more and more upset, though he could not have said why it was happening.

"The second explanation for my company on Monday night," I pressed, "is that he was a relative of yours, someone who knows the family history and is taking advantage of it for some reason or another, trying to scare up information, perhaps, about family money. I'm trying to understand it, but I keep coming back to the fact that the man himself seemed so confused. And why would he tell me that he was Truck and tell Lucinda that he was Jacob?"

"Brothers." Simple was rocking and not looking at anyone.

"What?" Andrews asked her.

But she would not even look up.

"Oh." I snapped a few of the pieces together. "Polly told me that Truck Jackson came up here to find out about his inheritance, and he was shot by his brother. And Jacob Jackson left his family and fought against his brother. And the dead man and the killer are probably brothers. Nice work, Simple."

She smiled but did not look my way.

"Right." Andrews joined in, attempting to needle the old woman. "Civil War. Brother against brother. You people in this part of America are still on about that, I'm told."

"You don't know anything," Mrs. Jackson snarled. "Let me set you straight. Robert E. Lee was Lincoln's first choice to lead the *Union* army. Did you know that? Lincoln only chose Grant after Lee turned him down! Did you know that Lee cried like a child when he made the decision to lead the Confederate army instead? Before the war, Lee was the Democratic Party's leading contender to run against Lincoln in the next election."

"Look, no argument you could ever make would convince me that slavery—" Andrews sneered.

"The war was not about slavery!" Mrs. Jackson's voice was nearly at the edge of the range of human audibility. "It was about economics. It was about what sort of country we were going to have. It was a war between agrarian ways, which are God's ways—living off the land God gave us—and industrial ways, which are Satan's ways—living off the stinking inventions of little men. Jacksons *never* had slaves—not since we came here in 1692. Never would. We do our own work, and we glory in the work. Why would we turn that glory over to someone else?"

"Dr. Andrews doesn't really need a lesson about—" I interrupted.

"And as for Jacob Jackson," she continued, turning her venom my way, "he was a traitor to the family. He suffered in his last hours—he lived in Chicago, a town of stinking industry. In a tiny rooming house in Chicago, he became obsessed by the notion of reuniting with his family in Georgia. He felt he must repair a rift before he died—a rent in the fabric of his family that he must mend. This consummation was all but extinguished, however, when every letter he wrote to us was returned unopened. He discovered that he was dead to his family in Georgia. So they would be dead to him, too. He forgot about us—and about almost everything else—by means of a carefully planned program of spending all his money on prostitutes and liquor."

"The man in my kitchen told me he was Truck Jackson, married to Polly Hutchinson." I stared back at Mrs. Jackson, hoping she would understand that I was interested in the present more than the past—admittedly an unusual circumstance for me. "If I could just—"

"That was Jacob!" she objected. "You've got it all confused. Jacob met that singing Hutchinson girl when he was up at Gettysburg; they married in Illinois."

Without warning, Simple jumped up and left the room.

Mrs. Jackson shook her head, as if shouldering a burden that would be too great for a lesser mortal. "That girl. Excuse her, if you can."

"I'm a bit confused myself," Andrews piped up. "I'm an

outsider. I don't quite understand this business of Truck Jackson—the real one, back in the fifties, and some inheritance that ended up provoking his demise."

"Truck Jackson was a war hero!" Mrs. Jackson rasped. "War hero. I believe I have a photograph of him in an album somewhere."

"You said that," Andrews told her slowly.

"I did?" A momentary chink in her armor appeared; she shifted in her seat, and it was gone. "He and his brother, James, got into an argument about dividing up this property. I would not stand for it. I will keep this property intact! It must remain as it is."

"What did Truck want?"

"No." She waved her hand at me as if she were casting a spell. "*James* wanted to divide it. Truck didn't care. He sided with me. They argued—"

"Did this James person have any specific division of the property in mind?" Andrews asked.

"What?" She had to take a moment to think. "He...I believe he wanted the bottom twenty acres for himself."

I turned to Andrews. "Where Hovis Daniels's shack is located?"

"Hovis." Mrs. Jackson said the name the way most people cursed. "Hovis killed little Barbrie. She was my great-niece once removed, and the sweetest flower of these hills."

Before I could pursue that line of thinking, Simple bounded back into the room with a piece of yellowed paper in her hand.

"Not all were sent back." She sat on her stool, flushed.

"What have you got there?" Mrs. Jackson nearly rose to a standing position.

"Some of the letters from Jacob were kept. Someone in this house, not Edna, has some. I found them. Here's one."

She held it out, a wildflower found in a darker part of the forest, to everyone's surprise.

"Give me that!" Mrs. Jackson demanded.

"Listen," Simple said to me, drawing the letter backward to her face. "'I told her I had not injured my leg in the battle at

Gettysburg. I told her I had injured it wrestling with an angel. That's what made Miss Hutchinson fall for me.'"

"Simple," Mrs. Jackson growled. "Where did you get this nonsense?"

"I'd like to hear it," Andrews said in a very jolly fashion.

A brief war played itself out across the face of Edna Jackson—it was a war between good manners and personal anger. Manners, for the moment, won out.

"Very well," Mrs. Jackson grumbled.

Simple smiled, and continued reading. "'She thought I was speaking metaphorically about the struggle of humankind. She looked into the well of my eyes, down to the bottom. There she saw a perfect reflection of her face, because that was all I could think about. We were mad for each other. Before the older women at her church could stop it, fire had seized us both.'"

Simple stopped reading for a moment and looked up at me with a face generally reserved for medieval portrayals of the Annunciation, and then she turned again to her letter.

"'Married, our passion exploded. I often ran from the field in the middle of the morning to be with Polly. I ran. Six years and four children later, I still can't go more than a few hours without wanting her close to me. She feels the same way. Our desire is not shamed by public opinion. We hold hands—no, we *clutch* hands—in church. We kiss on the street. We never let more than three sentences pass without a sweet name falling from our lips. And when I look at my babies I am often unable to make words properly. I think they are starlight. I think they are diamonds. When I pitch hay, I toss every other forkful onto them. It makes them shriek with laughter. Delight in the golden rain. You can always see us, the whole family, planting roses, painting the farmhouse, singing in the kitchen while we make dinner. There isn't a man in the world who loves his own family more.'"

I was wondering why some of the letter sounded vaguely familiar to me when Mrs. Jackson wrecked the gentler air in the room.

"That's why it must have been such a shock to everyone,"

Mrs. Jackson interrupted, her voice like an ungreased mill wheel, "when he ran off one day and never came back."

"The rain just wouldn't stop," Simple explained. "It says so in another letter. It started in March. By the last week of May there were two clear days in a row—but they were too late. The corn was ruined, along with the Jacob Jackson family. A great deal of Indiana was flooded. The governor declared a state of emergency. Jacob was inconsolable. His heart was broken by the ruin of his fortunes, and it set fire to his mind. Something is lost in that kind of a fire—a compass or a gyre—whatever it is that keeps a man like that on track. I believe his mind capsized."

"He was looking for some reason why his life had been heaped with travail and tribulation," Mrs. Jackson sighed with a kind of self-satisfied resignation. "He thought he was Job."

"He wasn't," Simple objected. "He was *Jacob*—but he didn't know what that meant. Anyway, it's easy to see how a confusion like that might have happened. All that stands between Jacob and Job are the little letters *a* and *c*—and those letters stand for 'alternating current,' as a child learns in school. Only this was the alternating current of the Universe, the electricity of the spheres."

Andrews stared at Simple, his mouth actually wide open.

"Jacob wrestled with an angel," I began, partly to explain Simple's line of thinking to Andrews, partly to support it.

"I know," Andrews said softly, "but *the electricity of the spheres*—"

"What I'm wondering," I said to Mrs. Jackson, "I mean, the question I have turning in my mind, is this: What did Jacob do about his economic travail?"

"He thought he could come home," Mrs. Jackson crackled. "He was desperate enough to think he could muster sympathy in the bosom of his family."

"That's what I was thinking." I nodded. "He came here."

"Came back for money," Mrs. Jackson coughed. "They chased him off the property with dogs. He never came back. He went to Chicago."

"He lived in a rooming house," I said, not certain why I was saying it—or to whom, "owned by someone named Madam Briscoe. There he met a woman, a prostitute, called La Gauchina and had a son with her—named Truck."

"I wouldn't know about that!" Mrs. Jackson exploded.

"But Jacob Jackson would never see Truck," I continued, "because one of his relatives from Blue Mountain chased him down all the way to Chicago and shot him at Mrs. Briscoe's to keep him from ever coming home to this house—"

Mrs. Jackson's face was a stern warning. "Dr. Devilin, I must ask you to stop this line of—" Mrs. Jackson warned.

"—to keep him from ever inheriting any of this land. He was murdered by his brother, just like Truck was murdered—over some alleged inheritance."

"That's it!" Mrs. Jackson howled.

"But what—" Andrews began, baffled.

"Simple!" Mrs. Jackson shrieked, getting to her feet. "Show these gentlemen the door. I won't stand for another second of this!"

Simple shot up and began making frantic gestures toward the front door.

"What is it that all these people think they're inheriting?" Andrews stammered, finishing his thought.

"Yes," I answered, rising to follow Simple. "That's the very next thing we have to find out."

"I'm warning you to stay out of my family's affairs," Mrs. Jackson shouted, already halfway out of the room and not looking back at us. "I'll have lawyers to see that you do! No more questions. No more answers. Simple!"

Simple jumped as if she'd been shocked by an alternating current, and flew to the doorway.

"I love these letters," she whispered to me, fluttering the yellow piece of paper in her hand. "I wouldn't trade them for all the gold..."

She could not manage any more words after that, but short bursts of incomprehensible sound bubbled from her mouth.

Andrews and I, for her sake, hurried past the threshold and into the sun washing the front yard. It was as if we'd passed through a portal between two worlds. The daylight seemed to have divided reality into portions—one was the inside of the Jackson house, the other was the rest of the world.

THIRTEEN

"WELL, I MEAN, JESUS CHRIST," Andrews said as he climbed into my truck. "That was chaos."

"Every encounter I've ever had in that house has ended with my being tossed out." I threw myself in behind the wheel.

"All right, but I mean," Andrews stammered, "that house is loaded to the *brim* with both heebies *and* jeebies."

He stared at the house as if it were some sort of huge animal that might leap up at any moment and devour the truck. I started the engine and backed away slowly—just in case.

"Mrs. Jackson certainly does drag around a certain aura, doesn't she?" I stared at the house for a moment. A curtain in the parlor parted ever so slightly, and I thought I caught a glimpse of Simple's odd dress.

"And that daughter," Andrews said, sensing her presence in the window as well. "What a spook."

"That's the first time I've heard her voice, except for singing. I've never known her to speak before today."

"Can you blame her?" Andrews rubbed the backs of his arms as if he were cold, though he certainly wasn't.

The truck complained as I shifted gears and headed down the road. It was a bit cold. A sudden blast of wind drove blood-red and mud-brown maple leaves across the road, the perfect imitation of a huge flock of male and female cardinals all migrating to a warmer clime. Sunlight failed to pierce those wings, and for a moment we were in the dark.

"I didn't get to ask half my questions," I said haplessly.

"At least you found out that the old bat didn't look at the dead body."

"Right. But I really wanted to know what inheritance the Jackson family could possibly boast that would merit murder. Aside from the part of the mountain they own, I can't see anything of value at all."

"It is a bit...eerie that several sets of brothers have fought over it. And that someone has died each time. It's like the family are all stuck in a loop, longing for this swag, killing for it, regretting it, dying; then the whole cycle starts again."

"Brother against brother."

"You don't just mean the Jacksons—you don't even mean *just* your Civil War." Andrews nodded. "I understand that."

The sun finally penetrated leaves and limbs and hammered the hood of my truck with golden mallets.

"Look," I said to Andrews, glancing up at the sun, "we're running out of time. I feel a certain pressure to help Hovis Daniels. He didn't kill anyone, and I'm afraid no one but me will help him."

"Aside from your noble nature," Andrews asked softly, "what would prompt you to feel that kind of responsibility?"

"No idea." I pressed the accelerator a bit. "But it's there, and I'll analyze it later, if you like. For the moment, I'd like to discover why the stranger, the false Truck Jackson, visited the exact three people that he visited on Monday night."

"Why?" Andrews turned my way.

"I'm coming to the conclusion that, despite clear evidence to the contrary, the man had a purpose. He was looking for something. Looking for information. I have it in my head now that his stories might not be wild ramblings but some sort of internal code, or metaphorical language. The story of one brother killing another seems clear enough: The visitor killed his own brother, or was about to. And what if all this talk all about war is actually about family dynamics?"

"This is exactly the trouble with your so-called academic discipline," Andrews complained. "Too many folklorists have in their minds a Freudian or even, God forbid, a Jungian interpretation of simple human behaviors. Sometimes a war story is just a war story."

"But you just said that the surreal recurrence of the same story over and over again is too much to ignore."

"No," he objected, "I said it was eerie. I was going for the autumnal spooky feeling. You're going for some sort of publishable journal article."

"Pa-*tay*-toe," I pronounced in as perfect and derisive an imitation of Andrews as I could manage, "pa-*tah*-toe."

"You're an idiot," he told me, unable to keep from laughing.

"Here's what I have in mind," I breezed on. "I'll drop you off at the jailhouse. You can flirt with Deputy Melissa Mathews—"

"Now you're talking," Andrews oozed. "She's so cute in that crisp uniform, and she has her own handcuffs."

"And I will go speak with Nurse Lucinda Foxe," I continued, doing my best to ignore Andrews altogether.

"Who is also cute in her nurse's—"

"Stop," I demanded. "Listen. You're going to talk to Hovis Daniels; see if you can get him to go over his recollection of the conversation with the visitor. See if you can figure out what the visitor was really after. I didn't know to ask about that before—I didn't think to look for it. I'm going to ask Lucinda the same thing. And in the meantime, I'm going to try to figure out what he wanted from me. You can help in *that* regard by asking Melissa if she's listened to my tape recording enough to find anything significant in his strange rambling monologues. Then we'll piece it all together."

"Brilliant." He settled back. "The game is afoot."

"Shut very much up, would you mind?"

My truck sped down the ruts and stones of the road, bouncing us like a cheap ride at a traveling carnival, until we hit the blacktop into town. Fifteen minutes later, we were in front of the sheriff's office.

I got out to make certain Melissa knew what we were doing, and to assure her that Andrews wasn't there just to bother her. She was sitting at her desk in the front room of the suite with headphones on, shaking her head. She took them off when she saw us come in.

"This guy was a real nut, wasn't he?" she asked, turning off the tape recorder.

"Dr. Devilin believes there is method in his madness." Andrews sat on the front edge of her desk.

"There may be," she answered, clearly in doubt of the concept, "but I can't find any. He thinks he's from another time, and he's talking about the Tango. It's kind of scary."

"We could listen together," Andrews suggested.

"Would you mind letting Dr. Andrews speak with Hovis?" I asked her. "I have some questions in mind. I'm going to speak with Lucinda on the same subject, to wit: Why exactly did that man visit the three of us? What's the pattern? What was he looking for?"

"You don't think it was just a random, wandering thing?" She squinted up at me. "Surely does sound like it on this tape."

"There's always a pattern, ma'am," Andrews told her, clearly mocking me—and the entire genre of investigative detection.

"I hope to find some sort of thread," I assured Melissa. "Is Skidmore…"

"No. He's over at the county lab in Pine City." She leaned forward. "He's trying to do a DNA analysis, see can he find out who the dead man is that way. Isn't that exciting? This surely is the age of miracles."

It was clear to me that Deputy Mathews was deliberately exaggerating the more *Hee Haw* aspect of her speech and character—in an effort to confound Andrews—or to put him off.

Alas, Andrews seemed to find it charming.

"It is exciting," I said, catching Melissa's eye. "But, as I was saying, would you mind if a leering Englishman saw Hovis?"

I tapped on the desk to make Andrews stand up.

He did not.

"I'll have to lock you in with him," she said to Andrews, all business. She stood quickly, reaching for keys on her desk. That made him get to his feet.

"Then I'll leave you to it." I patted Andrews once on his shoulder and beat, as they say, a hasty retreat.

FOURTEEN

THE MORNING SUN was rising quickly to meet the top of the sky. It was God's scourge, warning me to move quickly, or feel the sting of its coming down. Sunset seemed all too close.

I made it to the hospital cursing the fact that I hadn't worn my watch. I wasn't certain when I'd taken it off or where I'd put it, but I suddenly felt I was an idiot for not having it with me. No idea what time it was, I barged into the admitting area and stormed up to the nurses' station.

The luscious and redoubtable Nurse Chambers was on the phone and managed to continue her conversation about cholesterol medication while offering me the most significantly suggestive eyebrow raising in the history of Western culture. When she hung up the phone she deliberately leaned over in order to present cleavage the way Jayne Mansfield used to in the B movies.

As luck would have it, Lucinda rounded the corner just in time.

"My, my," she sang, "two days in one week. People will talk."

"People in this town," I reminded her, "can talk for a week about the shape of a toothpick. They're certainly already talking about us. And I like to help matters along every so often by using the word 'fiancée' in a sentence."

"Able to say it without stuttering yet?" she drawled.

"He just did," Nurse Chambers offered.

"Quiet, you," Lucinda teased, "I saw the way you were leaning over just now."

"Me?" She blinked.

"Oh, please." Lucinda shook her head. "I could see far enough down your dress to tell what toenail polish you're wearing."

"Look," I interrupted, "I really need to talk to you about something for a second, okay?"

Lucinda turned to me ready to continue playing, but when she saw the expression on my face, I suppose, she dropped her smile.

"There's a consult room right here." She started for it without another word.

I followed.

"Hurry back," Nurse Chambers whispered behind me.

I made it to the consultation room without looking back, thus avoiding being turned into a pillar of salt. Lucinda closed the door behind me.

The room was tiny; smelled strongly of rubbing alcohol. There was only space for an examination table, a rolling chair, a counter topped with several containers, and the low buzzing of fluorescent lights.

We both stood.

"What is it?" Her face was perfection.

"Sorry to barge in at your work," I began, "but if I don't figure something out by tonight, that Millroy person is probably going to come to one of two erroneous conclusions. One would be that the dead man killed himself, the other would be that Hovis killed him."

"But doesn't he know about the man who came to visit us?"

"I guess he does, but it isn't evidence. Skidmore arrested Hovis to keep him…to keep Millroy from filing the victim's death as a suicide. But now Hovis stands to be charged with murder."

"Hovis is pretty far gone," Lucinda said softly, "but he wouldn't kill anything that he wasn't going to eat."

Despite my tension—or perhaps because of it—I was able to laugh.

"True enough." I nodded. "But what I've got in my head now is that our mutual visitor came to the three of us—Hovis, you, then me—looking for something. He wasn't rambling; he chose us for a reason."

She looked at her shoes for a moment and took in a deep breath.

"Sweetheart," she sighed, "you always think…you often want there to be a reason for something when, for the most part, things just happen. I feel I have to say that you might be looking for a pattern where there isn't one."

"Where's God's plan in that kind of thinking?" I asked her, a smile nearly imperceptibly creasing my lips. "What the hell kind of mountain-girl Christian are you?"

"The kind that's worked in a hospital most of her life," she answered back more seriously than I might have liked.

"Right. Right. But could you humor me, at least for Hovis?"

"Well, I mean, we *know* he didn't do it. The man who visited us killed that other man."

"Clear to you and me," I agreed, "but invisible to Millroy and insubstantial for Skidmore."

"All right," she acquiesced. "Ask me what you want. But I really can't take all morning—"

"Besides talking about the Civil War," I began immediately, "I'm wondering if our visitor asked you any questions at all."

"Let me see." She sat absently in the rolling chair. "There was a lot of talk about that Hutchinson Family—"

"Right," I prompted, "I've looked into that."

"And there was all that about Gettysburg," she continued, concentrating. "I don't think—"

"You told me that he said his name was Jacob," I pressed. "And then you said something about how much he loved his family and ran off. You used some pretty specific phrases that stand out in my mind. You said...I think your exact words were 'before the older women could stop it, fire had seized them both.'"

"How do you do that?" she marveled. "How do you remember things like that? It really is a talent."

"Don't you think that's what you said?"

"I do." She sat back in the chair. "I think it's pretty much a quote from my visitor. Doesn't sound like something I'd say, really."

"Right."

"Why did you—"

"Because," I answered, leaning on the examination table, a bit drained of color, "Simple Jackson just read me those words in a letter from the Civil War not half an hour ago."

"You heard Simple *talk?*" That was what amazed her most.

"And she has a lovely voice, but the point is—"

"I see the point." She folded her hands. "Now I really have to think harder about what the man might have said, I guess."

"If you would."

She rocked a little bit, staring at the wall. After a moment, her shoulders slumped.

"It did seem like he was trying to get around to something," she told me at last, "but I think Stacy's phone call—you remember I told you she called about a prescription? I think that stopped him. He was gone after that."

"I remember."

"You heard Simple talk." She couldn't get over it. "What did she say?"

"She read a letter from the Civil War," I repeated.

"Oh. Right."

"Sweet voice. Very melodic."

"Like her father," she said softly. "Did you ever meet Mr. Jackson—Edna's husband? What was his name?"

"I think his first name was Mister," I answered. "I don't think I ever heard anyone call him anything else, including Mrs. Jackson—whom I can't call Edna."

"He was a sweet old guy." Lucinda sighed. "I looked after him during his last days. I was just out of nursing school. It's probably because I hadn't figured out how to put some distance between me and the patients at that point, but I really got to liking him. He was always joking, even though he was in pretty bad pain."

"He died of—"

"Lung cancer. Smoked like a chimney, drank like a fish, and lived into his eighties. Give me those genes."

"Hard to imagine a smoking, drinking, joking man married to Edna Jackson."

"You said 'Edna.'"

"I know, but—"

"I think Edna's the reforming kind," Lucinda offered, "the sort of person who thinks her job is to take a sinner and kick him till he repents. Mr. Jackson, dying in the hospital, told me he was happier than he'd been in years."

"I did meet him, to answer your question. I made a couple

of tapes of him when I was still in graduate school. He was part of my dissertation, in fact. He could sing about forty verses of 'Barbara Allen'—some that I'd never heard before. I think he enjoyed singing for me—he told me he never sang in his house."

"Where did you tape him?"

"Down in that little shack where Hovis stays now. I think Mr. Jackson might have kept his stash down there somewhere. He was always pretty loaded when I met him—ready to sing."

"He sang in the hospital, too," she said softly. "One of the last things he did was sing."

"You were with him—"

"Literally in his last moments of life," she told me sweetly. "I said I'd gotten a little too close to him. I was there when he died. We'd called Edna, but she didn't make it in time to see him—it was just me. He sang, he asked me for a cigarette—don't remember what all he talked about, but, you know, he eventually winked at me. Really. And then closed his eyes and went to sleep. Gone like that. Very peaceful."

"Give me those genes," I said softly. "That's how I want to go, falling asleep close to a beautiful woman. In a nurse's uniform."

"You?" she laughed, rousing herself from her reverie. "You'll go falling off a cliff close to a dangerous maniac, the way things have panned out for you since you've come back home."

"Sadly, you've got a point."

"Well." She stood. "Sorry I couldn't be of more help. I really have to get back to work."

"Okay." I looked around. "Although we do have this very convenient table here. Does that door lock?"

"Are you out of your mind?" She giggled. Giggled like a kid, headed for the door. "You really have to examine your predilections."

"*Examination table* right here," I insisted. "You could examine my predilections for me."

"God." She burst from the room laughing, which set every nurse in the station to whispering.

"Fine," I announced, emerging from the room and following her.

We walked back to the nurses' station in silence.

"Sorry I couldn't tell you anything more helpful. Really." Lucinda managed to put the imposing counter of the station between herself and me. "What'll you do now?"

"See if Andrews got anything useful out of Hovis."

"Did you really think Hovis would talk to a stranger?" She shook her head.

"Time's of the essence, and I'd rather talk to you—"

"But I mean, Dr. Andrews?"

"He can turn on the charm when he wants to. I mean, obviously he's not as charming as he thinks he is—"

"He's a big flirt." Lucinda shook her head.

"All right." I deliberately pushed myself off the counter and turned toward the exit. "Dinner later?"

"Of course."

I could hear the smile in her voice.

I could also hear Nurse Chambers behind me as I pushed the exit door. "Who's this Andrews? Is he a new doctor here?" Long may she wave.

FIFTEEN

SKIDMORE'S SQUAD CAR was still not in evidence when I pulled into a parking spot in front of the police station. I could see Melissa Mathews, listening to the tape, through the big front window.

I consulted the sky, which seemed to say that it was nearly noon. I hurried into the station.

Melissa looked up.

"That was quick," she said, turning off the tape recorder and glancing at her watch.

"What time is it?" I asked, leaning on the desk.

"Oh, it's almost lunchtime," she told me.

"So—Dr. Andrews?"

Melissa began fussing with the tape recorder in an utterly meaningless series of gestures, which led me to believe that she was trying to say something or ask me something but couldn't quite manage it.

"That Dr. Andrews," she began slowly, not looking up. "He's not much like you, for you'uns to be such good friends."

"How do you mean?" I thought I knew what she meant, but I wanted her to say it.

"He's a little too bold for my taste." Her lips thinned. "He makes me nervous."

"He made a pass at you."

"Did what?" She looked up.

"He came on to you, he heavy-flirted."

"Yes." She looked back down. "I don't like that. It makes me uncomfortable."

Melissa Mathews—thick chestnut hair, perfectly porcelain skin, insanely sky-colored eyes—was probably the most eligible bachelorette in town, if there could be such a thing in Blue Mountain. She was only several years out of high school, beautiful in the extreme, and too shy for any social situation. A short trip down Freudian Lane would probably have yielded some easy answers if anyone questioned her chosen profession. As a deputy she could wear a uniform, which acted as armor to hide behind and, in this case, even involved what was commonly called "a shield"—her badge. She had a gun and knew how to use it, though she was very gentle in general, only firm when she had to be.

She had also suffered some great trauma as an adolescent. Skidmore would never tell me what it was, only that it had scarred her, rendered her incapable of a relationship with any one of the thirty or so local boys who buzzed around her at any given moment. She spurned them all.

She had once been accused by gossipy spiders—people like Mrs. Jackson—of having an affair with Skidmore. It could not have been a more absurd accusation, of course: Melissa could never have a relationship with any man; Skidmore was the most monogamous man on the planet; and Skidmore's wife, Girlinda, would have found out if anything *had* been going on and killed them both about seven times with a shotgun. That's what Lucinda always said, that Girlinda would have killed Skidmore, then brought him to the hospital to bring him back to life just so she could kill him again. So: no infidelity there.

But the rest of Melissa's psyche was a mystery. It occurred to me at that moment that she was the exact opposite of Nurse Chambers—the perfect negative image.

"You want me to ask him to stop it," I concluded.

"Would you mind?" She was very uncomfortable.

"Consider it done."

She nodded, still not looking up. She wasn't finished.

"When I asked him how you two were such good friends," she said softly, "he told me you saved his life during the Academy Wars. I never knew you were in the army. And anyway, when were they?"

"When were what?"

"The Academy Wars."

"Oh." I managed to keep a straight face. "He was joking. Some people in university life, in academia, think of their difficulties as a kind of battle."

"So you didn't really save his life."

"No."

Further comment on the subject was interrupted by a sad call from the inner recesses of the office where the cells were hidden.

"Melissa?"

Andrews was ready to be let out of jail, and was, for some reason, using his most plaintive tones.

"I think Mr. Daniels is finished talking to me. Could you come here, please?"

She stood instantly, hand on her keys.

"Mind if I go with you?" I said softly.

She caught my eye for a second. "Thanks."

We wended our way through the brief, familiar labyrinth and found ourselves in the long hallway that boasted five cells. Four were about the size of a really large bathroom; one was big enough to hold, perhaps, ten people in a pinch. The previous sheriff, Maddox, had thought all that room necessary, and had contracted, with his brother, to build the facility—at relatively great expense to the city. I had never seen more than three people in the entire place at any one time.

We came to the cell from which Andrews had called and quickly discovered the reason for his odd tone. Hovis Daniels had collapsed on the floor and was breathing strangely.

"Could you let me out, please?" Andrews was pressed up against the bars of the cell door.

Melissa moved with supernatural ease and speed. The door was open, Andrews was out, and she was kneeling beside Hovis before I could get a good breath.

"What happened?" I asked Andrews.

I believe Andrews's expression could only be described as sheepish.

"Hovis?" Melissa shook the man.

Hovis grinned and mumbled.

Melissa's head snapped back. She stood, her face red and her fingers twitching a little.

"He's drunk!"

My eyes shot to Andrews.

"I thought it would help," he began, backing away a little. "I happened to have a little flask of that fantastic apple brandy—needing a hair of the dog for myself, see—and when he wouldn't talk to me, I thought I might loosen his tongue—"

"He's *drunk!*" Melissa repeated, not quite believing her own words.

"I really apologize—" Andrews began.

Melissa whirled around so fast it made Andrews take another step backward.

"I ought to lock you up in this cell with him." She actually had her hand on her gun. "Damn it, do you have any idea how mad this'll make Skidmore?"

"Maybe we just shouldn't tell him," Andrews said quickly.

"Hovis?" she said sweetly. "Come on, get up, sugar."

She reached down, grabbed an elbow, and helped the old man to his cot. He seemed not to know where he was, but he was very appreciative of Melissa's help as he fell back onto the bed.

"How much did you all drink?" I whispered.

"Not that much." Andrews sloshed the flask around, trying to peer into it.

But I was well aware that *not that much* to Andrews was *way too much* to many other mortals.

Melissa covered Hovis with a county blanket and shooed us away. She locked the cell door and pointed toward the front office.

Andrews walked meekly toward it; I followed, making certain Melissa could see me shaking my head.

Once we were back at her desk, Melissa engaged Andrews in a fairly brutal bit of eye contact.

"If you were a resident of Blue Mountain," she began, barely controlling herself, "you'd be in jail now. I expect you'd know that the substance you had in the flask was illegal. I've smelled it a hundred times. It's also against the law, of course, to have spirits of any sort in the county jail; and plus: I ought to kick your ass for getting that old man drunk. The only thing keeping you out of a cell is your friendship with Dr. Devilin, which I don't see why you have it, but *damn*."

That was her speech. She turned to me for comment.

"It's entirely my fault," I began. "Dr. Andrews is my guest, and I all but demanded that he come here with me, made him interview Hovis—"

"After Dr. Devilin saved your life," Melissa shot her stinging glance back to Andrews, "in the Academic Wars."

"Oh." Andrews managed a vermilion hue about his cheeks. "Yes. Well. That—"

"I don't know what kind of trouble he got you out of in your petty little university world," she snarled, "and I don't care. My guess is that you made a pass at the wrong coed, or worse, and nearly got yourself fired—but for the intervention of Dr. Devilin. That'd be your speed."

I had to admire how quickly Melissa had caught on to the phrase 'made a pass'—and how perfectly she had grasped both the university world and the character of Dr. Andrews. In fact, I found I was fascinated that she had absorbed, evaluated, and learned so much in so little time. I felt it was the closest I would ever come to a proud parental feeling. But there was also the matter of rescuing Andrews.

"In fact," I said, clearing my throat, "Dr. Andrews was *accused* of the crime you mention—"

"Fever," Andrews said softly, shaking his head.

"—with the daughter of our chancellor," I concluded. "In the university world, if you're an ambitious sort, you aspire to work your way up from professor to department head to dean through a few other steps and on to being the president of a university. The only place to go from there is the board of regents, the governing body of the whole system, kind of like the board of directors of a large corporation. At the head of that table, like a CEO, is the chancellor. Ours had a daughter that had grown accustomed to lightweight course content and easy A's. Andrews failed her in his Introduction to Shakespeare class when, among other things, she recorded on her final exam that

Shakespeare had written *The Odd Couple,* had been black-listed by McCarthy, and had played drums for a rock and roll band called the Holy Modal Rounders."

"He gave her an F," Melissa confirmed.

"He did," I assured her. "And when he did—I believe the expression is 'All hell broke loose.' She accused him of attempting to have an affair with her. She said that her F was a result of rebuffing his advances. He was set to be fired with a speed far beyond the ordinary capabilities of the university system."

"But you saved him." She drew in a healthy breath.

"I did, because I happened to have a graduate assistant who was working on some field research—a bit of urban folklore involving the preponderance of stories about body parts, usually fingers, found fried in foods and canned in soft drinks. This graduate assistant had, miraculously, recorded several conversations with the chancellor's daughter, who claimed to have found a thumb in her French fries, and on several of the tapes—"

"Dr. Devilin is a bit long-winded here," Andrews stammered. "Suffice it to say that the tapes revealed her lie and were used in evidence to support my innocence. I was *not* fired. However, the chancellor was quite upset and had to do something for his lovely daughter, so he set things in motion in order to close down the folklore department at our university, ensuring that Dr. Devilin would lose his job. Which he did."

"*That's* what happened to make you come back up here to Blue Mountain?" Melissa's face was burning red.

"*Someone's* head had to roll," Andrews said, eyes narrow.

"There was nothing to be done about it." I shrugged. "I'm happy to be home. Now. And anyway, the university was thinking about closing the department no matter what."

"That explains why he's your friend," Melissa said, at the end of her patience with Dr. Andrews. "But not the other way around."

"Dr. Andrews pulled a few strings for me after that." I looked at Melissa's desktop. "I didn't ask him to, he just did it."

"I should hope he did." She looked him up and down with an expression that could have skinned a catfish.

"He had a friend in the human resources department—" I began.

"With whom I *had* dallied, for the record," Andrews interrupted, apparently interested in full disclosure. "And she arranged it, all very legally, I'm told, so that Dr. Devilin would receive his full retirement salary—"

"Even though I was twenty years or more away from retirement," I inserted.

"And that means that he's receiving his full salary—as a full professor at the university—for staying up here in the mountains, drinking illegal spirits, and helping the local constabulary solve the more ghoulish crimes." Andrews nodded once, a final punctuation.

Melissa wasn't certain how to react, and kept her eyes locked on Andrews.

"If only the tape you've been listening to, Melissa," I said, mostly to take up the silence that followed our tale, "could yield such fruit."

"That." Melissa looked down at the tape recorder as if it were a dead skunk on her desk. "I've listened about fifty times, and it only gets more confusing every time I hear it. There's nothing I can find that could possibly tell us what he's after. I think you turned off the machine too soon."

"I agree," I told her.

"Maybe it would be better for all concerned," Andrews said, nervously eyeing the street outside, "if Dr. Devilin took me away from this place before the sheriff comes back."

"Amen to that," Melissa said immediately. She came around her desk, went to the door, and held it open for us. "I'll let you know if anything else turns up."

"You think Millroy—" I began.

"He'll most likely say it was murder if the sheriff charges Hovis with it, so your deadline is gone."

"Not really," I told her, stepping past the threshold. "It's just set back a bit. Now I have to prove that Hovis didn't do it before the sheriff can get a formal charge filed. Hovis can't take a trial, do you think?"

She was about to answer when Andrews pushed past her and rushed to the truck, still absently holding the flask in his hand.

"I'd put that away if I were you," she called to him.

He glanced down, realized what he was holding, and instantly jammed the flask into his back pocket.

"Sorry," I whispered to Melissa. "Honestly."

"Still not certain what you see in him."

"I'm hungry," he called out to no one in particular.

"For one thing," I confided to her, "he keeps me from taking myself too seriously—which I could do all day long and twice on Sundays."

"Hungry," he moaned to himself.

She grinned. "Plus, he keeps you from ever starving to death."

I turned to look at him. He was shivering beside the truck, despite the fact that he would have known, if he'd thought of it, that the door wasn't locked.

"There is that," I agreed.

SIXTEEN

I'D DECIDED THAT Andrews was a bit too inebriated for Miss Etta's public dining room, so I drove back to my place instead. He was very quiet most of the way, but as we were making the final upward climb he seemed to rouse himself from some deep well of thought, which I had mistaken for lethargy.

"I think I understand why you have to help Hovis Daniels." He was watching the leaves rain down.

"Really." *This ought to be interesting,* I thought.

Andrews turned my way. "In the first place, he didn't do it, in the second place, you know who did, and in the third place, no one else will help him. He's had the trials of Job heaped on him for most of his life, and he deserves to flag down a break."

"Agreed on all counts," I assured him, "but how did you come to such a compassionate conclusion in so short a time?"

I was assuming that the answer would have something to do with what had once been in the flask Andrews carried. Andrews surprised me—which was apparently becoming something of a habit for him.

"Hovis Daniels is more than a human being." Andrews folded his arms. "He's a time machine. I don't know if he's always been a time machine or if his tribulations forged him into one, but at this point in his life, he ought to be preserved as a national treasure."

"Why do you think I tape-recorded him so much when he—"

"I mean there ought to be films and television shows and a declaration from Congress."

"He made an impression."

"He did."

I turned the wheel and guided the truck into my front yard.
"Anything in particular—?" I started to ask.

"He talked about old man Jackson," Andrews answered.
"I'd asked Hovis why he would want to stay around a person
like Mrs. Jackson—I guess I was still a little spooked by her—
and he said he did it because he liked Mr. Jackson. Said they
used to get drunk all the time down in that little shack where
Hovis stays. One thing led to another and I eventually produced
the flask—you know, mostly in memory of the dearly departed.
Anyway, I wasn't just listening to him talk, I was transported.
I was there in the room with those two old men, listening to
them laugh and talk and sing. I could smell them. And the
manner in which he described Mr. Jackson himself—it broke
my heart; made me wish I'd known him."

Andrews sniffed. He might even have had a tear in his eye—
another by-product of our apple brandy.

"Hovis can have that effect," I said quietly.

"Yes." Andrews rallied. "And Mr. Jackson? He was, apparently, both happy *and* go-lucky."

"Go-lucky? That's your phrase? How much of that brandy
did you have?"

"Hovis had most of it," he said defensively.

"But you had enough. Let's get you some food."

He was out of the truck before my last syllable was finished.

Half a dozen scrambled eggs apiece and at least as many
waffles later, Andrews was napping on the sofa. I spent a few
idle hours trying not to wake him up while I was putting away
the rest of the tapes.

Shadows of the evening grew longer outside, and though it
was barely four o'clock, the daylight was ending. I was, embar-
rassingly enough, enjoying the process of alphabetizing them,
when a cannonball of a fact slammed into my chest. Some of
the tapes in the *J* section were missing. I looked frantically under
the sofa, the desk, in the corners to make certain they weren't in
the house. When it was obvious that they were gone, I couldn't
decide which to do first, wake Andrews or call Skidmore.

That decision was made for me.

"Christ, what are you doing?" Andrews rumbled. "Can't you play maid when someone's not trying to sleep on your sofa?"

"Wake up," I demanded, coming around the sofa. "Sit up."

Maybe the urgency in my voice made him sit up, maybe he was just angry that I'd awakened him, but he groaned his way to a seated posture fairly quickly.

"The stranger wasn't looking for his own tape," I said before his eyes were focused.

"What?"

"The guy who broke into my house and rummaged through the tapes, the same person that killed the dead guy? He wasn't looking for the tape I made of *him!*"

"Then what was he looking for?" Andrews craned his head around to take in the living room bookcase behind him, as if the answer might be on a poster there.

"He took the three tapes I made of Mr. Jackson a long time ago."

"You made tapes of Mr. Jackson?"

"Mostly singing," I said quickly, "but they're all gone. And nothing else is missing."

"You couldn't have just misplaced them?"

"Who are you talking to?" I glared at him until he nodded.

"Right," he agreed, "the guy stole them. But why?"

"Exactly," I shot back.

"Exactly *what?*"

"I don't know," I confessed, though my enthusiasm did not flag. "But I'm calling Skidmore."

I dashed into the kitchen and grabbed the phone. Andrews stumbled behind me, trying to form sentences.

"Isn't this a bit half-baked?" he mumbled.

"Melissa?" I barked into the phone. "Is Skidmore there?"

Alas, he had not returned from his mysterious "lab work" errand. Though it was barely past midafternoon, the sun was already lowering itself behind the western hills. I had always considered an early sunset the single depressing foible of autumn in the mountains. It would be getting dark in less than an hour.

"Well, would you mind telling him that I have some new evidence and to please not formally charge Hovis Daniels yet?"

"I'll tell him," she said, obviously in doubt of the efficacy of such a plea, "but, you know, he'll do what he does."

"As long as you tell him I'm certain about this, and I that have new evidence."

"What new evidence?" she wanted to know.

"I'll be down in your offices in just a little while," I answered. "Thanks, Melissa."

I hung up before she could ask any other questions, or insist on any more answers.

"Why didn't you tell her about the missing tapes?" Andrews was leaning on the counter where Hovis had bled. There was no sign of the mess he'd made; I had cleaned the place three times.

"Because," I answered, staring at the spot where the most blood had been, "it's not enough to...it doesn't sound compelling, 'Three tapes are missing!' I mean, does it?"

"Right."

"So are you awake?"

Andrews yawned and scratched his stomach. "I think so. Am I standing in your kitchen?"

"Yes."

"Okay, then I'm awake. Why do you ask?"

"I want to tell you the other thing I put together while you were napping."

"I *needed* that nap," he protested.

"Do you want to hear what I came up with?"

"Yes." He managed to sit down at the kitchen table. "Shoot."

"I've said all along," I began instantly, "that the visitor, the false Truck Jackson, was not befuddled, that he only wanted us to think he was—and that he was, in fact, looking for something specific. Something was important enough to him that he would kill someone else because of it, or for it."

"You've said that all along?"

"He wanted us to think that he was a bit like Hovis," I continued, ignoring Andrews. "He visited Hovis first. He got some information from that visit that provoked him to go to Lucinda's house and then to come here."

"All in an effort to find something, or to find out something," Andrews said slowly, trying to keep up.

"And one of the recurring themes we've seen is the struggle of brother against brother—"

"And the dead man looks like the killer's brother." Andrews was catching on.

"And when Hovis *told* me that the killer was Cain, I just thought it was the ramblings of a crazy old man, but now I think he was trying to tell me something important."

"That Cain killed his brother!" Andrews was getting into the spirit of things, even though he clearly wasn't awake.

"No, damn, I know that. Everybody knows that. Damn. He was trying to tell me where the killer might hide."

"Might *hide?* How would—"

"Where did Cain go after he killed Abel?"

"I don't know," Andrews objected, "into the desert?"

"He went out east of the garden of Eden, to hide there."

"Oh. Right." Andrews slumped in his chair. "And this helps us *how?*"

"You've been there with me," I said softly. "You've been to our town cemetery. You just don't remember that it's called Eden."

SEVENTEEN

DESPITE MIGHTY AND vociferous protestation, Andrews had agreed, in the end, to come with me to the cemetery. He thought I was crazy, and must have used the phrase "grasping at straws" at least seven times.

The shadows around the cemetery were quite long by the time we made it all the way up the hill. If there hadn't been so many taller mountains around, we might have been able to see better, in that kind of golden afternoon light, but the larger rises bullied sunlight, bent it, forced it away from valleys and gorges, and made dark scars over the landscape.

Still, it was easy to see why no one ever objected to calling the place Eden. City planners from the nineteenth century had taken the time and care to create a park where families could gather, mourners could find peace, and children could play. Alas, more than half the families in the area continued, long after the landscaping was in place and richer families had purchased acre plots, to bury the departed in their own backyards, near a significant tree or close to a convenient rock.

One of the larger plots was owned by the Jackson family, and ornate crypts had been built in the early 1900s to house important men and women with that name. The wife of Hovis Daniels did not find quite so grand a repose. She was buried on the periphery, near the rusted iron fence that separated the Jackson land from other prominent family plots. Her tombstone called her Bayberry because the company had misunderstood Hovis's grieving pronunciation of "Barbrie" and he could not afford a correction. No one intervened to help him, to explain to him that the company had made the mistake and ought to correct it at their own expense. He had already given up anyway. How could it matter, he asked me once, what it said on a stone? Barbrie wasn't there under it. She wasn't anywhere. She was gone.

Andrews and I had taken the shortcut up the hill, through briars and weeds. I hadn't turned on my headlights because it was still, technically, daylight, but lack of ground light made me hit a fairly significant rut in the road right as I turned into the entrance and headed eastward past the perpetually open gates. Just as I hit the bone-crushing crater, Andrews noticed a woman flying through the air, right toward the truck.

"Jesus God in heaven!" He ducked down.

"The Angel of Death," I reminded him.

"What?" He seemed dazed.

"The statue. You've seen it before."

He peeked out the window.

The large statue, pale gray and covered with moss and lichen, hovered around the first bend in the road. She had been strategically placed so that she would appear to be flying toward visitors. In fact, her feet were molded in concrete from which she had not extricated herself, as far as I knew, for 150 years or more, despite the efforts of her mighty wings.

We rounded the turn and saw her hovering in a small grove of weeping hemlocks. Blue juniper hid the base of the statue, and creeping ficus threatened to overtake her raiment. Her eyes seemed to gaze down upon the truck, and her sword was poised to smite. Andrews hadn't seen the thing in a few years, and I was always taken aback by the sight of her. The mood the angel created was impossible to ignore: blessed or cursed, holy or hated, righteous or fiendish—everyone would fall beneath that sword.

"I'd forgotten about it." Andrews managed, after a moment, to sit up straight.

"It even gave me a bit of a turn," I confessed.

Everywhere else we looked, we could see dead leaves falling or swirling in the wind, plaiting the ground and covering everything. Shocks of stark amber sunlight striped the ground between yawning black shadows. A murder of huge black crows, disturbed by the truck, suddenly took to the air, and it looked, in the first instant of their flight, as if a shadow had come loose from the ground, broken apart, and was bent on attacking the sun.

"The Jackson plot is over that way, just beyond the angel," I told Andrews, mostly to dispel the shivers.

"Ah," he responded, eyes glued to the raving birds.

"We're going this way." I turned the truck away from the last of the sunlight.

We were leaving the light behind us, and the eastern sky was already gouged by hard charcoal shards and the ghost of a near-full moon.

"You won't be offended if I just say, once more, that this is a useless waste of time, right?" Andrews folded his arms and slumped down in his seat.

I'd tried to encourage him to put on one of my coats over his impossibly wrinkled shirt, but some variety of errant testosterone had prevented him from doing it. He was obviously regretting it. The air had taken a sudden plunge through invisible caves of ice, everything had turned colder, and I was glad to have my leather jacket.

"Not if you won't be offended at my very emphatic 'I told you so' when we find the killer tonight," I answered him.

"Never going to happen."

The eastern rim of the graveyard ended at the farthest reaches of the Newcomb family area. It was the largest in the cemetery, but the really impressive crypts were at the top of the hill, not where we were headed. Blue Mountain had been called Newcomb Junction until 1925 when Jeribald "Tubby" Newcomb married his half sister and all the resulting progeny bore serious birth defects. After that, everyone in town unanimously agreed to change our name, calling it after the mountain we loved instead of the family we hated.

As my truck rolled up to the six-foot iron fence that divided graveyard from happier nature, Andrews happened to notice the name on one of the lesser tombstones.

"Newcomb," he mumbled. "Wasn't that the family that owned the show your parents worked for? What was it called?"

"Like a lot of other traveling entertainments of its sort," I said tersely, "it was called the Ten Show—ten in one."

My parents had provided the most popular of the ten acts. My father had been a relatively renowned magician in the South; my mother, his lovely assistant. Both were ghosts that wouldn't seem to rest. They often walked the rooms in my house, especially when I was given to darker thoughts. I didn't care to see if they also visited the Newcomb gravesites, so I deliberately changed the subject.

"But more to the point," I said to Andrews as we came to a halt at the edge of the cemetery, "this is where we get out of the truck and explore the far slopes."

"What?" He stiffened. "I have to get out of the truck?"

"There's a fence." I nodded in the direction of same.

"Push it down, run over it. I don't want to get out of the truck. I'm cold."

"You wouldn't take a jacket—"

"I didn't know we were getting out of the bleeding truck!"

"Bleeding?" I hoped he heard all of the deliberately mocking tone I was using. "You'll get nowhere with me using that kind of language. I mean, I know the girls go for the accent—which, incidentally, you always exaggerate when you're flirting—but it means nothing to me."

"Then you really won't like it when I tell you to sod off."

"I suppose I might object if I knew what it meant." I turned off the engine. "But at the moment, I really don't care."

"Knew what it meant? Seriously? I've said it to you enough times—"

"Oh, for God's sake, Winton, are you going to get out of the truck or do I have to go by myself to find the killer?"

He stopped squirming for a moment, tilted his head.

"Um…" He rubbed his nose.

One of the advantages of rarely calling him by his first name was that when I did, it meant something.

I only waited a second more before opening the door and plunging into the chilly wind. Without a word, Andrews followed suit.

"Wait." I sighed. "There's a raincoat under the passenger seat. It'll keep the wind out, at least."

I couldn't tell, in the fading light, if he retrieved the coat reluctantly, but fetch it he did, and was standing beside me at the iron fence in a matter of seconds.

"What's over that way?" He whispered the words.

I understood why his voice was hushed. The view of the landscape beyond the fence was strange enough by daylight, but sunset gave the crags and weeds and dying leaves a kind of animated menace. To make matters worse, some of the darker hollows were blazing with green flame.

"And what the hell is that burning over there?" he continued.

"I've told you about that." Despite myself, I realized I was answering him in a low voice. "It's usually called foxfire—a bioluminescence created by a certain sort of fungus or lichen. You find it on decaying wood. I used to believe that it was primarily a product of only one species of the genus *Armillaria,* but over the years I think I've found as many as forty individual species."

"You've told me about this?" He couldn't take his eyes off the eerie blue-green glow—and the darker the shadows, the brighter the fire.

"It exists everywhere. Pliny and Aristotle mention it. Ben Franklin suggested that the military use it to light the inside of one of our first submarines."

"I mean, but what *is* it?"

"Believe it or not, a substance called luciferin—same thing that lights up a firefly—reacts with an enzyme, luciferase, and that causes the luciferin to oxidize and make light."

"But why would nature do it?"

"Nobody knows. And I suppose you don't want me to give you the folk—"

"Not remotely." He turned to face me at last. "It's got something to do with fairies."

"Well." I smiled. "Maybe it attracts bugs to disperse the spores."

"There you go." He was satisfied. "Got something to do with procreation. I can buy that."

"But you did hear that the substance is called luciferin."

"So why isn't it called devil's fire, then?"

"Maybe it is."

"I'm getting back in the truck." He didn't move.

We both stood staring at the growing darkness and the glowing lights. In moments the sun was gone behind the western hills, and night had arched its back against the moon.

"All right," I sighed, grabbing a spine of the moldering fence, "God set the scene: perfect night to go lumbering through the poison berries and wake up a few copperheads to look for a murderer."

"Absolutely," Andrews agreed, tweaking his bravado. "What could possibly go wrong now? I mean, I've been shot, you've been attacked, Lucinda's been threatened, an innocent man's in jail, and there's a maniac loose. We're disaster-proof. What else could happen?"

He set his foot on the rail and hoisted himself up. Alas, that entire section of fencing instantly collapsed forward, sending Andrews plowing into the weeds and dirt outside the cemetery.

"There's a lesson in this," I said, stepping over the fallen fence and going to help him up.

"Bite me," he said, spitting leaves and clay.

I got him to stand up, but it didn't look like he was going to move. Somehow, outside the fence of the graveyard, he felt unprotected—I did, too.

We were standing near the top of the mountain. Straight around and upward, huge boulders loomed, black sentinels in the growing darkness. A few hundred yards below us lay a dense forest of pines and cedars and bare oak trees—the perfect home for genus *Armillaria* and the devil's own fire.

"We could start down there." I pointed toward the foxfire.

Four or five sections of the forest floor, each several feet square, were alive with the sick color. Small wonder that some people in the mountains would walk a mile out of their way to avoid it.

"What's over there?" Andrews pointed around the hill in nearly the opposite direction, toward the boulders.

"Not much." I put my hands in my pockets. "Some shallow

caves, a few really big rocks. If you keep going around and up, you'll eventually get to the Devil's Hearth."

"Caves?" He looked as if he might move. "Doesn't that seem like the most likely place for someone to hide?"

"About this time of year," I answered, "you're more likely to find a tired bear than anything else in those caves. You don't want to fool with a bear."

"I don't want to go down there." He pointed in the direction of the blue-green light.

And there it was: the human aversion to anything unfamiliar. Andrews, like most people, would rather face a real bear than imaginary fire. He understood what a bear was; he had no idea what made the fungus glow—even though I had offered him a perfectly good scientific explanation. He'd seen bears a hundred times. He'd seen foxfire twice. And even though the bear was certain danger and the luminescent fungus would never attack him, rake him with claws, or bite him with teeth, Andrews preferred the bear.

Something about that observation set off a chain of other thoughts. I must have seemed paralyzed to Andrews, standing there and staring into space.

"Fever?" He took a step my way. "What is it? Do you see something?"

"Not exactly," I told him slowly, "but I'm developing a theory about the man who called himself Truck Jackson."

"Now?" He seemed inexplicably impatient with me.

"I think he was acting strangely on purpose," I said, "to put us off. Lucinda and me, at least."

"You said that. Are you talking about something new?"

"Not certain yet."

"Then can we please get moving?" he whined. "This raincoat isn't very warm."

"And you'd rather go poke a bear than walk down in the woods."

"Let's go." He started upward in the direction of one of the largest boulders.

The moon began to offer its guidance; here and there in the

sky, a star blinked on. The wind kicked up dead leaves and dampened other, more subtle noises.

The boulder seemed to lean toward the forest, as if it had a longing for the shelter of the trees. Too much rain, too many windstorms; long cold years had sculpted its lonesome posture.

We rounded it and came to the top of a shelf, only a drop of several feet but a bit difficult to navigate. We scrambled down, loosening stones and clay and in general making a terrible clatter. At the bottom of the shelf and to our left we saw a series of caves. I couldn't remember how many there were. I could have kicked myself for not bringing a flashlight. I had one in the truck, and thought about running back for it.

Before I could even suggest such a thing, we heard a scrambling noise from inside the second-closest cave.

"There!" Andrews pointed.

I nodded.

"If that's our man, remember that he's a small man," I whispered, "but he's got a gun."

"Who better than I would know that," Andrews snarled.

"I mean we should…" I trailed off, finishing the sentence in sign language, trying to say that one of us should stand on one side of the cave entrance and the other on the opposite.

He seemed to understand. He took off toward the cave, head down, fists balled. I could see the look on his face: game face, a mixture of rage and delight. Never shoot a rugby player like Andrews—it wouldn't stop him, it would only make him angry. He won't die and he'll find you. And eat your liver. While you watch. All that was on Andrews's face.

I followed—my own face, surely, displaying a mixture more of fear and adrenaline than anything else, but I was ready nonetheless.

Andrews achieved his place on the far side of the cave's mouth; I stood at the other. The scrambling came again, as if the resident were trying to climb out through another hole in the mountain.

He's heard us, I thought. *He's trying to escape.*

"Now!" I shouted to Andrews.

We both growled and plunged into the cave. I tried to make myself as big as possible, waving my arms and shouting incoherently. Andrews ran at a crouch ready to tackle. I could barely see, and Andrews was feeling his way along the ground.

The scratching became even more frantic, and I thought I could make out movement at the back of the cave, only three yards away.

"Stay where you are!" I barked. "You can't get out."

I moved immediately after I spoke, in case he was thinking of firing his pistol again.

But nothing happened. The cave fell silent.

"Come on," Andrews growled slowly in the direction of the rocks.

The rising moon lit the entrance of the cave, but did little to reveal our target inside. Still, I thought once again that I could see a bit of movement, and began to inch toward it. Andrews nodded and moved, too, nearly on all fours.

Without warning, the cave's inhabitant flew past us, right between Andrews and me, and scrambled noisily out into the field—and he was much smaller than I remembered.

"What the hell?" Andrews stood.

We both strode to the mouth of the cave and looked down the weedy hill. A terrified raccoon, a very large one, was plummeting away from us, toward the eerie glow in the forest.

EIGHTEEN

ANDREWS AND I stood, two shadows in rising moonlight, watching other shadows move in the glowing woods until the raccoon disappeared.

"Nice work, Sherlock," Andrews sneered. "There goes my Daniel Boone hat."

"That's not a hat. That's a coat." My heart was thumping and I was short of breath; I realized then how much the thing had frightened me.

"I told you the guy wasn't here," Andrews muttered. He didn't seem remotely fazed by the event. "We're on a fool's errand. And do you know what errand that is? Chasing wild geese. *And*—"

"There are about twenty more caves," I told him, working to calm my breathing. "The night is young."

"God." He actually looked upward into the dark sky. "Please smite this man; he maketh a blight upon the land."

I only took a second to remember why that sounded familiar. "Isn't that—"

"It's from *The Producers*. The original movie. Not an exact quote. And I haven't seen the Broadway show or the new movie, so I don't know—"

"You're Zero Mostel?"

"No one," he intoned, "is Zero Mostel."

"Agreed." My panic was abating. "To the next cave?"

In spite of his heavy sigh, Andrews pulled the oversized raincoat tightly around his neck and lumbered forward.

"Lead on, McDuff. Not an exact quote."

"Misquoting Mel Brooks *and* Shakespeare—you're in a rare mood." I headed for the next cave.

"I have a bullet wound," he explained very carefully, as if he were teaching a class. "I am allowed a bit of *mood*."

The first cave in the cliff, the one we'd passed by, was barely large enough for a rabbit. The cave past the raccoon's home was larger—bear sized. It was about twenty feet away.

"Let's toss something into this one," I suggested, "and see if a raving bear comes charging out."

"You toss something in." He stopped walking. "I'll wait here. That way I'll have a head start in case I have to outrun the bear."

"You know the joke, don't you?" I headed for the cave. "You don't have to run faster than the bear. You just have to run faster than your friends."

"Nice." He still didn't move.

It was clear to me that Andrews and I were doing what some human beings have always done when they're alone in the dark: deliberately making light of the situation in order to keep the terror at bay. Underneath every syllable was an implication of danger, the possibility of death.

I slowed my pace and turned to Andrews. "I'm glad you're here."

"I'm not."

A soot-black cloud shot past the moon and plunged the landscape into complete darkness, reminding me how much light a moon was prepared to offer under the right circumstances.

I couldn't see where I was walking very well, so I waited a moment. The moon reappeared; so did the ground. I instantly found a softball-sized rock perfect for chucking into a cave to disturb a bear. I scooped it up and moved quickly.

About five feet from the entrance, I turned to see where Andrews was. He hadn't moved, but he waved, a bit halfheartedly. I nodded and turned my attention back to the yawning cavern. I got my footing, looked around to see where I could safely run if anything shot out of the cave, chose a path, and tossed the rock.

It clapped and cracked for a second or two, almost echoing, but nothing else happened.

"Go on in and look," Andrews offered from his place well behind me. "Maybe you hit the bear on his head."

"I tossed the rock," I told him. "*You* go in the cave."

"How about if I toss you in—" he began.

The rest of his suggestion was interrupted by the distinctive clap of a gun being fired.

Andrews dove to the ground. I, foolishly, stood looking around, trying to decide whence the shot had come. It took a second notification, a bullet fairly close, to shake me from my stupor and send me rolling behind a small crag.

"Where's it coming from?" Andrews demanded in a stage whisper.

"Can't tell," I answered.

"But he's not in that big cave."

"Right."

I tried to keep as flat to the ground as possible and still see along the upper ridge.

"Fever?" Andrews had somehow managed to get closer. "Did that sound like the same gun that shot me?"

I blinked. It hadn't sounded remotely like a pistol, upon reflection.

I held my breath a moment, thinking, and by the time I exhaled I realized what an idiot I'd been.

I sat up. "Red? Is that you shooting your gun at me? It's Fever Devilin. And my friend from Atlanta. He's on vacation."

For a moment the scattering of the wind and the pounding of blood in my temples were the only sounds.

Then there was a grumbling at the top of the ridge above the caves. "I wasted two good bullets on *that?*"

"It's Red Jackson," I told Andrews. "He makes a cheaper version of the apple brandy you like so much. He thought we were here to bother him. He does his work around here, and he doesn't like to be disturbed."

"He's a moonshiner?" Andrews whispered, fascinated, heading my way.

"Not exactly," I answered, "not in the way you mean it. But he is making an alcoholic substance, and he is producing more than the legal household limit. He works here at night because he works in a seed-and-feed store in the daytime."

Andrews arrived at my side. "How much is he making? I mean how much of the apple stuff—"

"I think the household limit is around a hundred gallons a year, for personal consumption. Red makes that much a week. And sells it."

"Ah."

"It's not as good as what you drink at my house."

"I'll be the judge of that." Andrews headed upward.

"Red?" I called out. "Is it all right if my friend Dr. Andrews visits with you for a moment? He's interested in purchasing."

There was a short silence, then another gunshot. This one came from below us, from the forest.

"Jesus." Andrews fell to the ground again.

"Who's that shooting now?" I called out.

"Toby!" Red hollered. "What the hell are you doing? It's Fever Devilin."

From down in the pines we heard the faint response. "You got to see this, Red. I shot me a raccoon the size of a bear down here."

"Hey." Andrews scrambled to his feet. "My hat!"

"Come on up," Red sighed.

Andrews and I wrestled with gravity, struggling up the ridge and over the caves. In a little clearing near the top of the mountain, Red sat tending a trio of witch-cauldrons, three hulking iron bellies filled with apples. They boiled over a low flame, and Red's face was only half-human in the hellish crimson glow. His hair had mostly gone to gray, but a strand here and there still evidenced the nickname by which everyone knew him. A shotgun lay in his lap so comfortably it looked as if it might have been his arm.

"You'uns make more noise than a cat down a well," Red grumbled. "And toppled a portion of the graveyard fence. You'uns got to fix that back."

"How could you have heard that from here?" Andrews asked, astonished.

"Family trait," Red answered tersely. "All Jacksons has ears like rats, and I been watching you'uns since you crossed into the open fields."

"Family trait." I walked slowly and hoped that Andrews would take a cue. Red wouldn't have minded shooting us if he thought we were there for any reason other than to buy his wares.

Andrews, alas, was too fascinated for caution. "This is fantastic!" His eyes flashed, trying to take in everything.

Red glared at me.

"Dr. Andrews," I said slowly. "Could you just stand where you are for a moment?"

"But look," he said. "Is this what you do? You boil the apples?"

"You have to make the cider first," I told Andrews impatiently. "Then you distill it. You're seeing the first part of the process here."

"How did you learn this?" he asked Red. "How do you know what to... I'd like to know how—"

"My family has been making apple brandy for nearly three hundred years in America." Red's face was sterner than a preacher's. "You don't *learn* how to do it. No learning to it at all. You grow up watching it, and by and by you do it yourself. You people from Atlanta and places like that, you don't know spit. *Moonshine.* I heard you say it. Moonshine is dung in a bucket—"

"'Moonshine' is generally the word used for spirits that have undergone only one distillation," I said to Andrews hastily. "It's a quicker process that doesn't get rid of potential poisons."

"That's right," Red growled. "We run twice. Always twice."

"Red and his family, I believe, collect the juice of milled apples in large barrels and ferment them with brewer's yeast. That apple juice averages around thirteen percent sugar, which translates to roughly six percent alcohol by volume. But if you distill it, you get something around eighty proof."

"I don't know about all that." Red shifted on his stool, holding his gun tightly. "We ferment in one of them caves down there. Takes two months. Then you take and use a pot still with the cider. Got to heat it enough to boil alcohol, not quite so hot as you boil water. Get you a vapor, collect it, send it through again, and there you go. Got something fine to sip."

"And your family has been doing this—"

"Three hundred years." Red was impatient. "How much you want?"

Andrews stared into one of the boiling pots. "When will it be ready?"

"This?" Red cracked a smile. It was more frightening than his stern look. "This won't be ready but for New Year's. I got some I done put together. You take ten gallons. That's worth my time."

"Ten gallons?" Andrews seemed stunned at his good fortune. "How long will it keep?"

"I expect it'll keep till you die," Red drawled, standing, "or till Judgment, which-one-ever come first."

"We can't carry ten gallons," I interrupted just as Red was getting ready to haggle about the price—which surely would have been triple what any local would pay. "I'll have to go get the truck and bring Dr. Andrews around to...well, where, exactly?"

Red squinted suspiciously at me for a moment. "If that truck of yours can make it up the Hearth, where Hovis and Barbrie used to live, you meet me up yonder. But I won't be done here for another three, four hours. And then I got—"

"Midnight?" I asked Red. "I think that would give us time for our work, and it would just about complete Dr. Andrews's experience."

"Absolutely," Andrews enthused. "Midnight at the Devil's Hearth for apple brandy. Damn."

"Language, boy!" Red exploded. "Don't take to that kind of talk!"

"What?" Andrews was so surprised by Red's vehemence that he stumbled backward.

I held up my hand. "Red—he lives in Atlanta. And, really, he's from England."

Red sighed, accepting that people from other worlds had strange ways.

"So." Andrews waved happily. "See you then."

"Let's go fix the fence," I said to Andrews, my tones a bit louder than they needed to be, "and get my truck."

"Um," Andrews began, "all right, but I thought—"

"We have to fix the fence. Red is right about that."

Andrews seemed momentarily confused by my sudden change of heart concerning seeking out the murderer, but when he caught my eye, he understood, at least, that we had to leave Red's encampment.

"Okay." Andrews turned his back on the man with the gun and started down the hill toward the cemetery. He seemed only too happy to be returning to the truck.

I nodded to Red. "Sorry to bother you at work, Red."

"Heard you, too," he answered, his eyes narrow slits. "You think somebody else's drink is better than mine. So why you to bring that'un up here to me?"

I cursed my loud voice—and his good hearing—before I realized that I might disarm him with, of all things, the truth.

"I'm certain you've heard about the dead body they found behind Edna Jackson's home." I stood my ground and folded my arms. "That's the real reason for my visit up here. Although Dr. Andrews would, in fact, be interested in a purchase from you."

"Sheriff arrested Hovis." Red shook his head and cradled his gun as if it were a baby.

"You and I know Hovis didn't do it. That's why I'm poking around up here after dark when I'd rather be at home in front of the fire. I believe that Hovis Daniels could stand to have somebody on his side, for once in his life."

"Well." Red closed his eyes. "Amen to that. He's had a power of misfortune."

"So what can you tell me?"

I watched his face demonstrate every thought and emotion that was playing out behind his eyes, a warring theater of jumbled impulses.

"Well," he sighed, "there was these two boys—they lived up past the Hearth, some kind of distant kin, they say. Never had much use for their like. They were part Deveroe."

The way he said the name Deveroe was the way most people talked about septic tanks.

"Wild boys; fought all the time," he continued. "No parental guidance. Heard they was gone to the army, but it might be them, come back."

I had no impulse to ask him how he could know so little about his relatives in such a small environment. Red kept to himself and his close family, and if he didn't like you, it was unlikely that he'd ever speak to you or even look you in the eye. You didn't exist to him. He'd treated me that way for the first half of my life. He was only conversant with me, finally, because I had recorded his nephew Toby—who had just killed a very large raccoon—singing songs about apples. The songs were all hundreds of years old, though Toby told me that he had made them all up himself. It had produced a great article: apple brandy and songs about making it.

"And you think," I prompted him, "that one of them might be the dead person, and the other might be the killer."

"Couldn't say." He was impatient for me to leave. He shifted his gun in his arms.

"Okay." I nodded once. "Take care."

I turned without any further farewell, and followed Andrews down the slope.

NINETEEN

ONCE I CAUGHT UP with Andrews and we were far enough away and around the curve of the mountaintop, I touched Andrews on the arm, stopped him, and put my finger to my lips.

"We're going back," I whispered. "I know where the killer is."

"What?" Andrews's voice carried, I was certain, across the mountain and northward to Carolina.

"Sh!" I insisted. "We have to sneak back around, hug the ridge, and get to the cave where Red keeps his fermenting barrels."

"We do?"

"I'm not certain if Red meant to tell me something, or if he was trying *not* to tell me something, but I think our guy is in that cave."

"You think *that's* what he was saying?"

"You have to know him—" I began.

"So wait," Andrews interrupted. "You want to tiptoe around in the dark, hoping that a man with a shotgun doesn't see us, break into that very man's secret stash, and confront a murderer who has both a loaded pistol *and* a history of shooting me?"

"Yes."

He took a single breath before he shrugged. "All right, then, off we go. In for a penny."

There was the quintessential English spirit, I thought, the attitude that made a small island community into a world power—and gave most of the original fire to the American belly as well.

I pointed out our route as best I could, and we set sail. The ridge would hide us from Red's view, and if we were a bit more careful than we had been earlier, we might avoid making too much noise.

There was Toby, in the woods with his big raccoon, to worry about. But I reasoned that he had not heard the conversation we'd had with Red, and would not be too suspicious, at least at first, even if he did see us still meandering around the caves.

The cave we were looking for was called, I knew from many a previous conversation with Red's brood, Barrel Cave. I'd never been inside, and hadn't realized until that night that its name came from its contents, not its shape. I had always wondered why it was called by such an appellation when it looked no more like a barrel than any of the other dozens of caves around it.

We hugged the lower edge of the rim; I was in the lead. Stepping over rocks and slippery moss made the way slow going. The moon dodged black clouds that shot past it in the high wind. Below us the harvest of weeds ran ragged; red clay and granite paved odd paths that started and stopped with no coherence. Farther down the slope, the woods seemed darker than they had been, and the pines swayed, creaking like an abandoned house and echoing up the mountain.

As we would come to a cave, I would peer inside to check for bears, snakes, and, with a bit of melancholy, raccoons. I felt responsible for the big animal's demise. There he had been, snug at home, when two maniacs broke into his castle and chased him out and, alas, into Toby's line of fire.

"The best-laid plans of mice and men," I said softly to Andrews. "One minute you're safe in bed—"

"You're feeling sorry for Rocky Raccoon," he whispered back. "Me too."

"Thanks for reading my mind."

"I only skim," he assured me. "I really don't want to read too much in there. I couldn't take the nightmares."

"I think that's it." I pointed to a larger cave about fifty feet to our left.

"What's the plan?"

He had a point. I came to a standstill.

"What if we sort of hide our faces," I suggested, "and just walk in, you know, as if we were Red's henchmen."

"Red does not have *henchmen*," he corrected. "He has *kin*—none of whom is tall and blond or as big as you are. And then there's your high-beam white hair to consider."

"If we had hats—"

"Good thinking," he snapped. "I'll just nip back to the truck and snatch up two, shall I?"

"Maybe we could crouch low and hide behind the barrels."

"We'd have to see the layout."

I glanced toward the cave. "Only one way to find that out."

I headed toward it, as carefully as I could. Andrews followed behind, only a bit more noisily. We both grew more cautious the closer we drew to the wide opening. The mouth of the cave was roughly the size and shape of an old Volkswagen, and the entrance floor was worn and smooth from thousands of boots walking in and out over who could say how many years.

As we inched toward the edge of the cave, I could make out old oak barrels close to the entrance. The moon broke through a chain of clouds and spilled a piercing silver over the mountaintop. I ducked down until my head was inches from the ground and moved to peer into the cave.

Filled almost completely with fermenting apples in their wooden houses, the cave smelled much more pleasant than I'd thought it would—a bit like wine and bread. At first glance there didn't appear to be anyplace for a man to hide. I beckoned and Andrews slid up beside me, lying completely on the ground.

"I'm going in," I mouthed soundlessly.

I had to repeat myself three times before he understood, and immediately he began shaking his head and scowling.

I ignored him. Feeling my way along the cave floor, I began to crawl on my stomach into the darkness. It was oddly warmer in the cave, and I wondered it if had anything to do with the fermentation process.

Past the first few barrels, I saw that there was, in fact, a little room in the center of all of them. A table with an oil lamp on it and two small stools occupied most of the space. I still couldn't see any human inhabitant.

The moon was suddenly gone again, and I could barely see

the table. I was about to back out when I heard a noise from further inside the cave. It sounded like a bear growling. My heart quickened. Andrews had apparently heard it, too, because he was tugging at the bottom of my pants leg.

The noise came again, a sudden snort, and I realized that it wasn't coming from a bear.

I contorted myself weirdly, working my way to a crouching position, and pointed to the back wall. Andrews was still shaking his head, and his scowl had become a grimace.

I beckoned him as insistently as I could without making any sound, and he relented, joining me in an uncomfortable hunker.

"That's someone snoring," I whispered into his ear as quietly as I could.

His head jerked back a little; he listened for a second, and obviously concurred.

We moved ridiculously toward the sound, a little like fat ducks waddling. As we came to the edge of the row of barrels, nearly to the table and stools, we could both see the pile of rags in the corner from which bear sounds escaped. The pistol lay on the stone floor in front of it.

Without warning, Andrews leapt, like a great ape, the distance between us and the snoring man. He landed with a crunching skid, swiped his hand across the pistol, knocking it my way, and had fistfuls of the man's clothing tightly in his grip.

The man blathered like a caged gibbon.

Andrews stood, dragging the man up with him. I managed to get hold of the pistol and march with great deliberation right up to them both.

Even in the near absence of light, I could make out the general features of the man's face.

"Hello," I said softly.

"Shoot this bastard right across the temple, would you mind?" Andrews rasped, shaking the man. "Then he'll know what it feels like. Teach him a lesson."

"All right." I glanced at the pistol, then pointed it directly at the man's skull.

"God in heaven, don't shoot!" the stranger exploded.

"You have a whole lot of explaining to do," I told him, still pointing the gun at his head.

"I'll tell you anything you want to know."

I held the pistol up for a few seconds more, then dropped my hand, shoving the gun in my pocket.

"You know the safety was on, right?" Andrews said, lowering the man so he could stand on the floor.

"I glanced at the gun before I pointed it at his head, if that's what you mean. I *think* the safety was on. I don't know that much about guns."

There was a sudden clicking sound behind us.

"But I do." It was a familiar voice.

I turned slowly to see both barrels of Red Jackson's shotgun aimed directly at my chest, the hammers cocked back, ready to blow me to Judgment Day.

TWENTY

RED COUGHED. It was the sort of sound a dying animal might make. It was impossible to see his face, backlit by the moon. Most of the light seemed to take pleasure in glinting off the cave-sized barrels of his shotgun.

"If your aim, Fever," he began, the words rattling in his throat, "is to fetch out a man from somewheres, you have *got* to learn you a portion of shut up."

"We were still too loud?" Andrews was checking to see if his translation of Red's words was correct.

"The thing about a cave," Red explained, "is it acts like a megaphone. You know what a megaphone is? A normal sound in here is thunder in them woods."

"You heard us?" Andrews asked incredulously.

"I heard somebody jump in here," Red confirmed, "and then a lot of jabbering. You might imagine I pay pretty close attention to this particular cave."

"And plus," said another voice behind Red, "I seen you'uns come up on this cave."

"Toby seen you," Red repeated.

Toby appeared, grinning. "Hey, guess what. You know how they say, like, you can make enough racket to wake the dead? That's how loud you'uns was. That fat old raccoon? He hear all that noise, open up his eyes, take one look of me, and scatter."

Andrews relaxed his grip on the stranger and his face lit up. "He got away?"

"That he did." Toby seemed almost as pleased.

By the next week there would be a nice story circulating in

the upper part of the mountain. Toby killed a giant raccoon; a man from England woke it from the dead. And somewhere out in those woods there lurks an invincible creature, still alive despite great wounds—and still growing.

"So who've we got here?" Red twitched his rifle in the direction of the stranger.

"I believe this is the man," I volunteered, "who killed the person that the sheriff found on Tuesday morning. It's a little hard to see him in here."

"Drag him out." Red backed away from the entrance, gun still leveled at us.

Andrews looked the man in the eye. "Come on, then."

The man's head was down, and he was sniffling.

"Red," I called. "I've got this pistol that he had. It's in my pocket. I believe it belongs to Hovis Daniels. Just wanted you to know. It's not mine."

"Show me," he demanded calmly.

I produced the gun immediately, holding it in the flat of my hand.

"That's an old'un." Red was still backing away. "I know Hovis to brag about it, or one like it. Put it away."

I did.

Andrews and I moved toward the entrance of the cave very carefully, ushering the stranger with us. Andrews still had a tight hold on the man's old army surplus coat.

Out in the moonlight, Red and Toby seemed a bit more relaxed, though their guns remained quite in evidence.

"Let me see him." Red lifted his chin in the direction of the stranger.

Andrews turned the man so that the light could show him more clearly. Instantly I saw that he was, indeed, the man who had invaded my kitchen. Red took longer in his assessment.

"Don't know," he said slowly. "Could be the one I'm thinking of. Got more hair and less meat on him. Mite older."

"I ain't never seen him," Toby offered.

Red dropped the barrel of his gun, pointed it to the ground. "Nope. Can't say for certain. Go on, take him."

Andrews shook the man he was holding. "You have nothing to say?"

He looked down. "I'm Truck Jackson."

Red and Toby froze. I started to speak, but thought better of it when I saw the mixture of curiosity and terror on Toby's face.

"I helped to liberate Paris." The man's voice was absolutely affectless, droning. "This is no way to treat a veteran."

"Truck Jackson's been dead for more than fifty years," Red said evenly. "You ain't barely old enough to be his great-grandson."

The man's head snapped up; his face changed. In the near-white ghostliness of the moon, I felt I could see a vivid, burning spirit inhabiting that body.

"That's where you're wrong," he said. His voice had completely changed. It was strong, certain of itself, and clear as autumn's air. "And I'll tell you why, if someone could get this limey dingleberry to let loose of my coat."

"What the hell is a dingleberry?" Andrews asked.

"I'll tell you later," I assured him, voice lowered. "It's not particularly nice."

"Then I'm not letting him go." Andrews clutched the man's coat tighter.

"I'd love to hear how you could be Truck Jackson." Red shifted his weight to his right leg and sniffed once.

"I stumbled onto a very important bend in the River of Time." The man turned to face Red with a look of such ferocious joy that it nearly knocked the old man over. "The River of Time is a roiling fountain, and it rushes in all directions at once."

"What?" Andrews glared at the man.

"But what I've discovered is that certain scenes from the Grand Theatre are doomed to repeat themselves over and over again until something is done to jar the cogs of Time. I have determined to do just that, kick the wheels until they come loose. That way I won't have to do my killing anymore."

"What's he talking about, Red?" Toby asked, his voice barely audible.

"Few human beings ever realize," the man roared, "that their true journey as a spirit in this world is to wade through the waters of Time, here and there bumping into the debris of History, until they are properly baptized! Then they can rise up out of the water, into the light, and move on. That's the metaphor of evolution—creation and evolution are as illusory as anything else, of course. It's the metaphor that counts. Each individual lifetime is barely the blink of the spirit's eye. We go rushing down those corridors frantically on our way to the Great Light. But we're distracted by things—a strain of melody, the sound of laughter, a gunshot, the smell of bread and coffee, the taste of a kiss upon the lips, the soft edge of a trellis rose. Sometimes it's even a face. A single face can distract us from our forward motion toward the light, and we'd dally. That dalliance is called life. Another life."

Toby was clearly terrified. Red had taken a step or two back as well. I, on the other hand, was beginning to remember how well this man had played the cazier-than-thou game in my kitchen, and I thought I knew what he was up to.

"I think that's about all for now," I ventured, moving closer to the man. "Let's get you back to my place. You can have a nice cup of something, and I'll call the sheriff."

"What makes you think I'd come with you?" the man asked, very congenially under the circumstances.

"You're the only one in this crowd without a gun," Andrews told him, clenching the man's coat lapels tighter.

"You don't have a gun," the man answered back, blazing a look of overwhelming intensity directly into Andrews's pupils.

"I have a gun in my mind," Andrews answered back with equal power, and just the right addition of barely controlled rage.

"Get on, boy," Red commanded. "Onliest thing to keep you from being shot dead and buried up under some rock is these two. I don't like a witness. I could kill all three of you, I guess, but ain't got the notion for that right now. It'd take up too much of my time. Maybe some other night, though."

"Maybe some other night," Toby repeated gleefully.

I couldn't tell if Red had said that for effect or if he was serious, but it seemed the perfect exit line.

"As I was saying," I began.

Andrews didn't wait for the rest of the sentence. He headed toward the cemetery, and my truck, dragging his captive along as if he were carrying oversized luggage.

"Good night, Red; Toby." I nodded once.

Red snorted, uncocked his shotgun, and offered me one quick wink. His entire face changed, and I realized that ninety percent of what he'd been doing—perhaps for the entire evening—was an act, a *Deliverance* parody of backwoods crazy. Andrews was so focused on getting his prey back to the truck that he was moving at a righteous clip, already yards away.

Just to see what answer he'd offer, I smiled as wryly as I could and asked Red, "How's business?"

"Good." He smiled back. He had all his teeth. "We're in five states now. And the stuff you buy that you like so much, from those people up behind Hek's church? You know they buy it from me, don't you? I'm the only one who crafts in bulk on this mountain. I make three grades, you buy the best."

"Are you serious?"

"Don't let it get out, hear? I need a certain reputation. The fact is, I am a state-licensed distiller. I'm ashamed to admit it, but all this is squeaky legal. I don't know what my granddad would say."

"I can't believe—" I began.

"Have a look," Toby told me, "at www.jackapple.com. Even got us a kind of a theme song I guess you'd call it. I wrote it."

Temporarily at a loss, I finally managed to say, "It certainly is the twenty-first century."

"Sad to say," Red agreed, nodding. "Enjoy the rest of your evening, if you can."

Red and Toby turned without further ado and headed back up the ridge.

TWENTY-ONE

I WATCHED THE Jackson family distillers vanish into the darkness at the top of the rim. For a moment I was transported back into the long past, a time when the Jacksons still remembered what their homes in England or Scotland had looked like; I despaired that every bit of the folklore I loved was gone from the hills of my home. Then I heard Andrews calling.

"Are you coming or am I going?"

I ran after, and arrived at his side not so far from the fence we'd toppled.

The prisoner was babbling, barely audibly, and seemed to be quoting Heidegger's *Being and Time,* but I could have been projecting—most of what he said was incoherent.

Andrews made it to the truck and shoved the poor man in while I managed to restore the portion of fence we'd knocked down. I couldn't fasten it to the rest of the fence, but I leaned it very neatly and called it a job well done.

I was in the truck in a matter of minutes, only to find our companion dead asleep.

"I didn't do anything," Andrews said nervously as I climbed in behind the steering wheel. "He just conked out like this. In a flash, honestly."

"I believe you," I told him, cranking the ignition. "He did this in my kitchen on Monday night. Although it could be a ploy. When I called Skidmore because I thought he was asleep, he vanished."

"Right." Andrews eyed the snoring man with intense suspicion.

The drive back to my place was bumpy and silent after that. I decided not to tell Andrews the horrible truth about Red's business. I knew that Andrews would enjoy his beverage infinitely less if he knew that it was all legal—not to mention available on the Internet. Which, of course, was what made Red's performance so spectacular: the knowledge that his clientele relished a certain romantic image. It was good for business. So much of American advertising is a game of playing to reductive stereotypes in the general television psyche, in fact, that Red's behavior may well have been essential to his sales.

That's what kept me silent on the drive home. Andrews used the time to perfect his seething mechanism. The third of our unholy trio appeared to dream his way through that short portion of the night.

The truck's headlights blared onto my front porch in no time, and I pulled closer than usual. I had the intuition that our prisoner might try something once Andrews opened his door.

"Here we are!" I announced happily, nudging the sleeping man with my elbow. "Wake up!".

He seemed to drag himself from the arms of nepenthe with great difficulty.

"Your house?" He licked his lips and swallowed. "I thought we were taking me to the sheriff."

"We're calling him from here." I opened my door. "I want to get some answers before he gets ahold of you."

"I see." He seemed to be waking up.

"Don't let go of him, Andrews," I cautioned, climbing down out of the truck.

"Not to worry," Andrews answered, clamping a vise-grip hand onto the man's arm.

"Oww," the man complained.

I hurried to the front door. The air had become bitter, and the moon was gone again. For some reason I was eager to turn on lights, start something on the stove, make noise.

I threw the door open with a jarring rattle and flipped several switches at once. Artificial daylight flooded the porch, the living room, and the kitchen.

"The kitchen seems the right place," I told Andrews.

In a relatively small number of steps, Andrews had marched

the man into the house and seated him, rather roughly, at the kitchen table.

"There," I said, pleased, "just as you were on Monday night."

"But it's not Monday night," he said, grinning. "Even if you can't see Time's water move, you still can't step in the same stream twice."

"Yes, about that," I told him, taking a chair on the other side of the table. "If you think you can outcrazy me, think again. Ask anybody. I'm pretty much the acknowledged master in this state."

"But to be fair," Andrews added, "Dr. Devilin's had training from childhood. His parents were monstrous lunatics, at least in his mind, and they bathed him in crazy from an early age."

"Look," the man said, leaning into the kitchen table, "you don't believe I'm Truck Jackson. That doesn't matter to me. It's only a name. I know who I am. What's got you nervous is that you don't know what to believe about me."

"Whereas it's not so difficult for me." Andrews took a seat at last. His face was red, and his hair was a crown of golden flames. "I know you're a lunatic, and a killer. You're about to be put far away, and I'm glad."

"No." The man sat back in his seat, face absolutely serene. "I won't be here much longer. Later tonight I'll lose my grip on this illusion, and I'll be back where I belong, in my own part of the River of Time—long before any of this happens."

"Oh." Andrews slammed an exasperated hand down hard on the red tabletop. "Now you're a time traveler? Jesus God in Cleveland—"

"Not now," he snapped. "Always. I've always been—"

"Stop!" I demanded. "I don't care about any of that. I need a few specific answers. If you give them to me, everything will be fine. If you don't, Dr. Andrews is liable to take one of my kitchen knives and see to it that you return to your own time with much less equipment than you had when you arrived here."

"With great glee," Andrews assured us all.

My kitchen was an odd setting for such a violent insinuation, and I was forced to reflect that perhaps the spilling of blood, specifically from Hovis Daniels very recently, had somehow contaminated the spirit of the room. I found myself distracted, suddenly, by the fact that I had threatened a man with a gun—a gun that was still in my pocket. There had been, I realized then, a very strange atmosphere in my entire house since Monday night when the stranger had first paid a visit. I felt the merest sliver of ice in my veins; the faint smell of gunpowder assailed my nostrils.

"Let me explain something to you," the man told Andrews suddenly, daggers in his eyes. "Time is easy to travel. Everyone does it."

Andrews was so startled by the force in the man's words that his head snapped back and he was instantly on the defensive.

"It can be something as simple as mowing the lawn," the man said, his demeanor changed again—he was filled with overflowing agape. "The smell of fresh grass, the way the air plays with that smell. One second you're mowing your own lawn and the next you're a boy at your parents' house in Indiana, lying on your back watching white horses made out of clouds race each other toward the end of the afternoon. Most people only experience it for a breath or two, because they can't hold on to it. They're afraid to. They're afraid they'll drown in the River of Time. But if you linger, if you grab a fistful of grass and forget, for just the blink of an eye, *what* you are, then you can better grasp *where* you are. And *where* you are is primarily a question of where you want to be at any given moment—in my experience. And these experiences are not novel."

"Yes, look," Andrews stammered extremely impatiently, "you're not Billy Pilgrim and this isn't that kind of novel."

"Billy Pilgrim?" the man said, confused.

"Isn't that the guy in the Vonnegut novel who came unstuck in time?" Andrews asked, turning my way. "I have to teach it next week."

"Slaughterhouse-Five," I confirmed. "But I'm not certain—"

"You don't know squat!" the man exploded at Andrews. "Not everything is in a book. Most things are in the human mind. I'm here in this kitchen because I chose to be, because I picked this time to wander in."

"But—" Andrews began.

"Why?" I asked the man suddenly. "Why this time? Why here; why now?"

"Are you out of your mind?" Andrews snapped at me.

"Seriously," I said to the man, ignoring Andrews. "What are you doing here?"

I had learned many times that the more you try to get people to deny their illusions, the stronger the illusions can become. But if you indulge those delusions instead, they often fall apart all on their own.

For a moment my trick seemed to be working. The man was at a loss for what to say. Andrews nodded, slowly understanding my ploy.

"I've come to stop the cycle." His voice had gone ghostly quiet.

In fact, his demeanor had shifted so dramatically that Andrews let go of him and drew in a shaky breath.

The man sat at my table, staring into space.

"Cain slew Abel," he began, "brother against brother. Ever since the world began, men have been killing their brothers. I can't stand it anymore. It has to stop. I have to kick the cogs of Time—kick the wheels until they come loose."

"So you said." I sat with him at the table. "But that's not what you did. You didn't stop anything. You killed a man."

Andrews took a few steps back, still wary.

"I guess I did." His face was snow.

"Why?"

"I am the one who murders his brother time after time. I've killed so many men. I was just in a war—just now."

"But why do you keep doing it?" I stared.

"The moon shivered behind a thick cloud, and there was a darkness over all the earth." He wasn't talking to me; he was reciting something. "Then, like black wings plummeting to earth, my hands darted to grab his shirt. I threw him sideways, hard, to the ground. I knelt on top of him, my knees in his stomach and chest, so he could not move or breathe. My face was nearly touching his. My teeth could have gnawed out his eyes. I had to know, why did he leave me?"

"He left you?" I whispered.

"To fight for strangers."

"The Civil War?" Andrews asked.

"Why did he kill our land and tear up our spirits and leave us all for dead?" the man raved on. "Why did he send me out into this world to be a wandering spirit? I was shaking him so violently that I thought his neck might snap. He tried to talk, but I cut him off. He was a traitor and a coward, and I wanted not one word from him. Not one! He ruined this land. He destroyed his own home. No crops, no land, no money, no food, no work, no clothes, no books, no music, no joy, no life, no health, no heart, no hope. Only rage and desolation. He left his family in their deepest time of need. He was my *brother*. God Almighty-damn-damn-*damn*, I ought to kill him a *hundred* times! A *million* times! He was my brother. I loved him so much."

Whatever the man was seeing in his mind's eye provoked tears.

"But what happened Monday night?" I insisted. "This Monday night?"

"Suddenly the moon broke free and a shower of silver light bathed his face. It was radiant. It was holy. It was beaming brighter than the sun and moon and stars. He threw his arms around me and pulled me so close to him I thought he'd crush all the life out of me, and I could not move. His voice was like small white wings beating close to my ear. 'I loved you too. I loved you too. I loved you too.' He kept saying it to me over and over again."

"What did you do?"

"I asked him my question: 'Then why did you *leave?*'"

"What did he say?"

"He nearly crushed me, holding me to him, but his voice was gentler than ever, and he said, 'Christ Almighty, brother—why did you *stay*!' And I only realized the answer to that question as I was saying it to him, in the moment I heard myself speaking the words. I said, 'You weren't the only one with a conviction. I stayed for *this*: This land—the ripe and growing fields. My God.'"

"Is he talking about Cain and Abel," Andrews whispered, "or the Civil War?"

I just shook my head.

"The wind picked up for a moment," the man continued, "and all about us a sort of rustle—the whisper of the healed land—rose up to my ears. I heard, at last, on Monday night, how the land had been reborn. I had, in a single terrible moment, veered wildly out into the yawning chasm of God's Footprint, a chasm so wide and deep I could have been swallowed up again by it, as I had, I supposed, in lifetimes before. But then, because my brother had held me fast, I had not fallen downward, and I was saved. Because my brother had held me fast. The land had already been reborn. It was only waiting for me to join it. Then, like God's Own Grasp opening up, we released each other from our mutual embrace. Time gave us up to its more ordinary slipstream: a world where we were essentially strangers and a little startled to be standing so oddly close in the autumn night. We were actors again, standing outside our characters for the moment, wondering at the strange scene we'd just played out. And in our wonder, we just stared. I have no idea what our laughter must have sounded like at a distance—demon curses or angel wings—but to us it was the sound two rivers make coming together again after long and separate journeys over many a rock and stone."

"So," Andrews hissed, unable to grasp it all, "you reconciled?"

"We did." The man nodded once, and a look of great beatification came over him. "Now I can go back home."

"But—" Andrews began.

"Who killed the man, then?" I asked bluntly.

"You don't understand," the man said sweetly, looking into my eyes with a Buddha's compassion. "He's not dead; he went home. That husk you found? That's just a conveyance. I just pulled away the husk and let the spirit go free. It doesn't mean a thing."

"Doesn't mean a thing?" Andrews was on the verge of exploding. "You sling around all this bleeding talk about ending the cycle of violence by *killing* someone? This is American thinking at its finest."

"All young people go through a period of naive idealism," the man snapped. "It's one of the things that keeps the wheels of Time well oiled, also one of the things that makes God laugh out loud."

"Fever!" Andrews demanded. "I renew my original request. Would you please shoot this man in the head? I don't want to kill him, because I think that would be playing into his little game, somehow, but I would like to shake him up a little—and give him a scar like he gave me."

"Look," I said to the man, "I'm a little in the mood to agree with Dr. Andrews here. I don't care about time travel or your cosmic mission. Since you don't seem to think you killed man, I want to know what you thought you were doing coming to my house on Monday night—and to Lucinda's."

"Research, my friend." He pounded the tabletop. His aspect had shifted again. He was hearty and boisterous. "Pure and simple. I'm something of a folklorist, like yourself, and wanted to gather a bit of interesting information before I went home. talked to Hovis because he was right there where my brother was. Hovis got me to Lucinda. She got me to you. That's about all I had time for. I had to get ready to go home myself after that.

"No." I sat back. "In the first place, you did all the talking. You didn't ask any questions. And in the second place, we found you hiding out in a cave, not getting ready—"

"Linear time," the man said, laughing and shaking his head as if he were amused by a child's inability to grasp an adult concept.

As he was laughing, he relaxed. As he relaxed, he leaned back in his chair. As he leaned back in his chair, his coat fell open. As his coat fell open, his clothes were revealed.

He was wearing a tattered Confederate army uniform from the Civil War.

TWENTY-TWO

OUR VISITOR SEEMED unaware of what he'd uncovered, that he'd revealed such a startling costume, but Andrews saw it, and shot me a glance that could have knocked me out of my chair.

"You can't tell me," the man went on, apparently oblivious to us, "either of you, that you haven't ever experienced some kind of time travel. I mean, just talking with Hovis Daniels, now, there's a human who travels time, don't you think? I listen to his stories and I'm taken out of the regiment of linear time and slapped down into whatever story that old man is telling. Aren't you?"

I could tell that Andrews was thinking a bit favorably about the concept—considering how he'd reacted to Hovis Daniels in the jail cell.

The man could see it, too: a look of confused concentration on the face of Dr. Andrews.

"So," the man said, very satisfied with himself, "what now?"

"Now," I told him firmly, getting up from the table, "Andrews watches you like a hawk while I call Sheriff Needle."

"Fine." The man seemed perfectly self-satisfied. "Call anyone you like. I won't be here much longer anyway."

"Call him now," Andrews said haltingly. "He's starting to make me very nervous."

I went to the phone, dialed, and turned back around to keep an eye on the man, half-wondering if he might vanish from my kitchen—again. The kitchen clock tried to make me believe it was only 7:05 in the evening. It seemed more like midnight. I dialed Skid's office, hoping he'd be there so I wouldn't have to call him at home. I was surprised to find a great relief in the sound of his voice.

"Sheriff," he sighed into the phone.

"You should get caller ID," I said back. "Then you wouldn't have to sound so deliberately weary when you answered. It's only me."

"Fever," he whined, "I'm really tired, and unless you have—"

"He's in my kitchen."

Skidmore was momentarily struck dumb, so I continued.

"The man responsible for the dead body you found Tuesday morning," I said deliberately, staring at the killer, "is right here in my kitchen. Would you like to come over and have a talk with him? Maybe take him back to the jailhouse with you?"

"How the hell did you find him?"

"Well," I began, "sort of... Hovis told me where he might be. Then Red Jackson—"

"Wait. Doesn't matter. This man you have in your kitchen—"

"Andrews is here, too, and I have a gun."

"You have a *what?*"

"I know." I smiled. "Isn't it amazing?"

"Do *not* shoot anything with that...where did you get a gun?"

"I'm pretty sure it's the murder weapon." I winced. "Which now has my fingerprints all over it. But this person, the one in my kitchen? It's his. Or he stole it from Hovis, I mean—probably."

"I'm trying to get—"

"The man had it, he pulled it on Andrews, Andrews knocked it my way, and I picked it up."

"All this happened in your kitchen?"

"No," I drawled, "it happened in Barrel Cave close to the cemetery. Hey, did you know it was called Barrel Cave—"

"Red let you go into his cave?"

"No," I said again, "we sort of snuck in—look, do you want to come up here and arrest the murderer so we can let Hovis go home, or not?"

"I'll be right up. By the way, the dead man? He was a Jackson."

"I sort of had that in mind." I nodded. "Which means this person here is probably—"

"All we know is that the fingerprints of the dead man belong to Son Jackson." Skidmore was ready to get off the phone. "His prints are on file because he's a deserter from the army—

very recently. I'll be up there in fifteen minutes. Try not to let him get away again—but don't shoot him, either."

"You think you're funny, but you're not." I hung up.

I stared at the stranger in my kitchen. "So you did kill your brother. I mean, in this time or this reality or however you would look at it."

"What did Skidmore say?" Andrews still had a bit of adrenal concentration, ready to tackle the man if he even twitched in the wrong direction.

"The dead man is Son Jackson," I announced.

"So this guy's a Jackson, too." Andrews narrowed his eyelids.

"Great work," he sneered back at Andrews, "I've only been telling you that for the past half hour."

"So what's with the Halloween costume you're wearing, chum?" Andrews snapped back.

"One man in his time plays many parts." The man smiled serenely.

"Why does that sound familiar?" I asked Andrews.

"It's from *As You Like It.* Act two, scene seven, to be specific. 'All the world's a stage, and all the men and women merely players. They have their exits and their entrances, and—'"

"'One man in his time plays many parts.'" I nodded. "Now I remember."

Andrews kicked the man's chair. "'What seest thou else in the dark backward and abysm of time?'"

"That's from *The Tempest,* I think," the man answered. "Not sure where."

"Act one, scene two," Andrews said slowly. "But you didn't answer the question."

"What do I see in the abyss of time?" He closed his eyes. "I see a nearly infinite line of men, all killing each other for reasons that Time forgets."

"What's that from?" I asked.

"That, my fellow travelers," the man said, eyes still closed, "is from the bottom of my soul."

With that his head drifted toward the table, and he was fast asleep and snoring before Andrews or I could say another word.

TWENTY-THREE

SKIDMORE ARRIVED ABOUT ten minutes later. The anonymous Jackson was still asleep. Andrews had barely blinked since the man had gone to sleep. It seemed to me that Skidmore could sense the atmosphere in my kitchen almost from the second he walked in.

He asked again how we came to have the man in our possession, and we told him the tale. I omitted Red's business confessions, but the rest was accurate. Skid sat down at the table and indicated that Andrews and I should do the same. We just sat there for a while, staring at the sleeping man. I'm not certain what we were thinking, any of us.

But when the man sat up with a start, all three of us jumped.

"I'm still here?" He looked around the room as if it were unfamiliar to him.

"He's expecting to go back to his original time any moment now," Andrews explained, each syllable dripping derision.

"Sheriff?" The man squinted at Skidmore.

"That's right." Skid folded his hands in front of him, at least an imitation of patience. "Would you prefer to talk to me here and now, or would you rather talk to me in jail?"

"It's a nice kitchen," the man began.

"Let's start with your name." Skidmore's face was carved in solid granite.

"Yes." He lowered his head in a manner that could only be described as sheepish. "I suppose it's about time I confessed that, at least."

"Now we're talking," Andrews mumbled, still tense.

"My name is Jericho Jackson, and I killed my brother, Jacob."

The man let go a heart-wrenching, groaning breath. "God, it feels good to say that out loud—at last. I killed Jacob Jackson."

It took me a moment, but I remembered. "In a brothel in Chicago."

"In Madam Briscoe's House in Chicago," the man confirmed, "after the Civil War."

"He was dancing the Tango with a woman who worked there." I looked at Skidmore. "It's all on the tape that Melissa's been listening to."

"And finding useless," Skid said tersely.

"If you look upon this world in a map," the man went on, seemingly oblivious to our conversation, "you find two hemispheres, two half worlds. If you crush heaven into a map, you may find two hemispheres, too, two half heavens; half will be joy, and half will be glory."

"That's John Donne," Andrews whispered, more than a touch of awe invading his voice. "One of Donne's sermons."

"Who?" Skid asked, irritated.

"John Donne," I said quickly, "metaphysical poet, contemporary of Shakespeare, roughly."

"My brother had no glory, and so tried to lose himself in degenerated joy; spent most of his last days in a house of ill repute. He drowned himself in perfume, spirits, and a newly invented erotic dance. His favorite companion there was a woman called La Gauchina, because she claimed to be the daughter of a gaucho from the pampas of Argentina. She had come to America with seven Yankee dollars, a small guitar that her father had given her, and the knowledge of a brand-new dance named the Tango. The dance was invented in the outskirts of proper society in Buenos Aires—in brothels. It was a way for men to have sexual stimulation with their clothes on, set to music, while they waited for the actual acts of sex with prostitutes. The Tango was abstract copulation accompanied by violin, flute, and guitar. La Gauchina taught the dance in this manner. She would grab a man by the waist and thrust her pelvis toward his, drawing him as close to her body as anatomically possible. All the men loved her, but none so much as my brother, Jacob Jackson. On the evening of January the twenty-sixth, Jacob and this woman made love with such a fury that, despite the fact that my brother was much older and very drunk, they conceived a son. They didn't know they'd conceived a son; they only knew they were exhausted. Instead of going another round, they just wanted to dance. So they danced the Tango."

"Stop talking about the Tango!" Skidmore seemed on the verge of hitting the man.

"I rubbed my brother's name out of the family Bible." It was clear the man was growing more and more agitated as he talked. "No relative was ever allowed to speak his name. It was my intention that there be no trace of the fact that there had ever *been* a Jacob Jackson in the family. I took money from a secret hiding place in my bedroom here in Georgia, walked to the Pine City train station, and purchased a round-trip train ticket to Chicago. I took seven Yankee dollars, a small pistol that my father had given me—which Dr. Devilin now has in his pocket—and a certain wicked plan."

"Wait," Skidmore interrupted. "How did you know where he was?"

"Letters," Andrews answered, amazed at the connection. "Jacob sent letters to the Jackson family in Blue Mountain. Simple read one of them to us."

"Some were returned unopened," I added, "and some are in the Jackson house to this day."

Skid looked as if he might ask us for more information, but our guest was anxious to continue his story.

"I arrived in the Windy City on the late afternoon of January twenty-sixth," he said, his words clipped and tight, his eyes staring into space. "I found the rooming house where my brother was staying. I banged on the door. Neighbors came into the hall. A bald man in his underwear growled at me. He said, 'He's not in, for Christ's sake. Can't you see that?' This man's undershirt had tomato sauce on it. I exploded. 'Then where is he, you Yankee son of a bitch?' And I drew my pistol to emphasize the question. The bald man barely acknowledged the gun. 'He's at the whorehouse. Jesus,' he said, then wandered back into his own room, mumbling. Others in the hall seemed more impressed with the gun. They scattered when I turned to them. 'What whorehouse?' I demanded to know. Then the bald man returned to the hallway with the biggest rifle I had ever seen and pointed it right at my pants. 'Out the front door,' he said calmly, 'take a left, two blocks down on the right. Can't miss it. Now get the hell out of here before I blow all your privates to kingdom come.' I was not afraid. I thought I might die that night anyway. I just nodded and left. The bald man went back to his spaghetti, I guess. I turned left out the front door of the rooming house, walked two blocks, saw the house that was obviously made for sin, and wandered in the front door. I wasn't sure I'd recognize him after all the time we'd been apart. Underneath a nude portrait of an anonymous woman, I saw a familiar-seeming face. Beside him was a woman pulling on his elbow. She was laughing. The two got to their feet just as the Tango music started. They crushed together, laughing and stumbling, and began a sad and funny parody of the dance. I stepped up close beside them. Anyone would have thought I was about to cut in. I tapped Jacob on the back; he turned around, unable to focus his eyes because of the enormous amount of whiskey he'd consumed. There is no way to tell if he recognized his brother or not. He had not seen me in years, and war changes a man's appearance. I said, 'Let us go out to the field.' Then the gun exploded, blood erupted, and Jacob Jackson lay dead on the brothel floor. I tried my best to spit on him as other men in the brothel laid hands on me, pulled me away from the body."

"I've heard enough." Skidmore stood up.

"He was a turncoat and a deserter," the man insisted, near hysteria, "and I'm glad I killed him."

"You have the right to remain silent," Skidmore began in a ludicrous parody of bad police drama.

I tuned out the rest of Skidmore's speech in favor of studying the man's face. It was a mask—a theatrical mask, I thought. In his time a man plays many parts—and this man had assumed yet another role.

TWENTY-FOUR

DEPUTY MATHEWS WAS still at the sheriff's office when we all pulled up in front of it. Andrews and I were not capable of letting the matter go, so we'd followed Skid's squad car.

The lights were on, and we could see Melissa clearly through the big storefront window listening intently to the tape I had given her, this time without headphones. The rest of the street was dark. At eight in the evening Miss Etta would be getting into bed, and most of the rest of the store owners would have finished dinner, put another log on the fire, and been settled in for the night.

I thought Skidmore was a little rough with his prisoner as he grabbed him out of the back of the police car. I found I was eager to get Hovis Daniels out of jail almost as much as I was curious to see what the strange man in the Confederate uniform would say next. Andrews was interested in that as well, but the prospect of another moment with Deputy Mathews was surely the icing on that particular cake, so before we got out of my truck I took a hold of the good doctor's arm.

"Look," I told him, my eyes glancing involuntarily in the deputy's direction, "Melissa Mathews is very uncomfortable with your flirtations. I meant to talk to you about it earlier."

"My flirtations are hardly any of your—"

"She asked me to speak with you. She wants you to stop it, and I do, too."

"She asked you to get me to stop—"

"You have no idea what her situation is," I said firmly. "And neither do I. Skidmore has hinted that something strange happened to her when she was younger that's made her uncomfortable around most men. You make her nervous in all the wrong ways. I'm telling you this as a friend. Find someone else to—"

"Who the hell else can I—"

"Are you two coming inside?" Skidmore's voice was a razor on slate.

The sound of his voice prompted Andrews and me to jump out of the truck instantly. Skidmore was in the doorway holding on to his prisoner, and we followed him into the bright fluorescent room.

Melissa looked up, and the prisoner stared at the tape recorder, listening to the voice.

"Hey," the prisoner said, delighted, "that's me."

"This," Skidmore said to Melissa, holding tightly to the man's arm, "is our murderer. We're going to book him almost immediately. Do you think you could call Millroy? I've got a mouthful of I-told-you-so and I'm dying to spit it out."

"How colorful," Andrews mumbled.

"Gosh." Melissa turned off the tape recorder.

"And could we get the paperwork to release Hovis?" I insisted. "I'd like to get him out of here as quickly as possible."

She looked to Skidmore; he nodded once.

"Which one should I do first?" she whispered to Skidmore.

"What?" He was made almost entirely of irritation.

"Booking form for this one, or release form for Hovis?" Her voice was barely audible.

"Well," Skidmore said, the oil of patience completely absent from his grinding gears, "shouldn't we release one man from custody before we book another man for the same crime? Wouldn't that seem to be the proper order of things?"

"Yes, sir," Melissa said instantly, rolling her chair toward the nearest file cabinet.

"Release Hovis into Dr. Devilin's custody." Skidmore leveled a look at me. "As Dr. Devilin will be taking Hovis home right now."

"Yes." I responded almost as quickly as Melissa had.

Best for all concerned to stand clear of Skidmore Needle when he was in full sheriff mode—though it was a little difficult to tell why he was so hard-edged that evening.

Andrews, sensing the tension in the room, remained uncharacteristically silent.

"I'm taking this one to the interview room," Skid mumbled, dragging his prisoner toward a short hallway.

Andrews looked around, quickly found a seat in what passed for a waiting area only a few steps from Melissa's desk, and sat down.

"I'll be fine right here," he said, nodding once in Melissa's direction.

Before I could determine what, exactly, he had in mind, Melissa was asking me questions and filling out some sort of form. Skidmore vanished into a room down the short hallway. Andrews slumped in his chair.

I surrendered to the moment and did whatever Melissa wanted me to, including following her to Hovis's jail cell.

The narrow hallway, covered in thin, cheap wood paneling, was darker than the outer room, and for some reason urged silence. We were almost to the cell before Melissa turned her head toward me a bit.

"Did you have a chance to speak with Dr. Andrews about...you know?" She was clearly embarrassed to ask such a question.

"I did," I assured her. "There's no telling how he took it, but at least he's on notice."

"Okay." She didn't sound certain.

Hovis roused himself from his stupor when he heard us coming.

"I'm hungry," he groaned.

"Hey, Hovis," Melissa said sweetly, "look who we got here?" She opened the cell door.

Hovis tried to sit up, and his eyes were unfocused.

"Who is it?" His voice rattled.

"It's Dr. Devilin, see?" She pointed to me as if I were an educational display. "He's going to take you home."

"Home?" He reached out his hand. Melissa helped him achieve a seated position. "I can go?"

"Yes." She patted him on the arm.

"How long I been here?"

"A day," Melissa answered.

"That's all?" Hovis squeezed his eyes shut.

"Seems like longer?" She took hold of his arm, trying to steady him.

Hovis finally managed to clear his head enough to piece together a few facts about his situation. He looked me in the eye; his gaze was firm as a hawk's.

"You done it, then." He nodded once, lips thinning. "You got me out."

"Yes." I was afraid to say more; Hovis seemed on the verge of tears.

"I'm obliged" was all he said.

"You're innocent," I corrected. "You have no obligation to me."

Melissa looked at the floor. She knew what an important exchange those few words had been, especially to Hovis. His nature, the predilection of most men and women his age in Blue Mountain, was to take a favor as a death-pledge. That was why it had been so hard for him to ask me for help—why so few people in our town ever asked for anything. I had done him an important favor, and he was already beginning to worry that he would have no way of paying me back. My releasing him from the bonds of reciprocity would not deter his attempting to set things even, but it would remove the pressure and scope of his commitment.

He let go a sigh to wake the dead, and nodded once.

"Can I go home right now?" he asked Melissa. "Is that what you said?"

"I've got my truck outside," I confirmed.

"Well, then." He stood, with Melissa's help, then held on to the cell door to get his legs under him.

"You take care, Hovis," Melissa said softly. "I'm sorry I had to shoot up your arm."

"Miss," he said, turning to face her, "I'm sorry I give you cause to do it. Won't never happen again."

"That's a deal," she told him, and smiled warmly.

"Let's get in that truck, then," he said, and without further ado began motoring with surprising agility toward the front room.

Melissa and I followed. He was in the front room in no time.

"Did he have some sort of coat?" I asked Melissa.

"No." She looked around trying to see what she might find to keep the old man warm on the drive home.

Before she had arrived at a solution, Andrews stood, shed the raincoat I'd lent him, which he had kept on even in my house, and held it out.

"This isn't very warm," he said, not looking at anyone.

Hovis just shook his head.

"It's mine," I explained to Hovis. "I keep it in the truck. Would you mind carrying it back to the truck for me while I finish up here? You know the one it is."

Hovis looked out the glass front of the office, but it was hard to see, the night was so black and the room was so artificially bright.

"Big old beat-up green Ford truck?" he asked, more to himself than to me.

"That's the one," Andrews sighed.

Without another word Hovis took the raincoat in one hand and shoved the door open with the other. He was gone.

I turned to Andrews.

"Behave," I whispered.

"Bite me," he whispered back.

"I'm just going to run Hovis home," I said much louder, turning to Melissa. "I'll be back in half an hour."

"Okay." She glanced once at Andrews, then sank to her seat behind the big desk.

I took another second trying to decide if there was anything more I could do or say that would prevent an uncomfortable moment in that room, but gave up in favor of getting Hovis home quickly and rushing back to save the day, if, in fact, the day needed saving.

"I'm off, then," I announced to the room, and pushed the glass and metal door into the night.

TWENTY-FIVE

HOVIS WAS ALREADY in the truck, and he was using the raincoat as a sort of blanket.

I climbed in beside him, started the engine, turned on the lights, and backed out slowly even though the streets were deserted. I wanted to give Hovis time to settle in.

I had barely gotten to the end of the street when he spoke.

"So you caught that boy, the one that was in my house the other night?" he said evenly.

I almost slammed on the brakes and turned the truck around. How could Skid and I have been so oblivious as to not let Hovis have a look at the man to confirm that he was our visitor?

"Yes," I answered him distractedly, trying to decide what to do.

"That's good," Hovis continued. "He wanted catching. Where'd you get him?"

I took a breath. If Skidmore was convinced that the man he had in custody was the murderer, he didn't really need to hear from Hovis on the subject. I relaxed.

"Top of the mountain," I told Hovis, "up there where Red works. You know Barrel Cave?"

"That I do," Hovis grinned.

"He was sleeping in there," I concluded, "the killer."

"Makes sense," Hovis nodded, looking out the side window.

We drove in silence for a moment before I actually registered what he'd said.

"Why does it make sense?"

"Him being a Jackson," Hovis explained calmly, "and one of them wild boys up there that don't know what time it is—he'd go up there to hide when he come back to the mountain."

"What are you talking about?" I hadn't meant to slow the truck; it just happened when I focused more on Hovis than on driving.

"I didn't tell you he was a Jackson?" Hovis turned my way.

"Maybe you'd better pretend that you haven't told me anything about your conversation with that person," I said slowly, "and start from the beginning. You know him?"

"No." Hovis shrugged. "But I know who he is."

"Who is he, then?"

"I believe he's Boy Jackson, Son Jackson's older brother."

Son Jackson—it took me a moment to recall, but that was the dead man's name. Brother against brother.

"Why didn't you tell this to anybody before now?" I almost raised up out of the driver's seat.

"Don't like to get nobody in trouble." He sniffed. "And nobody to ask me, so far."

"Even when you were arrested?"

"Sheriff didn't want to hear much of what I had to say. Plus, I was drunk and shot up—if you will recall."

If you will recall. There it was: continuing evidence of the man's schizophrenic nature, or at the very least a phrase that was said with a different voice and alternate diction. Hovis Daniels had spent more time in the county mental health facility than any other ten people, and still came out as troubled as he'd gone in—or worse.

"So, Hovis." I quickly tried to think of the perfect question, but all that came out was "What did you two talk about?"

"This and that."

His response was evidence that I had not asked the perfect question.

"What did he want from you?" I said quickly.

"Hard to say," Hovis answered, genuinely thinking about the question. "We talked a good bit about old Mr. Jackson."

"Edna's husband?"

"Edna," he growled, as if it were a curse word.

"Why was he—"

"Old man Jackson and I surely could drink," Hovis said, grinning, pulling the raincoat to his chin. "Sometimes he'd come down to my shed, once I moved in down there, and spend all evening until sunrise drinking and talking."

"I see."

"The boy found that interesting."

"He did?"

"He thought I was the last real person to see Mr. Jackson alive, on account of he had his seizure down in my place, Mr. Jackson did."

"The last *real* person?" I asked.

"He didn't count Edna any more than I did. But I told him that Mr. Jackson died in the hospital. I remember that. When I told the boy that, then he was interested in the hospital."

"Interested in what way?"

"This and that."

"Hovis—"

"I told him," Hovis snapped, "that Miss Foxe was the nurse on duty, so Mr. Jackson was treated best there is. Did I ever tell you that Lucinda Foxe was the one to look after me the last time the police shot me up? That was Sheriff Maddox. He shot my knee. Did it on purpose. Put the revolver pointed right at my kneecap and asked me a question. Didn't like the answer, so he pulled the trigger. That hurt bad. They fixed it up over to the hospital, but that's why I limp here today. I don't believe there's a kinder person in this world than Lucinda Foxe, do you?"

"No, I don't," I answered, "but you told this person, our visitor, that Lucinda—"

"Was most likely the last one to see Mr. Jackson alive," he concluded.

"What was his response to that?"

"Let me think." Hovis slid down in his seat an inch or two. "I believe he changed the subject after that. Got me to talking about...you know, telling stories. That's all I recall. Nor sure when he quit my place. I might have fallen out before he left—he gave me a whole lot to drink."

"I see." I was barely concentrating on the road, trying to pull together something in my mind that was just about to snap into place.

"Wait," Hovis said suddenly. "He did ask about the tunnel. 'Course I didn't tell him about that. Old man Jackson would raise himself up out of the ground and kick my ass if I told anybody about the tunnel."

"Tunnel?"

"What did I just say?" he asked me, irritated. "I can't tell nobody about the tunnel and that's that! I made a promise."

"To Mr. Jackson," I ventured carefully.

"Right." He shivered. "Damn. I got a chill. I do believe I will start a *hot* fire in my stove when I get home."

I thought I might try changing my tack. "You told the visitor some of your stories. Like the ones you told me—that I tape-recorded. That's why you had it in your mind that I ought to have my tape recorder when I visited you on Tuesday."

"Could be." He considered it. "I did tell him a power of stories. He was really interested. Told him war stories mostly, some gold rush stories—you know: the old days. That's what I know best. There's not a single today in life that can beat a really great yesterday. And do you know why?"

I shook my head.

"Because yesterday is polished by the rags of memory," he continued, "and it shines brighter, glows warmer. Hell. A man my age, especially, is more like to recall a penny's worth of ten-years-ago than a dollar's worth of earlier-today."

"And that's what Boy Jackson wanted to know? About ten years ago."

"He was curious about family history." Hovis sniffed. "I was happy to talk about it. I got to put in a mention of Barbrie. Always like to talk about her when I can."

"He asked questions about Edna and her husband?"

"Lots." Hovis nodded his head. "And now I think a mite about it, I believe I did mention that old man Jackson had some stories on your tape machine he might could hear. He really wanted to hear those. Reckon that's why he come to your place?"

I hit the brakes; the truck skidded to a stop. Hovis slammed into my side and grunted, pushing himself off me, greatly irritated.

"What the hell is the matter with you?" he demanded.

I'd gotten Hovis out of jail, but I hadn't nearly solved the murder. What it was really about remained a bafflement.

"I completely forgot about that!" Again I considered turning the truck around. "Melissa's been listening to the wrong tape. The visitor wanted Mr. Jackson's tapes. And he got them. They're missing."

What could have been on those tapes that was important enough to kill for?

"Fever Devilin!" Hovis was concerned. "Do you know you stopped your truck?"

"What?" I looked around. I realized that the truck was sideways in the road, and that I'd been talking out loud when I thought I'd only been musing silently. It happened occasionally that I would say things that I had only meant to think. Andrews referred to it as a bizarre by-product of self-absorption. I preferred to think of it more as a simple synaptic mishap.

"Sorry," I told Hovis.

"I'm damn cold," he complained, "and I need my little shack."

"Let me get you home."

I punched the accelerator and the truck jerked forward. We gained speed quickly. The engine complained and the tires objected. I was pushing sixty miles per hour on a dark, bending road that was unsafe at twenty-five.

"Look, Hovis," I insisted, "you've got to tell me everything you can think of that the man said to you. Really concentrate. It's important."

"Okay." He could see how serious I was. "Let me...okay. I got it."

That was all. He was silent.

"You've got *what*, Hovis?" I finally prompted impatiently.

"I got a way to pay you back," he answered firmly.

"You're going to tell me something that you just remembered about your conversation with the visitor," I said, excitement edging my words.

"No," he told me firmly. "I done told you most of what I can recall about that. This is much better. You come on in my house when you get me there. I got something for you."

No matter what I said or did after that, Hovis would not make a sound. His face was awash in holy satisfaction, as if he'd salved a painful burden.

We skidded up to his shack five minutes later. He was opening the door before the engine was off.

"Come on," he beckoned, practically running for his front door.

If I'd had my wits a bit clearer, I might have been wary of running into the dwelling place of a man who had pointed a loaded gun at me at least twice in one week. But he was so enraptured that it was hard not to be swept up in his Christmas-morning mood.

He hit the door hard, pounding it inward. I was only a few steps behind.

"Wait," he said, stumbling. "Let me get a light."

He knocked several things over in the nearly black room before he found a match, struck it, and lit an oil lamp. A hazy butter color filled the cold room.

"Okay." He looked up at me grinning like a jack-o'-lantern.

"Now, this is something I give to you in payment for what you done to get me out of jail. You got to swear that you'll not tell a living soul about it. Swear now."

"Look, Hovis—" I began, burning to get back to the police station.

"Damn it, Fever Devilin, swear this minute!" It was a command.

"I promise," I sighed quickly, "not to tell anyone whatever it is you're about to show me."

"Done, then," he nodded, satisfied with my halfhearted oath. His grin threatened to break his face. "Here it is."

Hovis set his lamp down on the floor close to the kitchen stove. He bent quickly and shoved his table aside. He dropped to his knees as if in prayer, and grabbed what looked like a nail that had not been completely pounded into his floor. With a deft tug and a sudden flip he pulled up several boards, and I realized that he was opening a trapdoor. A second later he had loosened a square of flooring and revealed a hole large enough for most people to slip down comfortably.

"Come on." He winked. "Follow me."

With that he dropped his legs into the hole and wiggled down it until only his head was visible. He grabbed the oil lamp and took it in, pulling most of the light with him down the hole. I moved to the edge of it, peering down. It appeared that the hole was short, and opened up into a much larger cavern.

I knew that if I thought about it too long I'd never follow Hovis, and it seemed important to him, at least in terms of paying me back, somehow.

So I sat on the floor, dangled my legs in the hole, and waited until Hovis disappeared below me and the light was almost gone.

"Slide on down," he encouraged. "It ain't a bad drop."

I took a deep breath and eased myself into the hole. I had the deliriously uncomfortable sensation of sinking into a bottomless pit just as my feet hit some solid flooring. With a bit of shimmying on my back, I was able to complete the journey down the hole and into what appeared to be a solid granite cave underneath Hovis's home.

The cave was well lit by the lamp, but Hovis busied himself lighting two more. The place was oddly homey. There were several wooden chairs, a strong table, a sleeping cot—and several dozen barrels that looked exactly like the ones in Red Jackson's favorite cave farther up the mountain.

At the side opposite from where I was standing, the cave opened up into a huge underground tunnel, also mostly granite.

I took another moment settling in before I realized the magnitude of Hovis's gift to me.

"This is your escape route," I concluded. "This is how you vanished from your house, how you got to my house so quickly, and without the sheriff seeing you."

"Right and right." The smile wouldn't leave his face. "This tunnel is the reason old man Jackson built the shack up there. It's the reason he hired me on to keep watch over it."

"To guard these barrels; to keep Mrs. Jackson from ever finding out about your hidden spirits." I nodded wisely.

His smile vanished at last, and he peered at me as if I were an idiot.

"Fever Devilin," he said slowly, his voice rich and deep, "this, what you're standing in, is the Jackson gold mine."

A sudden draft washed the air in the tunnel and the oil lamps flickered, making shadows and golden light dance on the walls of the cave.

"The *what?*" I thought I'd heard him incorrectly.

"The Jacksons," Hovis answered, a bizarre, stumbling parody of a tour guide, "first excavated their land in the last days of 1828. Everyone up here was talking about finding gold. The Jackson family home is, in a plain manner of speaking, sitting on a gold mine."

I looked around at the room. Bottles and kegs were in abundance. Gold, as far as I could see, was conspicuously absent.

"Are you sure this isn't just some story that the Jacksons—" I began.

"Old Mr. Jackson talked about it all the time." Hovis was turning angry—I had apparently challenged something important in his world. "Edna, too, but she was just...you want you some applejack?"

Without answer from me, he headed toward a row of bottles on the floor in front of some of the barrels. He scooped one up, unscrewed the top, and took a healthy slug.

"There," he whispered. "That's better."

"Hovis," I said carefully, "did Mr. Jackson ever say how much gold the family had gotten out of this mine?"

There was the grin again, returned at last. Hovis took another gulp from the bottle in his hand and sat down at the table between us.

"That's a good one." He shoved the bottle across the table, indicating that I should sit and join him in a cup of kindness.

"How's that?" I stood my ground.

He shrugged, took the bottle back. "That's one of the two or three best secrets of the Jackson family—about the gold. What you would call a well-kept secret."

People in Blue Mountain have always had, as far as I could

determine, a propensity for understatement. If, in fact, the Jacksons were actually gold rich, it would be the best-kept secret in the state. I had interviewed nearly everyone in town at one time or another, mining for my own kind of gold, and struck thick veins of information, stories that had lasted in oral tradition for hundreds of years. Never once had anyone mentioned or even hinted at a gold mine in our town. The so-called gold rush in Dahlonega had been short-lived and, beyond a lucky few, quite a disappointment. True enough, as I had mentioned to Andrews when we were there, tourists could still pan for gold in a Disney-style mill, and get a small vial of gold dust and sand to take home, so bits and flecks of gold were still around. But the big strikes that most people had hoped for had simply not appeared. Old-timers talked about looking in the hills in bear caves and hidden valleys, but it was idle gossip. Every once in a while someone would point out that if, after nearly two hundred years, thousands of people could still get a thimbleful of gold dust in a pan in Dahlonega, there must be a larger strain of the stuff farther up the mountains. Blue Mountain was certainly north of Dahlonega—but the entire notion was so absurdly far-fetched that I immediately began wondering why the Jacksons would foster such a conceit. I had no compulsion whatsoever to look around the cave for yellow stains.

Or was there something else hidden in the caves?

"Hovis?"

He looked up, swallowing.

"Would you mind if I explored this tunnel a bit?"

His grin got wider. "You want to see where does it come out. Sure. Fine. Go on. I'm warming up just fine right here."

"That's from the drink." I started toward the opening. "It's a false warmth."

"Don't you want you a lantern?" Hovis asked, holding up a box of kitchen matches he had magically produced. "Gets black as soot down there."

"Oh." I looked around, foolishly. "I guess that would be a good idea."

Hovis raised his head in the direction of several carrying

lanterns hanging on a nail close to the cavern opening. I fetched one and took it to Hovis, who lit it shaking his head at my witlessness.

Then, without the slightest fanfare, Hovis held up his pistol—the one I would have thought was still in my own jacket pocket.

"Thanks, by the way, for fetching this back to me." He stared at me evenly, all smiles gone.

"How the hell did you—"

"Felt it when I bumped up against you in the truck," he explained flatly. "When you clapped on the brakes. I pulled it out—you didn't notice. You have no idea how years in the nuthouse can make you light-fingered. I used to poach all sorts of things in the county home. Got real good at it."

"Be really careful," I stammered. "I think it's still loaded."

"It is." His eyes were locked on mine.

"Look, Hovis—" I began.

"You get on with your searching," he said, though I didn't quite understand what he meant. "I got what I need right here. Don't worry about me."

"I'm not worried about you."

Hovis cast a wary eye about his stronghold. "Come to think of it, maybe that boy already knew about this place. He did say something about a real good hiding place. You know how a Jackson is about a cave. Maybe I misremember."

He took another swig. He was done with thinking.

I was not comforted by his remarks, and stared down at the lamp he'd lit. "I'll just take this and head down the tunnel, then."

"Don't take too long," he warned me. "I'll be ready for bed by the time I get this bottle about halfway down. Hate to leave you all alone down here."

"Be right back," I assured him, backing away.

The thing about Hovis that made nearly everyone around him nervous was that there was no telling what was going on in his mind. Ever.

My lantern warmed, and sent a halo around me. I turned quickly and lumbered toward the darkness. Past the opening, the tunnel widened surprisingly, and the floor was well worn, easy to walk. The walls were a bit damp, but it was warmer in the rocks than I thought it should have been. Beyond the protective aura of the lamplight, the cave was invisibly black, so I moved slowly and made lots of noise. I had no intention of surprising anything else in a cave that night, and for some reason I thought a racket would keep Hovis calmer. After a bend or two, the ceiling lowered and I had to crouch a bit, uncomfortably claustrophobic. Just as I was about to decide to turn back, I thought I saw light up ahead.

I froze. I didn't know whether to extinguish my lamp, retreat, or make a bold foray ahead. I set the lamp down on the floor, thinking I should be ready for anything. I even considered calling out to Hovis.

I stood for a few moments more, peering through the darkness toward the light, before I realized that the light was not moving and was a completely different color from my lantern.

It was, in fact, moonlight.

I sighed, glad, for some reason, that Andrews had not witnessed my timidity, and stood. A few more steps ahead assured me that I was coming to an opening. I approached it cautiously, but the cave entrance, though covered over by rampant ivy that filtered the moonlight, was empty, and the moon was doing its best to light my way. From the outside the cave was perfectly concealed; there would have been no way for a passerby to know there was a cave entrance at all.

I emerged through a curtain of ivy into a field that looked familiar. Once I got my bearings I realized I was staring down the slope toward what would eventually become my backyard. The cave had cut past all the twists and turns in the winding road from my place to the Jacksons'. What would be the subterranean variant of "as the crow flies," I wondered. "As the mole crawls"? No matter. It was a very short cut around and down the mountain.

I turned back into the tunnel, headed for Hovis. Clever a tunnel as it was, evidence of gold was perfectly absent. Despite best efforts, my mind began creating questions. In no time I was back in the barrel room and ready to ask them. Alas—as he had on several other recent occasions—Hovis had disappeared.

I thought he must have gone back up to his shack, his cot. I blew out the lights in the cave and managed to grab my way up the hole through the trapdoor with only one lantern to guide me. Once I had achieved his kitchen area, however, I could plainly see that I was alone in the place. The mole had crawled; the crow had flown. I was standing alone in a very old shack. How and why Hovis had gotten away from me that night was a question I'd answer another day, I thought, suddenly exhausted. At that moment it seemed surpassingly sufficient that a murderer had been caught, and an innocent man had gone free—into the autumn night.

TWENTY-SIX

UNFORTUNATELY, AS ROBERT BURNS was wont to observe, even the best-laid plans of mice and men are often wrecked by the unintentionally brutish plow of circumstance.

Despite questions about the reasons for the murder, and my missing tapes, I was so tired that, in the end, I only went to the sheriff's office to pick up Dr. Andrews. We would both go home, drink, and fall asleep.

Unfortunately, when I pulled up in front of the place it appeared that Satan's Dominion had, in fact, broken loose and was doing its best to take over the sheriff's office.

Through the window I could see several deputies along with Melissa, as well as Andrews, all yelling at each other. Skidmore was on the phone and yelling louder than anyone, though I could not make out the words through the thick glass. It was a near-comic scene in its frenzy. Then I realized that the mayhem might well have been caused by something Andrews had said to Melissa, and what I couldn't hear were actually accusations and threats mostly directed at the only one from England in the room.

Much heavy sighing and personal aggravation got me out of the truck and into the fray. I couldn't have been gone for more than an hour, I thought. How could Andrews have caused so much fuss in so little time?

Inside, the room was impossible. Everyone was at top volume, and Skidmore was bellowing into the phone. I could only understand every third word, but it didn't take long to apprehend that Andrews was not, I thanked God, the cause of the ruckus. When Andrews saw me, he rolled his head violently and grabbed my arm.

"What the hell is—?" I began.

"He's gone!" Andrews blared.

"Who's gone?"

"He's *gone!*" Andrews repeated, louder.

"Swear to God if you'uns don't shut up now I'll take out my gun and spray this whole place!" The force of Skidmore's voice was like an explosion in the room. It left silence in its aftermath.

He saw me, pointed to Andrews, and then shook his finger violently at the door to the hallway. At first Andrews had no idea what it meant, but after a second he realized that Skid wanted us to go into the hallway so that Andrews could tell me what was going on.

Then Skidmore returned to the phone. "Okay, Donny, take it again, a little slower. You're not in trouble—this just now happened?"

The rest was lost to me because Andrews had dragged me into the dark paneled hallway.

"That wasn't Donny Deveroe on the phone with Skid, was it?" I asked, pointing backward to the office.

"Sh. Just listen to what happened," he commanded.

"What, then?"

"You're not going to believe it." Andrews was whiter than usual, which defied the laws of physics, or at least the dictates of English pigmentation. His blond hair was more disheveled than usual. He'd obviously been raking through it with his hands.

"Go on. Tell."

"The guy, the killer, Whatever-his-name-is Jackson—he's gone. He got out. He escaped." Andrews was in a weird form of shock. He was shivering, and his eyes were huge, pupils dilated.

"How is that possible?"

"No idea. Would you like to see?"

"See what?" I asked him.

"Come on." Andrews started down the hall away from the office, toward the cells. "You have to see this."

He opened the door at the opposite end of the hall, and I followed. All the cells were empty. He moved slowly toward one, then pointed.

I came up beside him and finally saw what he wanted me to see. In the exact center of the cot in the empty cell there was a perfectly folded Confederate uniform.

"That's all that was left when Melissa came back here to get some fingerprints or something." Andrews couldn't take his eyes off the uniform. "The cell was still locked."

"How could he have managed this?" I was a bit mesmerized myself. "And, I think I should mention: What's he wearing? It's kind of chilly outside."

"Obviously he had something on under the uniform." Andrews turned to face me. "But you haven't heard everything yet. That *was* Donny Deveroe on the phone. He just now called. The corpse is missing, too!"

"The corpse?"

"The victim, the other Jackson. Gone!"

"Wait." I was processing as fast as I could.

"Right," Andrews confirmed before I was really finished. "The killer is gone, and the body is gone. Melissa called Skidmore—"

"Wait." I tried again. "I thought Skidmore was here."

"He'd gone to shake up that Millroy character," Andrews explained, "with a fistful of forms and a relatively ugly demeanor."

"Millroy was still in his office?"

"I think so." Andrews wrinkled his brow. "I think that's what Melissa said—that he's on his way over."

"So he was just across the street," I said, more to myself than to Andrews.

"How does that matter?" Andrews was completely on edge. "The guy is gone and the body is gone, did you hear me say that?"

"Come on." I headed back to the office, and the noise.

Skidmore was still barking at Donny when I pushed though the door.

"He didn't just up and disappear, Donny," Skidmore was saying, a particular brand of rage threatening to break through the sheriff's thin fence of reason. "Somebody came to get him."

"I might know where he went," I told Skidmore.

He glared at me with an intensity that would have deterred a lesser mortal.

"Fever—" he began.

"I have a really good idea, Skid." My voice was steady, my eyes clear. "But we'd have to hurry."

He knew I was serious; he knew I had something in mind, even if it was a hunch. He'd trusted my guesses before.

Staring at me, he spoke softly into the phone. "Good-bye, Donny." He hung up.

Everyone else in the office followed his lead and stared at me.

"The killer is Boy Jackson," I said calmly, "the victim's older brother. Much as I would like to convince myself that the killer is actually Truck Jackson come back from the dead, locked in a wheel of killing and repentance, I believe I must come to the conclusion that we have all been, variously, duped by Boy Jackson. And I believe that the answers to this situation are sadly simple and base; they lead me to guess where he might be hiding right now."

Appropriately stunned silence followed.

Skidmore glared at me long enough to melt my resolve, but I didn't move. I really did think I knew where to find the killer.

"Most of the time," I said softly, "I'm right about this sort of thing."

Skidmore nodded once and said, "Let's go." That was the extent of his support, but the others fell in behind him as he headed out the door.

TWENTY-SEVEN

IMMEDIATELY WHEN WE stepped outside, Melissa Mathews made a sound I would not have thought possible from a human being.

"Melissa?" Skidmore glared at her.

"Look!" She pointed to an empty parking place. "That's where my squad car ought to be."

Two seconds later it was clear how the killer had escaped.

"My keys are gone." Her voice grated like granite rocks in a rolling barrel. She held up an empty flap on her gun belt.

"You can ride with me," Skid said, his voice cold.

Under her breath Melissa let go a carefully constructed string of profanities that soiled half the air in Georgia. I studied her face as she said them. She was a person who blamed herself first in every situation, though it clearly wasn't entirely her fault. I even considered that maybe Andrews had distracted her, made her nervous, thrown her off her guard.

"Come on," Skid said in answer to her whispered tirade.

Moments later we were speeding down a dark highway toward the killer's hiding place, toward the corpse of the victim. Andrews had agreed to ride with me in my truck. Skid and Melissa had taken one squad car; Crawdad and several other boys I didn't know were bringing up the rear in a third vehicle.

There was a certain surge of righteous leadership in my solar plexus when we'd all piled into our various conveyances. I had certainly saved the day, I thought. It had only taken Andrews seconds to quash the sensation.

"I guess you'd better be right about this," he said, buckling himself in. "If you're leading us all on a fool's chase, you'll never live it down."

That was enough to raise a demon of self-doubt—never far below any mask I wore.

So I turned the tables.

"You could probably figure this out yourself," I told Andrews casually, backing the truck out onto the road. "If the killer—"

"Boy Jackson," Andrews completed. "That's really his name?"

"All a part of the plot." I nodded. "If he's carrying or somehow transporting the dead body of his brother—as he has in metaphorical ways for most of this week, you understand—he can't possibly travel quickly. He'd want to go somewhere and hide out. So if you had to say—?"

"I guess he could be back in Red Jackson's cave?" he answered, but he didn't have any faith in his surmise.

"Someplace very much like it," I assured him. "I think I've just recently discovered the perfect place."

I roared up the back road that corkscrewed around the mountain. Mud and colored leaves sprayed behind me. The other cars kept a distance to avoid being splattered, but they were following at a good speed as well. As we rounded a particularly bumpy curve, I saw that we were near the spot I had in mind. Downward and to my left, the slope ran gently and eventually came to rest, roughly, at my back door. A bit up the slope and to the right, farther ahead, we would eventually come to the back of the Jackson place, near the spot where Skidmore had found the dead body. I was immensely relieved to see Melissa's squad car parked there.

I slowed the truck, turned off the lights, and peered at the side of the mountain to our right. Andrews was compelled by my intensity, and did the same.

"What are we looking for?" he whispered.

"A break in the ivy," I told him, barely audibly.

As I said it I saw the spot and stopped the truck completely. I looked back. Skid and the others had turned off their lights, too. They pulled up behind my truck as silently as they could manage. We all got out of our various rides. Skid got to my side immediately. Melissa went to her car, found the keys still in the ignition, and jerked them out with a violent gasp.

"Behind that wall of ivy somewhere over there," I told Skidmore softly, "there's a cave entrance that leads through a tunnel to a rock room directly underneath Hovis Daniels's shack."

Skidmore started to say something, stopped, bit his lower lip, and shook his head. He was realizing that the cave explained how Hovis had disappeared from him, and pulling together a few other deductions.

"He's got liquor down there," Skid said after a moment.

"He does. But he seems to think that the cave is actually a mining shaft." I watched Skid to see if his face would betray any recognition of the idea. It did not.

"What kind of mining shaft?" he asked me honestly.

"Gold."

"Oh, for Christ...you didn't believe that."

"I don't," I confessed, "but *he* was pretty convinced of it himself. Said that old Mr. Jackson had told him. Apparently they used to be drinking buddies."

"Hovis and Mr. Jackson?" Skid blinked. "I guess that would make a weird kind of sense. But you do know that there's no gold—"

"Look," I said impatiently. "The focus of the moment is that Boy Jackson and Son Jackson are in there, I think, and we should go get them."

Skid looked around for a moment. "This is right near where I found the body."

"Yes."

"Huh." He turned to the rest, who had assembled behind us.

"All right. I would like for Melissa to be the only one with a gun in her hand. I'm beside her. Crawdad, you're outside here, right at the cave entrance. Ted and Walter? You're back at your car, third line."

They moved immediately.

"Why is Melissa the only one—" Andrews began to ask me.

"She's the best shot," Skidmore snapped. "And she's got a reason."

Crawdad bobbed his head, but held up his hand. "Absolutely. Now, where is this cave entrance again?"

It was impossible to see. The upward slope, under a few loblolly pines and rampant weeds, was covered with near-black ivy. The opening was completely camouflaged.

"I'll take you to it," I volunteered.

"And then you'll wait out here with Crawdad," Skid said quickly. "I mean it. If you get shot and fall down, you'll really be in my way."

"I could wait in the truck," Andrews suggested. "I've already had my turn at being shot."

Melissa laughed. Crawdad just stared.

I was momentarily distracted from the task at hand by her laughter. It was like slow, clear water over round rocks—on a spring afternoon. Moonlight wasn't strong enough at that moment to make out her face, but something in her laughter made me think that Andrews had somehow set things right with her.

"Are you going to think about it some more," Skidmore insisted impatiently, "or are you going to show me to this damn cave?"

I headed immediately for the spot where I'd emerged from the cave. It was a bit more difficult to find, perfectly hidden. But in short order, there it was.

Melissa drew her pistol and a flashlight at the same time, checked her gun once, and started into the cave; Skidmore looked once to Crawdad, pulled out his own light, and followed her. Andrews had not moved from his place beside the truck. I stood there next to Crawdad, grinding my teeth.

Andrews stared at me, the occasional noisy blast of air escaping his nostrils. He finally rolled his head, said something very rude under his breath, and came over to me. "Let's go." That was all.

I turned to Crawdad. "I'm going in there."

"No," he said very kindly. "Sheriff would have my head."

"Think how much madder he'd be," Andrews explained reasonably, "if you shot Dr. Devilin yourself, right here. I'm guessing that's the only way you'll be able to keep him from going in. And, see, also: I have to go with him to keep him in line. I'm the only one who can do it. You see the predicament that you and I are in? It's not our fault. It's Dr. Devilin's. He's a very, very bad troublemaker."

"The thing is—" Crawdad began.

But before he could finish I was already through the curtain of ivy, and Andrews was right behind.

"Is that how he got here?" Andrews whispered. "How could he have used that to carry the body—"

The rest of his question was stopped by the blinding light of Skidmore's flashlight in his face.

"Turn right around," Skidmore whispered through clenched teeth. At that moment he was only the sheriff of a small mountain town, not anyone I knew: all business, no humor.

I folded my hands in front of me like a pallbearer; a more solemn face than mine did not, at that instant, exist on earth. My demeanor conveyed my determination, it seemed. In the ambient light I could see Skidmore shake his head, then turn back to his task exploring the dark cave. He knew I would follow.

Melissa was several feet ahead of Skidmore. I tried to stride quickly to tell him that the cave wasn't very long, and that Melissa would come to the cavern room very shortly, but it was difficult because the light was ahead of me, not where I was walking. I had to feel my way along the cave walls and step lightly, afraid I might trip over something.

Before I could reach Skidmore, it was apparent that his deputy had found her prize.

"Please don't move," I heard her say sweetly, her voice echoing a bit as if she were down a well. "I already had to shoot somebody else this week, and I'd rather not—"

A deafening explosion threatened to crack my eardrums, and I grabbed my temples. Skidmore dropped his flashlight. Andrews cursed.

Someone had fired a gun.

TWENTY-EIGHT

THE SILENCE THAT followed the gunshot seemed louder than the noise of the blast. My ears were ringing. No one was moving. I thought my heart might break out of its rib cage.

"Melissa?" Skid whispered desperately.

I held my breath. Andrews was frozen. No answer came.

"Boy Jackson!" Skidmore snarled at the top of his lungs, gun in hand. "This is the sheriff. You are under arrest. Put your gun down now and come here to me or I swear to God I will shoot you *very* dead."

More silence followed. I hadn't noticed, but Crawdad and the other two deputies had come into the cave. There was a good bit of illumination from their flashlights, and they were whispering to each other frantically, but I couldn't quite hear what they were saying.

Skid walked backward to me without looking and began talking in a loud voice. "What's that room like?" he demanded.

"Small, lots of barrels, a table, some chairs, oil lamps—but look, there's also the escape hatch into Hovis's shack just above him. Someone should—"

Crawdad was out of the cave and headed for Hovis's front door before Skidmore even looked at him.

"The man's got a great advantage in there," I continued. "There's no way you can sneak in on him."

"But he can sneak out." Skid sighed. "Ted, would you go on up behind Crawdad, back him up?"

Ted shot out of the cave after Crawdad.

"All right." Skidmore got his bearings. "Walter, would you go call the hospital and get an ambulance to come on out here? No siren, tell them."

Walter vanished.

"Seriously." Skid offered me the sternest expression I'd ever seen him wear. "You two stay right here, and I mean—"

Melissa appeared very suddenly from around the only bend in the cave. She looked like a shadowed specter in the light rising up from the cave floor where Skidmore had dropped his flashlight.

"Um," she offered sheepishly, "Sheriff? I think I just shot the dead man. The victim? And the killer, he might have gone up some sort of escape hatch—"

Skidmore grabbed her and crushed her to his chest. She was momentarily at a loss, then returned his embrace with equal fervor.

"God," Skidmore whispered. "I thought I might have lost you."

"I see that." Her voice was holy.

In that moment I realized that all the gossip about Skidmore and Melissa, no matter how hyperbolic, may have had some genuine basis in reality.

Their pose only lasted another second, and they were back to business.

"What happened?" Skid asked, full-voiced.

"You've got to come see this." She picked up Skid's flashlight and handed it to him.

She sauntered back toward the cavern room; we followed.

A single oil lamp was lit beside the body that was slumped over the table. It was dressed in a dirty army surplus coat, sported a pair of plaid cotton gloves, and gripped the pistol in one of its hands.

"I think Melissa's right," I surmised at a distance. "That's the victim."

"Why do you say that?" Skid stopped.

"Gloves," Melissa sighed.

"Those ridiculous gloves are from the Deveroe boys. Something about the victim's hands being swollen."

"Remember Donny told us about that?" Melissa asked Skidmore.

"They were going to fix it, he said." Skidmore nodded.

"I believe that the killer set up the body like this," Melissa offered, a little too loudly, "to hold us off. It worked—looked like a man with a gun pointed right at me. I fired a warning shot, you know, like I'm supposed to, but the body fell over. I knew something was wrong then, you know, because I didn't shoot the guy, and then I was afraid he had a heart attack or something. Anyway, so I looked around for a second and discovered that the killer probably got out that way."

She pointed to the trapdoor that led up to Hovis's kitchen.

"Damn it, I'm still having a hard time hearing," Andrews growled, sticking his little fingers in his ears. "Is anybody else?"

"I can't hardly hear a thing," Melissa agreed.

"Is that why you didn't answer me when I called out after you fired?" Skid asked.

"You called out?" She shook her head.

"Look, I'm the least qualified to ask anything of this sort," Andrews whined, "but shouldn't someone go after the murderer?"

Skidmore and Melissa both turned to him.

"You want to stick your head up that hole and see is he up there?" Skid asked. "I've got two people going up to the cabin and two more down here so he can't escape this way again. We're covered."

"Oh." Andrews looked at me.

"Should we...?" I pointed at the corpse, taking a step toward it.

"Leave that be," Skid said quickly. "God knows what Millroy will say now. I'd just as soon not touch it until everything else is settled."

There was a sudden commotion above our heads near the hole in Hovis's floor.

"Sheriff?" Crawdad called. "You down there?"

Skidmore shot to the place beneath the hole. "Did you get him?"

"No, sir," Crawdad answered. "Nobody here. Not even Hovis. You want to come on up?"

"Damn and damn," Skidmore mumbled, putting his gun back in his holster. "Come on."

Melissa put her gun away as well and was instantly at his side. Skid sized up the hole, looked around for a foothold, and worked his way upward. Melissa followed right behind.

I was still trying to decide what to do when Andrews poked me in the arm.

"Are all these barrels filled with that apple brandy?" His eyes were glistening; he was using his Church of England voice.

"Every one." I couldn't help smiling.

"What a wonderful country this is," he intoned, rapture in every word.

He went to examine one of the barrels with a reverence others would have reserved for the Grail.

I stood foolishly still, thinking that if I didn't say anything, the feeling of capturing the murderer would stay with me despite the fact that the murderer had actually gotten away—again.

"Hey," Andrews mumbled. "What's this?"

He leaned over one of the barrels, started to speak, then threw himself backward with a force so sudden he landed on his backside on the cave floor.

"Christ!" he stammered.

"What is it?" I started toward the place where he'd been.

A gravel-whispering voice from behind stopped my forward motion.

"He probably found a dead body."

I whirled around. The corpse that had been slumped over the table was now standing up and pointing his gun at me.

"Don't be too loud," he warned, a bizarre calm settling over his words. "I don't want to have to shoot everyone else."

Andrews made small involuntary noises that couldn't quite manage to become words, and I squinted hard at the face for a full minute before my pulse slowed a bit.

"Boy Jackson," I sighed. "Currently wearing a dead man's clothes—right down to the gloves."

"Dead body. Naked." Andrews tried to grab on to coherency, but his grip was not firm enough.

"Do you remember Red Jackson's telling us that his entire clan had supernatural hearing?" I asked.

"What?" Andrews seemed to think I'd lost my mind.

"I heard you coming, moron," Boy sneered. "Heard the whole caravan of cars."

"He heard the cars pull up outside." I smiled at the man with the gun. "He traded clothes with the dead man, hid the body behind those barrels, and hoped for the best. It was the act of a lunatic, really."

"Worked out pretty good." Boy began moving slowly around the table, coming toward me.

"So far," I cautioned him.

"But," Andrews stammered.

"Dr. Andrews has had a difficult evening," I explained to Boy.

"It was such a desperate thing to do," Andrews blurted out, finally rallying his cognition. "Anything could have happened."

"You forget that I don't care," Boy said. "I won't be here much longer. What was the line? I don't have to outrun the bear, I just have to outrun you."

Andrews, momentarily at a loss, suddenly seemed to remember the joke I'd told him.

Had Boy Jackson heard that, too, earlier in the evening?

"And the bear, in this case, is—?" Andrews began.

"Time," Boy explained. "Now, if you'll excuse me, I have to get back to my real home."

"But why did you go and get the dead body of your brother?" Andrews began.

"I'm through answering questions," Boy said calmly.

"If there's no body," I explained, "it's harder to prove a murder."

Boy declined to agree or disagree; he only indicated that I was to get out of his way by shaking the gun at me. It was persuasive. I stood aside. Andrews remained seated. Boy simply strode past us, waving his pistol, and disappeared into the tunnel that he thought would lead to his stolen car, and escape.

"Should we call out for Skidmore?" Andrews whispered.

I bit my lip, glanced at the hole that led up to Hovis's shack, and then abruptly started out the tunnel toward the escaping killer.

"Wait," Andrews said helplessly.

"Come with me," I whispered, moving faster, "or go get Skidmore."

Andrews began making his funny noises again.

I broke into a run toward the cave entrance. I couldn't hear anything ahead. I was trying to keep low, hoping I wouldn't bump into anything jutting from the cave wall or ceiling. I had plunged into obsidian, but I knew that once I gained the entrance of the cave I'd be able to see again.

A very few more steps brought me to vague light. The ivy was still quivering from Boy's egress. I followed, crashing through it, hoping he'd still be right there and I'd catch him off guard, tackle him, save the day.

The door to Melissa's car was open, but Boy was nowhere to be seen.

Odd dappled moonlight gave the landscape an eerie, unfamiliar sheen. I was near my own backyard but, suddenly, I seemed to be looking out on a stranger's land. I froze, hoping to take in the entire scene at once, sensing as much as seeing any movement.

I was startled first by a shushing of leaves a few yards down the hill, followed almost immediately, then, by the sound of Andrews breaking through the ivy behind me.

"Are you out of your mind?" he exploded.

"Sh!" I commanded in a stage whisper. "He's right down there!"

I pointed in the direction of the leaf sound.

"What the hell do you think you're doing?" he demanded.

"I think I'm chasing a maniac with a gun." *The truth is a complete defense,* I thought.

Of all things, that snapped Andrews out of the stupor that had begun moments before when he'd seen the dead body.

"Well," he told me, grinning, "as long as you have a plan."

There was another odd crackling of autumn leaves a little farther down the hill. Without any further thought, Andrews and I began running in that direction. I was trying my best just to run, not to think. I had no idea what Andrews was trying to do.

Stumbling across the road and seeing that my truck was parked where I'd left it proved reassuring. I couldn't have said why at the time, but there was something about it that convinced me I was still in my own reality, ridiculous as that may sound.

Once the road was crossed, the hill sloped downward at a fairly steep pitch and I didn't run so much as try to keep from falling down. Gravity pulled me toward the killer.

I could barely make him out, thirty or so yards below me, running and looking back. He knew I was coming. I wasn't sure why he didn't shoot his pistol, except that it was dark and I was moving in between trees. I didn't present much of a target. Flight was his best option.

I seemed to be gaining on him, possibly because he was looking backward so much, I thought. Something about his running seemed less a desperate escape than—what was it? Taunting? Did he want me to catch him? Or did he genuinely believe that he would vanish at any moment, leaving Andrews and me in the dark woods under an autumn's moon?

He came to a rock outcropping. It was too large to go over; he chose to go around in the direction of my house. If he kept going in that direction, he'd end up in my side yard just before the mountain took a more dramatic plunge downward toward the town below.

I realized that I had the advantage of knowing the terrain better than he did—maybe it was one reason I was traveling faster than he was. Also, he was being pursued; he chose the path and had to think about it beforehand, or at least make choices. All I had to do was keep my eyes on him and go.

As I veered around the rock outcropping, I realized I was close enough to hear him gasping for breath—perhaps only ten feet away. I also realized that my heart was pounding like a hammer on an anvil, and my chest felt like the anvil. I wouldn't be able to keep up the pace much longer.

People in the movies and on television manage those chases all the time, I thought deliriously. *How do they do it? No one has that much energy.*

Just as I was thinking it, a hulking mass hurled past me, took to the air, and flew directly into Boy Jackson. Andrews had tackled him. They rolled over several times, and Andrews wound up on top.

"Where's your gun now, you bastard?" Andrews taunted,

sitting on Boy's chest. Without another word, he balled his fist and slammed it like a pile driver into Boy's face.

"God bless!" Boy cursed. "You limey cretin. You broke my nose!"

"I'm just getting started," Andrews snarled.

"Dr. Andrews?" I asked, very politely, as I drew up beside them, panting. "Could I speak with you for a moment?"

"What?" Andrews had locked eyes with Boy, and it was a fight to the finish.

"I don't mind your pummeling this man," I said, my words absolutely breezy, "but you know how you get. Once you start, it's hard for you to stop, and if he's dead—"

"Get him off of me!" Boy demanded.

"Where's your gun?" I asked.

Boy was silent.

"Well, Dr. Andrews," I said, turning my back, "go ahead, then, but I can't watch. I can't take that much blood."

"It's in my right pocket!" Boy called out. "Right pocket."

Andrews rummaged for it, found it, and tossed it in my direction. I didn't catch it, and had to forage on the ground in the leaves for a moment.

"I'll take this back to Hovis." I grabbed it. "It is his."

"Yes," Boy admitted.

"Wait!" I stood bolt upright. "I gave this back to him tonight—or he took it. You didn't do anything to Hovis, did you? Because if you did—"

"Me?" Boy whined. "Why would I do anything to Hovis Daniels? Enough's been done to him already. He took off."

For some reason, I believed him.

"All right." I sighed. "Now. Dr. Andrews is going to continue to sit on you while I trudge back up the hill and fetch the sheriff. It may take a while, as I believe I have permanently compromised my lungs by chasing you *down* the hill."

"Not necessary," Andrews told me, and nodded upward, in the direction of the Jackson place.

I turned. Several flashlights were wending their way toward us.

"I'm not a moron," Andrews said to Boy. "Before I gave

chase, I hollered up into that shack for Skidmore and his cohorts to join us."

"Nice work," I beamed. "I don't know if I would have made it back up there before sunrise."

"God damn it!" Boy exploded. "Everything happens to *me*."

"Let's wait for Sheriff Needle," I offered politely, "before we discuss just what 'everything' means in that sentence, shall we?"

Boy moaned. It was his only answer, but it was a sound wrenched up from the center of his black heart.

TWENTY-NINE

MOMENTS LATER SKIDMORE, Melissa, and Crawdad were sliding on dead leaves descending the hill toward us. Skid managed a spot beside me; Melissa stood back and drew her pistol. Crawdad came close to the two men on the ground.

"Good," I announced. "You're probably wondering why I called this meeting."

Crawdad laughed.

Skidmore's neck snapped in Crawdad's direction. "Go put your handcuffs on the suspect, would you?"

Crawdad moved immediately, but Andrews refused to get up.

"I'm not moving." Andrews stared up at Crawdad. "This guy is slippery, and we can't chase him any more tonight. Dr. Devilin is old for his age, and he wouldn't make it."

"He needs to exercise more," Crawdad suggested.

"Look—" Skid flared.

"Let me tell you what I've pieced together," I said quickly, "and Boy Jackson can correct me when I'm wrong. When that's done, Andrews will get up, and we'll walk on down to my house for some apple brandy. I'll give my keys to Crawdad, and he can bring my truck around—if he wouldn't mind."

"Happy to." Crawdad's grin was vibrant even in the moonlight.

"Boy Jackson and his brother, Son, have been raised for years on stories of the lost Jackson gold mine," I began.

"There is no gold mine!" Skid interrupted.

"I know," I told him, attempting to soothe him. "This will take a lot longer if you interrupt."

"Why can't we take him back to the jailhouse and book him while you're telling your little story?" Skid asked tersely.

"Because I don't want to go back to your jailhouse again tonight," I snapped. "I'm tired, I'm hungry, I'm grouchy, and I was supposed to meet Lucinda for dinner. I haven't even called her. She'll be mad at me. I'm going to tell you what I know, and then you can do whatever it is you do."

I'd made my little speech with such force that everyone else nodded agreeably—even Boy.

"The psychology goes like this," I continued. "Boy was the oldest, but Son was the favorite."

"How on earth would you know that?" Andrews asked.

"A hundred reasons. Because 'Boy' is a de facto and merely descriptive name, whereas 'Son' is a possessive and affectionate name." I glared down at Boy. "I'm right. There's more to it, but I'm right about that."

Boy nodded.

"So when it came time for their father to pass on his inheritance," I told Skidmore, "a part of that inheritance was the mythology of the lost gold."

"Jackson fathers have told Jackson sons about the gold mine," Boy added, his voice pitiable, "for generations—since the middle 1800s."

"When they came of age," I guessed, "their father told Son about the gold instead of Boy—and told him how to get it, or how he thought it could be had. But Son didn't care, or didn't believe the stories. Son joined the army as a way out of the mountains."

"No!" Boy corrected with great vehemence. "My brother joined the army because he knew that our dad would like it. I joined up, too, but Dad was only proud of Son—with apologies to Freud and, I suppose, Oedipus."

"You both joined the army?" Andrews was baffled.

"He joined for honor," Boy growled. "I joined because I thought that the army would be a good place to get at my brother. I could talk to him, find out about my inheritance. Not to mention: Lots of things can happen in combat."

"You saw combat?" Andrews was also fascinated.

"We requested it." Boy closed his eyes. "Lots of things can happen in combat."

"Where?" Andrews asked.

Boy opened his eyes and looked at me imploringly. "Can you get this oaf away from me? It's humiliating explaining my life trauma with a large blond man sitting on top of me."

I could see his point.

"Andrews," I announced, "please let Crawdad put handcuffs on Boy Jackson and come over here, would you?"

Andrews didn't move. "Can I at least hit him a few more times?"

"Fine by me," Skid said, to no one in particular.

"Seriously." Boy looked directly at Andrews. "Get up."

Andrews sighed heavily, but stood.

Crawdad moved immediately to put handcuffs on Boy's wrists.

"Let's do his ankles, too," Melissa suggested. "Just in case. He is a slippery one."

She tossed her cuffs. Crawdad caught them with one hand, barely looking—even in shaded moonlight. He pulled another pair of cuffs from his own belt, locked them together with the ones Melissa had given him, and then attached the free cuffs to Boy's ankles. He was hobbled.

Boy rolled onto his side, sat up, looked around at his congregation, and nodded his head.

"Well," he wheezed, "I really gave it the old...what they used to call the old college try. But you've got me now. Where should I begin?"

Andrews folded his arms. "First of all, I don't even believe you're a Jackson. I've met several in the past few days. Your diction and demeanor don't remotely resemble anyone else's I've encountered—to say nothing of your vocabulary."

Of all things, that broke Boy Jackson. His face clouded pitiably. I could see a wave of despair wash over him. His shoulders sank and his eyes welled. To make matters worse, I knew what he was about to say—I could feel it in my cells.

"I know." The sound of his voice could have made an angel weep. "Do you have any idea what it's like to be smart in a cabin at the top of this mountain? What it's like to have brains in a school that prizes football scores and doesn't even notice test scores? An ability to lift big rocks was the clincher in the selection of the star student in our high school. My father thought of me as a freak of nature. He had no idea what to do with a boy who wanted to read instead of hunt, talk instead of drink. Son, on the other hand, was everything a Jackson should be: bold but polite, dumb as a stick of butter. When we went to join up, he had trouble spelling 'army.'"

"No." Andrews deliberately interrupted Boy's near-weeping confession. "I don't give a damn about your psychological motivation—especially since I think you're making it up to glean sympathy from Dr. Devilin, whose life story you could be telling. Shove all of that, and I mean shove it as hard as you possibly can. I want to know about the murder and the gold mine. That's the plot. Screw the Freudian digression."

Boy's head snapped upward as if he'd been slapped.

I took a breath to speak in Boy's defense, and Andrews shot me a look that momentarily prevented me from exhaling.

"All right, then." Boy shifted his body, sitting more upright. "The facts are these. Son and I are deserters from the army. I spent a moment or two in an army hospital as what is still sometimes called a Section Eight, not mentally competent to serve. Son visited me, and I escaped, taking him with me. He barely knew what time it was, let alone what we were doing. I told him we were on a mission, a special mission. We made it to Atlanta, recently. Do you want to hear those details?"

"God!" Andrews shrieked.

"Why were you in the hospital?" Crawdad asked softly.

"Well," Boy answered, a sickening grin growing in his face, "someone had it in for Son. Someone had fragged his digs in combat, and there was an incident of friendly fire that almost killed him. He was scared. Someone said I did it. Someone who, incidentally, didn't make it out of a firefight, so I probably would have gotten off."

"I see." Crawdad didn't realize it, but he'd taken a small step back, away from Boy.

"We came back up here with a plan," Boy continued. "My

plan, of course. Son was too stupid to build a plan for coming in out of the rain."

"It involved the gold mine," Andrews prompted impatiently.

"It did." Boy's grin reached monstrous proportions. "Son had decided to tell me about the gold mine, because he was afraid. I'd convinced him that he would die without passing on the secret. He only knew it was on the Jackson property somewhere. The rest was up to me."

"Son knew one other fact," I corrected. "He knew that Mr. Jackson and Hovis Daniels were drinking partners."

"Yes, that was part of our father's secret." Boy seemed astonished. "How did you know?"

"A guess." I tried not to look into his eyes. "It's not something you would have been interested in, since it involved the family business. You were not, as you hinted, interested in the family business."

"Any moron can crush an apple and let it rot," Boy responded.

"So your first visit, once you were back here in the mountains, was to Hovis." I stared up at the moon.

"It was. Son waited outside in the cold because I told him he'd give us away. He would have, too. He knew he was stupid."

"And Hovis wove a spell," Andrews said slowly. "He can do that; he did it to me."

"It was amazing." Boy lit up, agreeing. "Hovis Daniels is a genius storyteller. When he gets going, you're not listening anymore, you're transported. I wanted him to talk all night. He told me about the Civil War and World War II and all the Jackson troubles—God!"

"And you remembered—or partially remembered—most of what he'd told you," I interrupted, "to use on me."

"Yes, but you have to see the point of what I'm...what I'm getting at."

His eyes bored into my skull.

"Brothers in the Jackson family," I admitted, still avoiding eye contact, "do seem to have been somewhat at odds for the past several generations. You've certainly bought into that, if that's what you mean."

"At odds?" he snapped. "We've killed each other like snakes and rats. Damn. You don't get it. I *am* all of those brothers. I am the genetic property of those men. I am the reincarnation of every murderer in the family. I am doing my best to fulfill my—"

"Stop!" Andrews commanded. "I'm stopping you before you get all wound up in another poetic departure from the point. Get to the murder and the gold! Christ!"

Boy laughed out loud. "Well. Aside from the great family history, I learned from Hovis that only two other people around here might know something about the location of the gold mine."

"Lucinda Foxe," I interrupted, "because she was the last person to see old Mr. Jackson alive—he might have offered her some sort of deathbed information. And me, because I tape-recorded him talking about all sorts of things. You thought he might have, at the very least, given some clues as to the location of the mine on my tapes."

"But you called the sheriff before I could lull you into giving them to me," Boy said, "so I had to come back and steal them."

"We thought you were looking for your own tape," Melissa told him, shaking her head.

"My fault," I confessed. "But the facts are that Hovis told you nothing about the mine, Lucinda didn't know anything, and you left my place on Monday night without Mr. Jackson's tapes. So what happened?"

"Son wanted to go home," Boy answered. "He'd had enough. He kept trying to tell me there was no gold, that it was just a story—the moron. We had an argument about it. One last argument in a long line. I lost my temper and I killed him; killed him good. I realized while I was doing it, in fact, that I'd really been looking forward to it. I wish I could convey how absolutely great it was to watch him die—with that stupid expression on his face. He had no idea what was happening to him. I could have carved a better man out of a banana."

"And the rest of this," Skidmore butted in, "was smoke and mirrors, based on the stories you'd gotten from Hovis. You've got a good memory. You were deliberately going on about being Truck Jackson or someone else to keep us off guard—"

"To weird us out," Andrews suggested.

"Or to set up an insanity plea," I said, finally looking him in the eye, "in the event that you got caught."

Skidmore and Melissa nodded together, realizing that everything that Boy had said could confirm a psychological defense strategy at his trial.

"You got that from Hovis, too," I guessed.

"You really are batting a thousand," Boy said, genuine admiration in his voice.

"Hovis has been ill-treated by life," I responded; "but he's also learned that when times get really tough, a free place to stay with three meals and a nice warm bed can be had for the price of a bit of his sanity—something he doesn't care that much about in the first place. Or at least not since his wife died."

"Correct on all counts, I believe." Boy nodded. "Getting thrown into the state hospital was like a spa vacation to Hovis. Check and see, but I believe most of his incarcerations there have been during the winter months."

"Wait," Andrews interrupted again. "You had several contingencies, I'm realizing. You stole Hovis's pistol, and you killed your brother right outside Hovis's house. You intended to frame him for the murder."

"It worked, too." Boy's smile was now threatening to crack his skull—it was a terrifying expression. "For a while. It would have worked better, but I didn't have a chance to move the body closer to Hovis's hovel. I was going to, but Fate had a better plan. I saw Hovis—and someone else—emerge from the side of the mountain in the moonlight that night. Out of nowhere. I thought for a second I was hallucinating. I threw myself to the ground. They didn't see me. And that, ladies and gentlemen, is when I found the cave which I believe is the lost Jackson gold mine—the one that's crowned at the other end with the shack of Hovis Daniels."

"*That's* how you found it," I whispered, nearly to myself. "Hovis didn't give it away."

"But, then, what was all this changing clothes with the dead man to make everyone think that *you* were dead?" Andrews asked, almost to himself. "You did that twice."

"I've had enough," Skidmore said suddenly. "And I'm getting a chill. Let's have this man on his feet and take him into the office, hear?"

Melissa and Crawdad moved instantly.

"No," Andrews protested, "there's a lot more to be said *here*."

"Such as?" Melissa sighed.

"What was he thinking when he changed clothes with the dead man? Who was Hovis with on Monday night? A million things. I'd like a much better explanation of these wild identity impersonations."

"Don't care and don't care," Skid said, obviously tired. "He confessed to the murder in the presence of witnesses, and he's already set up a possible defense to it. My work is done. I don't have an idea what you think your work here is."

Crawdad and Melissa had Boy on his feet and began to move him up the hill toward the cars. It was going to take a while, moving the way Boy had to with his feet cuffed together.

"Dr. Devilin," Boy said softly, "could you come here for a moment?"

I looked at Skid. He shrugged.

I took the few steps to Boy's side cautiously. He inclined his head ever so slightly toward my ear and whispered several sentences.

"What?" I couldn't hear him properly.

"Okay," Skidmore complained, "that's enough. Take him up the hill."

"What did he tell you?" Andrews asked me.

"I'm not sure." I stared at Boy's back.

"I'm saying that's *enough* for one night!" Skid declared, a bit too loudly.

"But—" Andrews began.

"Okay, but no kidding," I said to Skidmore, "can I give my keys to Crawdad and have him bring my truck over to the house?"

Skidmore looked at Andrews and, exhausted as they were, they seemed able to share a moment of derision at my expense. It got Andrews out of his questioning mode, at least for a moment.

"Sure thing, Mrs. Devilin," Skid answered, barely holding

back the laughter. "Do you need somebody to walk you to your door, too?"

Andrews burst out with what is sometimes ridiculously called a guffaw.

"No," I told Skid, "but you could arrange to bite me sometime in the near future."

"When I get around to it." He turned and followed the others up the hill. "Crawdad, do you mind being a delivery service?"

"Sure thing," he answered immediately.

If it had been anyone else I wouldn't have tossed my keys on a dark night in the middle of the woods, but I knew Crawdad. A silver flash in the air caught his eye, and he had my keys with one hand.

"I'll leave it in your yard in a few minutes." He waved.

Andrews watched them go for a moment before he completely realized they were leaving. "Is that it?"

"What more do you want?" I asked.

"Hey!" Skidmore called back in our direction. "You realize that there is no gold, right? That's not a gold mine under the Jackson place."

"I want something like that," Andrews responded to my question. "More punch line."

Boy stopped dead in his tracks. He was only ten yards away, but I had trouble hearing him.

"Yes, it is," he insisted, the grin gone from his face at last. "It is a mine."

"No," Skid said firmly, "it's not. It was excavated in 1861, long after the so-called gold rush up this way. It was blasted. It's in the county record."

"What was it, then?" Andrews called up to Skidmore.

"You know how, in the 1950s, lots of people thought it was a good idea to build a bomb shelter in the backyard?" Skid's voice carried well in the night air. "When the Civil War looked like it could get up in these mountains, some people built their own version of that—a place to hide out from Yankees, an escape route from the house. Just in case. That's what the cave is. I say again, it's in the county records. I never knew exactly where it was, but old Sheriff Maddox, he spent some time looking for it. He might have believed the gold stories, or he might have been looking for illegal spirits. Couldn't say. I'm content to leave it a secret."

"But," Boy stammered desperately, "what about the gold?"

"There isn't any gold," Skidmore said, laughing at Boy. "There was never gold. Are you serious? A lost gold mine? Really?"

"Did Mr. Jackson say anything to Lucinda before he died?" I asked. "Did you find anything on his tapes?"

"I didn't get a chance to listen," Boy answered, his voice a ghost.

"Hey, where are my tapes?" I called.

"No gold." Boy's voice was the merest echo of a human sound.

"There's no gold." Skidmore was still laughing.

"You moron," Andrews whispered.

If Boy Jackson heard Andrews, he did not respond. He remained silent for the rest of the time his captors spent dragging him up the hill toward the police cars.

"God." Andrews leaned back on a tree.

"At least," I agreed.

"Can we go home now?" he asked, looking around. "Didn't you say that your house was around here somewhere?"

"Down that way." I nodded my head in the general direction of my place.

"Downhill: good." He began trudging his way toward my house. "And believe it or not, what I'm looking forward to is a cup of espresso, not a glass of that stuff."

"Had enough apple brandy for one visit?"

"Not nearly. But right now I think it might make me...something. Sad, maybe." He turned to look at me. "You know?"

"It's a season of melancholy," I answered, following him down the hill.

I drew up next to him, and we walked together in silence for a while—or staggered, grabbing pine trees on the way down, in a lumbering gravity-driven dance.

When the back of my house came into view, Andrews offered up an audible sigh of relief.

"I just realized it's cold," he said. "All that chasing around and the excitement of everything momentarily obviated the temperature, but damn."

"Nice phraseology."

"Boy Jackson did all this for gold that never existed," Andrews said softly—he'd obviously been mulling during our silence. "Killed his brother, shot me, terrorized a town. He's not just playing at being insane the way Hovis might be. He really is psychotic."

"You're not wearing a watch, are you?"

"What?" He stopped still. "No fancy summary, no poetic comparisons—nothing about how Boy's journey is like—"

"I was supposed to have dinner with Lucinda, and I wanted to know how late I was."

"Oh." He glanced at his wrist. "It's after ten-thirty. Will she still be up?"

"I have to call her." I quickened my pace.

"Jesus," Andrews said softly, falling in behind me, "you really are engaged."

The sound of his voice was strange, a tone I'd never heard from him. I'd nearly made it to my back door before I understood that his comment was, for him, a realization. Because my life would change sometime in the future, so would his. A bachelor's best friend could easily become a married man's occasional guest.

THIRTY

FRIDAY MORNING CAME late for me. I slept into the early afternoon. I woke up to the sound of voices downstairs in my house. Sunlight slanted through my bedroom window like a solid wooden beam, something propping up the impossibly bright autumn sky, and I wondered, as I was emerging from the dream state, if it would be possible to climb that beam—all the way to God.

I sat up, realized I'd slept in my clothes.

"Dr. Devilin!" Andrews called. "Are you awake?"

"Define awake," I mumbled.

"What?"

"Coming," I yelled down the stairs, sliding my legs over the side of the bed.

Generally given to insomnia, my muscles were reacting weirdly to an excess of sleep. I glanced at the watch on my nightstand. I'd slept for eleven hours. I had to hold on to the footboard of my bed for a moment to get my balance before launching myself through the door toward the stairs.

"You have company," Andrews announced.

I stood at the top of the stairs for a moment, unable to focus my eyes on the couple standing in my front doorway. As I came down, clutching the banister for all my life, I was certain my eyes were playing tricks.

"Hello, Hovis," I said uncertainly. "And Simple."

I made it to the bottom of the staircase and still didn't believe it. Hovis and Simple, arm in arm, were standing at my front door. Hovis had changed his clothes. His shirt was stunningly clean. Simple, on the other hand, was still dressed in her floor length Empire dress, though her dyed red hair was worn a bit more loosely than before. She was carrying a modern purse made of black leather.

Andrews had slept in his clothes, too. His hair had exploded about his head, and he wore an expression that surely mirrored my own absolute befuddlement.

"It was her idea to visit you," Hovis said quietly, his face different than I'd ever seen it. "Hope we're not a bother."

"No," I managed to say, still holding on to the stair rail. "Please come in."

I glanced in the direction of the living room sofa, and they headed for it.

"Can I offer you some—"

"We can't stay." Simple offered me a beatific smile. "We came to thank you, and I brought you a present."

They sat together on the sofa. It was clear that their relationship was…something more than I would ever have thought, but I couldn't wake up enough at that moment to completely decipher the riddle.

"Imagine my surprise," Andrews said, taking a seat on one of the overstuffed chairs opposite the sofa. "I haven't been up for more than ten minutes myself. I was doing my best to fathom the espresso machine, when suddenly there came a tapping, tapping at my chamber door."

Andrews, clearly, was not awake yet, either.

"And look who it was," he continued. "Hovis and Simple." He said it as if I hadn't yet seen them.

"Yes." That single syllable was all I could think of. I took the other large chair opposite the sofa and hoped that our guests would be more coherent than I would be—though their histories could not support that probability.

"We'll get right to the point, then," Simple said. "First, thank you for getting Hovis out of jail. Second, I brought you these."

She reached into her black purse and pulled out a packet of papers tied with a thin pink ribbon. She smiled at Hovis and then reached out her hand, offering the packet to me.

I leaned forward, completely at sea, and took them from her.

"There." She nodded once. "Done and done."

"What—" I began.

"It's every last letter I have from one brother to another," Simple announced to the room, smiling. "Accompanied by several photographs. I believe you will know what to do. I wish to have all wandering revenants put to rest. You will do that, won't you, Dr. Devilin? For my peace of mind."

Her voice was like steam from an old-fashioned teakettle, and Hovis looked at me so expectantly that I was forced to nod my assent.

"Oh, good." Simple sighed, obviously greatly relieved. She smoothed her dress over her legs, preparing to stand.

"Just...just a moment, please," I stammered, marshaling all my faculties. "Could I settle a few things in my head? Would you mind?"

She glanced once at Hovis, and her smile grew to solar proportions. "I expect you're wondering about me and Hovis."

"At least." Andrews gulped.

Hovis beamed. "We've been sweet on one another for a great many years now," he said softly, "but we like to keep it from Edna."

"You know how she is," Simple told me, each word rife with compassion.

With that phrase, the way it was said, and in an electric shock of comprehension, I realized that Simple tolerated Edna out of love and pity—which was quite a different scenario than anyone might have imagined. From the outside it seemed the other way around, that Edna tolerated Simple out of a perverted notion of Christian duty and some cruel joy worthy of Miss Havisham. It was clear to me at that moment that all of Edna's petty tortures were lost on Simple.

She was a candle flame of a spirit—and a woman in love.

"Poor thing," Hovis added, shaking his head.

"But, I mean, how did you two—?" Andrews finished the rest of his sentence by simply moving his hand in the direction of the happy couple.

"I was a mess when Barbrie died," Hovis answered immedi

ately. "Came to live with her kin. Edna did her best to make me feel worse, but every harsh word and cold-eyed look was counterbalanced by Simple. She's a God's angel and that's the truth."

"Hovis," she whispered sweetly, and momentarily placed her head on his shoulder.

"After a while," Hovis continued, "we become friends, me and Simple. And then friends become more than that. Now—"

"We can't decide if we should wait until Edna dies to get married," Simple began.

"Or to just go on and do the deed," Hovis concluded, a short laugh escaping between words, "to finish Edna off that way."

True, I thought, Edna might actually die if she saw Hovis and Simple get married.

"So that's where you were last night," I said, my head finally clear. "You went to tell Simple you were out of jail."

He nodded.

"And on Monday night," I continued, guessing, "you and Simple met, and you escaped out the cave. You wanted to tell her about your visitor."

"Pretty good," Hovis grinned. "Good guess."

"How did you know that?" Andrews scowled, leaning forward.

"Boy said it last night," I told him. "He said he wanted to move Son's body closer to Hovis's place, but he saw Hovis and someone else come out of the side of the mountain. That's how he discovered the secret cave."

"Oh, right." Andrews sat back. "Wait. Simple—about that cave. Everyone in the Jackson family thinks there's gold in it?"

"Not really," she answered sweetly. "My father's grandfather, I believe, started the family tradition about gold as a device to control his more unruly relatives. Some of the Jacksons, you may know, are not as sophisticated as the ones who live in the big house on the hill."

Hovis explained. "It was, 'Do what I say and I'll put you in the will and leave you a portion of the gold mine; go against me, and I'll cut you out.'"

"Money is power," Simple went on. "The idea of wealth is often as good as gold. After that first generation, the tradition was to tell the oldest son the truth so that he could use the power of it—wield it over the more wild sons."

"But," Andrews protested, "that's not what happened. Boy Jackson is older, and the father told Son Jackson—right?"

"Boy was always strange," Simple answered. "Their father didn't care for Boy because of it. That part of the family— they're a feral tribe; live in great seclusion at the top of the mountain, up close to where Hovis and Barbrie lived. They work for Red, now, most do. But they've always had their secrets up there. Who knows what they really do? I only heard, because Edna would go on about it, that Boy was considered wrong. He was too smart for this part of the world. That can be quite a curse."

Simple's eyes momentarily shot some sort of arrow into my brain, and then she looked down just as suddenly, the old sweet smile returning to her lips.

"I guess you ain't heard," Hovis said softly, looking at his knees, "but Boy Jackson killed hisself this morning. Swallowed a sock and stopped breathing. He's dead."

Andrews and I stared in stunned silence. Before either of us could muster a response, Simple clapped her hands once.

"We've taken up enough of your time," she concluded and stood suddenly. "We'll be going."

"Oh." I got to my feet.

Hovis got up and offered his arm to Simple, and they moved toward my front door.

"Don't forget," she said to me, pointing at the papers she'd given me.

"Right," I assured her. "I'll do it today."

She nodded once, and without another word from anyone, they were out the door and into the bright yard. Andrews and I watched them go; they were whispering to each other and never once looked back.

"Boy killed himself." Andrews couldn't believe it.

"I guess he wasn't setting up an insanity defense after all," I suggested foolishly.

"Or the news that there was no gold was too much for him?"

"Not really, do you think?"

"You've got to feel a little…" Andrews stammered, grappling with his diction, "I mean, what did he say? Something about smart being the last thing you'd want to be in a cabin at the top of this mountain."

"I can attest to that." I sighed, trying not to think about the fact too much. "You don't want to be smart in that kind of environment, or too aware of a larger world."

"He didn't really seem like a person from Red's family."

"Not that you want to indulge in any stereotypes," I chided.

"Well, it's too much for me before I've had my coffee," Andrews mumbled, turning toward the kitchen. "And I can't figure out your sodding-damn *machine* to save my life."

"It reacts to temperament," I explained to him, closing my front door and shivering a bit. "It knows you're cursing at it."

"Shut up." He sat at the kitchen table.

I went to the machine, turned it on, grabbed an unopened bottle of Evian from the counter, opened it, and poured it into the water reservoir.

"Only the best," Andrews mocked.

"Do you want espresso or not?" I glared at him.

"Sorry. Christ." He rubbed his eyes.

I pulled an air-tight canister of black, oily beans from the cupboard and poured half a cup or so into the machine.

"Oh," Andrews continued, "and PS: What the hell is all that about those letters or whatever it was she handed you? What's that?"

I still had them in my hand. I laid them on the kitchen table.

"Let's have a look, and I'll tell you," I answered him.

The espresso machine began to click and grumble, warming the water in its well. I pulled out two demitasse cups and set them down beside it.

"I need espresso," Andrews moaned.

"Help is on the way," I told him, distracted.

I looked upward, searching the exposed beams in the kitchen for the proper solution to Simple Jackson's trouble concerning her packet of letters.

"Here we are," I said to myself, finding what I wanted.

I reached up for several sprigs of sage. I'd just put them up there, and they weren't completely dried, but they would have to do. I took them in hand and sat down before the letters.

"Let's see what we have." I reached over to untie the bundle.

"I don't want that in my coffee," Andrews told me in no uncertain terms, pointing at the sage.

"Right," I assured him, "that's for what we find in this package."

I pulled the pink ribbon and spread out the letters and pictures in front of us on the red tabletop. Some of the pages were near decay, but all of the photographs were well preserved.

"Wait!" I said suddenly, jumping up from the table.

"What?" Andrews got up, too, staring down at the documents on the table as if there might be something poisonous on them.

"I nearly forgot," I told him, going to my good leather coat. "I lifted a photograph of Truck Jackson from the woman at Sunset Acres or whatever that place in Atlanta was called."

"You stole a picture from a poor old woman?" he asked, astonished.

"I thought I'd need it."

I got to my coat, found the picture there, nicely defined by its brown wood frame. I hurried back to the kitchen, taking the photo out of the frame.

"Now, then," I said, taking my seat again.

Andrews remained standing. "What the hell—"

"Shh!"

I reached behind me for the box of kitchen matches on the counter next to the stove and brought it to the table. I pulled one out and struck it.

"You're not going to burn these letters and pictures," Andrews said, a bit shocked.

"Would you sit down?" I instructed him, staring into the match flame. "I'll tell you what I'm doing."

I reached for the sage branches and lit several of the leaves. Instantly the scent of burning sage assailed the room. I held the smoking branch and touched it to the bottom of the photograph of Truck Jackson I had in my other hand. The smoke curled up around the picture; the burning part of the sage singed the border.

"Come over here," I whispered to Andrews, "if you're not going to sit down. You should probably see this anyway."

He moved silently, as if he might disturb some malevolent creature.

"Watch the face," I told him.

As the smoke continued to rise up in tiny silver-gray columns, the face in the photograph seemed to change—he seemed to breathe, to exhale. The expression became relaxed; the image blurred slightly. Truck Jackson even appeared to look upward for a moment, almost sighing. Then the face dulled, grew lifeless and gray.

"Done." I nodded once. "Did you see?"

I tossed the photo onto the tabletop.

"It looked like...his whole aspect seemed to...what the hell was that?" Andrews was barely audible in the bright kitchen.

"Simple would tell you that the sage smoke has released any remaining spiritual content from the photograph. That's why his expression changed. His spirit was leaving the image. Anything left of that person that might still have been clinging to the picture has now been set free, and won't need to return over and over again looking for bits of itself."

"What do you believe?" he asked.

"Oh, I'm with Simple," I assured him, "but another explanation, much less reliable because it is merely scientific, has to do with the way the sage smoke affects the oxides coating the picture—something about removing a thin layer of something. But, I mean, did it look like his face changed or not?"

"It did," he agreed, but the skepticism had already returned to his voice. "Nice trick. Nice parlor gag."

"If you say so."

We performed the magic on every single piece of paper and every last photograph. It took over an hour, and we'd both had several cups of espresso by the time we were finished. Each thing that Simple had given me bore a singe, a brand from the spice—and smelled like burnt sage.

The fact that every face in every photograph was the same—the very image of Boy Jackson—was left unspoken. Or perhaps Andrews simply hadn't notice the resemblance as much as I had.

"I'll give these back to her somehow," I told Andrews, sitting back with my fifth espresso. "She'll see them and smell them and her mind will be at ease."

"Good." Andrews sipped from his cup. "Maybe you could hand them over to Hovis and he could smuggle them into her house. I wouldn't want you going back in to speak to Mrs. Jackson again anytime soon. Not unless you had a crucifix and some holy water."

"Agreed," I replied serenely.

"It's nice about Simple and Hovis," Andrews announced in an uncharacteristic bit of romanticism, "don't you think?"

"I do." I wondered what was on his mind, feared he might be leading to some odd discussion of my relationship with Lucinda, a relationship I could not possibly have conveyed in human language.

"I was just thinking," he mused, staring down into his cup. "Hovis has his girl, you have yours—where's mine?"

He looked up, grinning.

"Good," I sneered, "I thought for a second there you might actually be thinking of someone besides yourself."

"Me?" he protested.

"But as it happens," I told him, holding up an index finger, "I may have the perfect person for you, and I don't know why I haven't thought of it before now."

"Wait." His face clouded. "I was mostly kidding, you realize. I'm not exactly the mountain-girl type."

"In the first place, you have no idea what that type is," I assured him, "and in the second place, you're an idiot."

"Really?"

"I'm telling you," I said, standing and going to the kitchen phone, "I have the *perfect* girl for you. I'm calling Lucinda. We'll go for a late lunch. She doesn't eat until two on Fridays."

"Stop, now." He was verging on panic. "I do *not,* emphatically, want to be set up on a blind lunch date with one of Lucinda's crook-tooth cousins!"

"I repeat my assertion," I sighed, dialing the phone. "You're an idiot."

"Fever!"

"Hey!" I said into the phone, "you answered. Let's go to lunch. Yes, twice in one week. I have a lot to tell you. But look, Andrews is coming along, so I'm wondering if you could invite the redoubtable Nurse Chambers to come along with us?"

"Nurse?" The hint of a smile touched Andrews's lips. "She's a nurse?"

"Yes," I said into the phone, "I thought you'd agree it was a good idea. Since Etta's will be closing soon, do you just want to—all right, see you in a bit."

I hung up the phone.

"All set," I told Andrews. "I'd clean up if I were you. We're to meet at one of Blue Mountain's finer eateries."

"Will she be wearing her uniform?" Andrews asked with an expression generally reserved for adult films.

"You're a troubled man."

"Rule, Britannia," he answered.

Little more than half an hour later, we were stomping out of my house and into the bright autumn afternoon. Crawdad, true to his word, had left my truck right where I usually parked it, with the keys in the ignition. Though the air was crisp and the sky was decidedly autumnal, we were bound for a more spring-time assignation: romance and fine dining.

THIRTY-ONE

THE EMPLOYEES' CAFETERIA at the hospital was nearly empty by the time Andrews and I arrived. Lucinda and Nurse Chambers were waiting for us. Andrews exhausted a great many jibes at the expense of the concept of cafeteria food—much to the delight of Nurse Chambers.

We spent a pleasant fifty minutes talking and dining on warmed-over canned corn and stringy Salisbury steak. Ultimately, the company made the food inconsequential, according to Andrews.

"No perfect meal can rescue an awkward moment," he declared, in a fit of poesy, "but fine companionship can save even the worst cuisine."

Nurse Chambers beamed.

"Well, then," Lucinda announced, standing, "I'm back to work."

"I'll walk you," I said immediately, picking up my tray.

We left the two combatants locked in mortal flirtation. As we placed our trays on the moving conveyer belt that led to the kitchen, Lucinda cast a surreptitious glance their way. They were equally matched players, and it was a wonderful game to observe.

"Hard to tell which one's worse," she whispered.

"I know," I said proudly. "I think they're perfect for each other."

"It was a little embarrassing to watch."

"A *little?*" I asked loudly. "They set up a flurry of libidinous intentions that is eating a hole in the ozone layer high above our planet even as we speak."

She nodded, heading for the elevator. "That was really something about Simple—her wanting you to burn out the spirit from those letters and photographs."

"Yes, it was."

The elevator came. It was packed; we were barely able to squeeze on. Someone complained loudly that the elevator had gone down instead of up. No one else commented, but the crowd prevented me from telling Lucinda everything I was thinking. Still, I couldn't hold back the most troubling item in my array of worries.

"Every single face in every photograph," I told her softly, "looked exactly the same. I don't mean there was a strong family resemblance. It was the same person."

"Who?"

"The man who was in your kitchen on Monday night."

The elevator door opened and several people pushed by.

"I don't know," she said vaguely, her mind already back at work. "Old photographs—they don't really give you much to go on. I have a picture of my great-aunt Rose that looks exactly like me in high school."

We arrived at her floor, stepped out, and I kissed her on the cheek.

"We'll talk about it more tonight?" She smiled very comfortingly.

"All right."

She was off.

I decided to take a moment to myself instead of going back down to the cafeteria right away. In the first place, the prospect of watching Andrews and Nurse Chambers bat the ball of innuendo back and forth was thoroughly unappealing, but more than that, I wanted a chance to think about what Boy Jackson had whispered to me just before he'd been carted up the hill the night before.

I took the stairs down to the front door of the hospital but realized there was no happy place outside to go with my thoughts, the hospital being located on a highway and surrounded by a parking lot. After a moment of disconcertion, I remembered that there was a small chapel on the first floor.

I found it in short order; it was empty and still—perfection. I took a seat on a firm wooden pew with a burgundy cushion.

At the front of the chapel there was only a translucent window, no pulpit or altar, and light was pounding through, battering the floor with white clues, hints of celestial observation.

I sat there for a moment. The sound of my breathing was loud in all that silence. I did my best to reconstruct exactly what Boy had said.

"A womb in Blue Mountain, a classroom at university, a distant star, a brothel in Chicago, a battlefield, a gold mine in a small Georgia town—they're all distractions. You have to stop being distracted if you want to get off the wheel of birth and death."

And Boy had made his bid, earlier that morning, to climb off.

Perhaps my knowledge of his suicide was making his ideas haunt me. I'd always thought that after all was said and done, when the play of this life was over, we only had to take off the costume, rid ourselves of the bloodlike rouge on our faces, turn out the lights in the theatre, and go home—to our true home and rest.

But suppose we bought Boy Jackson's ideas, thoughts stolen from dozens of world religions. Suppose that when the course of any particular life is done, we do find ourselves wandering down the corridors of Eternity. What is it that we should do in order *not* to be distracted, as Boy had said, so that we won't be sucked into a womb somewhere and be born again—another time around the wheel? How could we be swept, instead, onward toward light, toward God, toward our true home, a place not made by human hands? How are we released from the wheel of death and rebirth?

The answer in most religions, I thought, is simple—you just have to be willing to let this life go, once and for all. You have to refuse the distractions.

That's a great secret in those dozens of religions. If you want to leave this world behind, all you really have to do is say good-bye, and really mean it—and you will be released.

But there's the rub, I thought. If Boy Jackson kept coming back, maybe he didn't really want to leave at all.

As for myself, I started thinking about all the things I'd misin this life, a few of the things that would distract me, keep me, coming back. They, too, were surprisingly simple.

I would like, just one more time, to see a certain maple tree in the autumn of the year. I also need one more meal of *poulet sauté à la Provençale;* one more hearing of the second movement of Beethoven's seventh symphony; one more night in bed and talking with Lucinda; and five more minutes of light on the waters of the Seine. Maybe then I'd be able to say good-bye and go away from the beauty of this earth for good.

But not today.

My first realization as I sat there in the hospital chapel was that if I really wanted to be released from an endless cycle of cause and effect, I would have to stop causing things to happen, and to stop being affected by other things. I would have to genuinely want to get off of the wheel.

My second realization was a little disturbing but also, for some reason, profoundly warming. Obviously I was someone who understood the way off the wheel of Time. I just wouldn't do it—not yet.

Apparently, I was enjoying the ride.

Lord Nathaniel Lindsay,
the heir to the earldom of St. Auburn.

She could not believe it, could not quite take in
that her dangerous rescuer in Nay with his scarred
body and quick reflexes was now a dandified lord,
known across all of England for his wealth and his
power, the family lineage stretching back across the
centuries.

Away from the stares she was feeling a lot better,
and his coat was warm, her shivers lessened by the
touch of wool. She could smell him, too, here in the
carriage, the depth of him and the strength, and if
her sister had not been right there beside her she
might have breathed in further, allowing the colors
of his beauty to explode inside, tantalizing and
teasing.

The scent of a man who could ruin her.

* * *

Scars of Betrayal
Harlequin® Historical #1188—June 2014

Author Note

Scars of Betrayal is the third book in a series about three friends, Nathaniel Lindsay, Lucas Clairmont and Stephen Hawkhurst.

The themes of family, protection and betrayal have been features of all three stories (*Scars of Betrayal*, *Mistletoe Magic* and *Mistress at Midnight*).

I hope you enjoy Cassandra and Nathaniel's story.

Sophia James

—

Scars of Betrayal

HARLEQUIN® HISTORICAL

Recycling programs
for this product may
not exist in your area.

ISBN-13: 978-0-373-29788-7

SCARS OF BETRAYAL

Copyright © 2014 by Sophia James

Printed in U.S.A.

**Available from Harlequin® Historical and
SOPHIA JAMES**

Fallen Angel #171
Ashblane's Lady #838
Masquerading Mistress #875
*High Seas to High Society #888
The Border Lord #946
ΔMistletoe Magic #973
*One Unashamed Night #1005
*One Illicit Night #1046
Gift-Wrapped Governess #1063
"Christmas at Blackhaven Castle"
Lady with the Devil's Scar #1102
*The Dissolute Duke #1132
ΔMistress at Midnight #1152
ΔScars of Betrayal #1188

*linked by character
Δlinked by character

**Did you know some of these novels are also
available as ebooks? Visit www.Harlequin.com.**

SOPHIA JAMES

lives in Chelsea Bay, on Auckland, New Zealand's, North Shore with her husband, who is an artist. She has a degree in English and history from Auckland University and believes her love of writing was formed by reading Georgette Heyer in the holidays at her grandmother's house.

Sophia enjoys getting feedback at www.sophiajames.net.

Chapter One

London—June 1851

It was Nathanael Colbert walking down the wide staircase of the de Clare ballroom.

Cassandra Northrup knew it was him.

Knew it from the bottom of a rising horror and an unmitigated relief.

The same strength and height, the same dark hair, shorter now but every bit as black. She could barely take a breath, the guilt and the anger that had been stored inside and hidden for so long seeping out, winding her with its intensity.

Lord Hawkhurst, the heir to the Atherton fortune, descended beside Colbert, laughing at something Colbert had said. Disbelief made Cassie dizzy. Why would he be here in such company and dressed like an English lord? Nothing quite made sense, the wrongness of it all inviting disarray.

Shaky fingers closed around the small pottery shard

that she always wore around her neck, the heavy beat of blood in her ears making her feel sick. What could this mean for her?

Carefully, Cassie opened her fan so that it covered most of her face and turned from the trajectory the pair were taking. She had to leave before he saw her. She had to escape, but that was becoming harder as shock numbed reality. Maureen clasped her hand and she was grateful for the anchor.

'You look pale, Cassandra. Are you feeling sound?'

'Perfectly.' Even her sister did not know the exact details of what had happened in the south of France all those years ago, for she had never told another soul. A private torment, the details locked in shame.

'Well, you do not look it.'

The will to survive was flowing back, the initial jolt of shock receding under reason. She doubted Colbert would recognise her at a quick glance and resolved to leave as soon as she was able to without inciting future question.

Future. The very word made her stiffen. Could she have a future if he saw her? She felt as if she stood in the ballroom in nothing but the clothes he had once found her in, the events from almost four years ago searing into memory, all anger and fear and regret.

No. She was stronger than this. In a moment she would walk farther away, into the throng of people, carefully and quietly so as to draw no attention towards herself. She had become adept at the art of camouflage within society, the skill of obscurity in a crowd almost second nature to her now. It was how she had sur-

vived, washed back into the world she had not thought to be part of again, with its strict observance of manner and rule.

Cassie's gown mirrored her anonymity, the plain dove-grey unremarkable. All around the well-heeled young ladies bloomed like flowers, in yellows and pinks and light blue, tucks, ruffs, frills and flounces adorning their bodices, sleeves and hems. Her widow's weeds were another way to hide in full view from the notice of others.

As five seconds went past, and then ten, she started to feel safer, beguiled by the noise and movement of the very large crowd.

Everything is all right...it is still all right.

Her eyes scanned the room, but Colbert was nowhere to be seen. 'I should not have come, Reena,' she said, turning to her sister. 'You manage these things with far more acumen than I. It is simply a waste of my time to be here.'

Maureen laughed. 'I hate these functions, too, but Mr Riley was adamant about the invitation being for the both of us, Cassie, and his purse is a generous one.'

'Well, as he did not show himself I doubt he would have known if I had stayed away.' She needed to leave, needed to walk towards the door as though she did not have a care in the world. The ache inside intensified.

Once she had loved Nathanael Colbert, right from the bottom of her broken life.

The thought of what had happened next made her swallow, but she shook it gone. Not here, not now. Fixing a smile on her face, she listened to Maureen ramble

on about the beauty of the room and the dresses and
the lines of the small shaped trees set up near the band
to give the appearance of a natural grotto. A fantasy
world where anything was possible, a kinder world
away from all that was sordid and base and unclean.
All about her happy banter tinkled, the easy discourse
of people with few worries in life apart from what they
would be wearing to the next social occasion or the
generous inheritances they had garnered from the latest deceased relative.

A strange sound above caught her attention. Looking up, Cassie noticed one of the chandeliers lurch-
ing sideways, each globe spluttering with the motion.
Would the whole contraption fall? The horror of the
thought that perhaps it was about to made her mouth
dry. Had anyone else seen? To shout out would draw
the attention to herself she so wanted to avoid, but the
death of some unknowing soul would be for ever on
her conscience if she did not.

'Watch out! The light is falling.' Her raised voice
carried easily across the chatter around her, but a group
of girls to one side were not quite fast enough. With
a crash the ironwork of the leaves and flowers caught
the leg of a beautiful young blonde woman.

In the chaos Cassie hurried forward, kneeling almost at the same time as another did, bumping his arm
against hers.

Monsieur Nathanael Colbert.

Close.

A touch away, unbridled fury in his eyes. Grey eyes
with just a hint of blue. Unbalance hit and she felt

a jagged panic, her glance taking in the line of his jaw bissected with the scar she'd wrought upon him. When she had last seen this it had been opened red, blood falling across his shirt in a stream. She wanted to reach out and trace it, as if trying through touch to let him know of her sorrow. He would not welcome it, she knew, but betrayal always held two sides and this was one of them.

The sheer physical presence of him scorched at sense but as the woman's cries mounted the healer in Cassie prevailed. She could not deal with the ramifications of meeting Colbert now. Looking down, she placed her palm hard against the back of a shapely knee and the flow of blood waned, red dribbling on to her skirt, the colours mixing strangely.

'Keep still. There is a lot of bleeding and it needs to be stemmed.'

At that the young girl sobbed louder, grasping her free hand in a vice-like grip.

'Will I die?'

'No. A person is able to lose at least twenty per cent of their blood and still feel only mildly cold.'

Leached grey eyes raked across her own, no warmth whatsoever within them.

'How much would you say I have already lost?' The wounded girl's voice was breathless with panic.

Cassandra made a thorough check of the area, lifting her ankle to ascertain just what lay beneath.

'A little over half that amount so it would be wise to stay calm.'

The answering terrified shriek left her ears aching.

'I am certain that it is not so severe, Miss Forsythe.' The voice she had recalled in her dreams for so many years was measured. It was the first time she had ever heard him speak in English, the clipped and rounded vowels of privilege hanging upon every word. She hated the way her heart began to race.

'Well, as your shin has been badly cut it is most important that you...'

A shadow to one side caught her glance and then all she knew was black.

Sandrine Mercier? Speaking perfect English? Downed by the last falling remains of the chandelier and completely unconscious. The loathing he felt for her swelled in his throat. Another deceit. A further lie.

She lay on her side, her eyelashes magnified against the shining de Clare tiles, her hair shorter now, and sleeker. She was still thin, but the beauty once only promised had blossomed into a full and utter radiance.

Damn her.

He wanted to stand and turn away, but to do so would invite question and in his line of work such scrutiny was never a good thing.

Lydia Forsythe was screaming at the very top of her voice, but the bleeding from her leg had almost subsided. A doctor had scurried over as well as her distraught mother and a myriad of friends. Around Sandrine just himself and one girl lingered, an uncertain frown on her forehead and tears pooling in dark-brown eyes.

Albi de Clare, the host of the evening's entertain-

ment, crouched down beside him. 'My God, I cannot understand how this has happened for the lights were installed only a few months ago and I was assured that they were well secured. If you can lift her, Nathaniel, there is a room leading off this one that should offer more privacy.'

Another touch. A further punishment. When Nat brought her into his arms blue-green eyes snapped open to his, horror blossoming into shock.

'I never…faint.'

'You didn't this time, either. The debris from the chandelier hit you.'

She was vibrating with panic, her head turned away. On reaching the smaller salon he placed her down upon a sofa, wishing he could leave.

'My personal physician is amongst the guests, Nathaniel, and he is examining Miss Forsythe as we speak.' Albi de Clare's tone was muted and Nat saw Sandrine's glance flicker round taking in the presence of the others who had followed them in. 'He will come to you next.'

'No.' Already she had swung her feet onto the floor and was sitting there, head in her hands. 'Please do not take the trouble to call him, my lord. I should not wish for any fuss and I already feel so very much…better.' She stood on the word and just as quickly sat down, beads of sweat garnering on her top lip.

Albi, however, was not dissuaded from seeking a medical opinion, hailing his doctor as he came into the room.

'Mr Collins, could you have a look at this injury?

The back of the patient's head has connected with the remains of the lamp.'

The old physician placed his leather satchel on a table next to the sofa before making much of extracting a pair of glasses from an outer pocket and perching them across his nose.

'Certainly, sir. Those outside intimated that you were one of the first on the scene, Lord Lindsay. Was the young lady unconscious for long after this happened?'

'Only for a few seconds,' Nat answered. 'As soon as I picked her up she seemed to regain her mind.' Plain and simple. Everything complex and twisted would come later.

Sitting, the physician held up two fingers.

'How many do you see, my dear?'

'Four.'

The woman beside Sandrine shook her head and worried eyes went quickly to her.

'Three. Two.' Guessing for all her heart's worth.

'Do you have a headache?'

'Just a small one.'

'Is your right arm numb?'

She did not answer as she dug her nails into the flesh above her elbow. So numb she did not feel it at all?

At the doorway a group of interested onlookers had gathered, though Sandrine, marked by the blood of the other victim, looked bewildered and vulnerable. She had also begun to shake. Badly. Taking off his jacket, Nathaniel tucked it about her, for shock could

be as much of an enemy as injury. He hated himself for bothering.

'Warmth will help.'

For the first time he noticed the pendant at her throat, the one he had given her in Saint Estelle before she had betrayed him. The grey fabric of her bodice had drooped to reveal the roundness of one breast and the tall woman who had followed them in knelt down to pull the gown back into place, the skin on her cheeks flaming.

'Keep still, Cassie.'

Cassie? The anger in Sandrine's eyes was magnified by a deep and startling verdant green.

Albi's voice broke into his thoughts. 'If you bring Miss Cassandra this way, Nathaniel, a carriage is waiting. Miss Northrup, if you would collect her reticule and follow us?'

Northrup? Maureen and Cassandra Northrup? These were two of Lord Cowper's daughters? Hell.

A shutter had fallen across her averted eyes at the mention of her name, wariness and the cold surge of alarm evident.

'I need no extra assistance, my lords. My s...sister can help me to our conveyance.'

At that the other moved forward, pleased to be able to do something in the room with all its onlookers and the stark awkward silence.

Within a moment they were gone, both of them, only the scent of some flower he could not name left behind.

Hemlock? Foxgloves? Lily of the Valley? All poisonous and lethal.

Albi watched them go, a frown across his brow. 'The Northrup sisters may have their detractors, but it is my reasoning that with just a little time and effort they could knock the Originals from their perches. They seldom come out into society, but by all accounts their mother was beautiful, too. I think there's a third sister, married and living in Scotland. You will need to get your jacket back.'

'Perhaps.' Nat's tone was flat.

'They live in Upper Brook Street and you can't miss Avalon, the Northrup monstrosity.' Nathaniel did not wait to hear more, walking out instead to the ballroom and being instantly surrounded by the newest and most beautiful débutantes of the season.

Young women of impeccable taste and good breeding, their pasts unblemished and flawless. He smiled as he moved into their midst.

Cassie's head ached and her neck stung. She knew the wax from the candle globes had burnt her, but there had been too much to ascertain about the health of the young woman to spend time thinking about her own injuries.

Lord Lindsay.

The physician had called him that and de Clare had named him Nathaniel. Lord Nathaniel Lindsay, the heir apparent to the earldom of St Auburn. She could not believe it, could not quite take in that her dangerous rescuer in Nay with his scarred body and quick

reflexes was now a dandified lord, known across all of England for his wealth and his power, with family lineage stretching back across the centuries.

Away from the stares, Cassie was feeling a lot better. The borrowed coat was warm, her shivers lessened by the touch of wool. She could smell him, too, here in the carriage, the depth of him and the strength and if her sister had not been right there beside her she might have breathed in further, allowing the colours of his beauty to explode inside, tantalising and teasing.

The scent of a man who could ruin her.

As the skin at her neck smarted beneath the heavy silk swathe of her gown, Cassie longed to take off her clothes and walk into the shallow pool at Avalon. Her mother's pool, Alysa's gown still upon the hook and her beads draped across a single gold-leafed chair. Papa had insisted on them staying.

'Lord Lindsay has only recently returned to the social scene, but I have heard tales about him.' Maureen watched her sister carefully, and Cassie knew that she was curious.

'Tales?'

'He is said to have spent some time in France. You did not meet him there, did you? I gained the impression he knew you.'

Cassandra shook her head, the truth too terrible to speak of, and she pulled the jacket in tighter.

He had remembered her, she knew he had, and under the smile she wore to keep Maureen's avid cu-

riosity at bay she also knew she must stay as far from him as possible.

When the lights of Avalon came into view she was pleased to see them.

Nathaniel Lindsay watched the house through the night, the moon upon its burnished roof outlining the gables and the attics.

The Gothic style here in London. Even the trees had taken their cue from the stark outline of the building and dropped some of their leaves as though it were already winter.

He should not be here, of course, but memory had made him come, the calm treachery of Sandrine's voice in Perpignan as she had dispatched him into hell.

'I barely know him, but he is a soldier of France, so better to leave him alive. But do as you will, I really don't care.'

Swearing, he turned away, but not before the pale outline of a figure holding a candle moved through the second floor, down the stairs and out on to the porch, peering through the black of night.

There was no way she could have seen him, tucked into the shadow of a brick wall. But for a second before she blew out the flame the world seemed bathed in a daylight born from the candle, and she looked right into the heart of him.

Then there was only darkness and she was gone.

Sometimes his world disgorged ghosts from the past, but never ones as worrying as Sandrine Mercier. He'd been twenty when he had entered the heady en-

clave of espionage, his grandfather's distant demeanour a catalyst for him to become part of a close group of men who worked for the British Service.

His friend, Stephen Hawkhurst, had already been involved and when Nathaniel's grandfather, the Earl of St Auburn, had ranted and raved about his uselessness as the only son and heir, Nathaniel had joined as well.

Determining the likelihood of the rumoured marriages between the Spanish and French crowns had bought Nat into France, his expertise in both languages allowing him an easy access to the higher and lower echelons of its society.

The ties that were being forged between Britain and France were becoming strained, leaving a climate of suspicion and fear in their wake. A united block would render England isolated and make the battle for the control of Europe all that much harder to fight.

Nathaniel's mission had been to test the waters, so to speak, and to liaise with the handful of British agents who had been assimilated into the French way of life, keeping an eye on the workings of a political ally who was hard to trust.

Determining the likelihood of such an alliance had taken him to the court of Madrid. Returning across the Pyrenees to make his way up into Paris, he had been alarmed at the murder of one of his agents whilst on the road to Bayonne. Finding those culpable had led him into an enclave of French bandits near Lourdes.

And it was here he had met Sandrine.

* * *

Cassandra knew he was there, quiet and hidden in the night. It had been the same at Nay, when in the chaos the spaces around him had been full of a certain resolve, menacing and dangerous, the last afternoon light glinting in the dark of his hair as he had taken apart the minions of Anton Baudoin.

She shivered at the name and thought of Celeste. A week sooner and her cousin might have lived as well, might have been taken too, through the long night and back into warmth. She did not know Lord Lindsay was an Englishman then, dressed in the trousers of a peasant, skin sliced with the marks of war. The French bastards had not known it either, his accent from the warmer climate of the south and the musical lilt of a Provençal childhood masking all that he was.

Nathanael. He had named himself such. Monsieur Nathanael Colbert. At least part of his name had been true. His hands had been harder then, marked with the calluses of a labouring man and none of the softer lord on show. He still wore the same ring though, a gold chevron against blue, on the fourth finger of his right hand.

A movement behind made her turn.

'Ma'am, Katie is crying and Elizabeth cannot make her stop.'

One of the Northrup maids stood in the doorway, a heavy frown evident, and, forcing all the thoughts from her mind, Cassie hurried inside.

Tonight, chaos felt close and Lord Lindsay was a large part of the reason. She understood that with a

heartfelt clarity as the cries of the girl took Cassie from her revelries.

Elizabeth, her maid, was in the annex at the rear of the house, the place used when women needed a bed for a night or two before being rehomed elsewhere. She was bathing the burns on thin legs, angry red scarring beneath the soft brush of cotton; another small casualty owing her injuries to London's underbelly of child trading.

'Did you make certain your hands were clean, Lizzie, before you touched the wounds?'

'I did, ma'am.'

'And you used the lime solution?'

'Just as you told me, ma'am.'

The smell of it was still in the air, sharp and strong, crawling into all the corners of the room. Alysa, Cassie's French mother, had always been a vehement supporter of cleanliness when dealing with sickness, and such teachings were ingrained within Cassie.

Soaping up her hands, she dried them and felt the child's forehead. Fever was settling in, the flush in Katie's cheeks ruddy and marked. Removing a clean apron from a hook by the door, Cassie put it on and went to stand beside Katie, the folds of the child's skin weeping and swollen. Carefully Cassie took plump shards of green from her medical cabinet and squeezed the slime into a pestle and mortar before spitting into the mixture. Mama had shown her this and the procedure took her mind back unwillingly into a different time and place.

She had been almost eighteen years old, still a girl, still hopeful, still imbued with the possibilities of life.

Completely foolish.

Utterly naive.

And painfully heartsick from the guilt of her mother's death.

Chapter Two

Nay, Languedoc-Roussillon, France—October 1846

The stranger had forced himself into stillness. She could see it as he stood, his heart and breath calmed by pure will-power as he raised his blade and stepped forward.

So many were dead or dying; such a little space of time between the living and the departed and Cassandra expected that she would be next.

A knife she had retrieved from the ground felt solid in her fist and the wind was behind her. Left handed. Always an advantage. But the rain made steel slippery as he parried and the mud under her feet finished the job. As she fell her hat spun off into the grey and her plait unfolded into silence. She saw the disbelief in his eyes, the hesitation and the puzzlement, his knife angling to miss her slender neck, pale against all else that was not.

The shot behind sounded loud, too loud, and she

could smell the flare of powder for just a second before he fell, flesh punched with lead.

He could have killed her easily, she thought, as she scrambled up and snatched back her cap, angry with herself for taking another look at his face.

Mud could not mask the beauty of him, nor could the pallor of death. She wished he might have been old and ugly, a man to forget after a second of seeing, but his lips were full and his lashes were long and in his cheek she could see the dent of a dimple.

A man who would not bring his blade in battle through the neck of a woman? Even a fallen one such as she? The shame in her budded against the futility of his gesture and she went to turn away. Once she might have cared more, might have wept for such a loss of life and beauty and goodness. But not now.

The movement of his hand astonished her.

'He is alive.' Even as she spoke she wished she had not.

'Kill the bastard, then. Finish him off.'

Her fingers felt for a pulse, strong against the beat of time, blood still coursing through a body marked with wounds. Raising the knife, she caught the interest of Baudoin behind and, moving to block his view, brought the blade down hard. The earth jarred her wrist through the thin woollen edge of his jacket and she almost cried out, but didn't.

'Take your chances.' Whispered beneath her breath, beneath the wind and the rain and the grey empty nothingness. Tonight it would snow. He would not stand

a hope. Cleaning the knife against her breeches, she stood.

'You did well, *ma chère.*' Baudoin moved forward to cradle the curve of her chest, and the same anger that had been her companion for all of the last months tasted bitter in her mouth.

She knew what would come next by the flare in his eyes, knew it the moment he hit her, his sex hardened by death, blood and fear, but he had forgotten the knife in her palm and in his haste had left her fighting arm free.

A mistake. She used the brutality of his ardour as he took her to the ground, the blade slipping through the space between his ribs to enter his heart and when she rolled him off her into the mud and stood, she stomped down hard upon his fingers.

'For Celeste.' She barely recognised her voice and made an effort to tether in her panic. The snow would help her, she was sure of it; tracks could be hidden beneath the white and the winter was only just beginning.

'And…for you, too.' The sound was quiet at first, almost gone in the high keening of wind, a whisper through great pain and much effort.

Her assailant, his grey eyes bloodshot and sweat on his brow underpinning more extensive injuries. When he heaved himself up, she saw he was a big man, the muscle in his arms pressed tight against the fabric of his jacket.

'You killed him too cleanly, *mademoiselle.*' Not a compliment either as he glanced at Anton Baudoin. 'I would have made him suffer.'

He knew how much she had hated him, the prick of pity behind his eyes inflating her fury. No man would ever hold such power over her again.

'Here.' He held out a silver flask, the stopper emblazoned with a crest. 'Drink this. It will help.'

She meant to push it back at him, refusal a new capacity, but sense kept her quiet. Half a dozen days by foot to safety through mountainous land she held no measure of. Fools would perish and she was not a fool.

The spirits were warm, slung as the metal had been against his skin. The crest surprised her. Had he stolen it in some other skirmish? She could feel the unfamiliar fire of the whisky burn right down into her stomach.

'Who was he?'

'A bandit. His name was Anton Baudoin.'

'And these others?'

'His men.'

'You were alone with them?' Now his eyes only held the savage gleam of anger. For him or for her, she could not tell. Against the backdrop of a storm he looked far -more dangerous than any man she had ever seen.

As if he could read her mind, he spoke. 'Stop shaking. I don't rape young girls.'

'But you often kill men?'

At that, he smiled. 'Killing is easy. It's the living that's difficult.'

Shock overtook her, all the horror of the past minutes and months robbing her of breath and sense. She was a murderer. She was a murderer with no place to run to and no hope at safety.

He was wrong. Everything was difficult. Life was

humiliating, exhausting and shameful. And now she was bound for hell.

The tall stranger took a deep swallow from the flask before replacing the lid. Then he laid his jacket on the ground, raising his shirt to see the damage. Blood dripped through a tear in the flesh above his hipbone. Baudoin's shot, she thought. It had only just missed killing him. With much care he stooped and cut a wide swathe of fabric from the shirttails of one of the dead men, slicing it into long ribbons of white.

Bandages. He had tied them together with intricate knots in seconds and without pausing began to wind the length tightly around his middle. She knew it must have hurt him to do so, but not in an expression, word or gesture did he allow her the knowledge of that, simply collecting his clothes on finishing and shrugging back into them.

Then he disappeared into the house behind, and she could hear things being pulled this way and that, the sound of crashing furniture and upturned drawers. He was looking for something, she was sure of it, though for the life of her she could not imagine what it might be. Money? Weapons?

A few moments later and he was back again, empty-handed.

'I am heading for Perpignan if you want to come.' Tucking a gun and powders into his belt, he repositioned his knife into a sheath of leather. Already the night was coming down upon them and the trees around the clearing seemed darker and more forbidding. The cart he had used to inveigle his way into the

compound stood a little way off, the wares he plied meagre: pots, pans and rolls of fabric amidst sacks of flour and sugar.

She had no idea as to who he was or what he was or why he was in Nay. He could be worse than any man here ever had been or he could be like her uncle and father, honourable and decent.

A leaf fell before her, twirling in the breeze.

If it rests on its top, I will not go with him, she thought, even as the veins of the underside stilled in the mud. *And if he insists that I accompany him, I will strike out the other way.*

But he only turned into the line of bushes behind and melted into green, his cart gouging trails in the mud.

A solid indication of direction, she thought, like a sign or a portent or an omen of safety. Gathering up her small bundle of things, she followed him into the gloom.

There was no simple way to tie a neckcloth, Nathaniel thought, no easy shortcut that might allow him the time for another drink before he went out. Already the clock showed ten, and Hawk would be waiting. Catching sight of his reflection in the mirror, he frowned.

His valet had outdone himself with tonight's dress, the dizzying hues of his waistcoat clashing with the coloured silk of his cravat; a fashionable man with nothing else to occupy his mind save entertainment. People dropped their guards around men such as this. His fingers tightened against the ebony of his cane and

he felt for the catch hidden beneath the rim at the back as he walked downstairs.

He had returned from France in the early months of 1847 more damaged than he allowed others to know and had subsequently been attached to the London office. For a while the change had been just what he needed, the small problems of wayward politicians or corrupt businessmen an easy task to deal with after the mayhem of Europe.

Such work barely touched him. It was simple to shadow the unscrupulous and bring them to the notice of the law, the degenerate fraudsters and those who operated outside justice effortlessly discovered.

Aye, he thought. He could have done the work with his hands tied and a blindfold on until a month ago when two women had been dragged from the Thames with their throats cut. Young women and both dressed well.

No one had known them. No one had missed them. No anxious family member had contacted the police. It was as though they had come into the river without a past and through the teeming throng of humanity around the docklands without a footprint.

The only clue Nat had been able to garner was from an urchin who had sworn he had seen a toff wiping blood from a blade beside the St Katharine Docks. A tall and well-dressed man, the boy had said, before scurrying off into the narrow backstreets.

Stephen Hawkhurst had been asked to look into the case as well, and the Venus Club rooms five roads away towards the city had caught their attention.

'The members meet here every few weeks. They are gentlemen mostly with a great appetite for the opposite sex. By all accounts they pay for dancers and singers and other women who think nothing of shedding their clothes for entertainment.'

'So it could be one of them is using the club for more dubious pursuits,' Nat expanded. 'There are a number of men whose names and faces I recognise.'

He had kept a close eye on the comings and goings from the club across the past weeks, astonished at the numerous alliances taking place. 'Any accusations would need to be carefully handled, though, for some there have genuine political and social standing.'

'Hard to get closer without causing comment, you mean?' Stephen questioned.

'Exactly. But if we joined we could blend in.'

Stephen had not believed him serious. 'I don't think belonging to the ranks of the Venus Club is the sort of distinction one would want to be known for.'

'It's a place hiding secrets, Hawk, and privacy is highly valued.'

'Well, I'm not taking part in any initiation or rites of passage.'

Each of them had laughed.

'Frank Booth is reported to be a member. I will ask him to sponsor us.'

A week later they were given a date, a time and a place, a small break in a case that was baffling. Girls were ruined all the time in London, for reasons of economics, for the want of food, for a roof over the head

of a child born out of wedlock. But they were seldom so brutally hurt.

Sandrine. He remembered her ruined hand and the fear in her face when he had first met her.

The rage inside him began to build. Back then Cassandra Northrup had never given him any glimpse of an identity, though with each and every day in her company questions had woven their way into the little that she told him.

The first night had been the worst. She had cried behind him in small sobs, unstoppable over miles of walking in the dark. He had not helped her because he couldn't. The wound in his side had ached like the devil, fiery-hot and prickling, and by midnight he knew that he would have to rest.

Throwing down the few things he had taken from the cart after abandoning it many miles back, he leaned against a tree, the bark of its trunk firm behind him. Already the whirling circles of giddiness threatened, the ache at his hip sending pins and needles into his chest.

The girl sat on the other side of the small clearing, tucked into a stiff and inconsolable shape.

'You are safer than you were before. I said I would not hurt you.' He couldn't understand her weeping.

'I killed a man.'

'He was about to rape you.' Nat's heart sank at the implications of her guilt. God, how long had it been since he had felt anything remotely similar? He wished he had been the one to slide a knife into the French

miscreant, for he would have gutted him and enjoyed watching him die. Slowly.

Her hands crossed her heart and her lips moved as if reciting a prayer.

Had the bullet wound not hurt as much he might have laughed, might have crossed the space between them and shaken her into sense. But he could only sit and watch and try to mitigate his pain.

'I am sure that the wrath of God takes intent into account.'

'Oh, I intended to kill him.' Honestly said. Given back in a second and no hesitation in it.

'I was thinking more of your assailant's purpose. I do not think Monsieur Baudoin would have been gentle with you.'

'Yet two wrongs do not make a right?'

He closed his eyes and felt the bloom of fatigue, irritation rising at her unreasonableness. 'If you had not killed him, I would have. One way or another he would have been dead. If it helps, pretend I did it.'

'Who are you?' The green in her eyes under moonlight matched the dark of the trees. In the daylight they were bluer, changeable.

'Nathanael Colbert. A friend.' Barked out, none of the empathy he knew she wanted held within the word. She remained silent, a small broken shape in the gloom, tucked up against bracken, the holes in the leather soles of her shoes easily seen from this angle. 'Why the hell were you there in the first place?'

He did not think she would answer as the wind came

through into the hollow, its keening sound as plaintive as her voice.

'They caught us a long time ago.' He saw her counting on her fingertips as she said it, the frown upon her brow deepening. Months? Years?

'Us?'

He had seen no other sign of captives.

'Celeste and I.'

Hell. Another girl. 'Where is she?'

'Dead.' The flat anger in her voice was cold.

'Recently?'

She nodded, her expression gleamed in sadness. She had old bruises across her cheek and new ones on her hand. In the parting of her hair when her cap had been dislodged he had seen the opaque scar of a wound that could have so easily killed her.

As damaged as he was.

Tonight he did not have the energy to know more of her story and the thin wanness was dispiriting. If they could have a drink things would be better, but the flask he had brought with him was long since empty.

'Can you hear that stream?'

She nodded.

'We need water...?'

He left the words as a question. No amount of want in the world could get him standing. He had lost too much blood and he knew it.

'Do you have the flask?'

'Here.'

When she took it and left he closed his eyes and tried to find some balance in the silence. He wanted to tend

to himself, but he would need water to do that. And fire. He wondered if the young French captive would be able to follow his instructions when she returned.

He also wondered just exactly how those at Nay had gained their information on the identity and movements of a British agent who had long been a part of the fabric of French country life.

It was quiet in the trees and all the grief of losing Celeste flooded back. Her cousin's body rounded with child. Her eyes lifeless. The pain of it surged into Cassie's throat, blocking breath, and she stopped to lean against a tree. The anguish of life and death. What was it the man who sat in the clearing wrapped in bandages had said?

Killing is easy. It's the living that is difficult.

Perhaps, after all, he was right. Perhaps Celeste had known that, too, and put an end to all that she had loathed, taking the child to a place that was better but leaving her here alone.

Alone in a world where everything looked bleak. Bleaker than bleak even under the light of a small moon, the trickle of water at her feet running into the tattered remains of her boots and wetting her toes. The cold revived a little of her fight, reminded her how in the whole of those eight terrible months she had not given up, had not surrendered. She wished the stream might have been deeper so that she could have simply stripped off and washed away sin. A baptism. A renewal. A place to begin yet again and survive.

The flask in hand reminded her of purpose and she knelt to the water.

Her companion looked sick, the crusted blood beneath his nails reflected in the red upon his clothes, sodden through the layers of bandage. Without proper medicine how could he live? Water would clean the wound, but what could be done for any badness that might follow? The shape of leaves in the moonlight on the other side of the river suddenly caught her attention. Maudeline. Her mother had used this very plant in her concoctions. An astringent, she had said. A cleanser. A natural gift from the hands of a God who placed his medicines where they were most needed.

The small bank was easy to climb and, taking a handful of the plant, she stripped away the woody stems, the minty scent adding certainty to her discovery. She remembered this fresh sweet smell from Alysa's rooms and was heartened by the fact. The work of finding enough leaves and tucking them into her pocket took all her concentration, purpose giving energy. A small absolution. A task she had done many hundreds of times under the guidance of her mother.

An anchor to the familiar amidst all that was foreign. She needed this stranger in a land she held no measure of and he needed her. An equal support. It had been so long since she had felt any such worthiness.

He was asleep when she returned, though the quiet fall of her feet woke him.

'I have maudeline for your injury.' Bringing out the leaves, she began to crush them between her fingers,

mixing them to a paste with the water on a smooth rock she had wiped down before using. She saw how he watched her, his grey eyes never leaving the movement of her hands.

'Are you a witch, then?'

She laughed, the sound hoarse and rough after so many months of disuse. 'No, but Mama was often thought to be.'

Again she saw the dimple in his right cheek, the deep pucker of mirth making her smile.

'Maudeline? I have not heard of it.'

'Another name for it is camphor.'

He nodded and came up on to his knees, holding his head in his hands as though a headache had suddenly blossomed.

'It hurts you?'

'No.' Squeezed out through pain.

When he stood she thought he looked unsteady, but she simply watched as he gathered sticks and set to making a fire. The tinder easily caught, the snake of smoke and then flame. Using the bigger pieces of branch he built it up until even from a distance she could feel the radiating warmth.

'The tree canopy will dissipate the smoke,' he said after a few moments. 'The low cloud will take care of the rest.'

Half an hour later flame shadow caught at his torso as he removed his shirt, the bandages following. His wound showed shattered skin, the tell-tale red lines of inflammation already radiating.

'Don't touch.' Her directive came as she saw he was about to sear the edges of skin together with a glowing stick. 'It is my belief that dirt kills a man with more certainty than a bullet and I can tell it is infected.'

Crossing to him, she wiped her hands with the spare leaves and poured water across the sap. When she touched him she knew he had the fever. Another complication. A further problem.

'I have been ill like this before and lived.' He had seen her frown.

Lots of 'befores', she mused, lines of crossed white opaque scars all over his body. The thought made her careful.

'You are a soldier?'

He only laughed.

Or a criminal, she thought, for what manner of man looked as he did? When he handed over the flask of water, she did not take a drink.

'I will heat it to clean the wound. It might hurt for it has been left a while. If you had some leather to bite down upon...?"

He broke into her offered advice. 'I will cope.'

Stephen Hawkhurst's voice made Nathaniel start, the echo around the marbled lobby disconcerting as all the years past rolled back into the present.

'You look as though you have the problems of the world upon your shoulders, Nat. Still thinking of the Northrup chit, I'd be guessing: fine eyes, a fine figure and a sense of mystery. Her uncle, Reginald Northrup,

will be at the Venus Club tonight. Perhaps you can find out more about her from him.'

'Perhaps.'

'A few years ago when I was in Paris I heard a rumour about a woman who sounded remarkably like Cassandra Northrup.'

'What did it say?'

'That she was kept a prisoner in southern France and that she was not released for quite some time.'

'I see.'

'Her rescuer was also mentioned in detail.' The flint of gold in his friend's eyes was telling and there was a certain question there.

'It was you, Nat, wasn't it? And she was one of theirs?

'Whose?'

'The French. One of their agents.'

Anger sliced in a quick rod of pain. 'No, Cassandra Northrup never held loyalty to any cause save that of her own.'

'Others here might disagree with you. She is the chairwoman of the charity Daughters of the Poor.'

'Prostitutes?'

Hawk nodded, leaving Nat to ponder on how the circles of life turned around in strange patterns.

'She must have been a child then, and scared. God, even now she looks young. And you got home in one piece, after all.'

One piece? How little Stephen truly knew.

Taking his hat and cloak from the doorman, Nat

forced away his recollections and walked out into a
cold and windy London night.

They were all there, myriad affluent men gathered
in a room that looked much like a law chamber or a
place of business. Nat was glad that Stephen stood beside him because he still felt dislocated and detached,
thrown by the reappearance of a woman he had thought
never to see again.

He recalled Cassandra Northrup's eyes were exactly
the same as they had been, guarded in their turquoise,
shuttered by care and secrets. But her hair had changed
from the wild curls she had once favoured and she was
far more curvaceous.

If her eyes had not given her away her left hand
would have, of course, with the half-finger and the
deep scar across the rest of her knuckles.

It had been a newer wound back then in the clearing, when she had reached forward and laid one cool
palm across his back. He had flinched as she brought
the knife she carried upwards to cut away the badness.

The pain had made him sweat, hot incandescence in
the cool of night as she simply tipped the heated flask
up and covered ragged open flesh.

The camphor helped, as did her hands threading
through places on his spine that seemed to transfer
the pain. Surprise warred with agony under her adept
caresses.

The poultice was sticky and the new bandages she
bound the ointment with were from the bottom of her
shirt. Cleaner. Softer. He could smell her on them.

He wished that he had the whisky to dull the pain. He wished for a bed that was not on a forest floor, but some place warmer, more comfortable, some place where his heartbeat did not rattle against the cold hard of earth.

'If you sit, it should help with the drainage.'

He was shivering now, substantially, and went to drape his jacket around himself to find warmth, but she held it away and shook her head.

'You are burning up. The mind plays tricks when the fever rages and as I cannot shift you to the stream we will have to make do with the cold night air instead. I had hoped it would snow.'

Her accent was Parisian, the inflection of the drawing rooms and the society salons where anything and everything was possible. He wondered why the hell she should have been in Nay, dressed in the clothes of a lad, and when he inadvertently blurted the thought out aloud, he saw her flinch.

'I think you should sleep, Monsieur Colbert.'

His name. Not quite right. But he needed to be quiet and he needed to think. There was danger here. He wished he could have asked her who she was, what she was, but the camphor was winding its way into the quick pricks of pain and he closed his eyes to block her from him.

He would be sore in the morning if he lived. The wound or the fever could kill him, but it was the bleeding that she was most concerned about. She had not

been able to stop it. Already blood pooled beneath him, more hindrance to a body struggling with survival.

Tipping up the flask, she took the last drops of water.

She was starving. She was exhausted. The embers of the fire still glowed in the dark, but outside the small light the unknown gathered.

Baudoin had not existed alone and she knew that others would follow. Oh, granted, this stranger had hidden their tracks well ever since leaving Nay, his cart discarded quite early in the piece. She had watched him set false lures into other directions, the heavy print of a foot in a stream, a broken twig snagged with the hair from her plait, but she knew it would only be a matter of time before those in France's underworld would find them.

She held far too many secrets, that was the problem. She had seen some of the documents Baudoin's brother had inadvertently left in Celeste's chamber, documents she knew had been taken from the carriage of a murdered man on the road towards Bayonne. A mistake of lust and an error that would lead to all that had happened next.

Her fault. Everything was her fault and her cousin had not even known it. The same familiar panic engulfed her, made her lean forward to catch breath, trying in the terror to hold on to the reason of why Celeste had done as she did. Cassie still felt the sticky blood across her fingers, the warmth of life giving way to cold.

Softly she began to sing, keeping herself staunch;

the 'Marseillaise' because it was fast paced and because it was in French.

To arms, citizens,
Form your battalions,
We march, we march...

Celeste was dead. And the Baudoin brothers. How
quickly circumstances changed. In a heartbeat. In a
breath. She looked across to the stranger, Colbert, and
determined that he was still in the land of the living
before she shut her eyes.

The girl was asleep, her hat pulled down across
her head and her jacket stretched over the bend of her
knees. As Nathaniel looked at her in repose there was
a vulnerability apparent that was not evident when she
was awake. She was thin, painfully so, and dirty. On
a closer inspection he saw on her clothes the handi-
work of small, finely taken stitches covering rips and
larger holes. Her shirt was buttoned to the throat and
the jacket she wore was tightly closed. More than a
few sizes too large, it held the look of a military coat
without any of the braiding. He knew she still had the
knife, but it was not visible anywhere. Too big for the
pockets, he imagined it tucked in under her forearm
or secreted in one of the boots she wore beneath loose
trousers.

A child-woman lost into the vagaries of a war that
could not have been kind.

He felt stronger, a surprising discovery this, given

his fever, and although the wound tugged when he shifted it did not sting like it had. Still, his vision blurred as he stood from the loss of blood or his own body's heat, he knew not which.

Camphor. Perhaps there was something in the doctoring, some healing property that would confound even the best of physicians? He resolved to use it again.

She stirred across from him, wild curls escaping from the plait and falling around her face. In sleep she looked softer, the burden of life not marking the spaces between her eyes. Her ruined left hand sat on top of the right one and fire outlined the hurt in flame. Not a little injury and not an accident either. This looked to be deliberate, a brutal act of damage that would have taken weeks to heal. It was strange to see such a battle scar on one so young. His own back was filled with the vestige of war, but he had been in the arena of secrets for some time and such damage was to be expected.

Her eyes flicked open suddenly, taking him in, fear reverting to wariness.

'How do you feel?' Even fresh from sleep she was observant.

'Better.'

Her glance at his throat read the measured beat of his heart. 'Your temperature is still high so you should be drinking as much as you can. In a moment I will fetch more water.'

A frown of concern slashed the girl's forehead, but he was tired of thinking of her as 'the girl'. 'What are you called?'

'Sandrine Mercier.'

Rolling the name on his tongue, he liked the sound of it. 'How old are you?'

'Almost eighteen.' Surprisingly forthcoming, though she did not look to have as many years as she professed.

'And your cousin?'

Moonlight caught her face as her chin lifted. 'Celeste was twenty and she loved music. She loved everything beautiful and charming and good. She played the piano and sang like an angel...' Her voice came to a halt.

Nat knew what she was doing because he had done the same himself when those close to him had died. A memory they might be, but in speech they came alive, drawn for others to know, almost living.

'Did Baudoin kill her?'

Only the quick shake of her head.

One day she will be beautiful, he thought. One day she will take men's hearts and break them. For now she was young. Too young for him. For now the stamp of grace lay in her long limbs and her boyish defiance, the promise of womanhood only hinted at.

He turned away, not wishing for her to see his regard.

He was back to being angry, his eyes the colour of a storm, not dark, not light, but the in-between shade that spoke of rain and coldness.

'Are you a part of Guy Lebansart's circle of spies?' If she found out something about him, there might be protection there.

His interest ignited. 'Spies?'

'Men who would take secrets and use them.'

'For France?'

'Or for whoever is paying the most.'

His frown deepened. 'Did you ever know any of these secrets, Sandrine?' In his words she could hear exactly what she did not want to. Interest and intrigue. Eight months in captivity had taught her every nuance in the language of deception.

'No.' She kept her voice bland and low, shaking out the truth with effort. 'I was only a prisoner.'

'Where did they keep you?'

She did not answer, moving instead to retrieve the flask. Her mattress had been in a room off Celeste and Louis's chamber, a sanctuary she tried very hard to seldom leave. Lying low, she only ever ventured out when the early hours of the morning saw each inhabitant befuddled by strong drink, her cousin included. But Celeste had made her own bargain with the devil and had won conditions to make the tenure livable. Cassie's thoughts went again to Celeste's beautiful voice and her smile. When memory was selective, everything was easier.

'I will get water and then we should leave. If others follow—'

He cut off her worry with two words.

'They won't.'

The confidence of a victor. So fragile. So absolutely flimsy. Baudoin had said no one would ever dare to challenge him and look at what had happened. Her French uncle had been certain, too, of the route west and then lost his way into peril.

Everyone could be bought for the price of pain or promise or vanity. She wondered what Monsieur Nathanael Colbert's price might be. Her own was freedom and she would never give it up again for anyone.

'When we reach the next town, hide your face with this.' He tossed her a scarf, dirtied with dust and blood. 'And tuck your hair well into the crown of your hat. If anyone asks a question of you, look stupid, for there is safeguard in a simple mind. If you could walk with more of a swagger—'

She cut him off. 'I know what to do.'

He swore at that, roundly, and began to collect his things.

Reginald Northrup was a large man, his face florid and his smile showing a mouth with at least a few teeth missing. The brandy he had hold of was in a glass as oversized as he was. The sweat on his brow reflected the light above him.

'It is a surprise to see you here, Lindsay. I hear you aided my niece the other evening at the de Clare ball?'

The man who sat near Northrup turned to hear his answer.

'Indeed. The last pieces of a falling chandelier knocked her unconscious and a doctor was called.'

'I am certain Cassandra herself could have remedied any wound she received. She has a knack for the healing and her mother was just the same.'

'Her mother was reputed to be one of society's beauties, was she not?' Hawk's question. Nat could not quite

let go of the thought that he had voiced the query for
his benefit.

'She was, but Alysa Northrup died a good many
years ago when one of her science experiments went
wrong. Had she lived a century ago she might have
been burned at the stake as a witch, for there were
rumblings in all quarters about her unusual endeavours and none of them was kind.'

The easygoing stance of the man hardened, giving
Nat an impression of much emotion.

'She was a beautiful woman, Reg.' Lord Christopher
Hanley, sitting next to Reginald, had imbibed too much
strong drink, lending his speech an air of openness.
'None of the other débutantes that year could touch her
in brains or beauty. I thought for a time it was you she
was sweet upon until your brother snaffled her up right
under your very nose and made her his wife.'

Northrup seemed out of step with such a confidence.
'Both girls are as odd as their mother was. You will do
yourself a favour by staying out of the way of them,
Lindsay. Indeed, most gentlemen in society have done
so already.'

Hawk beside him laughed. 'I think it might be the
other way around, sir, for even though they seldom
venture into the social realm your nieces rebuff all interested parties with alacrity.'

'If they turn their noses up at everything, it is because their father has too little left of his wits to bid
them marry. Maureen has already reached a grand old
age and I fear that she will always remain a spinster.

Rodney, their brother, shall have to no doubt house them when he inherits the properties.'

By the look on Reginald Northrup's face Nathaniel judged that he was not pleased about the fact. The terms of an entailment, perhaps, that left him with little to fall back upon?

'The younger daughter was married in France, if memory serves me well? I remember it as quite a scandal at the time, Reg, and she never took on his name.' Hanley spoke again, and Nathaniel stiffened. Another ache hooking into the cold prick of betrayal. He wondered what she had done with the ring he had given her, his mother's ring, a single, pure, verdant emerald set in white gold.

'What was the story of her groom?' Nat addressed Reginald Northrup directly.

'Oh, up and gone by all accounts, for she arrived home in a melancholic state that took a good year to recover from. I doubt any new husband would have put up with such gloom for that length of time, though my brother was happy enough to have her back and never questioned the marriage. He lives in his own world of science and experiments much the same as his wife was wont to. It was this interest that drew them together in the first place, I suppose.'

The layers of truth peeled back and, within the Venus Club in a room gilded with ostentation and excess, Nat found himself disheartened. It was what had happened after that which Nathaniel failed to understand: the closeness and then the unfathomable dis-

tance. He shook away his thoughts as Hawk spoke again.

'Reginald is asking if we wish to join him at his country home for the Venus Club's August celebrations, Nat. I said we would be more than delighted to accept his offer.'

'Indeed.' The taste of bitterness in Nathaniel's mouth was strong, for nothing here made sense to him. Why had Cassandra Northrup never married again given the fragile and unorthodox legality of their nuptials?

She was beautiful. More beautiful than any other woman of the *ton*, even in the dreary guise of a widow. Aye, muted dove-grey suited the tone of her skin and the colour of her eyes and hair.

Her hair had been longer once, falling to the line of her hips in a single swathe of darkened silk as they had pulled themselves out of the river.

He had realised the danger the moment they awoke in the barn they had found in the late afternoon of the day before after walking for many miles. A sense of threat permeated the early morning air, and he was a man who had always relied on instinct.

Sandrine had stirred as he stood, straw from the beds they had fashioned still in the threads of her hair. Everything about her was delicate. Her hands, her nails, the tilt of her chin as she listened.

'Someone is here?'

'More than one. They do not know we are inside, however, or their voices would be quieter.'

He saw how she drew the knife from her sleeve and held it at the ready. Her hands were shaking.

Six of them, he determined, from the footsteps and the whicker of horses. By himself he would have taken them on, but with Sandrine to protect...?

Placing a finger to his lips he drew her to one side of the building and indicated a hole at the bottom of the boards.

'Crawl through and make for the river. If they see you keep running and jump. Stay in the middle where the water flows fastest for at least a mile. After that I will find you.'

Fear sparked in her eyes. 'I cannot swim well.'

'Just put your arms out to each side and relax...'

He did not finish because a shout interrupted them and Nat knew their tracks had been discovered.

'Go.'

A quick nod and the space where she had been was filled only with the scent of her and the sound of someone lifting the catch upon the door.

Unsheathing his knife Nat breathed out, another blade at his belt tilted so that the hilt was easily accessible. The dry straw also caught his eye. He would not make this easy for them and a fire would buy them some time. He hoped to God that Sandrine had reached the water way undetected.

She heard the commotion in the barn as flame leapt from straw, hot through the missing frame of a window.

Colbert had set the place on fire and as a diversion the plan was inspired. Already she saw two of the men retreating, their attention caught so firmly on the blaze

they did not notice her as she ran past a line of weeping willows to the river bank.

Where was he? Why had he not come out after her? How long could a person breathe in the smoke and flame of straw? The quick report of a gun sent her under into the cold, down amongst the green of weed and the dirty swirl of mud. She pushed up and away, using her hands as he had told her, spread out as wings, the surface finally in sight, a faint glitter of day where only darkness had been and then she was out, air in her lungs again, a promontory cutting off any sight of the burning barn and distance-dulling noise.

Warm tears of fright ran against the chill, the quick rush of water taking her faster and faster, and the bank a good many yards from her on either side.

Had Nathanael Colbert died in the fight? The wound in his side and the remains of the fever would have sapped his strength and yet he had made sure she had the chance of safety before seeing to his own. He only knew her from her time with Baudoin, a girl marked with the horror of it and yet he had done this for her. Without question.

She wished he was here, behind her, as she was forced along in the rapid current, dragged down with the heaviness of her oversized boots.

And then he was there, reaching for her as she went under yet again, the water in her throat making her cough.

'Put your arms around my neck.'

He was solid and sturdy, the muscles in his shoulders keeping her up in the cold air. His hair had been

released from the band he kept it secured with and was falling in wet strands down his back. She wondered how he could keep going as the water flow quickened and rocks appeared, the fall of the river changing and whitening into rapids.

'Don't let go,' he called over his shoulder, one hand fending off a jagged outcrop as they bounced into its path. Then they were free again, down onto a new level of river, softer and quieter.

Cassie could tell he was tiring, the gulps of air he took ragged and uneven. Blood from his wound stained the water crimson about them as damaged flesh opened to pressure. But still he did not stop, waiting until the bushes turned again to countryside before striking in for shore.

The mud under her feet was thick and deep as she gained a purchase. For a good long while they lay there, on the bank, the greyness of the sky above them promising rain. Freezing.

'Take...your clothes...off.' Even he was shivering.

The first soft drift of snow came unexpectedly, landing on her upturned face in a cold and quiet menace.

'Take your...heavier clothes off...th-then get into the base of the hedge and dig. The l-leaves will be warmer than the air and they will p-protect you.'

He made no attempt to move himself, the flakes of snow thicker now. Again red blood pooled beneath him.

She came to a decision without conscious thought. He had saved her twice and she could not leave him here to perish. Unbuttoning what was left of his shirt, she sat him forward and took away the sodden cot-

ton. His jacket was long gone, probably discarded when he first went into the river. A chain hung at his neck, a ring secured upon it, white-gold with a large clear emerald.

Was he married? Did a woman wait at home for him, hoping? His eyes this close were ringed in dark blue, grey melting into the colour seamlessly. Watching her.

'Go.'

But she could not. Unsheathing the knife along the line of her lower arm as strength returned, she stood and cut a pile of branches. The leaves that lay at the base of a hedge she fashioned into a bed and rolled him into it, placing many more leaves and plant stems on top and using the brush as a shield to keep the snow away. Then, climbing underneath to join him, she snuggled in, jacket and shirt gone, skin touching skin.

Already the day had darkened, the dusk misting in early with the weather, more clouds on the horizon.

'Will they find us?'

'Not today. S-snow covers everything and whoever is looking will have to w-wait it out.'

Their small lair was becoming darker as the snow caught, layering and thickening. The wind, too, had lessened and heat was beginning to build. She liked it when his arms came about her, holding her close, the beat of his heart even and unhurried and his breath comforting.

For this one small moment they were safe.

She was glad when he stopped shivering, their warmth melding together to create hope.

* * *

Nat had awoken from their lair of snow beneath the bushes to a room with a fire burning bright. An older man and woman sat observing them, a youth standing near the window.

'Our dog found your tracks leading from the river and we brought you here early this morning.'

Looking about, he saw that Sandrine and he had been placed on a bed together, a thick feather down quilt across them. He knew immediately that they were both naked, for she was tucked about him as if in sleep her body had sought the warmth she so desperately needed.

'Your clothes and boots have been washed and repaired and should be dry by nightfall. The doctor said you were to stay very quiet for the wound at your side would have taken much in energy from you and could open again if you are not careful.'

A headache pounded in Nat's temples, impairing his vision, the room swimming as their words were lost into a droning noise. Sandrine was still asleep, their voices making no inroad into her consciousness.

Shaking his head, he tried to distil the blurriness, but the pain only intensified and so he desisted. He could not even move a muscle; a heavy stupor anchored him to the mattress, and a tiredness that defied description seeped through. Alarm furrowed his brow, but when the dark claimed him he no longer had the vigour to question it, demand it different.

Sandrine was awake before him when he next surfaced and she had moved a good distance away, a rough

linen shift now in place across her shoulders. A grey blanket was wedged in the space between them and no one else was in the room. A fire danced in the grate.

'Madame Dortignac has just left. She brought chicken broth if you want some.'

'No.' The thought of food turned his stomach. Outside it was pitch-black and the noises of the house were stilled. Late, then? Around two, perhaps, though he had no real measure of time.

'It has rained heavily all day,' Sandrine said after a moment, 'and I heard them say that the river has come up.'

'Good.' The threads of protection began to wind in closer. 'Any sign of our presence will be long gone from the mud on the banks.'

'They brought in a priest for you. I think they were worried you might not survive.'

'When?'

'Yesterday afternoon. It has been a full two days since you last awoke.' Anxiety played in her eyes. 'He asked if we were husband and wife before he left. When I said that we were not he was displeased.'

'A result of our bedding arrangements, I suspect. They think that I have ruined you.'

'The priest tried to make me go to another room, but I felt safe here and told him that I would not.'

She looked so damn young sitting there, the dark beneath her eyes worrying him and the homespun in her shift showing up the fragility of her shoulders. Her hair had been pulled back into a loose chignon, small curls escaping around her face. Feeling the punch of

her beauty Nathaniel breathed out and glanced away, angry at the effect she so easily engendered on the masculine parts of his body, even in sickness. He could not remember any woman with such sway over him.

Safe?

If he had felt better, he might have laughed at her interpretation of security. Looking around for his sword and gun, he found them next to his carefully folded clean clothes and polished boots to one side of the bed.

'Did they say who they were?

She nodded. 'Farmers. They own the land between the river and the mountains behind, a large tract that has been in their family for generations. The Catholic priest who came was certain that God was punishing us for...for....' She did not finish.

He smiled. 'Our sins of the flesh?'

A bright stain of redness began at her throat and surged up across her cheeks.

'Life or death requires sacrifices, Sandrine, and if you had not removed my clothes and kept me warm I would have perished. An omnipotent God would know that, and I thank you for it.'

A myriad of small expressions flitted across her brow: humour, puzzlement and then finally acceptance.

'Are you always so certain of things, Monsieur Colbert?'

'Yes.'

At that she laughed properly, her head thrown back and her eyes dancing. Not the pale imitation of laughter that the society ladies had perfected to an art form, but a real and honest reaction that made him laugh, too,

the medicine of humour exhilarating. He could not remember ever feeling like this with another woman before, the close edge of a genuine joy pressing in and a camaraderie that was enticing.

But when he reached out to touch her fingers humour dissipated into another emotion altogether. Connection, if he might name it, or shock, the sear of her flesh burning up into the cold of his arm.

She had felt it, too—he could tell she had as she snatched her hand away and buried it into the heavy grey of the blanket. Her face was turned from his so deliberately that the corded muscle in her throat stood out with tension, a pulse beating with rhythm that belied calmness.

Nathanael Colbert was as beautiful as he was powerful and even with the fever flushing his cheeks and tearing into the strength of him he still offered her protection. Outside, the night clothed the land in silence and inside his warmth radiated towards her, the barrier of wool insubstantial.

If she had been braver, she might have reached over and removed it, so that their skin could touch again as it had done before, close and real, offering safety and something else entirely.

Urgency. Craving. A yearning that she had no experience of, but that was there in her flesh and bones, the call of something ancient and destined, an undeniable and inescapable knownness.

Shocking. Wonderful. She did not wish him to see the remnants of all she thought so she turned away,

pleased when he did not demand her attention or reach out again.

An impasse in a cold and wind-filled night, the mountains of the Pyrenees filling a darkened sky and a fire measuring out the passing moments in warmth.

One and then two. Enough to regain composure and push away the thoughts of what might have been between them should they have given it a chance. An ache wormed its way across her throat and heart before settling lower. Loss could be a physical hurt, she would think much later, but right now it was a wondrous and startling surprise.

Chancing a look at him, she saw he lay back against the pillows, the sheet pulled away from the dark nakedness of his skin, muscle sculptured under the flame light. Still sick, she realised, by the sheen of sweat across his brow and the high colour in his cheeks. She wondered how the wound at his side had fared from such exertion, but did not dare to ask him, given the state of her racing heart.

'I will protect you, Sandrine. Do not worry.'

The words were quietly said.

'From everyone?'

His lips turned up, the dimple in his right cheek deepening.

'Yes.'

She did not wipe away the tear that traced down her face, but waited to feel the cold run of its passage, the blot of moisture darkening the yellowed counterpane as it fell. As his breathing evened out she knew he was asleep, his body needing the balm of rest. Turn-

ing with as little noise as possible, she watched him, his breathing shallow and fast and his dark eyelashes surprisingly long.

The past few days rushed up at her, the chaos and the hope. Baudoin and his brother had been bandits whose livelihood was made by taking the riches from aristocrats travelling the roads towards the north and west, but Guy Lebansart was a different story altogether. He boasted about working for the French Government, though Sandrine knew enough about the houses and land that he had accrued to know that more lucrative pickings had taken his fancy.

Lebansart blackmailed people and he hurt anyone who got in his way—even Anton Baudoin had been scared of him. He had been due to arrive at the compound with a good deal of gold in exchange for information found on a man Baudoin's men had killed on the highway. But Nathaniel Colbert had arrived first.

A coincidence.

Sandrine thought not.

Glancing again at the stranger, she frowned. What were his secrets? Closing her eyes, she fervently prayed that Lebansart and those who worked for him would never catch up with them.

Chapter Three

Cassandra smoothed down the wool of her pantaloons and pulled up the generous collar of her jacket. It was cold in the London wind and it had already begun to spit.

Damn, she cursed, for the sound of the rain would dull her hearing and she knew that dawn wasn't far off.

Lord Nathaniel Lindsay had returned to his town house a quarter of an hour ago, and by his gait as he descended from the carriage she knew he had been drinking.

Perfect.

The thick line of trees in the garden surprised her. She would not have imagined him to sanction such a shelter, for intruders could easily use the screen to hide behind. Making her way through the green-tinged darkness, she sidled along the undergrowth until she came to the windows.

The first sash was rock solid. The next one moved. Unsheathing her knife, she pressed it into the crack

and shifted the lock. One second and it was rendered useless, clicking into access. With an intake of breath she lifted the wood, and when she perceived no threat she raised it farther.

Waiting, she listened to the sounds of the room. A single last fall of wood in the grate as the warm air greeted her, a clock in the corner marking out the hour.

She was over the barrier in a whisper, turning to the chamber and waiting as her eyes accustomed themselves.

'Shut the window and join me.'

He knew she would come for he had seen a shadow that was not normally there against the stone wall on the opposite side of the street. This window had always been loose, a trick of wet wood or poor craftsmanship, he knew not which.

To give her credit she barely acknowledged the shock. A slight hesitation, one less certain step. He wondered if she held a knife in her hand and thought perhaps he should have bothered to arm himself. But he would not have harmed her. He knew that without a doubt.

'Lord Nathaniel Lindsay, the heir to the title of St Auburn?' Her voice was tight, tinged with more than a hint of question.

'At your service, Mademoiselle Mercier. And now you are all grown up.'

'A fact that you hate?'

He laughed at that because her surprising honesty had always appealed to him, though the sound held lit-

tle humour. 'I survived, but others did not. The names I presume you gave to Lebansart made it easy for him to mark them off as English agents. Didier and Gilbert Desrosiers were like lambs to the slaughter. Good men. Men who had never wronged you in any way. Men with allegiances to England and who had only ever wanted to serve this country.'

The blood seemed to disappear from her face. One moment her cheeks were rosy from the outside cold and in the next second they were as pale as snow.

'You were a spy, too? My God, that explains why you were there in France and in Nay in particular.'

'They call them intelligence officers now.'

'You were a spy for the English army?'

'The British Service.'

'Not just the army then, but the quiet and hidden corridors of a clandestine and covert agency. Are you still?'

He did not answer.

'I will take that as a yes, then.' The blood had returned to her face, and she did not waver as she went on. 'I didn't come to offer excuses for what I did at Perpignan, my lord, nor for exoneration.'

'Then why did you come?'

'To give you this.'

She took a ring from her pocket and he recognised it immediately. His mother's, the emerald as green as it had been all those years before.

'I took it and I should not have. For all the other things that I was, I was never a thief.'

'God.' Thief of hearts, he thought. Thief of lives.

Thief of the futures of two good Englishmen caught in the crossfire of politics.

'Celeste died for nothing. At least those agents of England that you speak of perished for a cause they believed in. A righteous cause. A cause to take them into Heaven and be pardoned by our Lord for it.'

'You came tonight to tell me this?' His voice shook with bitterness.

'No. I came to say that nothing is as black and as white as it seems, and the documents I saw were there for others to see as well.'

'Yet you memorised them and gave the information back to the one person you should not have.'

'Guy Lebansart was only one man who might have wanted them dead. France was seething with those who would harm anyone with loyalties to England. Perhaps they held your name, too?'

'I doubt I was on any index of names.'

'Then you doubt wrong,' she said and turned to the window. 'From the moment you rescued me there was danger.'

And then he understood. 'So you traded our freedom for intelligence? Hell.' So many questions and so few answers. Yet something was not quite right. And then the penny dropped.

'I was the one you bargained for?'

The nod she gave him was almost imperceptible. 'Indeed, that was a part of the story, but now I need a favour, Lord Lindsay. I need the right to go on with my life without having to look behind at the chaos, waiting for it to catch up.'

'And nothing else?'

'Nothing.'

Her voice was measured. No extra emotion. No tell-tale sign of weakness or feeling. She had sacrificed the lives of others for his and she knew there was no honour in any of it. It was not thanks she had come for. Neither was it a penance. Celeste was probably more of a part of it than anyone, for Sandrine had always been like a mother lioness over any perceived tarnishing of her cousin's memory and she might have been fearful about the recount of his knowledge of her.

The complex layers of guilt and shame mixed in strangely with integrity. She had not needed to come. He hadn't further want for the ring and no explanation could absolve murder.

'You whored in exchange for my life?'

She shook away the words. 'You know nothing, Colbert.'

'Lindsay,' he corrected her with a cold and hard fury.

'If I had not traded the information, you would have been dead.'

'And instead...?'

'You lived.'

Her eyes flickered to the scar that ran across his jaw on the right side.

'Death might have been kinder.'

She raised her fist at that, the hand of ruined and knotted skin. 'You think I did not wish that, too, many times after I left you, the blood of those I'd named wrapped about the heart of my guilt? But there is no

book written on the rules of war, my lord, and I was a young girl trying to exist in a world that had forsaken me. Anton Baudoin had taken the documents from a man he had murdered a few days before you came to Nay. I had no idea as to who those mentioned within it were.'

Silence filled the space between them for the time it took the clock in the corner to chime out the hour of two. It was why he had come to find the Baudoins in the first place, pointed in the direction by intelligence garnered after the agent's murder. Then she spoke again.

'You think I should have trusted you enough to make a run for it at Perpignan and believed that the impossible might be probable there with a hundred enemies at our heels and many more behind? You believed in that option of faith?'

'Yes.' Simple. Heartfelt.

Her unexpected smile was a sad one. 'On reflection you may have been correct because what happened afterwards took away all my right of choice.' There was a new note in her words now. Resignation and acceptance mixed with an undercurrent of shame.

'Merde.' The French word echoed through the dark like a gunshot. One moment a history just guessed at and the next known exactly.

'But I have made a new life here, a good life, a life that helps those whom all others have forgotten.'

'The Daughters of the Poor?'

She nodded, but in the depths of her eyes he saw the truth of what they had each found out about the other

shimmering. Unspoken. The lump in his throat hitched in memory and it rested in the spaces after midnight, the weight of such knowledge making him turn away, pain lapping at all they could never say.

'I help ruined girls like me.'

He hated that pretence was no longer possible.

'Get out.' Usually he was more urbane and polished, but with her he had never been quite himself.

'Not until you agree to what I have asked.'

He did not speak because he did not trust in what he might say, but when he nodded she was gone, the whisper of the velvet curtains as they fell against the sash and a faint eddy of wind. Placing his head against the wall, he closed his eyes and cursed.

No one can get back what is lost.

That is what she had whispered then, that last time, as she had untwined his shaking fingers from around her wrist and gone with the French spymaster, her laughter on the air as rough hands wormed into the young promise of girlhood.

The sacking shield had come down as her footsteps receded, the twine it was held in place with tight at his throat. He remembered the sharp blade of a knife pressed into his ribs just below his heart.

'Sandrine, the whore.' Someone had drawled the words behind him as he had been pushed into midair and then he could remember nothing.

Cassandra was shaking so much she could barely untie her trousers and unbuckle her boots. Two good men had died because of her disclosure and Nathaniel

Lindsay hated her now as easily as she had loved him, then. A young girl of shattered dreams and endless guilt. The hero in Nathanael Colbert had beckoned like a flame and she had been burnt to a cinder.

She was so utterly aware of Lindsay; that was the problem. Even now, safe in her room, the thrum of her want for him made her body vibrate. She forced stillness and crossed to the mirror above the hearth, its rim of gold leaf scratched by age. The woman who stared back was not the one she felt inside. This woman still held on to promise and hope, her eyes dancing with passion, heated skin sending rose into pale cheeks.

He had no reason to assent to all that she asked, no obligation to the betrayal and deceit lingering beyond the limits of honour. And yet he had assented.

She thrust her hand instinctively against one breast and squeezed it hard. No joy in this, no pleasure. No reward of the flesh, but the broken promises of men.

Turning away, she swallowed, the anger of her life forming strength. It was all she had, all she could hold on to. Once, other oaths had held her spellbound in the safety of Celeste's bedroom in Perpignan, and under the light of a candle that threw the flame of curiosity on to two young faces.

'Papa said that we can all go to Barages. It has been so long since we have been anywhere, Sandrine, and taking in the waters would be something we can all enjoy.'

'Will David come, too?'

'If you are going he is bound to want to for I have seen the way my father's godson looks at you. But

be warned, although he is eighteen he is also far too boring.'

Cassie blushed, hating the red that often rose in her cheeks at the mention of anything personal. She had arrived in France four months earlier, travelling from London by boat into Marseilles in the company of her mother's brother and her cousin, and the warmth of the south had seeped into her bones like a tonic.

'I want to meet someone who will take my breath away. A rich man, a good-looking man, a dangerous man.' Celeste's voice held that thread of wishfulness that Cassandra had often heard her use. 'I am so very tired of the milksop sons of my father's friends.'

'But what of Jules Durand?' Her cousin's latest swain had been at the door most days, professing his love and his intentions, a strange mix of shyness and gall.

'He is not...manly enough. He tells me too much before I want him to. He kissed my hand yesterday and all I could think of was to pull away from the wet limpness of his lips.'

All of a sudden the conversation had gone to places Cassandra did not understand, the edge of virtue tarnished by a feeling that seemed...bruised. Celeste had grown up in the year since she had seen her, the lines of her body curvy and fuller. Tonight under the bed-covers some other feeling lingered, something wrong and false.

Her cousin's blue eyes flashed. 'Do you never wish for a man's hands upon your body, finding the places

that feel only magic? Do you not want to know the wonderment that all the great books talk of?'

'No.' Cassie pulled the collar of her nightgown full around her throat. Her own bedroom was down the corridor amongst the shadows and she had been scared to stay there, but this room suddenly held a fear that she could not comprehend.

'You are no longer in boring stuffy old England. Here women know the dance of love and they flaunt it.' Rising from her bed, Celeste simply pulled off her gown, standing against the flame of her lamp like a goddess.

'I want to know what it is to be passionate and wanton and brave. Only dull wits shall be for ever stuck with one boring husband for the rest of their lives and I certainly shall not be that. When we are young we should be able to know...everything.'

Cassie's eyes ran across the fat abundance of her cousin's breasts, breasts that were so different from her own. Celeste's waist had slimmed and her hips had spread and the hair between her legs had been trimmed back into the shape of a heart.

'You look beautiful.' The words came from the very depth of admiration.

'Too beautiful to be wasted on the boys that I am forever annoyed by here.' One hand cupped her breast and the other fell to the soft place between her legs. 'There is no power more durable than that of womanhood. No influence over men as strong as the desire for sex. Remember that, Cassandra, when you do finally grow up, and use it wisely.'

Draping a blanket around herself then, she smiled, turning again into the more-known cousin, the girl who would push the boundaries, but was kinder with it.

'You look shocked, Sandrine.' She began to laugh in earnest now. 'Shocked and stiff. I do not think you are made for such confessions.'

All the words fell across Cassandra. Words she had not heard before or thought of. Ideas that had been a part of a world far from her own, lost in the corruption of love. She wished she were home in England, Maureen in the chamber next door and her father not far away either. Rodney was too young to think much of right now, but even his presence would have been a relief.

'Come, let us sleep, cousin, and I promise I shall behave myself entirely. You have been ill, after all, and I should not tease you.'

In her bedroom in London all those years later Cassandra dashed away the tears that came so readily whenever she thought of Celeste. Her cousin's promise had been fulfilled in blood and in pain, the danger of Baudoin's brother Louis and the wildness within him no match for a slightly wayward French virgin steeped in the potential of adventure and romance.

'Romance.' She whispered the word into the room, and it curled into sin. Some losses were beyond comprehension and this was one of those. Some truths, too, were made mute by their sheer and utter horror.

Her truths.

No, she could never let Lord Nathaniel Lindsay

know the exact depth of any of them and after discovering today that he worked for the British Service she knew she would have to be more than careful. Just another gulf of difference between them that could never be bridged.

Lady Acacia Bellowes-Browne hung on to his arm at the Smithson ball and laughed, a soft musical sound that ran through tenseness and made Nathaniel relax.

'You said that you would come down to Bellamy for the hunting, Nat. I have held that promise for some weeks now'

'And indeed I shall,' he answered, liking the feel of her fingers on his skin, the many rings she wore decorative and colourful. He was about to speak again when Lydia Forsythe came across to the group.

'I am sorry to disturb you, Lord Lindsay, but I want to thank you for your help the other week. Mama said you were most kind in ensuring that I did not bleed to death.'

'I rather think that you would not have.'

'Well, Miss Cassandra Northrup said that I might and she is thought to be most proficient of all in the arts of medicine. When I visited her to give her my thanks she barely allowed my gratitude. Instead, she has asked for my help with her charity. Mama, of course, does not approve, but I think it is important...to remember about the plight of others, I mean...' She petered off as Acacia began to speak.

'Cassandra Northrup has lobbied us all in her pursuit of supporting those less fortunate.'

Interest sparked his question. 'You think she is too assertive in her search for patrons?'

'No, not that. She is known to delve into the shady corners of London when locating all the broken women and I think she understands neither the dangers nor the gossip associated with such an occupation. She looks as if butter would not melt in her mouth, but I have it on all accounts that she is well versed in the art of self-defence.'

'Isn't she just wonderful?' Lydia Forsythe's eyes were alight with hero worship, and the woman standing with Hawk, who Nat had not met before, also nodded her head.

A paragon and model of charitable benevolence. What would these people say if they were cognizant of the truth as he knew it? He had not told a soul about the names she had given to Lebansart. A questionable protection? A foolish guardianship? Even for England he had not betrayed her.

'She will never marry again, of course. She has made that quite plain.' Acacia's voice drifted into his thoughts.

'She won't?'

'No, my lord. The love of her life was lost in a terrible accident in Paris and she has no want to ever offer her heart to another.'

Nat's mind scrambled. Paris?

'Well, I think that it is romantic to tender thoughts for a husband long dead.' Lydia Forsythe for all her youth was most outspoken in her opinions. 'I have

asked the Northrup sisters to my ball and they have promised to attend.'

'An inducement of money for the cause would no doubt bring them running,' Acacia was quick to add. 'The Daughters of the Poor is a worthwhile charity, however. I have a maid acquired from that very organisation and she has been a godsend. Cassandra Northrup's benevolent society is both efficient and organised.'

'She has a school somewhere?' Nathaniel could not believe what he was hearing.

'In Holborn. When the girl was sent to me she was well equipped with clothes and books. Miss Maureen Northrup is apparently the one who sees to that side of the business.'

Hawk began to laugh. 'They sound formidable.'

'They are. Kenyon Riley is involved in the endeavour as well.'

'I thought he had lost a leg somewhere in America?'

'Lost a leg and gained a fortune.' Hawk took up the conversation. 'And his great-uncle, the old Duke, is about to die without issue.'

'A timely inheritance, then, for the Northrups.'

'Oh, indeed,' Acacia trilled. 'And Kenyon is most besotted by them.'

Nat looked away. Cassandra Northrup had a knack of landing on her feet after adversity and using others to the very best of her own advantage.

Of all the men in the world he was the one to know that.

'Maureen Northrup has her own worries.' A wide frown marred Acacia's brow.

Now this was new.

'She does?'

'She is virtually deaf. She lip-reads, of course, and speaks in her inimitable fashion, but it is the younger sister who runs the show.'

'And the father?'

'Lord Cowper is a man who has tried to carry on the life's work of his beloved wife. Something of tiny animals we cannot see that live on our skin and make us sick.'

Nathaniel's mind went back. Sandrine had insisted upon dousing his gunshot wound in the clearing all those years ago with water and she had cleaned her hands before she had touched him. She believed in these things, too, then. Every single fact he heard about her was more astonishing than the last.

'I have read of this. Such a hypothesis is gaining in traction in scientific circles as a credible theory.'

Acacia spread out her fingers and peered at them against the light. 'Well, I can see no sign of these things of which they speak and because of the wild claims of their science there are many here in society who do not view the Northrups with much kindness. Bluestockings frighten men of little brain.'

Hawk began to laugh loudly. 'Not quite the ideal of Victorian expectation.'

'By virtue of ornamental innocence, you mean?' Acacia shook her head as she said it.

Innocence.

The word stretched across the years, and Nathaniel was back beside the river in the small cottage of the

Dortignacs, his new wife's hair spilled across the pillow like living streams of fire and gold.

Madam and Monsieur Dortignac had insisted they both be up the next morning, bathed and dressed in clothes that were remarkably formal. It was therefore no surprise when a man of the cloth had appeared an hour later, although the blood had ebbed from Sandrine's cheeks as she had grasped the intention of his visit.

'Marriage? They want us to be married now?'

'They feel as though they have fallen from grace, so to speak, by allowing us the freedoms of sharing a bed. This is their way of making amends with God.'

'But you cannot possibly want this?'

He smiled. The light caught at her hair this morning and tumbled across the soft green-blue of her eyes. 'Sometimes when people need things with as much passion as they need us to marry it does not hurt to humour them. Particularly given that they saved our lives by their actions and probably put their own at risk.'

'You think it wise, then?'

'I do.'

'Well, I should never hold you to such a farce, Monsieur Colbert,' Sandrine said. 'If we are wed by simple expedience and obligation then who should need to know of it when we leave here?'

God. You. Me. The priest. Two names in a book that make this union traceable? Nat said none of what he thought, however, as he looped the chain over his head and unhooked the clasp.

'I received this after my mother died. It belonged to her mother and her grandmother before that.'

'Then you shouldn't risk it with me.'

Ignoring her protest, he lifted her left hand, the cold smallness of it within his warmth. 'Let's try it for size.'

It did not fit her ring finger, but it nearly held on her middle one. When they reached Perpignan he would have it resized.

'It almost looks as though it could be a real emerald,' she said quietly, and he smiled as the Dortignacs and the priest came into their room. Madam Dortignac had found some winter wild flowers and she handed the straggly bouquet to Sandrine with a smile.

'For you, my dear,' she said softly. 'The very last of the autumn purple crocuses.'

Much later, as Sandrine held her arm out so that the light glinted upon his mother's ring, it was impossible to clarify what he felt, the witchery of the sickness from the wound at his side still holding him prisoner, yet something else free and different.

But while his mind was ambiguous, Nat's body was not and the need in him surfaced beneath thin sheets. She had felt it, too, he thought, because she rolled over to watch him, a silent, wary question in her eyes and a hint of compliance. Her lips turned up at each end like the beginnings of a smile, a girl changing into woman right before his very eyes.

He could not help his want, nor could he rein in all that was left better unseen, the words of troth be-

tween them allowing whatever it was they might desire: warmth, relief, resolution.

Or nothing, with their sickness.

He wished he might touch her in quiet acquiescence, but instead he turned onto his back, sense winning out.

'They were more than happy to leave us alone this time.'

At that she laughed, joy enveloped in the dark closeness.

He remembered the feel of her in the bed when he had awoken that first time, the contours of her body, the thinness, the elegance. Like catching energy and holding it.

'You were a beautiful bride, Sandrine Mercier, with your hair let down.'

'And my bare feet. Don't forget those. But I think green suited me.'

'Indeed. The ancient gown was particularly flattering.'

'It was our hostess's grandmother's and it was twenty sizes too large. At least you had clothes that fitted.'

He held his tongue and wished that they were home at St Auburn, the English winter about them and everything familiar. When she had taken off the wedding gown after the ceremony the lines of her ribs had been drawn starkly on her skin.

'You are too thin.' He should not have said the words, he knew, a piece of paper gave him no mandate for such a criticism, but it was concern that made him speak, not disparagement.

'I was sick. For a long time.'

'At Nay?'

'Before that even.'

'And now?'

She shrugged and looked directly at him. 'Have you ever lost someone close to you?'

He looked away.

'My whole family, apart from my grandfather.' He wondered at what had made him say it, made him confess to a hurt he had always held so very far from others.

Her fingers crawled into his, warm and true, the honesty of the connection endearing. He coughed to clear the thickness in his throat and thought with all this emotion he must be more ill than he knew.

'My own mama died fifteen months ago. It was an accident.'

She stressed the last word in an odd manner, making Nat wonder if perhaps it wasn't.

'I was there when it happened and the doctor thinks my mind became damaged. Afterwards I could not be...happy. Papa grew impatient and I was sent on the journey south with my mother's brother and his daughter to recuperate and forget.'

Cassie swallowed and held on to him even more tightly. The fever made her head swim and her vision blurry, but she knew exactly what she was saying. She needed to tell him—there was no going back because in the past few days even under the duress of hiding from those who would want to find them she had sud-

denly felt free. At liberty to be honest and say all that had been held bound in her mind.

'It was my fault.'

He did not even flinch. 'The accident?'

'I added some liquid to her experiment before she had asked for it to be done and the vapour from it made her sick right then and there. She died three hours later.'

'How old were you?'

'Sixteen. Old enough to wait and listen.'

'The exactness of science is sometimes over-exaggerated and the emotion of blame is the same.'

His voice was quiet, unfazed. For the first time in a long while Cassie did not feel breathless.

'Did you intend to kill her?' he asked finally.

'Of course not.' Shock jagged through her.

'But you knew that those particular elements combined might cause a problem?'

'No. I have no true understanding of all the properties of things.'

Dropping her fingers, he stretched his arms above his head, linking them under his neck so that he could watch her with more ease.

'Once, when I was small, I took a horse and rode it for hours until the steed sat down and died. My father said the horse could have stopped running with my light and small touch upon it, or thrown me off into the brush. He said the stallion did neither because he wanted to keep running. His choice. Would your mother have added the next ingredient of her experiment if you had not been there?'

'I think so.'

'Then it was her choice.'

'But I ruined our family. Papa told me so.'

'No. I think if your father blamed you, it was he who did that completely by himself.'

Perception. Skewered into truth. It was all she could do to stop the tears of a relief that felt indescribable. Someone else believed that she was not responsible even with all the facts at hand. More of the inheld tension that she always felt melted away.

Colbert had saved her in the river, she knew, the water in her throat and in her eyes, the heavy panic of exhaustion pulling her down. He had saved her, too, when he had insisted on the hole covered in leaves and branches being made on the leeward side of the bush, tucked into calm. How would she have found shelter otherwise without his knowledge of survival?

Survival was marked on his skin, in the scars of bullet and knife. On the upper side of his fighting arm she saw the blue mark of indigo. A serpent curled about a stake.

A man who had lived a hundred hard lives and come through each one. She needed this certainty and this prowess because for the first time in years hope inside began to beat again.

Not all ruined. Not all lost.

A small refrain of promise.

When she smiled at him he smiled back and Cassie felt, quite suddenly, reborn. 'How old are you?'

'Twenty-three.' He added the word *ancient* in a whisper.

'Yet you haven't married?'

'I've been busy.'

The stillness in him magnified. He never fussed, she thought, or used up energy in movements that were surplus. For a big man there was a sense of grace about him that made one look again and wonder. The danger of a panther about to strike, the liquid stretch of muscle honed with a precision that was undeniable, jeopardy tethered to a strict and unrelenting accuracy.

She had seen it in Nay in the way he fought and again at the barn by the river. Someone had trained him well. The government or an army? No amateur could have forged such expertise, but a political mercenary might have managed it. Once a man similar to Colbert had come to Baudoin's compound in the company of a French General, and had been accorded much respect and esteem.

This was Nathanael Colbert's legacy, too. No one could look at him and fail to see the menace, even when he was sick almost to death and the fever burned. Glancing away, she felt her stomach clench. To have someone like this on her side...

She shook the thought gone. One day if she was lucky she would remember back at this moment and know that just for a small time he had been hers, her husband, a ring on her finger and the simmering potential of more. She wished her body had had the curves of Celeste and that she might have met him in Paris as a woman of an impeccable reputation and virtue. They could have danced then to a waltz perhaps, her dress of spun gold matching her hair and at her throat her mother's diamonds. She could have flirted with

him, held her fan in that particular way of a coquette and watched him through smoky eyes, the promise of all that might happen between them so very possible.

And instead? Her ruined hand on the counterpane caught her attention, the missing part of her forefinger and the long red scar easy to see in the moonlight.

'Could you kiss me?'

Her words were out, an entreaty in them that she had tried so hard to hide. But the emotion of the day was thrumming underneath everything they said and if she parted company with him, as she knew she would, she did not want to be left forever wondering. Or wishing.

For a moment she thought he had not heard or had not wanted to hear and her fists clenched by her side. But then he moved, balancing on his arm and leaning across her, his eyes the grey of the sea at dawn just after the sunrise.

Nathanael's lips were as she had imagined they might be, soft at first and then harder, searching for things that held a promise. Gentle and strong, harnessed by both power and care, his free hand caressing the line of her neck and bringing her closer.

Only them in the world, only this, she thought, as she rose up to him, her tongue meeting his and tasting. She allowed him to force her back against the pillow, the darkness behind her closed eyes calling for more. She felt him turn and come across her body, the outline of his chest meeting her breasts, though his elbows kept the bulk of his body away. The shiver of passion, the heat of want, the memory of this day quickening as he covered her mouth and kept her breath as his own.

A wife and her husband.

Then he broke away. 'When I am not so sick, Sandrine, I promise to take the kiss much, much further.'

Under the cover of darkness Cassie smiled because his heart was racing every bit as much as hers and when he turned away as if to quell all the thoughts his body was consumed by, she simply curled up into his warmth.

But it was a long, long while until she finally went to sleep.

They woke to the crow of a rooster outside, and inside Cassie could hear the movements of the Dortignacs preparing for a new day, the dawn only a little while off.

'We will leave with the first light,' he said as if he had been listening too. 'If Baudoin's henchmen following us find these people have been sheltering us...' There was no need for him to finish.

To the south, the mountains of the Pyrenees seemed to hold their breath, dark with the presage of rain. Another cold day. A further freezing trek towards Perpignan, many long and difficult miles to the east.

When Nathanael sat up on the side of the bed she saw the bandage across his wound was sagging. She should change it, she knew, but she did not think he would allow it and so she did not say. When he put on his clothes she understood he was in a hurry to leave and that the quiet moments of honesty between them had come to an end.

He looked healthier today. She could see it in the

way he stood, no longer favouring his right side in the way he was yesterday. She also saw in his expression a hint of the promise he had made after kissing her.

In the new day, Cassie suddenly understood the danger of a relationship. She needed to go on alone from here because she was certain Lebansart and his men could not be far behind, and if Nathanael died for her…

She shook her head.

If she struck out early across the hills, she could find a pathway and other travellers and make her way to any larger town in the vicinity.

Monsieur and Madam Colbert.

For one night of marriage only.

He had saved her so many times it was only right that she must now protect him.

Chapter Four

Cassandra came across the rooftops in darkness and down into the interior of the brothel on Brown Street without being seen by anybody. An easy climb given the footholds and the balconies, but on gaining the room the note had instructed her to come to she could tell that something was wrong. Very wrong.

The chamber door was wide open and the man Cassandra had been looking for was already dead on the floor by the window. Crossing to the glass, she tested the locks, but rust inside the catches told her nobody had come this way. With care, she dropped to her knees and checked beneath the bed, knife in hand and ready to strike. Only the empty space of blackness.

She was glad for the silence in the room for it gave her a moment to think. He had not taken off any of his clothes. There had been no struggle at all and he was unmarked save for the wound at his neck. Money still lay in his pockets when she checked and an ex-

pensive leather briefcase languished in full view beside the doorway.

His right arm was bandaged, the thickness of the casing beneath his jacket belying the injury. His other arm was positioned above his head, the gold ring on his finger seen in the light.

Not a robbery then. Not a targeted wealthy man who had come to the wrong place at the wrong time and run into one of the shady characters off Whitechapel Road. Someone he knew had done this, a strike from behind without a notion that it was about to happen.

Walking to the bed, she took the bag and flicked open the buckles. Surprise made her eyes widen. Nothing lay inside, every pocket emptied and all the compartments clean. The perpetrator had been after this then, the contents of the satchel, and for such information had been willing to kill. Loud shouting made her stiffen, the sound of boots coming up the steep stairwell and voices in the night.

With only a whisper of noise she crossed from the room to the doorway and let herself out. She couldn't be found like this—in the garb of a street boy with a weapon in her belt—and she did not have the time in hand to make it up the next flight of stairs to safety without being noticed. With care she picked the lock of the room opposite and eased herself through the door. No one was in the bed and for that she was more than thankful. Dulling the noise of the closing door with the cloth in her jacket, she jimmied her foot up against the wood and flipped the latch.

* * *

Nat did not move a muscle from the alcove he stood in by the window, his breath shallow. Outside the noises were getting louder and inside the intruder stayed immobile. Was the newcomer a child? A youth of the house, perhaps, trying to escape the nefarious pursuits as best he could? The glint of a knife told him otherwise and he was across the room before the other knew it, his hand hitting out at the arm that was raised and knocking the weapon away.

He knew it was Cassandra Northrup even before she turned, the scent and the feel of her, the knowledge of each other burning bright. Bringing her against him, he felt the lines of her body even as she fought him, the fuller contours unfamiliar.

'Stop, Sandrine.' Whispered. Danger was everywhere and the discovery of a lady within the confines of such iniquity would be scandalous. Her breath was ragged, the warmth of it against his hand where he held it flat across her mouth.

She stilled, as much to listen to the noises outside the door as to obey him, her head tipped to the wood, jumping as a heavy knock sounded against it.

'Don't open it. A man is dead and I cannot be found like this.' Whispered and frightened behind his fingers, the quicksilver change into a woman startling.

'Hell.' He let her go. She filled out the boy's clothes much more generously these days, though the thinness was still there, too.

'Take everything off and get under the covers.' Already he was peeling away his own clothes, throwing

each piece against a chair. Randomly. Trying to give the impression of haste and passion mixed in a room that was conducive to neither.

'Sex,' he said as he saw she was not moving. 'This place expects it.'

He pulled one dusty quilt off the bed and hung it over the other chair, hopeful in hiding the fact that female attire was missing. On a quick glance an observant onlooker would imagine them beneath.

'Open up.' A voice of authority. Probably the law.

It was enough to make her decide as her fingers flew to the buttons of her jacket and shirt, the lawn chemise beneath left on as she added her boots to the pile of clothes.

He brought those beneath the sheets with them, her body underneath his, concealed. He heard her gasp as the door opened, the correct key finally fitting the lock and giving way.

'What the hell...?' He barely needed to feign the anger as he looked around, two men in the uniform of the constabulary and the woman he had seen downstairs accompanying them. 'Get out, immediately.' He made himself sound breathless, the full blush of ardour in the words, a client in the middle of a 'paid for' assignation and surprised by the interruption. He also used his most aristocratic tones, the persona of a simple fellow disappearing into expediency. And carefully he shielded her from view.

He knew he had them as they faltered, a rush of apology. 'I am sorry, sir, but there has been a murder

just reported in the house. If you could get dressed and come downstairs, we need to ask you some questions.'

Releasing a long rush of air, Nat nodded. 'Give me a few minutes and I shall be down.' No entreaty in it. Just authority.

The door closed behind them.

Silence.

Warmth.

Her skin against his own.

And then a curse. In French.

He pulled away and stood, making no attempt at hiding his body. 'Did you kill him?'

'No.'

'But you know who did?'

She shook her head.

'God.'

'Why did you help me?'

'Misguided instinct, though I am certain I shall now pay for such kindness. Is there a way out of here that does not involve going downstairs?' He reached for his clothes and began to dress.

'Yes.'

'Then I would advise you to take it.'

Already she was up, her shirt and jacket quickly donned, the boots following.

'I will expect you tomorrow.'

'Pardon?'

'At eleven p.m. Through the window of my town house to explain all this to me. Properly.'

'And if I refuse?'

'Then I will come to see you instead.'

'I will be there.'

'I thought so.'

'Will you be able to manage…everything?'

'Easily.'

She smiled. 'I always liked your certainty, Monsieur Nathanaël Colbert.'

The music inherent in the way she said his name made him stiffen, and then she was gone.

His indiscretion was all over the town by midday, a lord of the first water visiting a brothel in the back streets of one of the worst areas of London and being caught out in doing so.

'You should have sent for me to come with you, Nat,' Stephen said as they sat in his library drinking brandy. 'Why the hell did you think to go there in the first place?'

'A man whom the prostitutes thought was acting strangely had been seen in the vicinity for each of the last two nights. They said he had slept at the brothel and was tall and well to do.'

'Was the dead man our murderer at the river, then?'

'No. He was short and stocky with ginger hair.'

'Memorable.'

'Exactly.'

Hawk suddenly smiled and leaned forward. 'There is something else I am missing here, Nat. It's the youngest Northrup daughter, isn't it? She was there at Whitechapel with you?'

Nathaniel ignored the query.

'The man killed at Brown Street last night was in the room opposite to mine and I heard nothing.'

'You paid for a room?'

'With a wide view of the street below. If the same man the girls spoke of was there, I would have seen him, Hawk, but I didn't.'

'Do you think the murder was related to our case?'

'Perhaps. The contents of the dead man's satchel was missing, though I found this in the corridor on my way down the stairs.' He dug into his pocket and brought out a single page of writing. 'Do you recognise the hand?'

Stephen looked carefully and then shook his head. 'Do you? It's a list for things from a chemist by the looks of it.'

'If I did, this case would already be half-solved. Will you do something for me, Hawk? Can you ask around to see if anyone saw anything? I do not want to seem interested because...'

'Because implication is only one step away from imprisonment and Cassandra Northrup's presence at Whitechapel will make everything that much harder again. Society does not seem exactly enamoured by her pursuit of the nefarious and a woman like that will only bring the old Earl's wrath down upon your head with even more than the usual vigour.'

'Remember that puppy we had at school, Hawk, the one we hid for a term in the woodcutter's shed, the one you found off the roadside on the way to Eton?'

'Springer. My God, he was the best dog I ever owned.'

'Sixteen weeks of sneaking out twice a day with the

food we had saved from the dining hall and then another jaunt for exercise. One hundred and twelve days before you could bundle him up and take him back to Atherton.'

'An unfortunate start to life, but he had the heart of a warrior till the day he died. But what is your point, Nat?'

'Cassandra Northrup is a fighter just like that dog and for some damned reason I feel compelled to help her.'

'You said she had betrayed you in France.'

'So did Springer. He bit you, remember, that time at the cliff....'

'Whilst trying to save me from falling.'

Nat drew his hand through his hair and wiped back the length of his fringe. 'What if Cassandra Northrup once did the same for me, Hawk? What if what she said she did and what she really did were two different things?'

'You are saying she might have betrayed you to save you?'

'I am.'

Cassandra had dressed carefully in a dark jacket and loose trousers, the cap she wore covering her face and her hair knotted in a bun at the back of her nape.

A caricature of Nathaniel Lindsay had appeared in the evening edition of a popular London broadsheet, one hand clinging on to the family crest and the other around the shapely ankle of a woman of the night. A poxed and toothless woman, her cheeks sunken with

the mercury cure and rats scurrying from beneath the hem of her ragged skirt.

Lord Lindsay could not have been pleased; she knew this without listening to any gossip. He had also remained quiet about her involvement in this whole chaotic and sordid affair which, given the history between them, was a lot more than she might have expected.

Why he had been there in the first place she had no notion of, but he had been alone in the room waiting and completely dressed and when he had first pressed her against the door she had felt the outline of both knife and pistol.

Another thought also came. She had imagined she had been followed when she came to the boarding house in the backstreets of Whitechapel. Could it have been Lindsay watching?

The web of lies that bound them to each another was closing in, sticky with deceit, and yet here she was again, moving through his garden for a further encounter in his library. If she had any sense at all, she should be turning for home and ignoring his threats or packing her things and moving north for a while until the shock of seeing him again eased down into reason.

But she could not. Every fibre of her being could not.

He was exactly where he had been last time as she climbed through the window, his long legs out in front of the wing chair by the fire.

The only difference this time was that he had catered for her arrival, two glasses filled beside him.

'I have had a trying day,' he said as he handed one

to her, 'and as you are the reason for it I hope you will join me in a drink.'

'A celebration of your notoriety?' Even as she gave the reply she wished she had not, but he only smiled.

'Yesterday the débutantes and their mothers were pursuing me with all the wiles in the world. Today they are…fleeing.'

'Sexual deviance may appear rather daunting to any woman, no matter the size of the purse an ancient family brings.'

At that he did laugh.

'How did you know the man who was murdered?'

'I didn't.'

'Then why were you there?'

'I had word of young girls being brought in from the country.'

'And you were attempting to locate them?' Lifting his glass, he held it up and waited for her to take a sip. Cassandra hated strong drink, but, not wishing to annoy him further, she took a mouthful and swallowed. The burning bitterness reminded her of Nay and of all that she longed to forget.

'The information I received gave a location, a time and a date, but when I got there the man was already dead.'

'With a knife in the back of his neck?'

'Yes.' She did not blink.

'What else did you see?'

'A briefcase that was empty of papers.'

'Papers like this one I found in the corridor outside the murdered man's room.'

He brought out a sheet of tightly written words. He knew she recognised it by her sudden stillness. 'Your father pens articles for a science journal. The editor is a friend of mine and I spent a few hours this afternoon with him. When, by chance, he showed me Lord Cowper's latest offering the two hands appeared identical.'

'That is what the person who put this there wanted you to think, wanted the constabulary to think. My father is the one person who can stop them.'

'How?'

'He funds the Daughters of the Poor, and we are making good progress in catching those who trade the lives of young girls for work in the factories and the brothels.'

'We, meaning you. You in your boy's clothes in the dead of night risking life, limb and reputation.'

'Gone.'

'Pardon?'

'My reputation is gone. You of all people should know that.'

'The redemption of a sinner then, brazen and unmindful. I expected more of you.'

'Oh, I have ceased trying to live up to any expectations save that of my own, my lord. Now prudence rules over heroics, which in itself is a timely lesson for all who might rally against injustice.'

'Society holds you up as a saint?'

'Hardly that.'

'But not as a whore?'

The quick punch of hurt and then nothing. By the time she had come out from that hovel of a building

in Perpignan Nathanael Colbert had long been gone and she had wiped all trace of sacrifice from her conscience since.

Just a small space of hours, blurred by pain.

She was glad he had not insisted on the removal of her chemise last night for even in that darkened room he would have seen and known. Her shame. She glanced away, knowing the black anger of it would be showing in her eyes and she did not wish for him to see.

The mark on his jaw shone opaque against the firelight, lost slightly in the growth of stubble. If he grew a beard, it would be gone entirely. She was glad he had not. Had he wanted to he could have erased all memory of her for ever. As it was he must look every day into his reflection and be reminded.

The futility of everything blended with the brandy, a melancholy covering all she had hoped for once. He was as beautiful as he had been then, in every way, strong and self-assured, although the mantle of aristocracy gave him an added allure.

Shallow, she knew, but it was a fact. With a man like this she could be safe.

Sense reined in fantasy. He was all but promised to the beautiful and clever Lady Acacia Bellowes-Browne, a woman who would suit him exactly and in every way. She wondered if he ever thought of the hurried marriage in the village by the river where Mademoiselle Sandrine Mercier had married Monsieur Nathanael Colbert, two names plucked from a half-truth and settled in the register like impostors.

At this very moment all he looked was angry.

'Every time you come into my life, Sandrine, it seems chaos follows.'

'I am no longer Sandrine.'

'Are you not?' He came closer, the largeness of him disconcerting. England seemed full of small men with the smell of a woman about them, the indolence of life written upon their skin in softness, the bloom of ease apparent. Nathaniel Lindsay had none of these qualities. He could have been transported here from an earlier time, the menace and threat of him magnified in a room filled with books and quiet pursuits. She would be most unwise to ever think that a lord like this could offer safety after all that she had done to him.

'What other woman of the *ton* would dress as a lad and walk the back streets of hopelessness in the midnight hours? Your father must be demented to allow it.'

At that she laughed. 'The days of a man's ordinance over me are long gone, Lord Lindsay.'

'Even a husband's?'

She had wondered when he would mention it, had been expecting him to from the very outset, but the word still made her blanch, the beat of her heart hurrying with the reference.

'If our marriage was deemed to be a binding agreement, then our years apart must allow grounds for question. But given the circumstances, I should imagine it was not.'

He smiled, but the steel in his eyes hardened.

'Why were you there, at the brothel?' She needed to know if he was friend or foe.

'Two women were killed a month ago beside the

Thames in Whitechapel. I was following up a lead to find the man who did it.'

Every word he said made their relationship more dangerous. 'Do you have names?'

'No.'

'Other clues, then?'

'I am looking for a tall and well-heeled man. His hair is dark.'

'Such a one has been seen by the children we have rescued on a number of occasions.' She wondered why she told him.

'Which is why you were at the de Clare ball, no doubt. Scouting?'

'You read my intentions with too much ease for comfort of mind, Lord Lindsay.'

'Do I, Miss Northrup?' Something had changed between them in just this single second. She felt the tension in the room shift to something less certain.

'What happened after I last saw you with Guy Lebansart?'

'I grew up. I paid the debts I owed and I grew up.'

'You sacrificed others to save me? Why?' Anger creased his brow.

She felt the breath in her hollow, felt the beat of her heart flatten into some new and risky unease, and did not speak.

'I never asked that of you.' Said in the manner of a man who was not comfortable with indebtedness. 'Nor did I want it from you.'

She had had enough. 'You think that you might control everything, my lord? You think that people should

only march to your drum, the drum of the morally justified? Are you now one of those men who cannot see another side of an argument, the side where good and bad mix in together to create a new word, an in-between word, that allows life?' Whirling around, she went to stand at the window. Part of her thought to slip through it into safety, but another part understood that without explanation she might never be free of him and he was dangerous. To the life she had built which depended to a large extent on her being accepted by those she mingled with.

'After leaving you I stayed in Perpignan. I was shocked by all that happened, you understand. Celeste's family needed time to know of the demise of their loved one and I needed a space to myself before...' She stopped.

'Before you returned to England?'

Jamie. Jamie. Jamie.

Under each and every word said his small and beloved face lingered and it was all she could do to hold him safe.

'I have forged a life here. My life. Once, a very long time ago, I was someone else.'

A traitor. A wife. A victim.

A woman who had used every part of her wiles to save the father of her baby. She did not flinch as he watched her. She did not think of the marks on her breast or the weeks of fever that had followed. She thought only of Jamie.

As if Nathaniel Lindsay's fingers had a mind of their

own they went to his chin and traced the damage. 'I thought that I knew you then, but now...'

'Now we are strangers travelling in different directions, my lord.'

Away from each other? Away to safety.

Turn and go now. Turn and go before he touches you and before the quiet way he gives his words makes you foolish. It is the only way that Jamie can stay safe.

With a quick snatch at the curtain, she lifted her leg across the sill and was gone.

Nat stood and watched her run, her shadow barely there against the line of trees, blending in the moonlight.

Even with Acacia he had never felt this connection, this need to protect her from all and sundry. Cassandra Northrup made him crazy, witless and sad, yet the feel of her slight body against his in the warm waters of the high pool above Bagnères-de-Bigorre lingered.

Shimmering against reason.

They had gone there by chance, a traveller's tale remembered, a small, ancient and lonely pool set amongst the mountain scrub, steam rising like God's breath from the very bowels of a restless earth.

She had forged on ahead from the little house by the river, trying to escape him, he was to understand with time, hurrying along the mountain passes without looking back, though when he had found her a good two hours later she had given no explanation and he had not wanted to ask for one.

After that they had moved with their own thoughts

across the landscape, always climbing higher. An image of Alph the sacred river running to measureless caverns and sunless seas took his imagination. Sandrine was like a sylph, light of foot and pure of heart, her hair in the grey mists the only bright and shining beacon.

His wife.

He had never been married before and the troth was surprising in its power. She was young, he knew that, but under her youth there was wisdom and discernment born from an adversity he could only wonder at.

His.

For better or for worse.

He quickened his pace. Already she was thirty feet in front of him and the slope was steepening, but to his left was the grotto he had found many years before, the steam even from this distance visible.

'There.' He pointed, and she shaded her eyes and looked, a smile rewarding his discovery.

'We can take a bath?'

He nodded and took her hand because the shale was treacherous and he did not wish for her to slip.

Later, in the cold winters of London, he would think of this time and try to remember each and every moment of it. Back then the relief of another chance at life after their sickness had made him feel exhilarated.

He could smell the sulphur as they came across the last rise, the warmth of air in the wind blowing towards them. Like an invitation, and just for a moment, he imagined them as the only people upon the entire planet, lost in the universe. He wondered if the fevers

had taken his reason because he seldom thought like this, the flowery rhetoric of the Romantic poets on his tongue. Perhaps it was Sandrine who made him such but he didn't like to think of what that might mean.

Nat's side ached, and he still felt hot, but a day out amongst the clouds had revitalised and settled him.

'Will others come?' Her voice was small.

'Not now.' Already the light was falling. Another hour and it would be gone completely.

When she smiled, he smiled back, his aching bones crying out for a warm soak in a mineral pool. She dipped in her fingers, the ruined hand swallowed by opaque water, nestled in heat.

'You have been here before?'

'A long while ago.'

'Is your home near?'

This time he merely shook his head and sat down, taking off his boots and placing his socks carefully within the leather so that they did not get damp.

She was watching him, her eyes filled with delight. A joyous Sandrine was so different from the one he more usually saw, the dimples in her cheeks deep and the quiet creases of laughter charming.

'Put your clothes under mine when you have them off. That way they will stay dry.'

Within a moment he was naked, wading into the water and dipping down. She had turned away, allowing for privacy, but he did not care. Closing his eyes, he waited till she joined him.

'I cannot ever remember feeling so good.' Her words were quiet as she lay back, spreading her hair across

the surface, like a mermaid or an enchantress, the colour in each strand darkened by the water. She had not pushed off from the bottom for every other part of her body save her face and neck was hidden from him.

Most women of his acquaintance would have simpered and hesitated, a lack of clothes precluding all enjoyment. But not her. She simply took what was offered with a brave determination, the mist beading her eyelashes and small drops settling on her cheeks and lips.

'It is said in these parts that this pool contains the soul of a sea sprite who lost her lover.' Another flight of ridiculous fancy. He grimaced.

'How?'

'The sprite changed him into a merman so that they might always be together, but his jealous wife threw flames upon his form and he dissolved into steam.'

'Water and steam. They still live together?'

Sandrine's hand came up from the pool and she cradled both elements. 'Legends and science. My mother would have peered into this pool to see what lived inside of each drop.'

'The new and unseen frontier of science?'

'You know of this? She looked puzzled and faintly incredulous.

'When I am not killing people I can be found reading.'

Her laughter rang across the quiet, echoing back. 'A warrior and a scholar. If you were to go to the salons of the wealthy, Nathanael Colbert, you would be besieged by women. Celeste would have been one of those had she lived.'

'How did your cousin die?'

'By her own hand. Baudoin's brother Louis was her first lover and when he was killed she had no more heart for life.'

'Difficult for you. The one left.'

She did not answer, but in her eyes there was such grief that he moved closer and took her hand, waiting till she regained composure. All the things that she did not say were written in hard anger upon her face.

'How did this happen?' His thumb traced the line of her ruined finger because he knew that to speak of such travesty would be a balm.

'Baudoin and his brother were always at odds with one another over my cousin. Once, when we first came to Nay, I tried to drag Celeste back from getting involved in an argument and Anton slashed out at me.'

Anguish solidified inside of him, and he attempted for her sake to push it down. 'I see you holding it now and then, rubbing at the finger that is missing?'

She smiled. 'It hurts sometimes, a phantom pain as if it is still there.'

The small fragility of her hand made the wound seem even more mindless. The ring of his mother's that she wore was far too big and he touched it.

'I will have it resized, Sandrine. So you do not lose it.'

Puzzlement in her eyes was tinged with surprise. 'I should not expect you to honour a marriage that was forced upon you when you were too sick to resist.'

'The church may disagree.'

Their world stood still, steam the only thing moving

between them, up into the growing blackness. Their shared night-time kiss also shimmered in the promise.

'A poor reward, no doubt, for all your endeavours to save me.' The grasp of her fingers slid about his own.

'Ah, but it could have been worse. You might have been old or ugly or had the tongue of a shrew.'

She laughed.

'No. I think on balance I was not at all hard done by.'

The lustrous colour of her hair caught at them, claiming him, binding them as one.

Alive.

She was still alive and so was he and she was pleased her attempt to escape him had come to nothing. In the silence above the world she allowed her head to rest upon his chest, listening to his heart.

The beat of vitality against her ear, the course of blood and hope and energy. It had been so long since she had been held this way, with care, like a porcelain doll shimmering in the wind. With only a small nudge she might shatter apart completely and she did not want to move. No, here she wanted to know what it felt like to breathe in the sensual and be rewarded by its promise. The lump in her throat thickened. She did not love Nathanael Colbert and he did not love her back but they were man and wife, a pair beneath the gentle hand of God, and in this, His place, a natural pool of light and water and warmth.

For so long she had been fighting alone. For all the months of Nay and then the year before that, her mother's death embedded in her sadness.

Could she not let it go for one moment on a hillside in the wilds of the Pyrenees and in the company of a man who looked at her as if she was truly beautiful?

No ties save that of a marriage that would never be real. If she survived this flight to Perpignan she would return to England, ruined by all the accounts that would follow her, she was sure of it. But would she ever again be offered the chance of this?

The skin across his arms was brown and hard, the indigo of his tattoo strangely distorted in the water. She touched it now, traced the curl of serpent with one finger and then leant her mouth to the task.

Tasting him.

He breathed in deeply, and Cassandra felt the power of which Celeste had spoken all those months before. Not a limited sovereignty or a slight one. When her fingers slipped higher to his face she outlined the features: his nose, his cheeks, the swell of his lips and the long line of his throat.

His eyes watched her, fathomless, twin mirrors of the sky and the water and the mist, but fire lurked there, too, and it was building.

'I am only a man, Sandrine. So take care that you do not cross boundaries you have no wish for me to traverse.'

'What if I do?'

There, it was said and she would not take it back, not even when the flicker of wariness crossed into grey and she saw in his soul the first thought of 'why?'.

If he asks, I shall walk straight out of this pool.

But he remained quiet and the turn of hardness, his sex, budded beneath the limed water.

It was what she needed, this truth of reaction, no whispered lies between them stating a future that could never be. For this moment she felt like a woman reborn, the girl in her pushed back by a feeling that was new, creeping into the place between her legs and into her stomach. Heavy. Languid. Damp.

Lost in the transfer of all she had suffered.

And in control of everything.

He did not speak because he was a man who understood small nuances. It was his job after all, seeking truth and finding exactly what it was those buried under the shifting tides of war needed to survive.

Sandrine needed oblivion, and he needed her to find it. It was simple. A translation of grief.

She was weightless against him, her thinness in the water disguised. He was glad he could only feel: the small mounds of her breasts, the flat plane of her stomach, her long legs draped around his waist as if they had a mind all of their own.

Opened to him. Waiting.

He wrapped the fine length of her hair about his wrist, tethering her, gentling her, the cold in the air and the heat of their bodies making light work of the joining, and when his lips came down upon her upturned mouth he did not hold back.

He was in her, tasting, her throat arched upwards and their breath mingled. He knew the moment he had

her assent, for she began to shiver. In her ardency her
fingers scraped down the side of his arms.

'I want to know what it is like to have a husband.'
The honesty in her words undid him.

No pretentiousness, the grandiose and flowery al-
lowances of various ladies he had known pushed aside
by a simple truth. She did not play games or set rules
or say one thing, but mean another. Danger and hard-
ship had done away with all the extraneous.

Hot. He felt hot from the pool and her skin and the
building need inside him. 'I would not wish to hurt
you.'

She smiled at that, the dimples in her cheeks deep,
and steam across the coldness of night lifting around
them. 'I know that you won't. It is why I want it to be
you.' -

With care, his fingers dipped, the softness of woman
and the heat there, and she tensed, her eyes sharpen-
ing as though pain might follow and when it didn't
she urged him further, a small sigh of release and
surprise.

She was tight and tense, her eyes a clear and startled
turquoise as she watched him, measuring, challeng-
ing, her hips lifting to allow him in farther though her
brow furrowed as he found the hard nub of her desire.

She stilled him. .

'What is this?'

'You, Sandrine, the centre of you.'

Relaxing even as he spoke, she allowed him closer,
the feel of her body against his, her breasts more generous than he had thought them.

'Beautiful.'

Exchanging his hand for his manhood, he pushed wide, edging inwards, filling the space of her. When her arms pulled him in he knew that he had her and, twisting his body, he came in deeper.

With the water and the bubbles and the steam about them, both lost their tapering hold on reason, the final absolution as she went to pieces, beaching waves of rigid need, and then was quiet.

He held her motionless as he took his own relief, his face held upward so that the fine mist of night cooled him, his groan of pleasure involuntary.

'God, help us.' He had never felt like this before with anyone, never wanted to start again and have her impaled upon him, for all the hours of the night and the dawn, only his.

He should have withdrawn, should have given his seed to the water where it would wither and die in the heat. And instead...

If she were fertile then a part of him would grow.

But she did not let him think. 'Take me again on the bank in the cold.' Her voice was soft and her tongue licked at the space about his chin.

A thin, brave and pale siren with no idea at all as to how much she had affected him. Lifting her into his arms, he came from the pool in a cloud of steam and laid her down in the nearly night and gazed.

'You are so very lovely.' He whispered the words, honesty in every syllable, and when she smiled he found the hidden folds between her legs and tasted her. Sandrine. Salty and sweet and young.

* * *

Much later he dressed her, carefully so that the cold did not creep into softness. He had marked her as his, the red whorls of his loving standing out on the paleness of her skin, telling the story of long and passionate hours. But already the dawn birds called across the wide mountain valleys, signalling in the light.

'I did not know it could be like that.' Her voice was guarded. 'After Nay I was not a virgin.'

The rawness of her confession grated against the new day. A confidence she did not wish to share, but had felt the need to? He frowned.

'No one could live in that hovel and remain...untouched, though Celeste soon worked out a way to protect me from them.'

'How?'

'She began a relationship with Louis Baudoin and insisted I sleep in a small room off their own.' Taking in a deep breath she continued on. 'I think she thought the accident in the carriage was her fault somehow. She had wanted to take a detour off the main road and it was there that the horses stumbled down the hill. Her father and his godson were killed and Louis Baudoin found us just before it snowed.'

'A saviour?' He hoped she would not hear the irony.

'He took us home, and Celeste was grateful.'

'And you?'

'I was grateful to her.'

When people lied they often glanced down before they did so. Their body language changed, too, the arm crossing the chest in an effort at defence. Nathaniel saw

all of this in Sandrine, and when she did not answer he did not press her, but the joy of communion wilted a little in the deception and in her confessions.

With the wind behind her and the shadow of her hair across her cheeks she suddenly did not look as young as she always had before. But she was not quite finished.

'My cousin was of an age when the adventures of life are sometimes sacrificed to the safer and more conventional. I could not save her.'

Nat stood and took her hand, holding it firmly as she tried to loosen the grip.

'It is over now, Sandrine, and the past is behind us.'

But she only shook her head. 'No, Nathanael, it is here right at our heels, and if you had any sense at all you would leave immediately and escape me.'

His laughter echoed about the lonely and barren hills.

Chapter Five

Maureen confronted her the morning after she had gone to the St Auburn town house, deep marks of worry across her brow and dark eyes fixed upon her lips.

'You were so late home last night. I can hardly recognise who you have become, Cassie, and I do not think you know it yourself, either.'

Her rebuke stung. 'This is not an easy task, Reena. There are so many who need—'

'To be saved?' A question. 'And what will be your salvation when you are caught in the lad's clothes far from home and I cannot find you?'

High emotion changed a careful diction so that the words slurred together unfinished and disjointed. Realising this, Maureen reined her anger in, the hands she used so much in communication hard up against her ears, pressing, and the guilt that had been Cassandra's constant companion since the accident bloomed.

'I cannot properly hear what people say any more,

Cassie. Mama was certain that I would grow out of my affliction, but it is worsening.'

'If Mama was still here she would know what to do, but she isn't. She's gone,' Cassandra shouted back, for after an evening sparring with Nathaniel Lindsay she was heedless. 'It was all my fault that she died. I was the one who did that.'

They had seldom spoken of the day of the accident, the memory too painful for them both. Their beautiful and clever mama falling down upon the floor, her eyes wide open with surprise and pain and then nothing. Save Reena with her hands on her ears in exactly the same way she held them now, her face creased with disbelief.

The laughter was unexpected.

'Mama's science is what killed her, Cassie. Mama and her foolish insistence on having us help her.'

The shock of the words kept Cassandra still.

'Alysa only thought about her experiments. Don't you remember that? She lived in her laboratory. Her scientific discoveries were her babies so much more than we ever could be and the thought of saving the world soul by soul through uncovering unseen sicknesses was what drove her. If she had not been killed in that particular accident, then there would have been another.'

Such revelations amazed Cassie. 'You never told me this.'

'I tried to because I could see that you thought it was your fault, but you loved her too much to listen and then you got sick.'

Heartsick. Body-sick. Soul-sick.

Leached of life by guilt and then by shame.

'I should be rejoicing in my affliction in any case and not decrying it. I would have never met Kenyon otherwise for I would have heard his horse behind me and got off the path. What a loss that would have been.'

The day just kept getting stranger.

'Kenyon Riley?'

'Of course. I am getting older, old enough to imagine I should never have the chance of a family. I love him and he has asked me to marry him.'

Pieces of a puzzle clicked into place. Kenyon's presence at the school, his interest in everything that they did, his generosity and his kindness.

'You have been distracted lately, Cassie. I wanted to tell you, but you were never here. You were always dressed in your boy's clothes and out in the night, helping others.'

Mama. Maureen. Kenyon.

My God, she had missed all the signs of change.

'There is a problem, however, and I think it is only fair that you hear of it from me. There are whispers in places that say you were the woman in Lord Lindsay's bed in that whorehouse in Whitechapel, and they are gaining in traction. Kenyon has tried to douse the rumour, but it seems you were seen.'

Maureen's careful diction made the accusations sound so much worse, each rounded word ringing out the ruin.

'Tell me it is not true, Cassie, and we can refute it together. I can say you were here with me and that they were mistaken...' Her voice petered off as Cassandra shook her head and anger lit her dark eyes.

'He forced you?'

'No.'

'You wanted him?'

'No.'

'Then why?'

Because I was abused once by monsters who held no mind for a young, thin, sick and frightened girl. Because Nathanael Colbert saved me from hell and we were married under other names in a town I can barely remember. Because I betrayed others to save his life. Because I have killed men by my hand and by my words and he hates me for it all.

That is what she could have said, might have even tried to had her brother not have chosen that very second to interrupt them and come tumbling into the room with a parrot upon his shoulder.

'I was given this by a sailor in the park who had come from India and wanted to go back again without the bother of a bird. Sixpence, he charged me, and he said I was to call him "Mine".'

At the sound of his name the bird lunged from his perch on Rodney's arm up on to the gold clip in Maureen's hair, pecking at the glitter to create havoc. And Cassie knew without a single doubt that any moment of truth was well and truly lost.

'Mine. Mine. Mine', she heard them both calling as she slipped through the doorway and left.

Cassandra lay in bed that night and thought of all that Maureen had said. If the gossip about her were to become widespread, what would happen? Nathan-

iel Lindsay would hardly be stepping forward with an offer of his hand. Again.

Wonderful and terrible.

The day had been that. Maureen's good news balanced against her bad. The guilt felt about her mother's death lost into the wonder of Reena meeting Kenyon Riley and all because she did not hear the hoofbeats of his horse as they came from behind her. Despite everything else, Cassie smiled and rubbed at the china shard Nathanael had threaded for her in the tiny village of Saint Estelle.

They had come down into the settlement late in the afternoon, the thin sunlight slanting on to their faces as they walked in silence after their night at the pools. Cassandra had not dared to break with words the magic that danced about every part of her body.

This was what she had heard of in the ballads and in the books. This crawling, sensuous, languid warmth that sifted through everything and left her different.

She wished they might find a room somewhere, alone, and begin all over again. The punching throb of need made her groan, and he turned.

'Are you hurt?'

The redness began at her breast and crept up on to her cheeks, a wave of heat similar to that she had felt last night. Unstoppable. She was like a woman in a story book, a woman with little will of her own and a singular wish for the feelings expressed in the works of the Romantic poets Celeste and she had read under the candlelight.

Thrilling.

Please.

The word coiled inside her like a snake waiting to strike.

Please. Please. Please.

She saw the moment he understood what it was she hid, blue darkening across silver in a will all of its own.

Lust it might be for him, but for her love held on at the edges, grasping tentatively. The feel of the ring against her skin deepened it, a circle that held them together, caught in the company of each other, pledged to God.

And by flesh now, the feel of him within her, the building joy of need, the hours of play and delight so different from anything she had known at Nay.

She shook away the darkness. No. She would not think of that again.

'I will find us a room.' His voice sounded strained and unnatural.

This time the feeling was different. This time they circled each other fully dressed in a chamber that was… comfortable. Now instead of a strange world far from the one they knew, a certain familiarity crept in. The crystal of the glasses. The bed with its feather quilts. A window where the blinds had been drawn across the remains of the day; curtains of floral damask much like the ones hanging in the library room at home. Bread and wine sat upon a gilded tray on the table.

The consequences of choices already made settled in. One day she would be back in London and this would all be a memory.

She began to unbutton her shirt, but he stopped her.

'We will eat first.'

First.

She shook her head. She was not hungry for food or wine. She did not want to wait until they had supped and spoken, all the normal things that happened in a relationship. This was not normal, the aching lust that coursed through her and made her want to lunge at him and take everything that his body could offer hers. She wanted him inside, moving; she wanted to feel all those things she had last night and this morning when her mind for once had flown away from thought and into a place that was only feeling.

No past or future, only now.

'We have time to—'

She stopped him. With her fingers across his lips. Pressed hard.

'No.' Her other hand unbuttoned his shirt and came inside, the warmth beguiling. Yesterday he had flicked her nipples with his forefinger and she had liked it. Today she did the same to him, measuring his heartbeat as it quickened.

'Tonight is by my bidding.'

The slate-grey darkened, the last light from a dying sun slanting through a gap in the curtains and reaching the skin on his chest where she had peeled away clothing.

'Like the daughters of Achelous?'

'The sirens?' She laughed. 'Dangerous and beautiful?' He knew the old legends of Greece and the names of the gods. For a second she wondered just exactly

who he was, this man dressed in clothes that had seen better days, but when she kneeled to undo his trousers she forgot about such intrigue entirely.

He was her husband and he was ready for her, sprung hard against lust, nothing hidden. A gift offered without payment or coercion. Or hurt. Legal. Sanctioned. Authorised.

She laid her fingers around his shaft and brought it to her tongue, licking the ridges and the smoothness, finding the essence; and when he swore roundly she brought him in deeper.

Hell, Nathaniel thought, his world spinning in a way it never had before, the sweet feel of yearning drumming in his ears. Wild curls hid Sandrine from him, trails in gold and red, her slender shoulders bent in concentration to all that she gave. He knew she wanted control, but in another moment his restraint would break and he had to give her back more than just his own relief.

Guiding her face away from swollen flesh, he lifted her chin and she stood. He had no clothes on and she was fully dressed, small webs of repaired fabric standing out against the light. Placing his mouth across hers, he slanted the kiss, his fingers running across the fine lines of her throat and bringing her closer.

'Love me, Sandrine.' Whispered. Gentle. Allowing more than simple lust.

'I do.'

She was so light as he lifted her, a shadow of a woman, but tall with it. He brought her to the bed and

sat her down, and when her hands went to the buttons at her shirt he stopped her.

'My turn.'

She did not argue.

Five buttons and one missing. Beneath the cotton was sheer lawn and lace, repaired like the rest of her clothes, but of a quality that told him of a life led before. The pad of his finger lingered on the stitching, complex, intricate, the sort of thing his mother might have worn had she lived.

The straps were thin and of satin and he slid them across her shoulders so that the chemise drooped and her breasts were there, peaked and perfect. He cupped his hand around one feeling its form, admiring the curve of skin and the unexpected smattering of freckles.

The tip-tilt of her nose as she looked at him made him smile. A girl who was the most beautiful woman in the world. The narrowness of her waist, the slender length of her arms, the elegance of neck.

This was Sandrine.

A goddess lost into the wilderness and now refound.

He traced his initials into the cream of her skin, *NL*, and she looked up in puzzlement.

'Once I was someone else,' he explained.

'And I was, too,' she responded, the rightness of their coupling underwritten by truth. 'But now all I want to be is loved well.'

He lifted her onto his knees, slipping off her trousers and socks and boots so that she sat naked and waiting.

He liked how she did not hold her legs together tightly or stiffen as his fingers came between them, exploring.

'Is this well enough?' he asked as he found the core of her in the hard nub of need. 'Is this what you want?' he added as he began to move faster and faster, the rhythm changing just as he thought she was about to come apart.

Wet for him and swollen. He could feel the throb inside and the heat.

And when she nodded he simply placed her upon his cock and drove in, the finesse transformed to something much stronger and more basic. It was not knowledge that brought them together now, but an ancient magic with no rational thought, and he cried out as her body clenched about his, taking all that he offered and more.

He took her again in the night and once in the morning when the first rays of sunshine woke them. He had not slept with a woman for so many hours in his life, his more normal caution and vigilance taking him from a bed well before they asked for more than he might want to give. But with Sandrine they spooned together in the cold and lonely hours and when they awoke their bodies called, the quick burst of need and the slow sating after relief.

Once on waking he found her looking at him, as though she wanted to remember every piece of who he was.

'Stay with me for ever.' The words were out before he knew them to be and she placed his hand upon her heart in answer.

'Here. You will always be here.'

'Do you promise?'

Nodding, she simply rolled over on top of him and all that had been magical before began again.

Cassandra awoke with tears running down her cheeks and the cold London morning bearing down. No longer in France. No longer in the place of dreams and promises, the steam bath above Bagnères-de-Bigorre and the curtained room in Saint Estelle.

Avalon. The vaulted ceilings and the shining marbled Gothic arches.

A noise made her turn, and James was at her doorway, a teddy bear held in one hand so that his furry legs dragged along the floor.

'Mummy.'

'I am here, darling.' She pulled back the sheet and waited until he came inside, tucking the warmth about him when he was settled. His small roundness pressed into her, the smell of slumber upon him.

'I dreamed we were in France.' His pale grey eyes watched her, dark hair standing on end from sleep.

'Once we were, my love. Once it was just you and I there and I knew from the very second I saw you that I should love you for ever.'

He giggled. 'You always say that.'

'And I always mean it.'

'Nigel said his daddy still lives in France. But I said mine was dead.'

The worm of dread turned. 'Well, you have so many

others who love you, sweetheart. Mummy. Maureen.
Anne. Granddad. Rodney. The cook. Nigel's mummy.'

'But a daddy is special. Nigel said that they were.'

Lord Nathaniel Lindsay. More than special. She
would have to tell him, she knew that she would, but
not yet. Not while Jamie was still hers to love and hold
like this, the secrets of the past hidden in a corner
where they were unable to escape and ruin everything.

And if Nathaniel took their son away...?

She shook her head and, drawing her fingers up into
the shape of a spider, began to recite a children's ditty,
liking the laughter that followed.

Chapter Six

'Chris Hanley said what?'

Nat tried to curb the panic in his voice as Stephen answered.

'He said that he saw Cassandra Northrup creeping from the Brown Street boarding house as though the very devil was on her tail the night of the murder.'

'What the hell was Hanley doing there?'

Hawk began to laugh. 'He was out on the town with a group of friends, but your question precludes other more pressing ones, Nat. If, for example, your lady was not present you might have asked if he was crazy to be so mistaken? As a judge, I would infer from your words that the accusation was true.'

'Cassandra Northrup is hardly my lady.'

His mind whirled as Stephen continued to speak. 'The ruination of her reputation might only be a minor concern when stacked up against such a killing.'

'Do people believe Hanley?'

'I'd like to say no, but I think that they are begin-

ning to. Reginald Northrup has made no attempt at silencing his friend either, which is telling. I took it on myself to find out a little of the Northrups and if Reginald himself stands to gain anything from any discrediting of the brother's family. One daughter is almost deaf, the second one is married and living in Scotland and the son is still a minor. Cassandra Northrup's ruination is irrelevant for I am certain Cowper would have made a will stating his preferred guardians for Rodney and for the trustees of his estate.'

'Is it the title he wants? From all accounts the Northrups are not as rich as he is.'

'No, not that. Just the influence, I am presuming, for the title is more than safe. Rodney is the direct heir, but there is another more pressing fact that you should know, Nathaniel, given your recent championing of the youngest Northrup daughter. Cassandra Northrup may not be the lady that you think she is. She is reputed to take many more risks than she should.'

'Risks?'

'She does not seem to give much account to her reputation. It seems she is not averse to wandering the same streets the prostitutes do in order to save some of them. Kenyon Riley was touchy when I asked him further about it.'

'You saw Riley?'

'Yesterday at White's. He bought rounds for all and sundry and I had the feeling some personal celebration was in the air. He spends a lot of time with the Northrups so perhaps he has finally decided to offer for one of the daughters.'

The wheel turned further and further. Cassandra Northrup had become the beauty Nat had predicted she would all those years before and even encumbered with two failed marriages she was...unmatched.

Swearing, he poured himself another drink.

She ransacked him with her beauty. That was the trouble. The history between them had also had a hand, their marriage, their trysts around Saint Estelle and the small villages before Perpignan, hours when he had imagined her as his forever wife safe at St Auburn and providing timely heirs for a title steeped in the tradition of first-born boys.

Lord, what groundless hopes. In every meeting thus far she had never given him an inkling that she hankered for more between them other than the safe keeping of hidden secrets arising from betrayal.

And now a further problem. She was innocent of the murder of the man at the brothel, but could he just leave her to fight the accusations herself? He knew that he could not.

'Is our membership in the Venus Club complete, Stephen?

'Yes?'

'When do they meet again?'

'This Saturday. I thought to go there after making a showing at the Forsythe ball.'

'I will accompany you then. I would like a chat with Christopher Hanley.'

'So you will still be involving yourself with Cassandra Northrup's plight?' The laughter in his friend's eyes made Nat wary. Sometimes Stephen had a knack

of finding out things from him that he did not wish to divulge.

'There may be no one else to help her.'

Hawk raised his glass. 'Then I drink to an outcome that will be of benefit to you both.' Nathaniel wondered what Stephen might have made of the fact that they had once been married and that high up on the foothills of the Pyrenees their troths had been consummated with more than just a nominal effort. He wished he might speak of it now, but there would be no point in the confidence. Sandrine had chosen her pathway and it had wound well away from his. Still, he would not want to see her made victim for a crime she had not committed.

He swallowed, for his logic made no sense. She had betrayed England and then carried on with her life with hardly a backward glance. He should not trust her.

A ring of the doorbell brought his butler into the library.

'There is a Miss Maureen Northrup here to see you, my lord. She will not come through, however, but would like a quick word in the foyer.'

Standing, Nat looked at Hawk, who lifted his glass with a smile. 'A further complication?'

Outside, the same dark-eyed girl at Albi's ball stood, her maid at her side and her hands wringing at the fabric in her skirt. Underneath a wide hat he could see her face and she looked neither happy not rested.

'Miss Northrup.'

'Thank you for seeing me, Lord Lindsay. I will be

as brief as I can be. Is there a room where we might have a moment's privacy?'

'There is.' He opened the door to his left and shepherded her into the blue salon, wondering at all the conventions being broken for an unmarried woman to be alone here. He did not shut the door.

'I wish to know what your intentions are regarding my sister, my lord?' She did not tarry with the mundane.

'I have none.'

He thought she swallowed, and she paled further at his reply.

'Then I want you to stay well away from Cassandra, sir. She does not need your dubious threats.'

'Threats? She told you I had been threatening her?'

'Not in as many words. But unless you have some hold upon her I cannot see why she would have been willingly in your bed in that house of disrepute off the Whitechapel Road for any other reason.'

This Northrup daughter was as brave as her sister, her eyes directly on his face and no blush at all upon her cheeks.

Her voice was strange, he thought, the diction so precise. Then he saw her glance upon his lips and he remembered. She was deaf. Deaf and brave, he corrected, and trying with all her might to protect her family.

'I was helping her. A man had been murdered in the room opposite and San...Cassandra would have been implicated had she been found there. I bundled her into my bed and pretended...'

He could not go on. This was the strangest conversation he had ever had with anyone before.

'Pretended...? You said "pretended"?' She mulled the word over, the light coming on in her dark eyes as she did so. 'I see, my lord. I had thought...' Again she stopped. 'Thank you for your time, Lord Lindsay. I do appreciate it.'

With that she simply glided out through the door, gesturing to her wide-eyed maid to follow and was gone, the clock in the hall ringing out the hour of one in the afternoon. The butler looked as puzzled as he did.

'If Miss Northrup returns, do you wish to know of it, sir?'

'I doubt she will be back, Haines, but if she comes send her through to me.'

Stephen still sat where Nat had left him and from the look on his face he had heard the whole thing.

'If Cassandra Northrup was with you, Nat, I should imagine your intentions are nothing like those you regaled the oldest Miss Northrup with? You have not taken a woman to bed in years.'

A reprimand. Given with the very best of intentions. He could no longer lie to Hawk.

'Once, Cassandra Northrup and I were married. In France.'

By the look in his friend's eyes this was the last confession that he had been expecting. 'Are you still?'

'It was never annulled.'

'I see.'

The silence in the room heightened, a heavy blanket of question.

'She had been captured by a group of bandits in the Languedoc region and dealt with badly. I was trying to protect her.'

'Something that you are still doing here.'

'Perhaps.'

'Then take care, Nathaniel, for society can be most intolerant to a woman who would live outside its rules. Even one who is both beautiful and clever.'

Saint Estelle had been small and run-down, a mountain town of old buildings and kind people.

In the morning after they had eaten they had walked along the river and he had found a shard of blue-green pottery at the water's edge.

'If I could buy you a tourmaline, Sandrine, I would, because that gemstone is the exactly the shade of your eyes. But as I am penniless, this will have to do.'

She took it carefully, with the hand that was not ruined, and held it up to look at. 'Gemstone pottery?' Her laughter hung in the earliness of the day and warmed his heart. 'A priceless gift that I will keep for ever.'

'For ever is a long time.' Sadness had settled in the corners of his mind. He wanted to hold her away from danger and keep her safe. He wanted to take her to St Auburn and make her understand exactly whom she had married, the coffers of the place filled with the treasure of the past in an unending array of wealth, diamonds, gold and silver and every gemstone in between. He wondered what she would make of the ex-

pectations inherent in his title and conversely what those at the castle might make of her. Especially his grandfather.

'Tonight I will find some leather and fashion a hole through the top so that you can wear it as a pendant.'

Her hair had caught the wind and the many-coloured lights of it tumbled wild with her curls, the length reaching the contour of her hips.

'Mama always insisted that one gift required another in return. She said that in the giving of a present there should also be the taking of happiness.'

He stood still as her hand came against his cheek, tracing the line of his throat downwards.

'The gift of the power of womanhood is one I could bestow upon you if you should so desire it, Nathanael.' Beneath the laughter in her words there was another cadence, full of promise. 'My cousin Celeste used to say that I should find it one day, this knowledge of the sensual, and that men would not be able to refuse such an authority from me.'

'She was right.' Gravity had crept in under humour and he could hear the steady beat of his own heart in his ears.

'So you accept?'

'I do.'

They were far from the village and he had seen no sign of others for many miles. Besides, the road out of Saint Estelle lay upon the opposite bank of the river, past the line of trees, out of sight.

Last night had been frenzied and passionate and

furious. Today a languid peace reigned, a quiet acceptance of each other's needs.

'Come.' She held out her hand and he took it, following her into the shadow of the trees until they
reached an overhang of cliff, the rocky outcrop of the
Pyrenees sheltering a little bowl of meadow. It was
noticeably warmer.

'Here, away from the wind we can love each other.'
Bringing two blankets from her bag, she laid them
down as a bed.

Within a moment she had removed her clothes,
lying on the wool without any sense of shame, burnished like an angel from one of the old religious
paintings that graced his grandfather's library.

Reaching for his fingers, she placed them upon her
right breast and leaned into the touch. His other hand
she splayed in the warmth of the space between her
legs, her thighs apart and waiting. 'I am yours for the
day, *monsieur*. I am yours until the sun lies upon the
horizon and the dusk is reached. My gift for your gift.'

Positioning the other blanket to keep out the cold,
his fingers began to move with a will of their own, up
into the warmth of her, up into the swollen wet darkness where feminine magic lingered. She did not draw
back. He slipped in farther and heard her sharp intake
of breath. Playing her tenderly and feeling the answer
of her muscles against his hand, the first tremble of
release as frenzy tightened. Taking ownership. He did
not let her move away as her whole body shuddered
into climax, roiling waves clenching skin to muscle.

She cried out, once and then again, her head arched

back so that daylight filled her, the sweat of climax dampening her skin and making her rigid with lust.

The scent of her between them, the hard erectness of nipples, the loss of self into a frenzy of feeling. Shivering need brought her arms about him, her nails gouging trails into his shoulder. Joined. For ever. Locked into union.

Moments passed in silence, the heat of her slackening to limpness.

When he brought his mouth onto the peak of her right breast, she simply clasped her hands about his head and nudged him closer. Like she might do a suckling baby, guided to the source.

Quiet. Still. Primal. The reclamation of all that had been once before and now was again. The gift of belonging. The heavy punch of sex and now the softer pull of place. Home. With Sandrine. He shut his eyes and took the offered gift, grateful and indebted.

In all of his life he had never felt as loved.

They woke to the sound of evening birdsong, the dusk across their blankets. With slow care she moved atop his manhood, filling herself with the largeness, moving in her own rhythms and refusing any help.

Her gift, she had said, and his taking. When she pinned his hands against the earth and told him that she was in charge he had allowed it, the sky above and the meadow beneath. She did not let him come until the sun had fallen almost to the horizon, the tension in him stretched to the full ache of friction, a thin hot pain of need.

And then she had taken each of his nipples between her nails and pinched. Hard. Jarring.

He had climaxed as he never had before, emptying himself into her, wave after wave, involuntary, uncontrolled. And she had taken him in, wanting his seed, drawing him up as the final gift of the day. He felt the undulating motion of her insides around him and knew without a shadow of doubt that he could love her. For ever.

On their return to Saint Estelle the tavern keeper was full of the news of a group of men who had come into the town looking for two strangers.

'The leader was a big man with dark-brown hair and a scar across his cheek. Here.' His fingers drew the shape of a crescent. 'He appeared very angry.'

Lebansart. Cassie drew in her breath and knew that Nathanael had felt her fear.

'Did they say where they were going next?'

'They didn't say and I didn't ask, but they left Saint Estelle before the noon hour and there was no talk of a return.'

'We will stay here then for a few days longer.' Nat dug into his jacket pocket and pulled out a handful of coins. 'If they should return at any time at all, I would like to be told of it.'

'Who exactly is this man, Sandrine?' The question came a few moments later when they were once again back in their chamber.

'Guy Lebansart. He was an acquaintance of Anton Baudoin.'

'What does he want?'

She shrugged her shoulders and turned away. *Me.* She almost said it, almost blurted it out before biting down on the horror. The document she should never have read shimmered in her memory.

Cassandra spent the morning at the school at Holborn. Kenyon Riley arrived around midday and walked into her office.

'Is Maureen here, Cassandra?' His voice was tinged with the accent of the Americas, and he sounded happy.

'She went to run an errand in town. I should not imagine that she will be long.'

'You look busy.'

Cassie observed the large pile of papers that littered her desk. She tried to be organised, she really did, but with the amount of work she had, such a thing was never easy.

'My sister told me the good news about your betrothal.'

'Did she? I was wondering if she would ever get around to mentioning it to anybody else.' His smile was wide.

'Reena is more contented than I have ever seen her.'

'She deserves to be.'

'I agree and I don't think she could have chosen more wisely.'

He watched her, his dark eyes perplexed. 'And what of you, Cassandra? Is there someone in your life, too?'

'You have been listening to rumour, I think?'

'More than rumours. Lord Christopher Hanley,

. your uncle's friend, claims he saw you in Whitechapel with Lord Lindsay. A large section of society is heeding him.'

'Well, I have never played a big part in the life of the *ton* so it will suit me to be even more reclusive. What can they do, after all?'

'Believe me, attack is the best form of defence. Come with your sister and me to the Forsythe ball and stare the naysayers down.'

'Apart from sounding risky, did you consider the possibility you might be ousted because of your association with me?'

He laughed. 'My uncle is one of the richest men in England and he is dying. No one would chance offending the next heir to the dukedom.'

In that moment Kenyon Riley seemed more like Nathaniel Lindsay than he ever had before. Powerful. Certain. Unafraid.

Perhaps he was right. Cassie had already flouted convention with the keeping of her maiden name and no true proof of her being at Brown Street existed anywhere save with Lord Lindsay. She did not believe that Nathaniel would abandon her as she had him in Perpignan.

'Maureen is having a fitting for a new gown this afternoon. You should go with her for you have worn the shades of mourning for all the months that I have known you. Perhaps it is time to branch out and live a little?'

'You sound just like Reena.'

'If I do, it is because I care about you and because Lindsay is a good man, an honourable man.'

She nodded her head. 'I know.'

'He is also a man who would not ruin a woman's reputation lightly.'

'He didn't.'

'Good.'

When he left her office she leaned back in her chair and looked out over the street at the front of the house.

Nat was indeed much more honourable than he would think her to be, in the light of what had happened on the outskirts of Perpignan.

They had remained in Saint Estelle for almost two weeks, always putting off their leaving for yet another day so that they could walk to the hot pools above the village or to the abandoned cottage on the other side of the river and pretend that this was their house and their life. Entwined in each other's arms, the particular glow of lovers blocked out the rest of the world and the world became blurred and ill defined.

Until one morning when Cassie awoke to the knowledge that her menses had not come and her breasts felt sore and full and heavy.

Pregnant? She counted back the days and the weeks and always came up with the same conclusion. She was overdue and her body was telling her that things were changing inside.

Elation was her first thought and then caution. Caught out in the countryside in conditions that were hardly conducive for an early pregnancy she knew Nathanael would worry. So she said nothing.

In Perpignan she would see a doctor and then she would tell him. She knew the town and the people there. She felt at home in the narrow streets by the river. Her hand with the ruined finger crept to the secret she held in her stomach and she cradled the joy. Their child. A child born of love and of passion. Tears threatened, and she swallowed them away.

Five days later on the way into Perpignan she began to bleed. Only a little, but enough to make her understand that she needed to be somewhere quiet and peaceful, to simply stop and relax. Each morning for the past week she had felt sick on awakening and the nausea had not abated till the noon. She wanted a hot bath and a hot meal and a bed that she could stay in that was comfortable and safe.

She wanted a doctor's reassurance and the time to tell Nathanael that he would be a father, in a place where they were not looking over their shoulders for any sign of who followed them.

They had seen no trace of another since they had left Saint Estelle, always keeping away from the main roads and shadowing the rivers as they ran from the mountains down onto the plains below.

Perhaps they were safe now and whoever had been following them had given up completely. She knew Lebansart hailed from a place farther north. Had he realised the futility of chasing them and had returned home? She prayed that it might be so.

Taking the shaded alleys, they came into the outskirts of Perpignan at sunset and stopped on the left bank of the Basse River. The fortified walls stood

before them and in the distance on a high citadel the Palace of the Kings of Mallorca sat, its limed walls pale in the last rays of sun.

Cassandra loved this place, with its warmth and its gentle winds off the sea. When first she had come she had been entranced to finally be able to speak the language of her mother and to feel the heat of the sun on her hair, the colours of this part of the world so different to the greyness of London.

Perpignan and the busy Mercier household had been a revelation, and the fact that she was only a cousin had made no difference to the generosity of her uncle. Celeste's mama, Agathe, had been dead a good two years so that was yet another thread that held the cousins together.

Another time.

A lost life.

A whole family gone.

She turned to look at Nathanael who sat leaning against a low stone wall, watching her.

'This was where I lived with Celeste's family. I came here to get well.'

'Hell!' His expletive was round as he stood. 'You never told me that. Would those at Nay have known of this?'

She shrugged, his anxiety seeping into her contentment. 'Perhaps they may have.'

'Then we cannot enter the town, Sandrine.'

'You think those who followed might find us here?'

'I know they will.'

The shadows around them moved in a way that was

suddenly dangerous, the branches taking on the outline of shapes of men in her mind. Never again. Never
again would she allow herself to be under some other
person's rule.

He must have seen her fear for he moved closer.
'We will strike north tomorrow along the coast and
find a ship to take us to Marseilles. I have friends
there.'

She shook her head. Another trek across the countryside and with the further promise of snow. The
reserves she had been storing up were suddenly no
longer there and now it was not just her life she had
to protect. She had to stop, the cramping pains in her
stomach no longer able to be denied and ignored. 'You
should leave, Nathanael. While you can. I cannot go
on.'

*It is me that they are after. Lebansart could pass
you on a street and not know your face. Thus far you
are safe.*

She wished her voice did not sound so afraid, the
cold air of an oncoming night making her shake. She
had killed Baudoin with her knife. She could not be
responsible for the death of Nathanael Colbert, too.
Not him. Breathing in, she suddenly knew just what
it was she must do. With all the effort in the world
she smiled.

'You have bought me home and it isn't as unsafe
as you imagine. Celeste's family has a position here,
a power. I can be protected.'

She should take off the marriage ring held in warm
white gold around her finger and give it back, but she

could not quite make herself do that. For the first time in a long while she felt virtuous.

'You cannot possibly think that a group of bandits whose secrets you know would stop pursuing you because of some aristocratic courtly authority? These people exist under far more brutal rule.'

Shaking her head, she placed one hand across his. She would go to the home of Celeste's father's best friend and his wife. She knew without doubt that they would keep her safe.

It all comes down to this, she thought, *his life and her child's safety. There was no room in any of it for her.*

The ache around her heart physically hurt as she gave in to all that she knew she must do.

'We have been flung together out of expedience and I thank you for the protection you have given me and for the things you have taught me, but...' She swallowed away the 'but' and began again. 'We are different in everything that we are and I want to go home, back to a life that I know. I am not used to such...a lack of luxury, you see, and eventually we would both feel embittered by our differences.'

Stifling grief, she looked directly at him, the stillness in him more worrying than any anger.

'Just like that?' he finally said, flatness in the words.

She nodded. 'It will be better for us both. I am sorry....' She could not go on, her hands spread in front of her gesticulating emptiness. Her smile was so tight it hurt the muscles in her cheeks.

They do not know you yet. They have no idea of exactly who you are.

'I have a comfortable life in Perpignan and I am tired of the squalor that we have needed to exist in.'

'I see.'

No, you do not see at all, Nathanael. You do not know what this is doing to my heart.

'We could meet sometimes, if you wish. I wouldn't be averse to that.'

'For what reasons, Sandrine? To demand my conjugal rights?'

She shook her head, his anger gathering in the storm clouds of his eyes. 'To reminisce.'

'Reminisce about all these weeks of memories that mean nothing to you or about the importance of material acquisitions? I think I shall say no.'

She could only guess at what he must think of her, one moment this and the next moment that. Disbelief flourished amongst fury as he lifted the blanket he slept on from his bag and rolled it out underneath a thick bush. 'We will talk again of this tomorrow when you have come to your senses. By then you may see the wisdom of my arguments and the half-witted nonsense in your own. The church, too, has strict and particular ideas about the sanctity of marriage.'

Then he simply turned away.

Cassandra's eyes felt heavy but she made herself stay awake, the moon much higher now and the true silence of early, early morning upon the grotto. They had made their beds on opposite sides of a small field

of grass and he had not spoken to her again, but now he was asleep. She could hear it in his breathing and feel it in the way he had been so still for all of an hour.

She watched him from her place across the clearing, the strong lines of his body, the dark of his hair. She could not see his face because even in sleep he had not let go of his anger and had turned away from her, the knife on a bed of leather beside him. Readied.

He would protect her to the death. She knew this. He would give his life for her without even thinking of the payment.

Her chance. To escape. Her chance to leave him here, safe against the darkness while she attempted to creep into Perpignan alone and disappear. She did not know why she had not thought that Lebansart and his men would be waiting in the one place they guessed she might have returned to.

Stupid, she chastised herself. *You knew how dangerous they were, but you did not think and now you have placed Nathanael in danger also. Mortal danger.*

Carefully, she sat up, each fraction of movement as slow as she could make it, her breath shallow and light. Then she stood, again stopping as she came fully upright, only the wind in the trees and the far-off call of a night bird.

One step and then two, the shadows taking her beneath them, blocking out the moonlight and then an open space on the banks of the Basse, a track to a bridge across the river and the gate on the old fortified walls. Open. It had not been defended for hundreds

of years, a relic of a medieval past when nothing was as safe as it was now.

She smiled at her thoughts given all that she was running from and kept to the dark side of buildings as she came into the town proper. She hadn't brought her bag because she did not want to lift it and hear the rustle of thick canvas. But she had brought her knife, tucked into her right sleeve in leather, the hilt extending from the thick fabric of her jacket.

Almost to the Rue des Vignes. Almost there.

Then a noise. Close. An arm snaked about her throat, cutting off breath, and the face of Guy Lebansart appeared next to her own.

'We thought you would come, Sandrine, although perhaps not quite so soon.'

The warmth of his palm as it caressed the line of her cheek made her skin crawl.

Nathaniel came awake to emptiness. He knew Sandrine was missing before he even looked, though her bag still stood beside her blanket.

Only a few minutes, he determined, the wool covering still slightly warm when he checked, but the wind had come up and she had used the noise from the trees to depart.

Last night they had not spoken at all after she had told him she needed to go on alone. He swore at the absurdity of everything and the nonsense of her beliefs. Did she truly think she could just fit in again to all that she had been and forget what was between them? Had all of the past days been some kind of elab-

orate deception to allow her passage into Perpignan, his presence a necessary one to alleviate the sense of danger? Only that?

Nat could not believe this to be true. There were other things that she had not told him, and he needed to find out exactly what they were.

Bundling all their things together, he stuffed them into an empty space between one of the bushes nearby. He would come back for them later, but it never hurt to cover your tracks, no matter how much of a hurry you were in; spying had at least taught him that.

She would have cut along the river, he was sure of it, to cross at the next bridge. From memory the Basse had more than one bridge spanning it and was swimmable in places, though he could not see her wanting to get wet. From there she would move inwards, and the town was not so big that a good search would be impossible. No. He just had to look carefully and hope like hell that she had made the place of her destination safely.

He tipped his head, listening, but there was no sound that was different from the wind on the water and the trees, no sound that alerted him to danger or compromise. Three o'clock. The quietest hour of the night. Jogging along the track until the first bridge, he then went down on his knees.

There he had it. A fresh print in the mud showing damaged soles. She had come this way. Again he tipped his head. Now there was only the noise of the water and the first spots of rain in the wind. Tracking. His forte. He had done this so many times over so

many years, following so many quarries. This time, though, the stakes were raised and he knew he had to be very careful.

'What was in the document, Sandrine? The one Baudoin wanted me to see? Pierre said that he saw you reading them.'

'I do not remember.'

'Liar.' There was an unexpected laughter in Lebansart's voice as if they were playing a game that he liked. The taste of fear and panic was bitter in her throat, but there was something else again. Triumph, if she could name it. They had not mentioned Colbert at all.

Guy's voice was close as he loosened her hair. 'Perhaps you might tell me when we are alone, *ma chérie*?' His fingers digging into her arm belied his nonchalance and around him others lingered. More than a few others. Ten or twelve, she supposed, and behind them in the shadows more would be waiting.

'Silver-tongued Leb', he was called back at the compound. A man who spun a web around his prey without fuss or contretemps. He had not even drawn his own knife, leaving that to those about him, their sharp blades seen against the dimness.

She had lost. She had rolled her dice and lost. But she had kept Nathanael safe and away in the arms of sleep.

The commotion started as a low roar and then a louder clatter. The sound of a neck breaking and a

knife jammed into breath and he was there, beside her, reaching out, the touch of him breaking her heart.

Nathanael. Already the others were circling behind him, quiet in the early dawn, like a pack of wolves waiting for the command to attack.

She did not let him speak; one word and they would kill him. One wrong sound and it would all be over.

Instead she got in first, swinging her left hand around to his face and opening his jaw with the sharpened edge of her marriage ring at exactly the same time another hit him from behind, the sound of metal against his skull crunching.

He bent over, shaking his head as he did so, trying to find vision.

Do not speak, Nathanael. Do not claim me.

She thought quickly. Lebansart had ties with the government that he would not wish to jeopardise. 'I have seen him before. He is a soldier of France so better to leave him alive. But do as you will, I really don't care.'

Looking away, she tipped her head towards her captor, trying to bring forth all of her womanly powers. If they killed Nathanael she would die as well, but the threat of the might of the military seemed to have done its job.

'We don't need the army after us. So blindfold him and bring him along.'

Another thump against flesh and she turned back, the blood from his jaw spilling over his shirt and his lips red raw from a wallop. He looked dazed, barely

conscious. No blades though, no telltale sign of an injury that he would not recover from.

She laughed in relief, the sound bringing the attention of Lebansart back to her before he had the chance to change his mind. 'Perhaps we might find a place to speak, Guy.'

When his arm threaded round her and his hand cupped her breast she simply snuggled in.

'Sandrine, the whore.' She heard the voice of a man behind and knew that Nathanael would have known exactly what she allowed.

A whole lifetime of his years for a few moments of her shame. A tenable payment. She did not look back again as Lebansart led her away, his fingers closing in around the small shape of her ruined hand.

Nat came awake in a bed and a room, a priest at his side and the light of morning on his face.

'Finally you have woken, *monsieur*. You were found beside the river Basse six days ago and have been in and out of consciousness ever since. In truth, we did not think that you would survive, but we prayed and God has answered us our call.'

Six days.

Sandrine would be long gone.

His head ached and his sight seemed compromised. The wound on the side of his jaw smarted, and he put up his hand to feel it.

'We stitched it and it is healing.'

Sandrine. He remembered the look on her face as she had led the Frenchman away. Pleasure. Flirtation.

Relief. She had not even glanced back at him as she allowed the enemy everything.

Sandrine the whore.

He hated her, this woman who was his wife, hated her lies and her easy betrayal. He had not known her at all in the days of their flight from Nay. A stranger. A harlot. A cheat.

'There is someone waiting for you outside. He is an Englishman and he would like to talk with you. Do you feel up to this yet?'

When Nat nodded the priest rose and left. A moment later a tall man with sandy hair came through to stand beside the bed.

'I am Alan Heslop,' he said quietly, 'from the British Service, and I have come to see what you know of the Baudoin brothers. It seems you were at their compound and a fight ensued? I ask this of you because two of our agents were targeted and killed this past week, brothers whose names were on the letters taken by the Baudoins from the overturned carriage of Christian de Gennes. Letters that were known to have been in the compound.'

Didier and Gilbert Desrosiers were dead? Sandrine would have seen the documents and told of them, then. He stayed silent.

'My sources say there was a woman. A woman was reputed to have been there.'

He opened his mouth and then closed it. Even now, after all that had happened, he could not bring himself to betray her. If the British Service had word of

her involvement they would hunt her to the ends of the earth. Garnering breath, he tried again.

'I saw no one. I left after Anton Baudoin shot me.' Lifting his shirt, he noticed the heightened interest of the newcomer. 'By all accounts, de Gennes's letters were at the compound, but I could find no trace of them.'

'Did you speak with Baudoin?'

'No. I was there in battle and there wasn't a chance of conversation before I killed him.'

'I see. You will start back for England next week. The Home Office has made arrangements for you to travel by ship, though I suppose you will need to answer more questions when you return.'

'Of course.'

'But for now you must rest. I will have warm broth sent in from the kitchen for you have lost a good deal of weight from the beating you received. It seems you were dropped in the river to drown, but your coat snagged on a pillar as the current took you away and a group of youths found you.'

'A lucky escape, then.'

'Perhaps.' The man's glance caught his own and without another word he left the room.

When he was gone, Nathaniel began to take stock of the wounds he had incurred. A heavily bandaged head, a broken right arm and two eyes that were so swollen it was hard to see.

Sandrine Mercier had betrayed both him and England to save herself.

Closing his eyes, he shut everything out and willed himself to survive.

On returning home, Nathaniel went straight to the family seat. His grandfather, the Earl of St Auburn, stood before him, a heavy frown upon his brow.

'A further scrape that you have no explanation for, and a newly made scar on your chin that looks like you have been in another fight. And to top it all off you have lost your grandmother's ring. An heirloom. Irreplaceable. I am almost seventy-three years old, Nathaniel, and you have never stopped disappointing me.'

Nat stood and finished his drink. It had been a bad idea to expect that William Lindsay might have welcomed him home after hard, long and lonely months abroad. Tonight, however, with the portrait of his father upon the wall above his head, Nat had had enough of such hostility.

'I shall be at Stephen Hawkhurst's for the next few weeks before going back to Europe, William.'

'Running away as usual. The St Auburn inheritance does not simply see to itself, you know. A small interest on your behalf as the one who will inherit the responsibility would not go unnoticed.'

'I am certain you are quite competent at the helm. I am also certain that any changes I made to the estate would only incense you, after all, for we have tried that track before.'

'Then take a wife, for God's sake, and settle down. You are old enough to be giving the estate some assurance of longevity, some hand into the future.'

A wife.

Nat almost laughed. He had a wife already and if he could have produced Sandrine Mercier at that moment he would have dearly loved to, if just to see the look of horror and disgust in his grandfather's eyes. But she had been lost to him in Perpignan, gone into the ether of betrayal, a woman who had not given trust a chance and who had flouted every principle of integrity.

Placing the glass carefully down on a small oak table beside him, Nathaniel tipped his head in parting and left the room.

Chapter Seven

Cassandra Northrup had come to the Forsythe town house on Chesterfield Street with her sister and Riley, just as Nathaniel had hoped she would not.

Tonight she had forsaken the colour of mourning and adorned herself in muted gold, like a flag of defiance, her eyes shining with fight. With her hair dressed and the gown complementing the sleek shades, she was the embodiment of all that Albi de Clare had once predicted.

Unmatched.

Original.

The girl in southern France only just seen through the woman she had become.

She neither fidgeted nor held on to her sister or Kenyon Riley for support, but stood there, chin up.

He doubted he had ever seen her look more beautiful than at this particular moment and when her eyes finally met his, Nathaniel knew without a shadow of

doubt that the swirling rumours of a relationship between them had reached her ears.

Her sister appeared less certain, but Riley, positioned in the middle of them both, gave the impression of a cat who had just been offered a bowl of cream. Nat wanted to hit him.

'Let the games begin.' Hawk was hardly helping matters, and Reginald Northrup to one edge of the room was watching Cassie intently, as was Hanley.

Undercurrents and anticipation. Nat did not make any move towards the Northrup party whilst he waited to see what would transpire.

The older Forsythes reacted first, moving from Kenyon Riley to Maureen Northrup without a glance at the one beside them. Then Lady Sexton and her husband turned their backs. A cut direct from a woman who was known for her own dalliance was hardly lethal. But it was the next snub that did it.

Lydia Forsythe, the young hostess who had the most to thank Cassandra for given her recent brush with the chandelier, simply stood, right in front of her, the slender wine goblet she held tinkling to the ground, shattering into pieces.

The band ceased playing.

Silence descended, the inheld breath of a hundred guests slicing through movement, ruin taking the physical form of a woman in a glorious gown and sharp blue-green eyes. She stood very stiffly, the horror of all that was transpiring barely hidden upon her face, her mutilated fist tight wrapped in the folds of her golden skirt.

Despite trying not to, Nathaniel moved forward, the only motion in a room of stillness and those all around craned their necks to see just exactly what might hap-pen next.

'Unfortunately, Miss Lydia Forsythe is a woman prone to histrionics,' he said as he reached Cassie, then he lowered his tone. 'However, if you act as if you do not care you might be able to salvage something of the evening yet.'

Cassandra was silent, dumbfounded, he supposed, by the way things had plummeted from bad to worse. Worry had furrowed a deep frown in the space be-tween her eyes.

'The trick in it is to converse as if you have all the time in the world or at least smile. Your face at the moment suggests you believe in the ruin of your name and this is exactly what others here have come to see.'

To give Cassie her due, she did try, the glimmer of humour showing where before only a frown had etched her brow.

Her sister, however, picking up the undercurrents, began to help, droning on about the seasonal changes and the new buildings in Kew Gardens. Riley stood silent, the grin on his face infuriating.

'I always love the Palm House, of course, but I think the Water Lily House will be every bit as beautiful. They say when it is finished the giant Amazonian lily will flourish within it and that a child might sit on a leaf like a boat and not get wet at all. Imagine how huge it will be.'

Amazonian must have been a difficult word to say

for someone who could not hear properly, Nat determined, though Maureen's unusual pronunciation did have the effect of making Cassandra's lips turn upwards.

Around them the silence was beginning to change into chatter, the terrible scene that some might have hoped for fading into something unremarkable. Even Lydia Forsythe had pulled herself together, her mother signalling to the band to begin to play again and the young hostess making an overture of civility towards the Northrups in the form of a genuine smile.

A waltz. Without waiting for another moment, Nat asked Cassie for the dance and they stepped on to the floor.

'Thank you.' She held him away as they moved, a large space between them, circumspect and prudent. They did not dance as lovers might, though beneath his palms the warmth of the old Sandrine lingered. He tried to ignore it.

'Your uncle appears to welcome the demise of your name.'

'I think his enmity has something to do with his relationship with my mother.'

'It was his friend Hanley who told the world he saw us together.'

Her direct glance faltered. 'I have heard.'

'What would Reginald Northrup have to gain by discrediting you?'

She shook her head. 'Not the title, for Rodney is the heir apparent.'

He might have asked of her movements after Per-

pignan then, just to see what she might tell him, but the colour in her cheeks was returning. Besides, the middle of a crowded dance floor was not a place he wanted to hear an answer in.

'He is far more wealthy than my father, so money cannot be a factor.'

'A man with no obvious motive is more dangerous than those who have one, and if your nocturnal wanderings are known to him then it would be wise to be careful. Or cease altogether.'

She tipped her head, her expression puzzled, and his fingers tightened around hers in a will all of their own.

He was so beautiful and so known.

The corners of Cassie's heart squeezed into pain as he watched her, grey ringed with just a touch of dark blue. In his arms, here in the middle of a crowded ballroom, she felt completely safeguarded, even given the poor start to the evening. No one could touch her. No one dared. The exhilaration was surprising.

'Come with me next time, Nathaniel. Come and see just what it is that the Daughters of the Poor do.'

His lazy smile was lethal. 'I have already discovered some part of it in the bawd house off Whitechapel Road.'

'No. Not that. It's the successes you need to see.' She thought of the toddler Katie, her injuries fading and her smile blooming again. It was these things that she wanted him to know of. A new beginning. Another finer path away from the chaos that had once consumed them.

'Please.' She did not wish to beg, but this moment might be her only chance to make him understand that sometimes with endeavour honour could be reinstated.

'When?'

The anger in the room and all her problems melted away with that one small question. He would allow her a chance? For the first time that night her breath was not tight and the beat of her heart quickened from something other than fear.

'As soon as I know I shall send you word.'

'Very well.'

'Wear black.'

Nothing now was the same between them as it had once been, but inside of her a bright warmth bloomed. The papers that held them together had probably long been lost and she no longer had his ring, but there it was, that same feeling from France that pulsed in every part of her body.

Love me. Love me. Love me.

Just a little. Just a bit. Just enough to allow the possibility of an understanding and forgiveness.

'How long has your charity been running for?' His question cut through all her fantasies.

'Two years now. I found two young girls wandering in Regent Street and on enquiry discovered they had been brought in from the country and then lost.'

'So you took them home?'

'Actually, no. I found out the place they had been stolen from and returned them. That was how it all began. Sometimes, though, it is not so easy. Sometimes young women are lost to us or put to work in the seedy

houses of London and it is hard to recover them again. The only real chance of saving anyone is finding them before they are sold.'

'That sounds difficult.'

'It is. People do not want to know that this is happening. Here in the grand salons of London they turn the other cheek because looking would be too harsh upon their sensibilities, and if Lydia Forsythe almost swoons away on seeing me, imagine what might happen if she were to confront such a truth. It is my belief that the Victorian model of virtue strips females of the things they should be capable of knowing.'

'A fierce criticism?'

'But a true one.'

'I heard that you were in Paris after...us.'

Had he not been holding her she might have tripped, the danger of letting her guard down so very real. It was the seeing him again and gaining his help in a moment when she might have been crucified without him. Everything they had been to each other imperilled all she had become alone, and the decisions she had made after he had been dragged away by Lebansart's men influenced things again.

It was foolish to imagine they could go back to what they had once had for it was far too late for that.

'I heard that you and Acacia Bellowes-Browne have an agreement.'

The muscle in his jaw tightened. 'My grandfather's hope, no doubt. I have no wish to be married again.'

The words were underlined with a raw harshness, and Cassie had cause to believe him.

Once was enough.

The dance lost some of its appeal and she pulled back. She wished she might have been able to ask him other things, important things, things that might have led to a discussion on how he perceived her ability to look after a child. His child. She took a deep breath, smiling at her sister as she swept past them in the arms of Kenyon Riley.

'They look pleased with themselves. Riley was buying all the drinks at White's the other evening and alluding to a happy event that might be occurring in his life soon. Perhaps this is it?'

'I hope so. My sister deserves each contentment that comes her way. She is sweet and kind and true.'

'Unlike you?'

Now the gloves were off.

'If it helps at all I would do things differently if I was able to begin again.' Her eyes ran across the scar that snaked down from the side of his mouth.

Unexpectedly, he laughed. 'Do you ever think back to the days before we reached Perpignan?'

All the time. Every day. Many minutes of every day.

She stayed quiet.

'I returned to Bagnères-de-Bigorre last year when I was across the border in Spain. The high bath was still as beautiful.'

'With the witchery of steam?'

Their eyes met, etched with a memory of the place. Together, close, lost in each other's arms through all the hours of the night and day. The delight of what had been jagged through her stomach and then went lower.

'What happened to us, Sandrine?'

Loss made her look away and she was happy when the music ground down to a final halt. After shepherding her back into the company of her sister and Kenyon Riley, Nathaniel quickly left. She saw him move across to stand with Stephen Hawkhurst, interest in his friend's eyes as he glanced over towards her. It was said that Hawk was entwined with the British Service, too, and there was more in his perusal than she wanted to see.

Raising her fan, she glanced away, the balancing act of appearing all that she was not and within the company of her sister, who positively glowed with delight, taking its toll.

Acacia Bellowes-Browne was here, too, standing next to Nathaniel with her hand lightly resting upon his arm. Cassandra heard the tinkle of her laugh as she leaned closer and saw Nathaniel's answering smile.

A beautiful, clever woman with her past intact. The bright red of her gown contrasted against the dark brown of her hair. The hazel in her eyes had had poems written of them. Maureen told her that once, on returning from a weekend away at a friend's country home, and Cassie still remembered the astonishment that the eyes of a lady might incite such prose from grown men.

She was certainly using her eyes to the best of their advantage at this moment, flashing them at Nathaniel Lindsay with a coquettish flirtation and using her fan to tap him lightly on the hand as if in reprimand for some comment he had just made. Intimate. Familiar. Congenial.

Turning away from it all, Cassandra recognised with a shock that envy was eating away at her.

What happened to us, Sandrine?

Life had happened with its full quota of repayment and betrayal. Jamie had happened, too; the responsibility of a child and the overriding and untempered love that would protect him from everything and everyone. No matter what.

'Could I have the pleasure of this next dance?' Stephen Hawkhurst stood before her, his eyes probing. 'Though perhaps I should warn you I am no great mover before you give me your reply.'

'Thank you.' She liked the quiet way he spoke. 'I, too, have not had a lot of practice at these things.'

'Then we shall bumble around together. Nat was always the most proficient dancer out of the three of us at school,' he said as they took to the floor, another waltz allowing them the ease of speech.

'The three of you?'

'Lucas Clairmont was the other, but he has been in the Americas for years now making his fortune in the timber trade. None of us have families that we could count on, you see, so the connection was strong.'

He looked at her directly as he said this. 'Adversity can either pull people together or it can tear them apart, would you not agree?'

Cassie dropped her glance. Words beneath words. Nathaniel had the knack of using this technique, too.

'Indeed I would.'

'Could I give you a bit of advice, then?' He waited till she nodded.

'Sometimes in life risks can deliver the greatest of rewards, but do not be too patient about the time allotted to reap them or you may lose out altogether.'

'I am not well received in society, sir. Tonight is just a small taste of that fact. To reap anything apart from disparagement might be impossible for me.'

He laughed. 'Look around you. How many men do you see who would not take risk over the mundane, who would not say to themselves if only I hadn't played it so safe as they look in the mirror in their preparations for yet another night out in society in the company of manners and propriety?'

Cassandra breathed out hard. 'Do you know anything of what went on between Nathaniel and me at Perpignan?'

'He once told me that what you did and what you said you did were two different things.'

She shook her head.

'In that he is wrong. There were others...others who died because of the mistakes that I made.'

The names of those she had consigned to the afterlife came to mind, people planted through loyalty into a land that was not their own and then murdered for their service. Aye, the world ran red with the blood of martyrs and hers had been included in that.

Lebansart.

Silver-tongued Leb.

His knife had been sharp and his words were sharper still.

Bitch. Traitor. Murderer.

Once she had been none of those things and now she was all of them, marked for anyone to see. Her penance.

She smiled through the anger and held Hawkhurst's returning puzzlement as though it were only of a small importance, a trifling consideration.

'Do you ever think, my lord, that when the world shifts in its truths sometimes one just cannot go back?'

'Often,' he replied, 'and I believe it is a shame.' As they turned with the music, Cassandra caught the face of Nathaniel watching them, his eyes devoid of feeling.

'Cassandra Northrup is nothing like I expected her to be,' Stephen said as they stood to one side of the room beside a pillar. 'In fact, I would go as far to say that after that conversation I am half in love with her myself. But she's hiding things. Big things. You can see it in her eyes when she looks over at you, Nathaniel, and she does that often.'

Nat did not want to hear this, for the cords that had held them together had been cut so irrevocably.

'Why did she go to Paris after Perpignan, Nat? She did not arrive back in England until eighteen months after you did. Why didn't she just come home?'

Lebansart. Sandrine's face turned up to his as she had left, his hands curled into hers. He wished he did not care any more, but the days beneath the Pyrenees had defined their relationship, and he found he could not let her go.

He hadn't slept with another woman since. Not one. Just that single thought made him furious. Was he destined to be for ever trapped in his feelings from the

past, unable to move on with all that was being offered now? A man for whom the holy words of matrimony meant a loyalty that remained unquestioned and unbroken.

'Well, I think it is safe to say that the youngest Northrup daughter has weathered her rocky start this evening, Nat, and I can well see why. Dressed in gold she looks like something out of a fairy tale.'

A line of young swains milled about Cassandra, though she did not seem enamoured with the fact, for her frown was noticeable even at this distance.

But Nathaniel had had enough of conjecture and, excusing himself summarily, he wound his way through the substantial crowd and out of the wide front door.

Hailing his coachman, he settled into the cushioned seats and closed his eyes. For the first time ever in his life he was at a loss as to what he should do next and he didn't like the feeling one little bit.

Cassandra Northrup threw him completely, that was the trouble. And when he had held her in the dance all he had wanted was to bring her closer. Her scent, her eyes, the feel of her skin against his.

She was a lethal concoction of beauty, brains and betrayal, but something else lingered there, too. Vulnerability, sadness and fright. What was it she was hiding? What had happened after Perpignan?

Stephen had liked her and so did Acacia. In fact, even given the collective anger of society against her earlier in the evening, he had never met a soul who did not admire her personally, apart from her uncle.

An enigma.

And she was still his wife despite all that she thought to the contrary.

He shouldn't see her again, but he knew that he would, her invitation to accompany her at night through the back streets on her charity business too tempting to turn down. What if she was hurt? She was not strong enough to rebuff a grown man who meant business, a fact he had found out in the house in Whitechapel when he had easily subdued her.

Another thought surfaced.

She had changed in four years. He could see it in her stance and in her eyes and in the way she had held the knife in the room on Brown Street in the darkness.

He had tried to teach her a few of his best tricks of attack in the final days before they had come down into Perpignan. The blade she had taken from Baudoin was a good weapon, light and comfortable in her fist.

'Grip hard and keep it upwards for this one.' He had turned her slightly, one foot away from each other. 'Position your body behind the knife, for if you lose concentration even for a moment you will be dead.'

'Like this?' She had taken to the lesson with a surprising accuracy, her footwork balanced and the line of her arm strong. Perhaps it was the legacy of months of being a captive, *never again* stamped into every movement.

'Being left-handed will give you an advantage because your attacker will not expect it so use this quickly before he has time to define it and go in under the arc of his forearm. Close contact negates skill to some ex-

tent so aim for the artery here on the outside of the leg. He will be protecting everything else.'

So far he had explained the rudiments in the slow motion of tutelage, but now he grabbed a stick that looked solid and stood before her. 'Try it on me.'

She shook her head. 'I can't.'

'Why not?'

'I might hurt you.'

He began to laugh, the sound echoing around the small clearing, and Nat thought right then and there that this is what it felt like to be happy, here, with a beautiful girl dressed as a boy in the mountain passes of the Pyrenees.

'You are a woman,' he managed to say when he finally found his breath, 'and I have been at it a while.'

'Why did you start?' She had lowered the blade and faced him, small curls of gold-red that had escaped her plait dancing in the wind.

'Belonging, I think.' He could not believe he had been so honest and that an answer to a question he had often asked himself should have been as self-evident. 'My parents died when I was young and after that...'

'You had trouble finding yourself.' Sheathing the knife, she came forward and wrapped her arms about him. Tight and warm. 'I was the same. After Mama it seemed as though I had no compass.'

'No true north,' he answered softly.

Her eyes fell to his lips and the smile she gave him held invitation as he brought his mouth across her own. They knew nothing of each other and everything, the truth of their bodies speaking in a way words never

could, telling secrets, finding the honesty. They had been hurt and they had survived. Right now it was enough.

All he could do was to keep her safe.

Chapter Eight

The note came on the third day after the Forsythe ball.

Tonight: 11:00 p.m. Wear black.

That was it. No directions. No meeting point. He held the letter up against the light and looked at her handwriting. Small and evenly shaped, no flourish of curve or wasted embellishment. No signature.

She would come here, he was sure of it, because there was no other place that had been mooted. Perhaps she expected trouble and to give an exact location might have exacerbated it. Black clothes indicated hiddenness and the fate of the man murdered at Brown Street came to mind.

The Daughters of the Poor seemed to be involved in more than the usual charity work of supplying funds. The faces of the women found near the Thames pointed to the dangers those antagonising the underbelly of London posed. One wrong move and Cas-

sandra could be joining them, her throat cut from one side to the other.

Swearing, he crossed to the cupboard and unlocked his guns. He would be prepared for the same force others hadn't been and if anyone crossed his path and threatened Cassandra... For the first time in a long while he felt a sense of energy and release, and a vitality that had been lost in France. His eyes went to the clock. Almost six. Five hours to wait.

He was dressed in black from head to foot as she came through his window, the effect making him appear even more dangerous than he normally did.

'We will be back well before dawn and I do not expect trouble, but if it comes then I should probably warn you that...' She made herself stop babbling by an enormous effort of will. She was nervous, of him, of being here, of Nathaniel Lindsay looking so much like he had done in the Languedoc, the battered edge of a soldier in his clothes.

'I have nothing else planned,' he drawled and smiled, the languid, beautiful smile he had given her in Saint Estelle and in Bagnères-de-Bigorre before they had made love and she had forgotten that the world existed.

Shaking her head, Cassandra tried to clear her mind of the past. The past years had been so busy with taking care of Jamie and of trying to protect others that she had barely left a moment for herself. The woman in her ached for Nathaniel's touch, even though she knew she had long since forfeited the desire for him to care.

'I have been told of a place where young women are being kept against their will.'

'Who informed you?'

'The woman who lives in a house across the road.'

'And you can trust her?'

'As much as I can trust anybody.' She hoped he could not hear the hollow uncertainty as well as she could. Last time at Whitechapel a trap had been set and she hoped that it would not be the case again tonight.

'Are you armed?'

'Yes.' Lifting the material of her sleeve, she allowed him to see the knife in a leather sheath. He was good at hiding surprise, she determined, for not a single muscle in his face changed in reaction.

'Dangerous?'

The word had her chagrin rising. 'I am not the same person you met in France and I do not wish to be either. I shall never again be beholden to another and if you want to rescind your offer of help because of such an admission then I will understand.'

'I don't.'

Swallowing, Cassie tried to regain a lost balance. She was seldom off guard with anyone other than him, her certainty coming easily and without too much thought. 'I will be in charge.' She needed to regain the lead.

He nodded.

'Good.'

Sometimes, she mused, *I do not like who I have become, this person who is hard-hearted and tough-minded.* Her thoughts went to Acacia, the beautiful

woman whose eyes had had poems written about them, and she frowned.

The crossroads in life had taken her in directions that had not all been her own choice and once she had traversed some pathways there was no going back. The burning boats of chance. Ludicrous to wish for some literary offering from a man, but there it was. She did. And not just any man, either, but the one who stood before her now, his pale grey eyes shaded, dressed entirely in black.

She gathered her words in carefully. 'I do not expect trouble, but sometimes it comes anyway. If it does, I will hold you in no account for the protection of my life.'

Nat could hardly believe the detachment she laced those words with. 'Because you no longer see me as your husband?'

The rush of red upon her cheeks surprised him before she turned away, a scarlet tide rising from her throat. Not all indifference, then. Already she had opened the window and climbed through into the cold darkness.

A carriage was waiting at the end of the street, a hackney cab with a driver who did not turn to greet them, but looked straight ahead.

'I pay him well for silence,' she clarified as they got in. 'The fewer people involved in this the better.'

'Does your sister ever help you in these night-time sojourns?'

'Of course not.' Shock was inherent in every syllable.

Suddenly he understood. 'How ruined does society imagine you to be?'

He caught the deep frown on her forehead through the gloom. 'Very. Societal judgement on the moral poverty inherent in prostitution holds a power that is difficult to fight.'

'But you are trying to?'

She shook her head. 'I help those without prospects or a place to live and most of these young women see their chosen profession in very different terms than those of wealth and power have a wont to.'

Nathaniel paused, trying to understand exactly what it was she was saying. 'You condone this activity? I thought you rescued such women.'

'The Daughters of the Poor encourages financial and social independence. Sometimes the only way of doing that is to make certain that those we aid are safe in their work.'

'You help them remain on the streets?'

'As opposed to leaving them in the throes of a fourteen-hour day inside a cold dank sweatshop run by punitive men.'

'That, I suppose, is another way to look at it.'

'The ideal of refined and protected ladies who are not only good, but who are to know nothing save for what is good is workable only for the rich, though some might say it is repression with a different face.'

At that he did laugh because he had never had a conversation quite like this with a woman. Such discourse was freeing and he wondered how far she would take her arguments.

'You are an advocate of sex for pleasure rather than for procreation? A dangerous threat to male authority?'

'Look around you, Nathaniel. Women, making their way in the world by the use of their bodies, are a highly visible aspect of our society now. The hope of the Daughters of the Poor is to keep them unharmed.'

Her use of his name was soft and familiar and when the carriage lurched to throw Cassandra against him, his arms closed around her in a movement all of their own.

Protected. Like you were not.

The scent of soft knownness was intoxicating, a small familiarity amongst everything that was changing as the carriage hurtled through the darkness of London's poorer areas.

Cassandra smiled. Nathaniel had never been a man to step back from risk—she had seen that again and again in France, and now even after a conversation of ideas that he could not have been brought up to believe in, it wasn't debate he was offering, but comfort.

A generous man. A generous lover, too. She sat up and away from him. 'You did not marry again?'

'No.'

'You did not wish to?'

He was silent.

'I thought you might be dead after Perpignan.' Cassie tried to keep the terror from her tone.

I went to Paris to look for you, to scour the streets for every face that might have been yours. I stayed

there for as long as I could manage it and even as I left I looked back.

'Lebansart's men made certain I could not call for help when they dumped me by the river. When I finally awoke I was in the company of friends and taken by boat to Marseilles.'

'But you never told anyone about me?'

He shook his head.

'I am half sick of shadows,' said The Lady of Shalott.

These words went around and around Cassandra's mind, the refrain plucked from Tennyson as he balanced desire against reality. With more courage she might have told Nathaniel of Jamie and of Paris and of searching for him ever since he was lost to her. She might have reached out, too, in the darkness and simply laid his hand upon her heart so that he heard the strong beat of want and need. And reply.

But Cassie did none of these things as the carriage drew to a halt and the seedy backwater streets came into view—the call of the driver, the light rain against the cobbles making everything slick-wet and the moon far behind a bank of clouds ensuring darkness.

Her world. The mirrored shadows. And beyond that the river, sludge-grey as it ran sluggish out to a freedom at sea; neither Camelot nor any other kingdom of dreams.

'Be on your guard,' she whispered as they made their way on foot down an alleyway, the high and close

buildings leaning in, every window hung with the remains of dirty washing flapping in a dirty breeze.

A woman met them almost instantly. 'There,' she said and pointed to a door, the paint peeled and the knocker broken. 'They have been here a few days and they are back now. I seen a tall man go in there a while ago and he has not come out again since.'

Nat pulled a knife from his boot.

'He were dressed well, too,' she returned. 'He will be in the room at the rear.' Taking a coin, their informant left, her shawl high up around her hair as she scurried off into the night.

Nathaniel looked around to make certain no one else was watching them. 'Stay behind me, Sandrine.' She had insisted that she would be in charge, but he was pleased to see that she obeyed instantly and moved to let him pass. A tall and well-dressed stranger who was up to some nefarious deed. Could this be the man the urchin by the river had spoken of? The corridor inside was narrow, many closed doors leading off it.

Raising his hand, Nat pointed at keys dangling in a door that was left partly ajar. These people were not expecting any company. They were also patently amateurs. His hopes faded.

He was inside in a moment and he knew without asking a question that the two youths before him were insignificant within the chain of command. Both were young and both were unarmed, the expressions on their faces frozen.

On a bed no bigger than a cot a young woman sat crying, her hat beside her and her hair unbound.

'Who the hell are you?'

'Will Fisher, sir,' the one nearest to him stammered, 'and this is my brother. He was stupid enough to believe the Lytton gang might pay him a sovereign for a girl new in from the country and he brought her here. Now that I have talked some sense into him we don't know what to do with her.'

'Is this right?' He addressed this query to the girl and she nodded. 'Did they hurt you?'

'No, sir.'

'Why did you bring her to this place?' He addressed this question to the older brother.

'Kyle Lytton uses it as a hideaway. Jack saw them here over the past few days and thought they were still about.'

'How old are you?'

All three answered at once. The brothers were seventeen and eighteen, respectively, and the girl but fourteen.

'Get out.' This was said to the brothers and they did not tarry for a moment, moving past with the look of felons unexpectedly excused from the gallows.

Cassie was already at the girl's side. 'So you are not hurt in any way?'

'No, ma'am. The coach was late and they only just brought me here. Or the younger one did. His brother was furious and arrived straight away after.' She burst into loud and noisy sobs. 'And now it's dark and I don't know where to go or what to do...and Da will be furi-

ous if I arrive back again with nothing in me hand...'
At that thought she could barely carry on.

'What is your name?'

'Sarah Milgrew, ma'am.'

'Well, Sarah, you can stay with me tonight and tomorrow we will find you a place. We have our carriage
outside on the next street.'

'I canna afford much for a room, ma'am, but I can
sew like an angel, Miss Davis says, and am quick with
it.'

'A useful trade and most sought after.'

'My sister came to London some weeks ago and
we have not heard from her again. I had hoped to try
and find her.'

Nat's mind went back to the two girls pulled from
the river. 'Did you sew for her?'

He saw Cassandra's eyes fasten on his face, a small
frown building on her forehead.

'I did, sir. She left with one of my dresses on and another in her bag. She said she would show people what
I do here and find a room for both of us. Da took her to
the coach up to London and we had no word after that.'

Both the girls from the river had been well attired,
but there was a touch of the country about them. Could
this be the lead that he was after?

'And the coach comes into...?'

'Gracechurch Street, sir. It's five hours' travelling in
good weather from Wallingford and more if it is wet.
That's where the young man met me and said he could
help, but when he brought me here I was afeared...' She

clutched her small bag tightly and looked around the room, drab and furnitureless save for the bed.

What connection could these girls have with a man who was obviously from London? Could something have happened in their home town to lead them to each other?

Wallingford was just outside Reading. He filed the name in his mind to be considered later, but right now he wondered how often Cassandra Northrup took it on herself to bring girls like this one home. Many times he surmised by the ease in which she gathered her up and showed her through the door.

In the carriage the young woman seemed to fold into herself and lean against the far corner, a pose which spoke of hopelessness, implying the difficulty of all she had been through. But at least they had arrived in time. Observing Cassandra's care, Nat knew that circumstances had not been anywhere near as lucky for her.

The same awareness that he had experienced back in France all those years before wound into the middle of his chest, and he forced it down. These thoughts were nonsensical because he had no place in her life now, nor she in his.

He felt anger as she raised her eyes to look at him, the street lamps illuminating the deep shadows of dimple in her cheeks, and was glad to see the gates of the Northrup residence when they came into sight, the fat-bodied hawks on each side swathed in vines.

As the carriage stopped the front door was thrown open and two maids hurried down the stairs to greet them. They had done this before, Nat thought, as Miss

Milgrew was dispatched without fuss or bother into their capable hands, the trio then disappearing up the wide front staircase and into the house.

Cassandra was still sitting in the carriage, but had moved on to the seat opposite, pulling the door closed in a way that suggested she required privacy.

'If your estate or town house has any need of competent staff, we have a number of girls I could recommend who could well do with a job.'

This was the last thing he thought she might say, though as he leant forward he had to stop himself from drawing closer.

'Accompany me to the Herringford ball next week, Sandrine.'

'Why?'

'Because I want you to.' And he did. Desperately.

'Acacia Bellowes-Browne may object, my lord, and the rest of society will almost certainly be astonished.'

'You would let that worry you?'

'I try to stay out of the notice of others. I have limited the occasions that I come into the public sphere and the two times I have done so lately have both been difficult.'

'Society does not quite know what to make of you, which could be a bonus if you use it wisely. I am certain that your charity would benefit.'

'I am not so sure. The Daughters of the Poor relies on the generosity of those of wealth to give donations towards ruin without ever having to confront it.'

She always surprised him, he thought, always made

him feel alive in a way he seldom had been in years. Her dimples. Her hair edging her face in curls.

'I can protect you.'

His words fell into the silence as she pushed the door open and escaped outside in one fluid movement. Once there she stopped and spoke quietly.

'I can protect myself, Nathaniel, but I thank you for your help tonight.'

But he did not leave it there. 'If a ball is too public, come to a private dinner, then, and tell me why I should make a donation to your endeavours.'

'I am certain that would be most inappropriate...'

'A hefty donation...' he added when she still hesitated.

'Very well.'

'A carriage will be sent for you the day after tomorrow at eight.'

She nodded quickly and then she was gone, pacing towards the front stairs of the Northrup mansion with the singular purpose of retreat. He watched her until the door shut and her shadow flitted briefly against the thin curtains of the downstairs salon.

My God, she should have declined his invite, she thought as she gained her room and leaned against the doorframe. She ought to be downstairs in the room off Alysa's laboratory, helping the others settle Miss Milgrew in for the night, but she could not risk letting anyone see the panic that was making her hands shake and her heart beat faster.

Nathaniel Lindsay made her careless and he made

her feel things that she should not: warm things, hopeful things, things that held her both in thrall and in
fear. Running her fingers across her brow, she felt the
clammy sweat of dread. None of these hopes were for
her and to imagine that they were would be to simply
ruin everything that was.

She had a life, a good life, a worthwhile life. In the
past years she had managed to find a way through adversity and to experience…contentment.

Cassie smiled at the word. Contentment. To anyone
else such an emotion might be perceived to be a bland
and worthless thing. But to her it was everything; a
way forward, a light after the darkness and the beacon
that called her on each and every day. After Nay part
of her had shrivelled up and died and after Perpignan
joy was an emotion she thought never to know again.
But she had known it with Jamie, holding him close
against her breast in Paris where she had delivered him
at night, the cold fear of aloneness failing to douse the
warmth and love she was consumed with.

Jamie had allowed her a purpose, a new beginning,
a way back.

And now here in London all these years later another chance was being offered. Nathaniel had held her
in the carriage as if he would like to offer more than
a donation, but she did not dare to believe in such a
promise. Not yet. Not now. Not when anyone on seeing
father and son together would realise that there was no
question of paternity.

The risk of everything had her sitting, her head be-

tween her legs, trying to find the breath she had forgotten to take.

'I can protect you.'

What did Nathaniel mean when he spoke of protection? The protection of marriage? The protection of being a mistress? The protection of lust and need translated into the flesh, a transient and momentary connection that would wither as soon as he saw the marks upon her breast.

Traitor.

No man could want to make love to an embodiment of betrayal. Not even one who had seen her before, whole and beautiful.

She crossed to the mirror, making certain that the door catch was on before she undid the buttons on her shirt. The cuts stood out, dark red against pale, three long slices of agony.

Lebansart's legacy.

'Tell me what was in the documents, Sandrine. Tell me and live.'

She had recited the names without further hesitation: her child's safety or that of two faceless men whom she had never met? There was no real struggle, a fact that she was to relive over and over in nightmares that wouldn't fade. She had stood there with the blood from her breast sticky against her fingers and she had itemised all that she had seen.

He wrote her words carefully in a book with a brown leather binding and a quill whose feathers had seen better days. The ink had stained his finger with black.

Little details. Remembered. Her voice had shaken as she spoke.

'Good. Very good. You were worth the trouble.' Those were his words as he had left the room.

Leaving her to die, slowly, from a loss of blood. But he had no notion that she was her mother's daughter and that she would know exactly what to do to lessen the flow and survive. A heavy wad of sheet and two long belts wrapped tight across them before lying face down on the thick mat and willing herself out of panic.

Survival. She breathed as shallowly as she could and tried not to move at all. And then after a few more hours she began to feel less lightheaded and warmer, the quilt she had heaped upon herself an added comfort and the noon-day light at the window spilling across her.

It had taken her another hour to find the energy to leave the room and make her way into the street. A doctor on a visit to a patient had found her and bundled her into his carriage and after that she struggled with living for a very long time.

Except for Jamie. Except for the growth of a child, Nathanael's child, the only thing anchoring her to the world as everything spiralled into despair and hopelessness.

Her uncle's friend had bought her a ticket to Paris as soon as the fever left out of respect for the Mercier family. He had arranged for his small house in Montmartre to be opened for her and sent two maids and a butler along to help her in her quest for independence.

She did not mention her pregnancy and allowed

him no notion of her own family back in London. She needed to think and to plan. She needed to find Nathanael if she could and she needed to be well away from Lebansart.

The house was quiet and situated in a street not far from the Sacré-Coeur, with a view across the rooftops of the city. Even with the beauty of white marble washed in rain she was lonely and sad, shock reaching into the depths of her soul.

And then one day whilst sitting in a park, wrapped warmly against the capricious springtime winds, a colourful bird had come to sit on the branch of a shrub in front of her and her baby had moved.

Life returned. Hope blossomed. The want to survive overrode the desire to simply cease to be, and she recovered.

Rebuttoning her shirt, Cassie looked back at herself in the mirror. No longer as thin. No longer as sad. No longer hobbling into each successive hour with the burden of betrayal heavy on her shoulders. The Daughters of the Poor had given her life a purpose and Jamie had given her body a heart. She could not endure uncertainty again. If she went to Nathaniel's dinner tomorrow night she would tell him she couldn't.

It was that simple.

Chapter Nine

Nothing was simple.

Nathaniel was dressed down tonight, his clothes less formal, the unbuttoned white collar of his shirt bold against the dark of his skin, a loose garment that gave him a sense of danger and familiarity. Cassie knew that it was more than scandalous to come to his house at night and alone, but both want and need had brought her here. Shaking away doubt, she moved inside. She was not about to give in to the narrow confines of Victorian rules, and besides, in the eyes of God they were married.

'I am glad that you came.'

His house was well appointed, every piece of furniture in sight beautifully wrought. Because she was so nervous she picked up a small bowl on a side stand, admiring the colourful flowers that marched around the rim. It was the one thing that did not look eminently English.

'I remember these designs from the marketplace at Perpignan. I always liked them.'

His eyes today were the shade of well-worn slate and warmer than usual. She wished he had been plainer, less intimidating and wished, too, that she might have worn some other dress than the one she had on, the starched blue silk too grand and stiff for this occasion.

'I have a fire going in the middle salon and some white wine.'

Nodding, she followed him. The fire sounded inviting though she was determined to refuse any drink at all. *Keep your wits about you*, she said to herself, *and understand that he will want explanation of what happened in Languedoc.*

The new room was more imposing than the last. A rich floral carpet was laid on the floor, the deep colour in it matching the heavy curtains at the windows. All around every wall mirrors and pictures abounded and, as in his library, there were shelves of books stacked almost to the ceiling. A generous fireplace blazed at one end and it was here that he led her. Two leather seats had been positioned opposite each other, a small table between them with fluted glasses upon it.

The apprehension of being here was growing by the second. A portrait of a woman in full riding regalia graced the nearest wall, and when he saw her looking he smiled.

'My mother loved horses.'

'She was very beautiful.'

'Indeed.' The talk then tailed down into silence, a thousand other things to say beneath the polite banter and no way to voice them.

I love you. I never stopped loving you.

For one horrible moment Cassie thought she had blurted the words out, bare and naked in their truth, and shock crawled up her spine, caught in the gap of honesty.

'Please, do sit down.' He waited until she complied before doing so himself, pouring two drinks and placing one before her. 'How is Miss Milgrew settling in?'

A different topic completely and one she was pleased to speak of. 'Sarah has been a godsend and has begun teaching the other girls the fine art of sewing.'

'Is there any sign of the sibling?'

'No. It seems she has quite disappeared. You asked if she sewed for her sister the other night and I thought the question odd. Why was that?'

'The bodies of two young women were pulled from the Thames a month back and no one claimed them. Both were dressed in finely sewn gowns.'

'You think it could be her lost sister, then? I see.'

'Do you, Sandrine? Do you see how searching out the damaged women of London may have more consequences than you can imagine? One day you could end up in the river yourself.'

'I take every precaution...'

'And you think that is enough against an opponent who is bigger and stronger than you.' He no longer sounded as mellow. In fact, now when she caught his glance she looked away quickly, so much of Nathanael Colbert before her. The soldier. The lover. The man who had watched her betray him, blood running down his chin.

'Where is the Colbert part of your name from?'

'It is a lesser title of mine. The St Auburn earldom contains many and as the heir I have an entitlement to them.'

'A real name? Not made up?'

'Made up like Sandrine Mercier was, you mean?'

'My cousin Celeste often called me Sandrine and Mercier was her surname.'

'I know. I went back and spoke to what was left of the family. An uncle, Gilles Mercier, informed me of the demise of Celeste and her father, though he said nothing of you.'

'Celeste had that knack of making everyone around her look invisible.'

'Or you barely went out?'

This was running too close to the bone. Depression had kept her in bed for a long time, but she did not wish to recall that.

Even sitting, the breadth and height of Nathaniel Lindsay was substantial. She remembered how she had loved his largeness after the small men of Languedoc. She remembered his scent, too, an evocative mixture of plain soap and maleness.

'Your sister visited me last week. Did you know that?'

'Maureen came here?' She could not keep her astonishment at bay.

'She wanted to be assured that I was not threatening you in any way. She stood her ground and cautioned me that she would not tolerate anything that may hurt you. When I told her that I had pretended to bed you

in order to help you from being discovered and compromised, she was happy.'

More unspoken words shimmered in the chasms.

*Were pretence and lies all that once held us to-
gether?*

Here it was harder to maintain the falsehood, even
with the arguments Cassie could muster for carrying
on with such a charade. She felt a choking want in the
back of her throat and swallowed it down. The wine
helped, a fine dry white that gave her hands something
to fidget with and her mind something other than him
to dwell upon. But secrets could be as damaging as
any wound and her fingers tightened around the crystal glass.

All of a sudden she wished he might just reach out
and take away choice. She wanted the feelings she had
discovered in Saint Estelle and in Bagnères-de-Bigorre
here in London, in the quiet warmth of his beautiful
house, far away from others and from the responsibility of her everyday life.

Nathaniel made her believe in fantasy. That was
it. He had before in southern France and he did again
now, the muted sounds of the city far away and the
clock showing eight-thirty in the evening. Still early.
The blue in her gown shimmered as she shuffled back
and sat up farther.

'My sister feels it is her duty to protect all those
about her.'

'Then such obligation must run in your family.'

At that she laughed. 'Perhaps it does in Maureen,
but Papa is too busy with trying to understand the

complexities of science and my other sister Anne is too preoccupied with her brood of children.'

'There is also a brother?'

'Rodney. He is the youngest.'

He had told her once that he was without siblings.

Alone. The word came with a forcefulness that made her blink. He was still like that; the solitary detachment of one who was careful not to anchor himself to another for fear of being disappointed. Oh, how well she knew that feeling.

The clock in the corner boomed out a further passage of time, and Nathanael finished his first drink and poured himself another, eyeing hers as he did so.

'You do not like the wine?' he commented.

She looked nervous and her hand shook as she made herself take a drink. Not just one sip, either, but three. Fortification. He wondered perhaps whether it had been a bad idea to invite her here because the ease that had always existed between them seemed dissipated tonight into a sheer and utter nervousness, her eyes skirting away from his and her body ramrod straight.

'Albi de Clare is of the opinion that you and Maureen are two of the most beautiful women in London.'

She smiled. 'Is his eyesight hampered, my lord?'

'Many I have spoken to would agree with him. But they also say you are prickly and distant to any advances that come your way. Most make a point of telling me that you in particular seldom venture out to partake in any of the entertainments that most are fond of.'

'There are other things that I need now more than a man, Lord Lindsay.'

He reached out and stroked a finger down the soft skin near her wrist, measuring the beat when he had finished. She often wore gloves, the left-hand fingers specially fashioned so as to show no signs of her old injury.

'Indifference requires a less rapid pulse, *Sandrine*.'

Cassie did not pull away, but watched his thumb as it moved up her arm and he had the sudden and unexpected thought that she might allow him more.

'I would like to know you again as I did once.' Firelight was reflected on the smooth skin at her throat and it was now there that his touch lingered.

'No. It cannot be as before.' She said the words slowly, enunciating each one, and he did not quite understand what she meant.

'Before?'

'Only a kiss. Nothing else.'

God. His body leapt with her words, shock warming everything. She did not turn away, but met his glance full on, the depths of burning need and pain inside them making his breath catch, for the Sandrine of old was so easily seen.

New secrets lingered there as well, he was too much of the spy not to recognise that, but they would have to wait. For now he pulled her up towards him as he stood, the length of their bodies touching. He did not wish to frighten her or make her call a halt so he was cautious. It was enough to feel her against him, will-

ingly fitting into the contours of his body and to smell her particular and sweet scent.

Strands of hair that had loosened from the knot at her nape lay across his arm, bright against the darkness of his clothes.

Night and day. Lost and found. Lies and truth. All were there as he brought his mouth down across hers, the limit of a kiss shrugged away by the blinding honesty of connection. They were back again in the hot pools of Bagnères-de-Bigorre and in the shadowed room at Saint Estelle, a thousand days of apartness lost into union.

No careful kiss this, after all, but a full-blooded connection of want. Slanting his lips, he brought her closer, the stark heat of his body tightening with desire. Sensation washed through reserve and instead of the judicious touch he had promised he ravished her mouth with his tongue, trying to make her understand the futility of boundaries and the depth of his need. The savage movement of years of memory and betrayal lingered there, too.

This kiss was different from any they had shared in France, the play of anger on one edge and a trace of hate. Once, as a girl, Cassie might have been frightened by such an emotion, but now she relished it, the woman in her responding to their complex and circuitous layers of history. She wanted to punish him back, too, for not being there when she had Jamie and for the all the loneliness she had felt ever since; for the pain of

his birth and the cold hard hours afterwards of isolation and solitude.

A shared and desolate despondence.

Her fingers raked across the bare skin on his neck and held him closer, the breath between them hoarse and rasping. Hardly proper. Barely kind. She wished she might tell him everything even as she knew she would reveal nothing.

But for this moment Nathanael Colbert was hers. She could not think of the earldom or of society or of the duties that would drag Lord Lindsay from her as soon as they broke off their kiss.

Nothing but now, but, oh, how she yearned for more, his body moving inside her and that particular moment of release when all the world fell away to the beat of pleasure and purpose, the dark, hard power of sex mitigating everything.

When the kiss was finished, as she knew it must, she laid her head against his chest, feeling his heart pounding in her ear, like the beat of some song that was played too fast for the melody.

Their lives. Out of tune and spinning into chaos again.

Jamie.

She made herself stand alone. For now she needed the time to think. Her smile was false when she finally looked up at him—she knew it was, and yet it was all she had left.

'I do not think this was a good idea.'

He laughed. 'Then you have not had many other kisses or you would recognise the magic in it.'

She was pleased he did not comment on the anger.

'I am older now, Nathaniel, and wiser. What I think I want and what I need are now two different things. I cannot make a mistake again.'

'Come to bed with me, Sandrine. Now.'

Shocking. Enticing. Impossible.

'And if I did, what then? Can you honestly say that without reservation you have forgiven me for what happened at Perpignan?'

His smile faded and he remained silent. When he looked away she knew that she had lost him.

'I think I should go.'

One minute of silence and then two before he simply reached down and rang a small silver bell she had not noticed on a table. Footsteps outside could be heard immediately.

'You rang, sir.' The servant was all a good butler should be, circumspect and prudent.

'Miss Northrup is just leaving, Haines. Could you find her coat and see her out?'

'Yes, sir.'

Lord Nathaniel Lindsay did not move as she pushed past him and followed his man from the room.

He punched his hand against the hardness of the wall behind as she left and liked the pain that radiated up his arm.

What the hell was wrong with him? Why could he not have given her the soft words she was after, the oaths of forgiveness and absolution? Lebansart's face drifted into his mind and the anonymous visages of two

men who had never known what was coming. The last words at Perpignan were there, too, as she had curled her fingers into those of his enemy.

Sandrine the whore.

He hated the truth of it, but he could not change. An impossible future moulded from an old and familiar hurt. How long had she stayed with Lebansart? It had been eighteen months later that she had returned to England according to Hawk. That long? A lifetime compared with the paltry weeks that they had been allotted. Lifting his glass, he finished the lot and his body ached with the loss of her.

Chapter Ten

'Lord Lindsay was at the Venus Club the night before last, Cassie, and according to our uncle he was enjoying all that was on offer there.'

Maureen gave her the information over the breakfast table the week after her meeting with Nathaniel, the anger in her voice lancing the words with repugnance. 'I would have thought him to have had more taste,' her sister added as she helped herself to a plate of scrambled eggs from a heated silver dish on the sideboard.

Cassandra was shocked, the shame that was still substantial from their last meeting now compounded by Lindsay's obvious lack of regard for women. He had sent a sizeable chit, too, with a servant the day after she had seen him. The bribe for the Daughters of the Poor now felt like a severance token, a way of apologising for a relationship that he did not want and could not pursue.

Nathaniel Lindsay was a bounder and a cheat; that was what he was, a man who would prey on the hard

times of others and yet pretend an interest in her work with the Daughters of the Poor; a man without the courage to chance her offering of more than a kiss. She was suddenly glad that he had dismissed her from his company if this was what he had become, though anger and disappointment made her shake.

'Kenyon said he could not imagine Lindsay in such seedy places when he has all the women of society to choose from, but as Uncle Reg was adamant in his identification, I presume it must be the truth. Stephen Hawkhurst accompanied him by all accounts.' She stopped then, a worrying look in her eyes. 'I had hoped you and Lindsay might have been friends. I noticed him watching you closely at the Forsythe ball, and he was certainly helpful there.'

'Perhaps he feels responsible for me somehow. Lords of the peerage have an inflated view of duty towards others in need.' Cassandra prayed that her sister might take her explanation as an end point to the conversation, but she was disappointed.

'Kenyon thinks he is a good person. He also said that his grandfather is a mean-spirited old miser who needs a hearty talking to.'

'Your husband-to-be has strong opinions, Reena.'

'I know. Isn't he wonderful?'

Unexpectedly, Cassandra found herself laughing. Her sister had changed from a woman who often questioned masculine dominance to one who was allowing Kenyon Riley every right of persuasion. It was heartening because Maureen looked so very happy, a smile pinned on her lips almost permanently now and noth-

ing and no one could dull it. Not even their father when he joined them in the breakfast room looking irritated.

'Reginald was here again yesterday and he is becoming more and more of an interfering and bombastic bore. I shall instruct the servants not to let him through to the laboratory again because he cannot help touching the experiments even when I ask him not to. Your mother was always exasperated by him and I can well see why.'

'I think he was after the watch Grandfather brought home with him from South Africa, Papa. He said the other week that he was certain it was supposed to be given to him.' Maureen sounded distant, as though the problems of this household were becoming less and less of a concern to her.

'The acquisition of family heirlooms is the only reason he ever comes calling and Lord knows he has more in the way of chattels than we do.'

'Why do you give him things, then?' Cassie joined in the conversation now, interested in his answer.

'Because he never loved a woman like I did or had children. Offspring. Heirs. His life is as barren as a moor and as empty. It seems he uses the clubs selling pleasure these days as a reason for living. God knows he is always trying to deter me from funding your charity.'

Cassie frowned. 'He told me at the Forsythe ball the other week that I should be placing my efforts into the marriage mart and that the frippery of charitable works would put any man off an alliance with our family.'

'And yet he himself has never entertained the idea of a bride?' Maureen's words were laced with question.

'Oh, he did once. He asked your mother to marry him and she refused. I don't think he ever forgave her for marrying me instead.'

Cassandra had heard this before from her mama. Alysa was a woman who barely spoke of the personal, but once when Uncle Reginald had come to the door she had pretended she was out and had given an explanation for the lie. Her love of science was the reason. Reginald for all his money and handsome looks could never abide a woman with a brain and if Alysa had a goal in life it was to understand the theory behind the small and unseen badness in a sick person.

'She had a lucky escape, Papa, and I am certain she knew it.'

'But it has made him mean and small-minded.'

Their father was usually far more reticent about discussing any of his feelings so Cassie determined that he must be worried about something. She had no further opportunity to ask questions, though, as he finished his breakfast and left the table. Back to the laboratory, she thought and watched as he left, a man slightly bent over by life and loss. She hoped she would not be like that in thirty years.

A few moments later a knock on the door took their attention. These days any unexpected caller had the effect of making Cassandra's heart race wildly just in case it was Nathaniel Lindsay, but when their butler showed in Elizabeth Hartley from the school, a new worry surfaced. She looked alarmed and anxious, her

more usual languid demeanour disappeared beneath a flushed face and bright eyes.

'Another girl has been pulled out of the river. We have just been informed of it and we think it may be Sarah Milgrew, for she has not returned home for two nights.'

Both Cassie and Maureen stood.

'When did you last see her?'

'She said she had to go out around six the day before yesterday and never came home. She had some information of her lost sister, it seems, and was hurrying out to find her.'

'How did the word come?'

'A young boy came to the front door and asked for her by name. When I looked in her room there was no note or anything. After we heard the news this morning, though, Mrs Wilson said I was to fetch you and that you would know what to do.'

Both sisters looked at each other. 'We will come, of course,' Cassandra said. 'Where has the body been taken?'

'To the police station in Aldwych.'

'Then I need to be there. If you stay here, Maureen, until I return we will all go to the school together.'

Twenty minutes later she was pulling up in front of the Aldwych constabulary in a hired brougham. God, how she hated what she had come to do, but as there was no one else for the job she took a deep breath and stepped down from the carriage, walking right into the path of Lord Nathaniel Lindsay.

Because her mind was on the dreadful business of the discovered body it took her a second to register his presence and react. The bloom of anger and discomfort could be felt on her cheeks.

'It is Sarah Milgrew, Cassandra. I have just identified her.' His words replaced embarrassment with a deep and shocked horror. 'Her throat was cut just like the last girls'.'

He was not being careful with his facts and for that Cassie was glad. She did not wish to be treated like a woman who would need the truth filtered and sanitised. His grey eyes were filled with the sort of anger she had seen them to contain in France.

'The constabulary said that there is nothing else that they can do at the moment. I have asked them to keep me informed of any new developments, however, and they said they would send someone over if there was other information uncovered. I have my own leads, too, that I shall want to investigate.'

'You have an idea of who it might be?'

'Sarah Milgrew's home town of Wallingford might allow us some answers. I will travel across there in the morning.'

'If you could keep us up to date, too, we would be most grateful.'

'Of course. Would you like me to drop you at home?'

'If you have the wish to.' Sadness had hollowed her; sadness for Sarah and for the other girls who had died.

'My carriage is this way.' For the first time he touched her, his hand at her elbow guiding her past a group of people walking the other way; an aloof and de-

tached touch that was discarded as soon as they reached the conveyance. Once inside he kept talking.

'Surely someone else could have been sent from the Daughters of the Poor other than you to identify the body?'

'There are no men on the pay roll, if that is what you are suggesting.'

'Older women, then. Married women.'

The barb dug deep, lancing all the hurt and anger. 'I might remind you, Lord Lindsay, that I was married even though you seem to have forgotten the fact entirely.'

'Hardly.' His eyes ran across her body in the way of a man who remembered everything.

'Well, as someone who spends his evenings in the bosom of the Venus Club you give all the impression of otherwise.' My God, she thought as soon as it was out of her mouth. What had made her say that? The sharp edge of hurt probably and the wasted loss of hope.

His laughter surprised her. 'You think I should stay at home and read instead?'

'Rumour has it the girls there are very young.'

All humour fled. 'Enough, Cassandra. You have no idea of my reasons for being there.'

'Oh, I am certain I have, my lord. Do not all men have the same purpose once they set foot in such hallowed halls?' Her temper was at full flight now, irreversible and unstoppable as years of her own loneliness and ruin came flooding in. 'I just had expected better from you, the unwise hope of one who has made choices that come back to haunt, I suppose, and your

penchant for such places makes a mockery of any history between us.'

'The history of you abandoning me in Perpignan for the arms of Guy Lebansart, you mean, and staying in Paris for the whole of the next eighteen months with him?'

'Who told you that?'

'Nobody had to. I was there, remember, as you happily went off with him. A woman who looked as though she could barely wait to be in more than his arms.'

She hit him then, full across the face, the sound in the carriage terrible and absolute. But he did not pull back. Rather, he grabbed at her shaking hand and yanked her forward, his mouth coming down on hers in a single frozen angry grimace.

And he took exactly what he wanted, bearing down with a force she could not deny. One hand threaded through her hair, tethering her to him, and the other gathering both wrists, bundling retaliation into stillness. He did not hold back either, ravaging her mouth with fury, barely allowing breath. At first she fought him, and then before she knew it another feeling altogether arose and she clung to his kiss as though her very life depended on it.

With a curse, he let her go.

'I am sorry.' He didn't sound at all like he usually did, and the scar across his chin stood out in a raised white line. Neither did he look sorry. Rather he appeared as though with only the slightest of provocation he might act in the very same way yet again.

Unbridled and rampant. A lord who was used to an

easy domain over others and was trying now to find a normalcy that had never been part of their relationship together in order to survive.

'We bring out the worst in each other.' More of his words slung with insult, though a small edge of them held another emotion. Shame, if she might name it, for his behaviour and for her own, each marooned in a half place of regret.

The silence was welcomed. The clip-clop of the horses, the call of the driver, the sounds of a busy London street. Normal and proper after everything else that was not. Her lips felt rough and dry, but she did not dare to lick them in case he interpreted such an action wrongly. With eyes downcast she swallowed back tears and sat perfectly still, pleased when the horses were called to a halt and the door was opened to the Northrup town house.

The footman helped her out. Nathaniel did not touch her or look at her. It was as if three feet were a thousand miles as she climbed down onto the white pebbles.

'If I hear any other news about Sarah Milgrew I shall let you know, Miss Northrup.'

'I would be indebted, Lord Lindsay.'

The polite manners of society hung across an undercurrent of weariness and then he was gone.

White's was busy when he flung himself down on a leather wingchair opposite Hawk half an hour later and ordered himself a double shot of their strongest whisky.

'A run in with the mysterious Miss Cassandra Northrup, I presume?'

Nat ignored Hawk's jibe because the whole fiasco was just too confusing to dwell upon right now. 'Another woman has been brought out of the river.'

'Lord.' Hawk sat forward. 'Who is it this time?'

'A girl whom the Daughters of the Poor had found and given a home to. The sister of one of those dragged from the Thames last month, I am guessing.'

'Was there a meeting of the Venus Club that night?'

'No.'

'Damn.'

'But the girl had made enquiries the evening before at the Sailors Inn concerning her sister. The tavern keeper remembers her asking. I also know the name of her home town, so perhaps something happened there?'

'Bits and pieces dropping into the jigsaw. God, how I love this game.'

'I doubt the youngest Northrup daughter would see it in those terms, Stephen. She was furious to hear I had been at a meeting of the Venus Club.'

'You did not enlighten her of your true purpose?'

'And run the risk of having her poke her nose into the whole conundrum? It is getting more dangerous by the day and she seems to think she is indestructible.'

'I see your point.' Hawk leant forward and frowned. 'Have you been in a fight? Your face looks bruised.'

'Cassandra Northrup hit me. Hard.'

Stephen began to laugh. 'She makes you foolish, Nathaniel, and it's about high time that one of us found a woman who managed to do that. Besides, she is your wife.' He raised his glass and drank, his smile laconic. 'It's been years since you have given any

woman the time of day and this one...' He stopped as though picking his words carefully. 'This one makes you feel again.'

Anger. Wrath. Irritation. Frustration. Helplessness. Fear. For what she was involved in and for the risks she took. Aye, Hawk was right in his summation of strongly feeling something. Nat stayed quiet.

'There is another matter that I have heard amongst the whispers of gossip, Nat, and I am not sure if this is a good time to tell you of it.'

'Something about Cassandra Northrup, you mean?'

'Yes.'

Nathaniel took a breath in because by the tone of voice that Stephen was using he knew the news was bad. 'What is it?'

'She has a son.'

The bottom fell out of his world in one dizzying and frantic sort of disbelief. Of all the things he had expected Hawk to say this was not one of them.

'How old?'

'Word is that she returned from Paris with him in tow.'

Nat's hands scraped through his hair as he tried to recover a lost composure.

Was the child his?

Anger filtered his world with a red haze, the beat of his heart drumming in his ears as he put down his glass. Had Sandrine been pregnant in Perpignan and not told him? His mind skirted back to the timings.

After his behaviour in the carriage he felt it unwise to confront Cassandra with this new question, for the

answer she gave back would determine everything. He wished that he could have gone then and there to her and sworn that the parenthood of her son did not matter to him.

But he knew that it did. With care, he straightened in the leather seat.

'Is it yours?'

Stephen's voice came through a billowing loss and for the first time in a long while Nat found himself unable to formulate even the smallest of thoughts.

Cassie held her son close against the night and listened to his breathing, the moon coming in between the curtains of patterned velvet, illuminating the bed with its paleness.

Jamie came to her room in the night with a wail of worry, another dream disturbing slumber and leaving him upset and frightened. Often she instructed his nanny to let him come to her in the early hours before the dawn if he awoke for she liked sleeping with him.

She wondered if he remembered his time in Paris, the uncertainty, the desperation. She hoped he held no recollection of her crying out for Nathanael and searching for a face that might look like his in the Place des Vosges or the busy markets of Les Halles. She had walked the length and the breadth of the city, hoping that she might see him once in the uniform of an army officer, in the Luxembourg Gardens and the Parc du Champ de Mars opposite the L'Ecole Militaire. Just to explain. At the Hôtel des Invalides she had waited on the esplanade and searched. This face and that one.

Men ravaged by battle and memories, but none of them were Nathanael Colbert.

Today in the carriage she had hated him. No, she shook her head for that was not quite true. Even membership in a club renowned for its debauchery could not dull the hopes she harboured. His kiss had been full of anger, a savage punishing caress, but underneath the fury, passion simmered. She had felt it sliding beneath intent and taking root, anger compromised by lust.

Crying over the loss of Sarah before finally going to sleep and then being woken when Jamie had padded into her room in the small hours of the morning, Cassandra felt dislocated.

Life and death was entwined irrevocably and now, as the moon waned and the dawn called she knew that she would have to be honest no matter what the consequences. Jamie was a boy who needed a father and it was only right that she gave Nathaniel Lindsay the chance to get to know his son.

Their son. A child born from love and from passion.

Tears pooled behind her eyes. Jamie was the reason she had lived, a calling hope when everything else had been lost. He had looked like Nathaniel from the first moment he had been born, wise eyes staring up at her under a shock of black hair. And every single year the resemblance had grown.

Turning over, she looked at the ceiling and remembered the kiss in the carriage. She wanted that feeling again, pounded by strong emotion and rescued from the inertia that had made her feel so flat for all the months and years without him. But she could not blackmail

him into loving her by offering their son as bait. No.
She would have to let Jamie go and trust Nathaniel to
be the sort of father she imagined he would be. Then
she would need to step back. The realisation brought
her arms in an involuntary protest around the small
sleeping body and she dozed with him snuggled in beside her until the morning.

She would tell him as soon as she saw him next.

Nathaniel was waiting for her by his carriage outside the school in Holborn two mornings later and it
seemed to her as if he had been there a while.

'I want to talk to you.' He did not bother with the
niceties of greeting, cold grey eyes levelled at her with
more than a hint of anger.

'Here?'

'Perhaps the park opposite? Could you accompany
me for a walk?'

A tight request, just holding on to politeness.

'Very well.'

She was unsettled by his demeanour. She had sworn
to herself she would give him the truth about Jamie
and yet now the thought of actually broaching such
a topic made her feel sick. Today he looked nothing
like the man she had made love to in the high passes
of Languedoc. No, today plain fury seemed to radi-
ate from him.

A few words and her life might be completely different and torn apart. Jamming her teeth together, she
did not say a thing, watching him as he shepherded her
behind a small green hedge and turned.

'Why did you take so long to return to England? From what I have been able to gather it was almost two years before you came back.'

Her eyes snapped up to his. Something had changed. He knew of Jamie. She could see it in his face and in his stillness. He always had that, a crouching sense of both calm and danger. His silence had its own voice, too. She had known this moment would come, of course, through four long years of imaginings. How often had she sat in the dead of night and wondered how this secret would be told.

'Hawk implied you had a child in France.'

Not like this. Not like this. Not asked with anger. Not out in the open where anyone might interrupt and the time to explain was not on her side. She cursed Stephen Hawkhurst for imparting the information.

'Was there a child from our union, Sandrine?'

Ah, so easy to simply lie given his uncertainty, but she found she could not.

'There was. There is,' she amended and heard breathlessness in every syllable. 'Jamie is three years old and will be four at the end of next month. He was born in Paris at the end of July in 1847.' All the facts for him to place together, the answer hanging in any interpretation he wanted.

The quiet continued for one moment and then for two.

'He is mine.'

Cassie had never heard such a tone from Lord Lindsay; the hope was audible as was the shock, but it was the simple yearning that got to her.

'Ours.' She could not say more, the tears in her eyes welling with the relief of her admission.

'And Lebansart?'

The ugly name crept in to all that should have been beautiful. 'He never touched me in that way.'

Emotion was etched into every hard line of Nathaniel's face. 'It certainly looked like he wanted to from where I stood.'

'The names I gave him put paid to that. He was too keen to use the information I had recited to think of anything else. He left with his men ten minutes after you last saw him.'

'Did he hurt you?'

Turning her face away, she was glad not to see the question in his eyes. 'James Nathanael Colbert Northrup is our son's name. I could not think of another way to make sure you would know you were his father if anything was to happen to me.'

He breathed out loudly, a tremor in the sound, all other thoughts washed away. She was pleased for it.

'When can I see him?'

Cassie was quiet. She was, after all, not certain just what sort of a part Nathaniel wanted to play in his son's life. Or what kind of a role *she* might be placed into.

'Does he know about me?'

'He thinks that his father died in France. I thought that, too.'

With a curse, his glance took in the far horizon. Allowing himself time to take in the enormity of all that she had told him before he needed to give an answer, she supposed.

'Why was he born in Paris?'

A different tack. Beneath such a question other queries lingered.

'My uncle's best friend had a house there and allowed me the use of it. He sent servants to help me settle.'

'You did not think to come back to England?'

Shaking her head, she took his hand. 'I wanted to have Jamie first. I wanted to have our baby without the pressure of all that would transpire in London had I come home alone. I was sick for most of the pregnancy and I did not trust a sea journey. I also believed that I could find you in Paris and explain.'

His grey eyes sharpened. 'Did you know you were pregnant before Perpignan?'

Looking straight at him, she nodded.

His anger was immediate. 'You knew and yet you still left?'

'Much has happened since we were young, Nathaniel. Good things and bad. But Jamie is one of the good things and that is where our focus must lie.'

Relief filled her when he nodded. A relationship held by the smallest of threads, the past between them a broken maze of trust. Sandrine Mercier and Nathanael Colbert had been vastly different people from Cassandra Northrup and Nathaniel Lindsay. But each of them in their own way was now trying to find a direction.

'Where does this leave us, then?' She heard the tiredness in his words.

'If we were to be friends it might be a start.'

* * *

Friends?

Nathaniel mulled over the word, hating the limitations upon it, yet at a loss to demand more. She had borne him a son in a place far from home. Jamie. James. The word budded within him like a prayer answered.

But it was Cassandra whom he needed to think about now. In France they'd experienced lust and passion and avidity as they had made their way through the high mountain passes. Now she needed friendship. It was what she was asking of him, this quieter calm after a storm. Friendship, an emotion he held no experience of with a woman. Did it preclude touching? He moved back, for the expression on her face looked as uncertain as his, eyes shaded equally in worry and hope.

Taking a breath, he smiled as he saw her hand shake when she pushed back the curls that had escaped from beneath her bonnet. 'Does he have hair your colour or mine?'

'Yours. I am constantly amazed that my sister does not see the resemblance and comment upon it.'

'A St Auburn, then.' The words slipped from him unbidden, and she sobered instantly.

'A piece of paper all those years ago was easy to sign, but a father should be for ever. You will need to meet him first, Nathaniel, and understand what it is you offer.'

'Then let me, Sandrine. Let me get to know both of you again in a way we did not have the chance of before. In fact, let us begin right now. I can tell you

something of my life as a child and then you can tell me yours.'

Her smile was tentative.

'After my parents died my grandfather found it hard to cope. He left me in the hands of a nanny and myriad servants and went to Italy for three years. When he returned home I was sent straight up to Eton. From the age of nine to the age of eighteen I barely saw him. When I did I found he was a man I couldn't like and I am sure that the feeling is mutual.'

'Where is he now?'

'At St Auburn. He rarely leaves the place and I seldom go there. Such an arrangement works for us both.'

'You never had sisters or brothers?'

'No. My mother had a difficult birth with me and could not have other babies. Perhaps that was a part of my grandfather's dislike.'

'Surely a grown man could not blame a small child for such a thing.'

His smile widened. 'My point exactly.'

With the wind in his hair and the sun on his face Nathaniel Lindsay looked to Cassandra like the epitome of a wealthy and favoured lord of the peerage. He also looked maddeningly beautiful, a fact that worried her even more than the détente that they spoke of.

She wondered if she could withstand such a thing and not give in to the feelings that swirled inside her. This time she was no *ingénue* with a hard-luck story as the unfortunate victim of crime. No, now she was the one who had betrayed honour and had the scars to prove it. With only the shedding of clothes would he

see the living, breathing marks of treason branded into her right breast.

Hence she moved away. From touch. From closeness. From temptation. His confession about his relationship with his grandfather was worth more to her than all the gold and riches in the world because for the first time she saw the child who had made the man.

'I don't know what it would be like to be an only child. Through all the years of our early childhood it was my siblings' presence that made everything seem bearable.'

'You think that Jamie needs a brother or a sister?'

Despite meaning not to she laughed. 'A gentleman should not mention such a thing, Lord Lindsay.'

The dimple in his right cheek was deep and whilst he was speaking so candidly of his past she did not wish to waste the chance of knowledge. 'What is St Auburn like?'

'The house was built in the sixteenth century by a Lindsay ancestor and has been added on to ever since. It sits in the midst of rolling farmland and there is a lake it looks down upon.'

'It sounds like a home that needs to be filled with family and laughter.'

Nathaniel smiled. 'Perhaps you are right. Are you always so wise, Cassandra Northrup?'

'If I was, I doubt I would have needed to go to France in the first place. I might have recovered from my mother's death like a normal child and been a proper lady of society with all the airs and graces.'

'I like you better as you are.'

The blush began as a small warm spot near her heart and spread to the corners of her body. Out in the air in the quiet winds of late summer it was so easy to believe in such troth.

'You do not really know me at all, Nathaniel.'

'Then let me. Come to St Auburn. Bring Maureen and Kenyon Riley. Bring whomever you like to feel comfortable, and come with Jamie.'

The grey in his eyes was fathomless today, a lover who would show her only what he might think she wished to see. He was good at hiding things, she thought, the trait of a spy imposed upon everyday life. She wondered how easy that would be, to live with secrets that could result in the downfall of governments if told. Her own had been a hard enough task to keep hidden.

When a group of well-dressed ladies accompanied by their maids walked into the park they were forced to return to the road, though once there awkwardness enveloped her. On the street she saw others watching him, a well-known lord with the promise of an earldom as a mantle around his shoulders. With Nathaniel Lindsay she could not afford to make a mistake or go too lightly into the promises that he asked of her.

Jamie's welfare rested on good decisions and proper judgement. No, she would rest on his suggestions for a while until she had mulled them over.

An hour later, Nathaniel sat in his leather chair behind the large mahogany desk in his study and looked about the room without really seeing anything.

He had a son. Jamie. James Nathanael Colbert Northrup, she had said, his name sandwiched in between her own.

He should have asked Cassandra other things, should have found out what Jamie liked and what he didn't. Did he read, did he love horses, did he play with balls, did he have a pet?

Almost four years old. For a man with little contact with children the number was difficult to get his head around. What could a nearly four-year-old boy do? Sitting back against the seat, he closed his eyes.

God, he was a father. He was a father to a child conceived in the wilds of the Pyrenees above Perpignan.

He took a silver flask from the drawer and unstopped it. Cassandra had been on edge, the usual flare of awareness between them doused by responsibility and worry. Did she think he might take their son away or insist upon the legality of their marriage?

Legality.

The child was a legitimate heir to the St Auburn earldom and fortune. Nat wondered just what his grandfather, William Harper Wilson Lindsay, would say to that.

The past few days had been full of surprises. Yesterday in Wallingford he had discovered another girl had been murdered in the exact same way as those in London. He also had the name of the tall and well-dressed Londoner who had left his room at the inn the day the body had been discovered.

Scrivener Weeks.

Nat had spent a good few hours since last night

trawling through the names of all those in society, but come up with nothing.

His mind reeled with all that had happened and as he took a sip of his brandy he smiled.

Chapter Eleven

Jamie was sick, the temperature he ran more worrying by the hour, and Cassandra was increasingly beginning to panic, something she seldom did in any medical emergency.

Her mind would not be still as she imagined all the possibilities and problems that could befall her son if the fever didn't begin to abate. Maureen had helped her with the nursing for most of the day, but had gone now with Kenyon Riley to a dinner with the old duke in Belgravia. His nanny, Mrs Harris, had also been here for the past hours, but Cassie could see that she was tired and so sent her off to bed.

Hence she was alone, the weak and pain-filled moans cutting through all sense and making her as fearful as she had ever been. By eleven o'clock she had had enough. Scrawling out a note, she asked for one of the Northrup servants to deliver it immediately to the Lindsay town house and wait for an answer.

She wanted Nathaniel here. She wanted a man who

might love her son as much as she did and who could bring some sense and calm into a situation that was spiralling out of control for her. A tiny whisper that predicted Jamie might not recover was also part of the reason. If her son died, then Nathaniel would never have seen him. She shook the thought away and ordered back sanity.

It was a simple fever with a high and sudden temperature probably brought on by the dousing he had had in a rain shower in the garden. Visions of young children who went on to develop rashes and stiff necks came too, however, and she had seen enough of life in the past years to know that things did not always turn out happily.

Yesterday in the park Nathaniel had offered her the chance of reconciliation. Tonight all she wanted was his strength and his composure. She tried to regulate her breathing so that Jamie would not pick up on her panic, but found that the beat of her heart was going faster and faster, a clammy dread beginning to take over completely.

She should have called the doctor, she knew she should have, but the Northrup physician was a man who still believed in doing things in his way and even after she had stressed a number of times to him the importance of clean hands and tools he had not taken up the learning. Her father had wanted to replace him, but the traditions of the Batemans attending the Cowper family in the capacity of medical practitioners had been a difficult one to break and so he had given up. Usually Cassandra dealt with any sickness and she did

it with such acumen and success they seldom asked for
the physician's attendance.

Jamie was so deathly still, that was the problem, and
the lukewarm water that she sponged his little body
with was making no inroads to a gathering heat. She
had used infusions of camphor, basil and lemon balm,
angelica and hyssop, yet nothing seemed to be making any difference.

The sound of footsteps had her standing, heart in
mouth, and she turned to the door as Nathaniel walked
through, his shirt opened at the collar as if he had not
even had the time to find a necktie, pale eyes taking in
the scene before him without any sign of panic.

Cassie burst into tears, an action so unexpected and
unfamiliar that she even surprised herself for having
done so. He did not break a step as he gathered her into
his arms and brought her with him over to the bed, his
eyes hungrily taking in the features of his son.

'How long has Jamie had the fever?'

'All…day.' She swallowed, trying to make her voice
sound more like it usually did.

'You have bathed him?'

'Many times, and I have used up all my remedies.'

Jamie's fit began with a twitch and a quiver, the right
side of his body tensing and moving in a rigidity that
spread to his legs and feet. While paralysing fear held
Cassandra immobile, Nathaniel whipped off the thin
sheet and spread it on the floor, lifting Jamie down to
lie on his side and crouching by him.

He did not restrain him or hold him in any way,
but let the shaking take its course for ten seconds and

then twenty, just watching to make sure that he did not injure himself with the movement. Finally, when Cassandra thought it might never pass, Jamie relaxed, vomiting across the boots of his father.

'So this is what it is to be a parent?' Nathaniel turned towards her, his hand passing across the forehead of his son and relief evident.

Nodding, she thought that she had never loved Nathaniel more than she did at that moment, his certainty and strength edged with gentle compassion and humour.

'I had the same sort of fits when I was a child, Cassandra, and the St Auburn physician assured my mother and father that they would disappear as I grew older. Which they did. He will be fine. Better than my boots, at least.'

He leaned over to wipe the traces of moisture from his fine dark-brown Hessians, the gleam of leather a little tarnished. 'If you straighten the bed, I will lift him back up for I think the worst is over now.'

Nathaniel felt as though he were lifting treasure, his son, the small and damp body smelling of sickness and fatigue. Yet he was beautiful in the way only small boys could be, a scrape upon his left kneecap as if he had been running somewhere too fast and his colouring exactly that of a St Auburn heritage.

The same dark hair and skin tone, the same line of nose and cheek he had seen in the drawings of himself as a child. His heart turned in his chest and squeezed with a feeling that was foreign, half fear and all love,

the utter storm of fatherhood beaching upon him, winding him with its intensity, fervour and suddenness.

'Thank you for calling me.'

'Thank you for coming.'

'He is beautiful.'

'I think so.' For a second a smile tweaked at the corner of her lips, the worry and fright beaten back a little, the tears drying on her cheeks.

'Is it the first time this has happened?'

'It is. Jamie is usually so well and full of energy. It was the fright of the difference, I think.'

'I had three of these fits across the space of a year when I was about his age and, according to my mother's diary, she was always as worried as you appear to be.'

Jamie suddenly opened his eyes, the pale grey confused. 'Mama?'

'I am here, darling.' Cassandra took his hand and brought it to her lips, kissing the fingers one by one. 'You have been sick, but you are getting better now.' The small face came around, questions contained within it.

'This is Nathaniel Colbert Lindsay, Jamie.'

'Nearly my name?'

'He is your—'

'Papa.' Jamie finished the sentence, and that one word sealed a lifetime of loyalty. Glancing over, Nathaniel saw Cassandra nod, and he came down on his knees beside the bed to take the offered hand of his son. Warm fingers curled into his.

For ever.

'I used to get sick like this when I was little, so I know exactly what to do and you will soon feel a lot better.'

'Did you come from France?'

'Pardon?' Was confusion a part of this sickness?

'No, Jamie. Your papa lives in London now so you may see him when you want to.'

'Can you stay here now?'

'Can I?' Nat looked over at Cassandra and smiled when she nodded. 'It seems that I can.'

'Good.' With that Jamie simply closed his eyes and went to sleep, his breathing even and the fever that had ravaged his body less than a few moments past, broken.

The silence stretched around them all, the gratitude of seeing a small child's recovery being a big part of that. His wife clasped Jamie's hand on one side of the bed and he held the other, a link of family and vigilance and concern. Outside distant bells chimed the hour of twelve, as the night softened into quiet.

'Would you like a cup of tea? I could go down to the kitchens and make it and then bring it back here.'

Tea? Nat would have far rather had a stiff brandy, but he wondered how she might feel about drinking in a child's room so he nodded at the offered drink. He felt as if he had been plunged into a different world where everything was altered and extraordinary. But right somehow. He smiled at that fact.

Left alone with his son, Nathaniel observed every feature, every part of a child who had been conceived out of love. He was sleeping now, his lashes dark against his cheeks and one arm curled beneath

his head. He had slept like that, too, as a child, he remembered, and smiled as he noticed a ragged teddy bear on the floor, a well-loved companion by the looks of it. Picking it up, he tucked it beside his son. Just another one of all the small moments of a childhood he had missed, he thought, and resolved not to lose more.

When Cassandra bustled back a few moments later with a tray in hand she gestured to him to follow her into a sitting room close by and then proceeded to set out the cups, sugar and milk on a table.

'I thought if we had our tea here it would not disturb Jamie and yet we are still near enough to hear if he calls out.' She tipped her head to listen, but no noise was forthcoming. 'His nanny and the servants are all in their beds and I did not wish to wake them again so if you need something to eat...?'

'Just tea would be lovely.'

A flash of humour answered him as she understood his meaning. 'Papa does not drink at all and so our house isn't well stocked with liquor. But I will make certain that some is brought in for you next time.'

'Next time?'

'Jamie wants you in his life. Even being so sick he told you he did.'

'And what of you? Do you want me here?'

She lifted her cup carefully and looked at him directly. 'I do.'

'Then let us begin with that.'

The tea tasted like an elixir the way she made it with a dollop of milk and sugar. It was steadying after a night of emotion. He wondered why he had never taken

to the brew before and resolved to instruct his staff
to get this particular leaf into his house for drinking.
Everything seemed heightened somehow: the scent of
Cassandra's perfume, the colour of her hair. The small
touch of her skin against his thumb as she had handed
him the cup and the earthy aroma of tea.

Tonight lust did not rule as it usually did when they
met, although in truth it simmered beneath the conversation. No, this evening a shared responsibility had
engendered new emotions. Contentment. Peace. Gratitude. The quieter humours that Nat had seldom experienced before. The joy of sitting in a room with family
around him and being a part of a tradition that stretched
back through the ages.

'I could buy him a horse, a small one with a good
temperament. One that did not kick. A safe steed.'

She smiled. 'You cannot protect him from everything, Nathaniel. What was your first horse like?'

'Wild. A real hellion. I learnt almost immediately
where to stand and where not to.'

'The lessons of life. These are what Jamie needs to
know from you.'

'Is it always this hard? Being a parent, I mean.'

'From the very first moment when the midwife
handed him to me my heart ceased to be my own.'

'You had others there with you?'

'No.'

He swore softly so that the sound of it would not
inadvertently reach the ears of his son. 'I wish I had
been present.'

'I did, too, but I thought you were dead. I looked for

you in Paris and asked after you. No one had ever heard
your name, of course, and you were probably already
back in England. But I did not know any of that then.'

'When you came to London you did not arrive as
Mrs Colbert?'

'I thought it too dangerous. I had no idea as to what had
happened to Guy Lebansart and his men and I wanted to
keep Jamie as safely away from them as I could. I thought
placing your name within his would be enough for you to
know what had happened if anything should go wrong
with me and you were still alive to find him.'

'And you were condemned for not using the name
of your husband because of it?'

'Oh, that was an easy sufferance for I seldom strayed
into society and finally the gossip lessened.'

'If you had used Colbert I might have found you
earlier.'

'Then that would be my only regret.'

'Come with me to St Auburn when Jamie is better.
I can show you both the beauty of it, the solidness.'

'You said your grandfather was there.'

'Come as my family and he can meet you.'

Nathaniel wanted Jamie and her to go to St Auburn.
He wanted things that she could not promise just yet
with the scars at her breast and the guilt in her heart.

Tonight it had been easy to pretend with Jamie between them. Tonight he had come like a knight in shining armour through the darkness to rescue her. But
tomorrow...?

Reality would creep back with the anger and then

she would be at the mercy of pity again. She needed to make sure that the feelings in France could be translated here away from any pressures before she followed him into a place that neither of them could come back from. She needed him to love her wholly with his body just as he had done once in the southern mountains and she wanted to love him back in the same way. But could she risk asking that of him? Now, after Jamie's sickness and the care he had shown, would the scars ruin everything?

The thrall of memory took her breath away. 'Do you live alone at your town house?'

'Yes.' His voice was quiet, underlaced with question.

'Then perhaps I could come there first. Just me...'

She left the rest unsaid, but he had picked up on the implications instantly.

'When?'

'Tomorrow night. At eight.' That gave her a day to make certain that Jamie was fully recovered.

'I would like that.'

'And it will only be us?'

'Yes.'

'I will need a carriage later...to bring me home before the morning.'

'It shall be at your disposal.'

'I am half sick of shadows,' said The Lady of Shalott.

Cassie just hoped that by leaving her sanctuary and following her heart into the arms of her Lancelot the result would be much happier than the one in the poem.

> *Out flew the web and floated wide;*
> *The mirror crack'd from side to side;*
> *'The curse is come upon me,' cried*
> *The Lady of Shalott.*

The three scars from Lebansart's blade burnt like hot ribbons of shame upon her breast.

After such a night Nathaniel was unable to sleep and so he sat at the desk in his office and worked on the case of the girls found near the river. Rearranging scraps of paper before him, he took away this one and replaced with that.

The list contained the names of every member of the Venus Club. The clues had to be here somewhere, he knew, the intuition that had served him so well in his years of working with the Service honed and on high alert.

Scrivener Weeks would be here somewhere hiding amongst the detail, he just had to find out where he was concealed. Removing each member who was neither tall nor dark, he was left with the names of fifteen men. Reginald Northrup's name caught his attention, but so did the name of Christopher Hanley.

Another thought occurred. It was Hanley who had told the world that he had seen Cassandra in the environs of Whitechapel Road and Hanley who had been disparaging about the role of the Daughters of the Poor trying to save every wayward girl in London. Could the existence of Cassandra's charity be threatening him in

some way; threatening his preference for sexual experiences with very young women?

Placing the name in the very centre of all the others, Nat determined to find out more about his family circumstances and his night-time habits. He would visit Hanley, too. Sometimes it just took a more direct approach to flush out a guilty quarry and make them run.

Meanwhile, he would make absolutely certain that Cassandra came nowhere near the vicinity of her uncle's friend.

Chapter Twelve

Cassie could barely settle to anything for the whole of the next day, a sort of wild excitement that verged on panic underlying everything she did.

Jamie was so much better, leaving his bed and eating large plates of whatever the cook tempted him with. Maureen was astonished at how much improved he seemed, though it was another matter entirely that she quizzed Cassandra about.

'There is word you had a visitor late last night, Cassie. Lord Nathaniel Lindsay was an unexpected caller?'

Cassandra knew her sister's ways. Maureen obviously had found out a lot more about the unusual happening and was waiting for Cassandra to unravel it for her.

'Lord Lindsay looks familiar somehow. I cannot quite put my finger on how I should know him, but...?'

At that precise moment Jamie ran past playing with a small train, and it was if a shutter had suddenly been raised.

'Oh, my goodness, Lindsay is Jamie's father? Nathanael is his second name?'

Horror stood where a humorous playfulness had lingered a moment before. 'He ruined you?'

'No. We were married, Reena. In France, almost five years ago. Everything is perfectly legal.'

'Then why...?' She could not even formulate her next question.

'One day I will tell you everything, but not at this moment. If you could keep my confidence for a little while longer, I would be most appreciative.'

'He will not break your heart again?'

'Again?' She could not quite understand what her sister alluded to.

'You came home from Paris like a half person and never looked at another male with any thoughts of interest although there were many good men who were offering. I knew there was someone. I just thought he was dead.'

There are worse ways to be separated than in death, Cassie thought as Jamie came over to her to demand a cuddle. Her sister's dark eyes watched carefully.

'Kenyon likes him. I do, too.'

'Who does he like?' Jamie's voice put paid to any further conversation.

In the late afternoon Cassie fussed about which gown to put on and finally decided on a dark yellow silk, a little outdated but beautifully cut. She fashioned her own hair into a bun at her nape, decorating the sides with two ornate tortoiseshell combs she had procured

in the Marais. Cassie reasoned that if the night was to play out as she hoped she needed a style that would be easily unpinned and quickly redone when she left in the early hours of the next day.

Even the thought of it all made her apprehensive. Such a premeditated and deliberate choice. The hands of the clock seemed to race towards eight, and her stomach felt agitated and jittery.

She was twenty-three and she had had just one lover for only a short time. She did not count the Baudoins' rough handling of her in the first days of Nay, preferring to forget about the violence and hurt of the place. No, all she remembered now were the weeks between Saint Estelle and Perpignan, and the utter need they had felt for each other, the desire and the passion.

Breathing, she held in her hope as an aching desperateness. Could this happen again or had she ruined it with her choice of sacrificing others so that they might live?

She turned to the mirror and looked at herself. She was not a bad person or a deceitful one. She had done her best ever since the betrayal at Perpignan to make amends for the harm that she had caused. Would Nathaniel see that of her? Would he be able to look beyond the past and see a future?

'Please, God, let it be so,' she whispered and hurried to find shoes, stockings and a coat to match her gown.

Cassandra arrived on the dot of eight-fifteen, the ornate clock in the corner of the front entrance still calling out the quarter-hour. She had come. Dismissing

his man, Nat went out to the carriage to open the door, the large black cape she wore hiding much, though her eyes shone through in the dark, anxious and fearful.

'Is Jamie better today?' A topic other than this want that hung between them was welcomed, and she smiled.

'He is, my lord.' She allowed the Lindsay servant to take her cloak.

'So formal, my lady.'

At that she blushed heavily, and would have tripped on the hem of her yellow gown had he not placed his hand beneath her arm. God, all he wanted to do was to snatch her up and take her to his bed, to assuage a pummelling need that was gaining more traction with every single second.

Friendship.

The word came back, loud with inherent meaning. He needed to slow down and calm down, for Cassandra Northrup deserved so much more than a quick tumble of lust, devoid of chivalry and consideration.

'Dinner is waiting in the dining room. After that I shall dismiss the servants and...' He did not finish.

'A meal sounds lovely.' She smiled at him then, as though she understood in his unfinished sentence some shared disquiet.

'The French chef from St Auburn followed me down to London and is very competent. I hope you will enjoy the fare.' Lord, why was he rambling on like this? He sounded like a green youth in the first throes of pleasing a girl, so he bit down for silence. He hardly rec-

ognised himself in his concern for making the right impression.

When he had visited Hawk earlier in the afternoon to tell him his worries about Hanley he had also mentioned the proposed dinner with Cassandra Northrup. With all good intentions Stephen had instructed him to smile a lot and be most attentive, but for the life of him Nat couldn't seem to make his lips curl upwards and empty compliments had never been his style.

Instead, he pulled the chair from the table and invited Cassandra to sit and then he took his own place a good few feet away. Distance made him less edgy and the procession of kitchen staff with tureens of soup and entrées turned his mind for a moment from the reason as to why she was here alone tonight.

'I don't think I thanked you properly for your help with Jamie the other night, Nathaniel. I do not normally panic.'

'I was glad that you called me, and if he is anything like me and has another fit it should be months away.'

'You only had three episodes, you said.'

'Indeed. I outgrew them exactly as the St Auburn physician had predicted that I would.'

'A family trait, then?'

'My father was prone to the same as a child. He did not have brothers or sisters, however, so I am not certain if it would have been something that ran through the whole line.'

'Well, it is reassuring to know that you recovered.' She drew a spoon of soup to her mouth and sighed.

'Onion soup. This is a taste I remember, though I have not had it since Paris.'

'You did not think to send word to your father after Perpignan and ask him to help?'

She shook her head, the red-gold catching the light from the chandelier above in a sparkling cascade of colour. 'Papa would have found the situation trying, and as a family we attempt to shelter him from anything that is difficult. After Mama died he was...brittle and I am not certain if he will ever be truly happy again.'

'So you managed alone?'

'I did.'

'You do that often.'

Her spoon hovered above the plate. 'I believe in myself more now.'

'I am glad for it.'

'I believe that atonement goes a certain way in alleviating past mistakes, and that what was, is not always the same as what will be.'

'Wise of you.'

'I have made errors, Nathaniel, big ones that I wish every single day I had not, but in the end one cannot wish life away. One has to confront it with courage and go on.'

'And you have.'

She nodded. 'For Jamie's sake, I had to.'

The strength of her washed across him. She sat there and told him that in adversity she had found a version of herself that she liked. He wanted to reach over and bring her ruined hand to his lips and kiss each finger one by one. She was no empty-headed maiden trying

to fit in with others' perceptions of her and whereas
Acacia had been hardened by the problems in her life,
Cassandra had been freed by them.

He wished he had skipped the course of soup and
gone instead for more simple fare because the hours
were running away with the task of eating and there
was still dessert. He was glad the removes of soup had
been taken away and hoped the offering of lobster,
ham and venison might disappear just as quickly. He
could not remember a meal taking quite as long as he
helped himself perfunctorily to one of the many plates
of vegetables.

Cassandra felt hot and uneasy. The food was beautifully cooked and expensive and yet she could barely
eat it. A clock in the house kept striking out the minutes
of every hour and time seemed to be racing towards
the real reason as to why she was here.

She wanted to sleep with Nathaniel Lindsay, she
did. She wanted to feel him inside her moving with the
passion only he could engender and she longed for the
quiet repose of skin against skin, their bodies speaking in a way words never did.

But the scars of Lebansart were a reminder of all
that had gone wrong between them and she dreaded
him seeing them and asking about what had happened.
She breathed out heavily and knew that he watched her
with his beautiful pale-grey eyes, the dimple in his
right cheek seen under the bright candelabras.

She would not survive again if he turned her away.
For all her bravado and independence she understood

that. The lobster felt dry in her mouth as she tried to swallow it, helping herself to a generous sip of white wine with the taste of summer in its bouquet. She seldom drank anything stronger than tea, save for in his company, where fortitude was as necessary as breath.

Cassie wished the meal would end and that the servants might disappear. She wanted him to lead her to his chamber with the minimum of chatter and undress her with the maximum of speed. She wanted to look into his eyes when he saw the scars and see acceptance or indifference, it did not matter which. It was the bewildering bloom of distaste that she hoped so fervently to avoid.

He suddenly stood. 'Perhaps we might leave the rest for later, Cassandra.' Those attending to the table stepped back and waited while he helped her from her seat.

As they reached the hall leading to the stairwell he petitioned her to tarry for a moment whilst he returned to give his instructions to the staff. She could hear his voice asking them to clean up and then retire for he would not be requiring their services further this evening. The resulting silence was full of question and speculation, but even that did not worry Cassie.

Then he was back again, taking her hand and escorting her up the wide marble staircase into the second floor of the house. His room lay at the end of a corridor, a set of French doors with an ornate gold handle and a substantial lock. As she walked through she heard him turn the key. Privacy. She was thankful for it.

His chamber was decorated in all shades of pale,

a restful luxurious interior that threw her off balance. The heavy brocades of paisley and floral at the Northrup town house looked tacky and overdone in comparison. This room was one of bleached furniture and patinas harking back to the age of a faded beauty. She wondered if he had had a hand in choosing the decor.

A whole line of leatherbound books sat on the table beside the bed. When he saw where she looked he commented, 'I read a lot.'

She remembered he had told her of that once and she had wondered. No amount of guessing could have placed him as a cultured English lord, however, with the lineage of an old family on his shoulders and a library of books at his disposal.

'You keep surprising me,' she managed to say.

At that he laughed, loudly, the first truly free emotion of the evening. A frisson of need made her stiffen. 'I could say the same, Cassandra. Few people manage to keep me as intrigued as you do and so effortlessly.'

He had come closer now. If she stepped forward she could have rested her head against his heart. With all her willpower she stopped herself doing just that.

Not yet, a voice inside her called. *He needs to understand exactly who you are.*

Her fingers came up to loosen the ties at her bodice. They were shaking in their pursuit of truth as fire began to build behind the slate of his eyes. The yellow silk had been chosen carefully. With just a few twitches of fabric it fell from her shoulders, the thin

bodice of lawn the only thing now that kept his glance from her shame.

Then that was gone, too, three slices of raised red skin at the top of her right breast on show.

'I did not give the names as easily as you had imagined, Nathaniel. I paid for their lives in my own blood, too. I knew that I was pregnant, you see, and if I did not give him something he might...'

'God.' One finger reached out to trace the injuries, horror and anger on his face.

But not at her. It was Lebansart his wrath was directed at.

'The bastard did this to you?'

She nodded because suddenly she could not speak, the back of her throat closing in an aching heaviness.

'He could have killed you. Both of you.'

'I th-think he thought he had.'

'Ah, sweetheart.' His voice broke as he simply leant down and kissed the scars, one by one. Healing their ugliness, she was to think later, and dissipating their power over her. Forgiveness was a quiet and gentle emotion, the light and earnest feel of his tongue and the smooth sweep of his lips, but it held all the weight of a new beginning.

Her hand came through his hair, shorter now than it had been in France, the dark sheen of it almost blue.

'Love me, Nathaniel, and make me forget.'

In response he lifted her to him and brought her to his bed, the wide velvet counterpane beneath her as he peeled the dress and bodice away. Her stockings were next and the small slippers bought only a few days be-

fore. Then he loosened her hair from its tie and draped the length of it down beside her.

Caught in the light and in his gaze she stayed very still. 'You are even more beautiful than I remember.' His voice held reverence and awe.

He was fully dressed as he stroked one breast, smiling when the nipple puckered at his ministrations. Then his fingers fell lower, across her stomach and down into the place between her thighs, pushing into the wet warmth with a gentle insistence. And all the time his eyes never left her own, the fire within them banking and a look that said she was his. Need made her loins rise from the bed to meet him, her legs opening wider to allow him in, and she looked away because she knew that the roiling waves of release were about to come and she did not want to see his reaction to such a surrender.

Her muscles caught around his fingers, stilling the plunder and keeping him there inside her tight, and when she began to shake he pushed in farther still, eliciting a groan that held a primal relief.

She was no longer cautious or circumspect. All she could think of was the aching craving urgency in her body and the balm and ease of tension.

They belonged together, Nathaniel and she, and it had nothing to do with marriage or legality or expectations.

It was far simpler than that. It was how their skin called to each other and how the shape of his body so perfectly fitted hers. It was in the scent of him and the beauty and the strength. It was in his honesty and morality and bravery and forgiveness.

A single tear traced its way from her left eye down onto the pillow beneath. She had not expected absolution, but how she had wanted it. From him. From the only other person in all of the world who might understand what she had lost and what she had gained.

Her saviour. Now and then.

'I will love you for ever, Nathaniel.'

Cassandra's eyes were clear and her voice was strong as she said it, no half-meant troth given with a lack of honesty or intent.

'For ever?'

This time he was ready and there was no question in his reply. With care he crossed the room and opened a drawer, pulling out his mother's ring from a velvet box. The emerald glinted in the light as he walked back and he saw she was now perched on the edge of his bed, watching.

With care he bent on one knee and the smile that he had missed so much came easily to her lips.

'I never stopped loving you, Cassandra Northrup. Will you marry me?'

'I already have, Nathaniel Lindsay.' The words were wobbly and tears pooled in her eyes.

'Again then. Properly this time. With everyone around us.'

'Yes.'

Bringing her hand up, he placed the ring upon it. His mother's ring was still oversized and the ancient gold needed a good polish, but on Cassandra's finger it looked completely right.

A circle. Of life. Lost and found. He knew his mother would have loved Cassandra, loved her rarity and her honesty. The only thing she wore was a smile and this ring and she looked to him like a goddess sent from above. To heal loneliness and doubt, to bring laughter and adventure and truth.

When her hands came to the buttons on his shirt he stood still, tugging the garment off on completion and then doing the same with his trousers and boots. Life had marked them both. Inside and out. But it had also melded them together into a shape that could not withstand the world alone. He smote the candles above and the one on the stand near the bed and in the light of the fire he turned. They came together as husband and wife, his seed spilled without a care for caution.

Home. Safe. The night outside and the warmth within.

'I want as many more Jamies as you might give me,' he whispered finally when sense had returned.

'Starting tonight, Nathaniel.' The light in her eyes danced as her fingers closed around his shaft and all that had been wonderful before began again.

Much later they spoke. She leaned against him, her head upon his chest as he lifted himself to sit against the cushioned bed end.

'Lebansart left the minute after I gave him the names on the document. Louis Baudoin had already died from having allowed me to see the paper and in the end it killed Celeste, too...'

His finger came across her lips, stopping the flow

of words. 'You don't have to tell me any more if you do not wish to. It doesn't matter now.'

'But I want to. If I had not interfered, my cousin's soul may have been saved, for she died by her own hand less than a day later.'

'Guilt has as many lives as you wish to give it, Cassandra. You were young and trying to do your best to save those you loved, but it's time now to stop the blame.'

'I hated her sometimes,' she whispered, the very words so dreadful she could not give them the full power of sound.

'Celeste?'

'She made me stay there with her. I could have escaped, but she held me there with her weakness and her need. In the end she understood just how foolish she had been, but for a long while she revelled in it. The wine. Louis Baudoin. The danger. I could never trust that she would not be harmed by her lack of foresight and so I stayed.'

'To protect her?'

She nodded, the brisk anger in the movement revealing. 'And finally I could not even do that.'

'Voltaire once wrote that "no snowflake in an avalanche ever feels responsible". Perhaps you should allow your cousin more of the burden of blame.'

Cassandra mulled his words over. Celeste had grown up reprimanding everyone except herself when things went wrong and in every situation had put her own needs first.

'You think each person is accountable for their actions.'

'I do. I am the next in line for the St Auburn title and all it entails, yet the duties that came with my job in Europe were never the ones my grandfather wished for me to entertain. It was his way of life or no way of life and he harboured a resentment I could never understand.'

'Sometimes people disappoint you.'

He laughed. 'I try to allow them not to.'

Lifting her head on to her hands, she looked at him. 'Did your work in France teach you the knack of knowing what it is that others wish to hear?'

He frowned. 'Hawk and Lucas helped me more with that. You have not met Luc Clairmont yet for he is in the Americas, but without them I wouldn't have survived the loneliness of my childhood.'

She ran her finger across his chest, circling the skin around his nipple and liking the way it tightened. 'I often worried that someone might come from England and arrest me after Perpignan, and in my dreams the punishment was always death. Perhaps that was a part of the reason I didn't come home for so long. You worked for the British Service, but you never told anyone about me.'

His hand clamped down across hers. 'I couldn't. I never asked another question of that time because if I had found out you were dead....'

'You kept me safe. Us safe.'

'Then I am glad. But enough of talk, my beautiful

wife, for there are still some hours before we need to rise.'

When he rolled her beneath him she simply relaxed, opening her mouth as his lips came across her own.

He heard the birdsong at dawn but remained perfectly still. Cassandra lay against him, one leg draped across his thigh and her head tucked into the crook of his arm. Her hair cascaded around them in all the shades of gold and red, wildly tangled and curling. He lifted up one tress and felt its softness.

His wife. They had slept for much longer than she could have wanted to and for that he was pleased.

No covert sneaking back home. He did not wish for only night-time trysts. He wanted to see the sunshine play across her skin and know the ecstasy of every hour of the day in bed. Not quite the slow-building friendship she had had in mind, but then nothing about their relationship had ever been ordinary. He wondered how she might explain this night away to her family.

Her breathing changed and her eyes opened, sleep filled and disorientated, but widening as they recognised daylight at the window. Yet still she made no attempt to leave.

'You kept me up too late, sir,' she whispered, and there was a smile in her rebuke.

'Can I do so again tonight, Lady Lindsay? Or today if you should so will it?'

'I cannot think your servants would be pleased at such a prospect.' Lifting her head, she listened for a

moment. 'They are at work already, yet they have not come in?'

'And rest assured that they will not, my love.'

Her left hand pushed back the heavy length of her hair and the ring of his mother glinted in the light.

'However, the grapevines of those in servitude will be ringing and my name, undoubtedly, shall be bandied around the salons in shock.'

'I'll announce our wish to marry in *The Times* tomorrow and everyone in the *ton* will recognise you as my intended. No one then would dare to criticise.'

'And your grandfather?'

'Who knows? Such a pronouncement may even bring him from St Auburn as he has hoped for such an occasion for ever. Jamie's existence will make him delirious.'

'You almost make me believe that it could be this easy for us.'

'Well, we have waited for years to be together again and that must be some kind of a miracle.'

She curled into him, holding tight. 'I have missed you. Missed this. Missed talking and loving. Missed closeness.'

He felt her breath at his throat, gentle and honest. Like his life was now with her in it. He wanted to protect her for ever and love her until they were old and grey with a million memories shared between them. The harsh and raw realities of the past faded into this new serenity, Cassandra and Jamie in the very centre of a world reformed.

Her finger traced the tattoo on his forearm. 'What does this mean?'

He smiled. 'It's one of the symbols from the healing temples of Asclepius. At the time, in the backstreets of Marseilles, I was looking for resurrection and renewal. Later on it always reminded me of the thin line between life and death.'

'Being a spy must have been dangerous work. Your body is covered in scars.'

'It's the price one pays for not carrying arms and being out of uniform. Blending into a community is not always as easy as it might sound.'

'But you have stopped?'

'Almost.'

'I am glad for it.'

'And for the first time I think I could settle at St Auburn and run the place, farm the land, sit as a judge at the country courts, grow vegetables. All the things I once would not have seen sense in.'

She laughed.

'With you and Jamie there it all feels possible.'

Cassie turned then to look at him, the light in her eyes bright and clear. He could never decide whether they were more green than blue. Today they seemed an exact mixture of both. 'I think I loved you the first moment I saw you in Nay, with your dimple...here.' She touched his cheek.

'Show me,' he returned and brought her against him, the sunlight from the new day creating a river of warmth on their bed.

* * *

They renewed their vows two days later in the chapel to one side of the Lindsay town house and it was a small and private occasion. Stephen Hawkhurst was the best man and Maureen the bridesmaid. William Lindsay, the old Earl of St Auburn, had sent a note declining his attendance. Cassandra's sister Anne had not been able to make the journey down from her home in Scotland because she was expecting her fourth child.

'You look beautiful, Cassandra,' Nathaniel said as she came down the stairs, her gown of cream silk shimmering in the new day.

'The seamstress you organised was wonderfully fast and this time around I even have shoes.'

He laughed and took her hand, but poignancy lingered beneath the humour as both thought of the small house by the river.

'Now and for ever,' he whispered, brushing his lips across her cheek despite the onlookers, and Jamie standing between them wriggled in delight.

When the clergyman called them to an altar fashioned with flowers, the three of them linked hands and walked forward, her father, brother and Kenyon Riley just behind them.

'Dearly beloved, we have come together in the presence of God to witness and bless the joining together of this man and this woman in holy matrimony...'

They looked at each other. This time they would be married under their own names, properly formed and completely legal.

* * *

A few hours later Stephen asked if he might speak to them both in the library where they would not be disturbed. After shutting the door he brought forth a leather satchel and took out a wad of documents from within.

'I have a wedding present for you both.'

Nat stepped forward, the frown on his brow giving Cassie the inkling that he might know what was held within the papers. They looked important. Her own heart began to beat fast.

'It is the official report from the British Service about the events that transpired in Perpignan after you were hurt in Languedoc, Nat.'

'God.' Her husband's curse was soft.

'It is not what you might think,' Hawk said quickly and handed him over the account. 'I have underlined the most crucial parts. Perhaps your wife might like to hear them.'

'No.' Her own voice, stiff with shock. How could Stephen Hawkhurst do this to her? She knew what would be within the letter, knew it to the bottom of her breaking heart. But Nathaniel was smiling and there was the suspicion of tears in his eyes as he began to read.

So it is concluded that on the fifth of November 1846 at about nine p.m. two masked men broke into the house of Mr Didier Desrosiers and Mr Gilbert Desrosiers in Toulouse, France, and killed each of them with two shots to the head.

> *Our agent in Languedoc, Nathaniel Lindsay,*
> *was also found on the right bank of the Basse*
> *River in Perpignan in the afternoon of the sixth*
> *of November 1846 with injuries to his head, stom-*
> *ach and right arm received by unknown enemies*
> *of England.*
>
> *Despite extensive searching the perpetrators*
> *have never been brought to justice.*

The fifth of November? The day before they had reached Perpignan. The day before she had told Lebansart the names. The day before she had branded herself a traitor. The day before shame had been scorched into memory.

'It was not me, after all.' The words slipped from her, tentative and unbelieving. 'They were already dead?'

'How did you know to find this?' Nat spoke now directly to Stephen, the relief in his tone evident.

'When you said you had married Cassandra Northrup in France I knew that you would not have done such a thing lightly. When you then went on to say that she had betrayed you, I realised there must be more to the affair than you had told me. At the Forsythe ball your wife made it known that there were others who died in Perpignan because of her actions and so I decided to find out exactly what it was she meant. After much searching I located this in a box that had been lost amongst others in the record room.'

'Lost?'

'Discarded, I think. Unsolved deaths. Cases closed to further enquiry.'

'But their deaths were not my fault?' The room felt farther away than it had been and a spinning lightness consumed Cassie as she groped for the chair at her side and sat down upon it. Hard. Nathaniel perched before her, taking her hands in his own.

'This is the best wedding present anyone could give us, Hawk,' he said, fingers warming her coldness. 'Cassandra was already pregnant when Guy Lebansart caught us at Perpignan. By reciting the names she had seen on the letters in the place she had been captured, she was trying to save both me and our baby.'

'But her confession and your injury took place the day after the Desrosiers died and at least a hundred miles to the south, so any information she gave was useless.'

'I didn't kill them.' Tears of deliverance fell down her cheeks. 'I didn't,' she repeated, the beauty of what the words implied washing across her like a balm.

'You have both been to hell and back on a lie. But you married her again, Nat, even knowing this?'

'When you love someone, you love them, Hawk, and there would be no argument in the world that would keep me from Cassandra. But this…this allows us peace.'

Standing up, he faced Stephen Hawkhurst. 'I should have tried to find out all that transpired after that day, but I could not. I never wanted to sift through the files and know the betrayal.'

'Yet you kept her name out of everything. I am not

certain, had it been me, that I could have done that. King, country, oaths and all.'

Nathaniel laughed. 'They are all nothing against love, my friend. Wait until you find it.'

Gathering the documents, Stephen replaced them in the book. 'If Shavvon knew I had removed these...' He left the rest unsaid. 'But if I have them back tonight he will never need to know anything of it. He sends you his best, by the way.'

Cassie looked up at her husband and wondered just exactly who this Shavvon was that they were speaking of.

'Our boss,' Nathaniel explained quietly. 'At the Service.'

'But now this case is closed. For good.' Stephen faced them both as he promised this and then he was gone, the documents in hand as the door closed behind him.

'A marriage and a reprieve,' Nat said as he drew Cassandra up against him. 'A binding and a freedom. It has been quite a day, Lady Lindsay.' She could feel his breath against her cheek, soft and known.

'Lady Lindsay. I like the sound of that.'

'My wife. An even better resonance.'

'And what of the marriage night?' she whispered, watching the flare of complicity and question in his pale eyes. 'I think we should celebrate Hawk's gift.'

'I am completely at your disposal, my beautiful *Sandrine*,' he returned, lifting her into his arms and taking her to bed.

Chapter Thirteen

The past week had been a whirlpool of activity. Maureen's delight at her news, her father's quiet pleasure at having three daughters now in advantageous unions and Jamie's thrilled disbelief that the papa he had so often spoken of was promising to buy him a horse when they arrived at St Auburn.

After their wedding Cassandra had been inundated with calling cards, every door into society now open to her, though Nathaniel seemed distracted by his own work with the Service. She confronted him about it late on the third night after their marriage when she had gone down to the library to find him surrounded by papers.

'You look busy.'

'Busy missing some clue that I am certain is right in front of me,' he returned and stood.

'It is the girls from the river and Sarah?'

He nodded. 'Have you ever heard of the name Scrivener Weeks?'

'No. He is the man who you think killed them?'

'I do. I went to Wallingford and discovered that a few months ago another young woman was murdered there. A tall, dark and well-dressed man signed into the tavern late on the night the body was found, using the name of Scrivener Weeks. He left on the London coach early the next morning. No one can truly remember what he looked like.'

'He could be anyone.'

'Not quite. I think he is a member of the Venus Club.'

'Like Uncle Reginald?' Another thought occurred. 'That is why you and Stephen Hawkhurst joined up in the first place?'

He smiled. 'It is easier to keep an eye on people at close quarters. For what it is worth I have discounted your uncle.'

'Why?'

'He was ill with some sort of a chest infection when the girls were found on the riverbank here in London. He has the same physician as Hawkhurst does and the doctor was adamant Reginald Northrup could not have left his sick bed for a fortnight.'

'How many members does the club have?'

'Sixty-eight, and I have a group of thirteen names who fit the description of Scrivener Weeks.'

'We leave for St Auburn tomorrow. Could Stephen Hawkhurst take over until we return?'

'He will. I have told him my thoughts and given him the names. Perhaps he will see something that I have not.'

'Sarah would be thankful to you for your time and effort in finding her killer.'

'I haven't yet.'

'But you will.'

At that she took his hand and led him upstairs.

Late the next afternoon Cassandra could barely believe that they were almost at the principal country seat of the Lindsays, the fields about them rolling and green.

'Will we be there soon, Papa?'

She smiled. Jamie never spoke to Nathaniel without adding on 'Papa'. He had lost four years of his father and now he was making up for it. Sitting on Nathaniel's knee, he looked at the various landmarks that were pointed out.

'I used to swim in that river when I was very young. My father made wooden boats and we would sail them in the summer. Often they got stuck so I would jump in to rescue them.'

'Can you make me a boat, Papa? We could do that, too.'

Cassandra's heart swelled as her husband looked over at her, kissing the top of Jamie's head as he did so. Maureen, Kenyon, Rodney and her father would be arriving the day after tomorrow and she was pleased to have a couple of days to settle in. The only cloud on the horizon was Nathaniel's grandfather for they had not heard a word from him.

'The first sight of the house can be seen past this rise,' Nathaniel said and lifted Jamie higher. Cassie

leaned forward to see it, too, and an enormous Georgian mansion materialised out of the distance, the six pillars across the front edifice flanked by two plainer wings, sitting on a hill. The tree-lined driveway wound towards it, a lake of grand proportions to one side.

'St Auburn is beautiful.' She could not keep the worry from her words.

'And big,' Jamie added.

'It's home,' Nathaniel said and reached for her hand. 'Our home.'

He had placed three of his staff into running the ledgers for the Daughters of the Poor and with his sizeable cash donation Cassie knew that all the work she had done would be left in competent hands. She would still hold regular meetings with Elizabeth and the staff, but the night-time rambles had ended and part of her was glad. This was a new chapter of her life and one she relished.

A line of servants had come out to greet them and there at the front door was an elderly man who Cassie reasoned would be Nathaniel's grandfather. He leaned upon a stick and watched them carefully as the conveyance drew to a halt.

Jamie was out first, the sun on his hair mirroring his father's and a sense of urgency and life on show that he had inherited as well. He looked right at home here, the tall yellow walls behind him with their meticulously pointed stone and inset windows. No small task for the masons, this building would have taken years and years to construct.

The old man came forward, his face devoid of expression. 'You have come back,' he said.

'We have come home,' Jamie cried. 'This is going to be my home now with the lake and boats.'

'Indeed?'

Such curling indifference had the effect of bringing Jamie closer to Nathaniel, fingers entwined in the expensive superfine of his father's trousers.

'William, this is my wife, Cassandra, and my son, Jamie.'

Pale silvered eyes whisked across her, calculating and assessing, and then they travelled over Jamie, the first glimmer of emotion showing.

'Well, at least he looks like a St Auburn. Does he like horses?'

'I have not ever ridden one, sir.'

'Grandpa,' he corrected. 'Call me Grandpa. Your father used to.'

A rebuke coined within the softness of memory. Nathaniel's hand tightened about her own, and Cassie hoped that whatever had gone wrong between them might soon be resolved.

After being introduced to the housekeeper and butler they walked along the line of other lesser servants, each one in a crisp and spotless uniform and all with generous welcomes. Once inside the Lindsay patriarch gestured for them to join him in a salon that ran along the front of the house, a room decorated in blues and greens.

'I was surprised that you finally realised St Auburn to be a duty you could encompass in your busy life,

Nathaniel. Have you had enough of lying around in foreign taverns?'

Her husband's languid smile did not quite reflect his words. 'Protecting England from its enemies requires more than a nominal effort, William, though I do admit to a few drinks.'

Strong brandy to quell the pain of a gunshot wound in his side, but only water a few hours later as she had tried to clean it.

She wanted to say this to an old man who had much to thank his grandson for. She wanted him to see the hero in Nathaniel that she so often saw, a spy who had spent years undercover and in places that had hardly been kind. But she did not say any of this because she had no idea as to whether her husband would thank her for it or not. So she stayed quiet.

'The rooms on the first floor have been made up for you. Dinner will be at eight.'

With that he simply got up and walked away, the tap of his stick on the polished tiles becoming fainter and fainter.

'My grandfather has never been a man to show his feelings. This attitude, I suppose, was the reason my father and mother left here when I was young. They probably got the same sort of welcome we just did.'

'Does he not like us, Papa? Is he angry we are here?'

'No, he loves you, Jamie, but he is old and has gone to his quarters to have a rest.' Pulling his son up into his arms, he turned towards Cassie. 'Shall I show you to our room, my lady?'

'Certainly, my lord.' Suddenly all the politics of

family squabbles did not matter at all. Tonight they would be together in a home that was theirs for good. She couldn't wait for the evening to come.

The chamber Nathaniel led them to was beautiful, with wide French doors leading out to a substantial balcony, pots festooned with greenery and flowers. Like in France, she thought, and looked across at the view. It was majestic. The far-off hills. The lake. The trees. The farm fields that went on and on for ever.

Jamie's room was a little farther down the corridor, flanked by the smaller nanny's quarters and a maid's room. To one side of Jamie's bed a whole row of old wooden toys were arranged on low shelves.

'They were once my father's. William must have instructed the servants to bring them down from the attic.' Nathaniel looked surprised.

'Did you play with them, too?' she asked as Jamie bent to draw a wooden train along the parquet flooring.

'I did. My grandfather was never very keen on the idea, though, for he thought I might break them. Perhaps he trusts you more, Jamie.'

'I will be very careful, Papa.'

'I know you will.'

Nat thought that the smile on Cassandra's face looked tightly drawn. She was obviously shocked by his grandfather's behaviour and by St Auburn, too. Most people on first seeing the place had the same sort of disbelief, but it was one of those houses that

had grown over generations and there had always been plenty of money in the coffers of the Lindsays.

Plenty of money and not a lot of love. William had seen to that. He would get Cassie and Jamie settled and then he would go and find his grandfather. It was one thing for William to be rude to him, but quite another to be contrary with his wife and son. He would simply not put up with it.

But other things began to play on his mind, too. The way the sun slanted in upon Cassie's hair and the beauty of her face in profile. Crossing the room, he brought her close.

'Thank you for coming here with me. I am not sure if I would want to face it alone.'

'I think he is sad, your grandfather. How old were your parents when they died?'

'Thirty-four and twenty-eight.'

'Young, then. Imagine what that must have been like. Did he have a wife?'

'No. Margaret Lindsay died after my father left St Auburn.'

'Two terrible losses. And then the loss of you, as well, to the British Service and the further worry of the only family left to him never coming home.'

He smiled into her hair. 'I was about to go and growl at him. Now I am not so certain I should.' Nat had seen William's lack of feeling in terms of his own grief when he had lost his parents, but with Cassie's words a different understanding dawned. Imagine if he were to lose both her and Jamie. Would he still be able to function? He doubted it. Across her shoulders his son played with

his new toys and beyond that again through the window the great lands of St Auburn spread out before him.

Home.

Here.

In Cassandra's arms, the scent of violets and woman and the promise of the passionate hours of night not far off.

'If this doesn't work we don't have to stay. There are plenty of other Lindsay properties.'

'But there is only one great-grandfather, Nathaniel, and Jamie needs to know him.'

Dinner that evening was a myriad of different emotions: William's distance, Cassandra's wariness and Nathaniel's equanimity. The room itself was beautiful with its carved table and tapestried chairs. On the wall around them were paintings from ground to ceiling displaying the images of relatives long dead. Their facial expressions looked about as happy as William's did as he sat at one end of the table.

'It is strange that you did not bring your family up to meet me sooner, Nathaniel.'

'We were married in France almost five years ago, but lost one another soon after. We resaid our vows a week ago.'

That brought a light to the old Earl's eyes and for the first time that evening a gleam of interest showed.

'There was a battle and a misunderstanding. I thought Cassandra had perished and she thought that I had, too. We met again only a handful of weeks ago by chance.'

'So you did not know your son?"

'I didn't.'

'He looks exactly as you did when you were that age. I should have some likenesses that were drawn at the time somewhere if you want to see them.' This was addressed at her.

'I should love to, my lord.'

'I will have them found tomorrow. There are other things, too, that I remember, a swing and a slide and a small rocking horse. Did he enjoy the toys in his room?'

Nat cleared his throat. 'He did. Thank you for thinking of it.'

'The boy and his mother can come with me on the morrow and we will go exploring for the rest of the toys that you and your father used to play with.'

A generous allowance and the first step into a truce from the battle of wits that Nathaniel and his grandfather seemed to be playing. Cassandra hoped that there would be many more across the next few days and weeks.

Much later Nathaniel and Cassandra lay in bed, holding each other and listening to the sound of a large house settling for the night: a clock in a distant hallway ringing out the lateness, the last swish of a maid's skirt as she went by on the final errands of the evening and a log in the fire shifting into a quieter burn. Jamie was fast asleep in his room. Nathaniel had tucked him in, all the love and concern of a father who wanted to savour the small moments he had so far missed in his care.

An hour earlier Nat had lifted her up in his arms,

too, and placed her on his bed, positioning the frothy nothingness of her lacy nightgown just so.

'You cannot know how much I have longed for this moment, Cassie. To see you here at St Auburn as my wife.' He clasped her hand and turned the wedding ring that he'd had resized in London. 'We have done everything so far all the wrong way around. But from now on I mean to get it right.'

She shook her head. 'You have, my darling, all the way through. Ever since you first found me and took me out of Nay with a bullet hole in your side.'

Standing naked in the half-light of the fire, he looked like a large, strong panther, circling for all that she might give him, muscles shadowed and harsh. The tattoo stood out as did the white scars of battle. Her knight. Her hero.

Opening her arms, she brought him against her. This was the bed and the room that they would live in together for all the rest of their lives. When tears welled in her eyes and spilled down her cheeks, he pulled back in question.

'It is happiness, Nathaniel, only that.'

His forefinger came up to gently wipe away the moisture. 'I will love you for ever, Cassandra Sandrine Mercier Northrup.' The troth was given with a solemn honesty before his mouth closed down on hers.

The belltower attic was a place of wonder, a high-beamed room of generous proportion and a thousand forgotten things in it. With a new morning the old Earl seemed more fleet footed despite needing to manoeu-

vre around rolls of material and piles of papers. The toys were stacked on large, low shelves, numerous versions of balls and trains and soldiers and forts. One look at Jamie's face told her that they might be here a while.

'I like the big train best, Grandpa.'

The word *grandpa* seemed to sink into the deep lines of his face and flatten them out. 'I think if I look there are tracks for it somewhere.'

Cassie glanced around. 'I am sure Jamie feels as if all his Christmas days have come at once.'

'I think he may deserve it. Three years without a father is a long time.'

'Almost four,' she said quietly. 'His birthday is soon.'

They were interrupted by a squeal of delight. 'Look, Grandpa, look what it can do.' He pulled the string behind the head of a large wooden puppet and the garish mouth opened to reveal a full set of yellowing teeth.

'That used to be my favourite, too,' William replied, bringing a large white kerchief from his pocket to dab at his eyes. As Jamie continued to explore, William started to speak of the past. 'Nathaniel is very like his father was, and forgiveness is not an easily won thing. When Geoffrey died, a part of me did, too, and I lost the little piece of him that I still had left in Nathaniel. Now it might be too late to find each other again.'

Cassie shook her head. 'Family should always be forgiven no matter what happens between them, for

blood is thicker than insult or misconception. It only takes honesty.'

He smiled. 'My grandson was indeed lucky to find you.'

'He rescued me from a desperate situation and he did not judge me as he could so easily have done. His job there in France was a hard and dangerous one and if he hadn't come when he did...' She stopped, the horror of what might have been evident. 'England is fortunate to have someone like your grandson protecting its interests, and you should be proud that he carries your family name with such honour. I know I am.'

'I should have known, of course, for Geoffrey was a good man, too. It was just after my wife passed on that I felt so marooned and lost, and in my sorrow the happiness of my son's family gave me no relief. I pushed them away and never got them back.'

'Nathaniel did not come here to St Auburn again?'

'Oh, indeed, he did for a time after his parents died but by then we were set in our distance from each other and we barely talked. Later he wanted to modernise the place and I was determined to leave things as they were. After a while he hardly ever came home.'

'Well, we are here to stay now, and you will have all the chance in the world to talk with him. If you told him what you have just told me...'

She stopped as he nodded his head, and Jamie came up to him with a small boat complete with sails and ropes in his hands.

'Papa spoke about this in the carriage.'

'He did?' William took the craft and turned it this

way and that. 'Your father's father made this, Jamie. If you bring it down we might be able to have a try at sailing the craft on the lake.'

'I will jump in and rescue it if it gets stuck, Grandpa.'

'Then we certainly have a deal.'

Maureen, Kenyon, Rodney and Lord Cowper arrived in the middle of the following morning, her uncle Reginald and his friend Christopher Hanley unexpectedly behind them in another conveyance. Nathaniel looked less than happy with the new arrivals as she glanced up at him. Something seemed wrong.

'I saw your father in London yesterday,' Reginald explained when the carriage stopped, 'and told him of my plans to head to the coast. When he asked if I would like to call in here at St Auburn for an hour or two, I was most grateful. I hope having Hanley here, too, will not upset anyone.'

The old earl looked about as pleased as Nathaniel did, and the arrival of Stephen Hawkhurst seemed to heighten the awkwardness yet again. Cassandra did not fail to see the look that went between her husband and his friend as they turned inside, and the tension seemed to emanate from the presence of Christopher Hanley.

Christopher Hanley sought her out an hour later as drinks and a light repast were being served in the front salon.

'You will not be so involved with your charity from now on, I suppose, Lady Lindsay? Being here should take up much of your time.'

'No, in that you are wrong. I shall be as busy with it as I ever was, and London is not far.'

'Was there ever any sign of Sarah Milgrew and her sister's killer?'

'No, nothing, though we are still hopeful of finding some clue to help us.'

'Your father continues to fund the Daughters of the Poor, then?'

'Indeed he does, and Nathaniel is involved, too. My husband has brought Stephen Hawkhurst in for added assistance.'

Hawk watched them now, Cassie saw, his eyes devouring Hanley's stance and face and a small worm of uneasiness turned in her stomach. Something wasn't right, but she could not quite put her finger upon it. She was pleased when her uncle came to claim his friend in conversation, allowing her to move away.

'You look worried.' William had joined her over by the windows. 'I knew Hanley's parents and they were not a happy couple. The father had a way with women of the night and the mother ran off with an Italian merchant and never returned to England.'

'A difficult upbringing for him, then?' Nathaniel had heard the last of the conversation as he came up behind her.

'You have had dealings with him?' William sounded interested in his grandson's answer.

'He has the unfortunate habit of poking his nose in other people's business. Suffice it to say he did Cassandra and me a favour in Whitechapel, but it could have been different.'

Uncle Reginald seemed to be making much of conversing with her father and for the first time in months Papa appeared happy. She supposed she should overlook the presence of the others here for an hour or two for it was good to see Papa smiling.

When Kenyon asked Nathaniel for a tour of the grounds of St Auburn everyone decided to go with them. Outside the sky was blue and the sun warm, and having partaken of food and drink a small exercise was desirable. Cassie was interested to see how Nathaniel shepherded Hanley, in particular, out through the front door.

Jamie was fractious though with all the excitement and so Cassie decided to stay back with him. A rest might see him through the afternoon pursuits and then he could have an early bedtime.

Bedtime.

She wished it were later already and that the hour to retire was here. Catching Nathaniel's eyes, she saw he watched her mount the stairs and she blushed with the warmth of his observance. Would there ever be a time when she could stand on the other side of a room fully dressed and in the company of others and not feel...desperate for him? She hoped not.

William, too, had decided to stay indoors because he found the heat oppressive. Concern marred Cassie's happiness. She prayed he would stay well and healthy enough to be a part of their family celebrations and outings for many years to come. They had only just found him again, after all, and underneath the gruff exterior was a man with a soft heart.

* * *

Half an hour later, sitting next to her sleeping son and thinking about her day, a new thought surfaced. Christopher Hanley had mentioned something about Sarah Milgrew, and Cassie sought to remember his words exactly.

He had asked about Sarah and her sister's killer. She sat forward, trying to pinpoint her uneasiness. The sister? Horror filled her. How had he known anything about Sarah's sister? The police themselves had not mentioned this and there had never been an identification carried out on the bodies of the earlier victims.

Oh, granted, Sarah had spoken of her sister's disappearance and Nathaniel had been interested in the gown of one of the drowned girls, but there had been no other information offered. Besides, the note that had arrived for Sarah the day she had disappeared alluded to information about knowing the whereabouts of her sibling, not the demise of her.

'My God.'

Standing, she indicated to a maid outside in the corridor to come in and sit with Jamie. Christopher Hanley was the tall, dark and well-dressed man. She was suddenly sure of it. He had been in Brown Street off Whitechapel Road when Nathaniel and she had found the body in the brothel, and the toff seen at the St Katharine Docks matched his description exactly.

Peering out the window on the stairwell, she noticed the group with Nathaniel to be perusing the formal gardens, but she could not see Christopher Hanley with them.

Fright made her heart beat faster as she hurried towards the front door. She had to get to Nathaniel to tell him what she suspected.

She had almost come into the wide hallway when a voice stopped her.

'I had a feeling I should return.' The sound came from behind and with all the effort in the world Cassandra made herself turn. She barely recognised the urbane and civilised lord, a sneer on his face and cold outrage in his eyes. Fear congealed in her throat and she could not hide her fright. 'I made a mistake talking to you earlier and I can see that you picked up on it.' Hanley's voice lacked any remorse whatsoever.

'You killed Sarah Milgrew and her sister. Why?' An explanation might buy her some moments for surely Nathaniel would be returning soon.

'They knew who I was. I thought after the first one I was safe and then the second girl turned up. I had killed their cousin in Wallingford, you see, and they remembered me.'

'And the man who was found dead at Brown Street?'

'Had come to London at the behest of their father to ask around and find out what had happened to the older sister. I couldn't let him ruin things.'

'So you tried to ruin me instead. It was you who sent the note asking me to come to the boarding house.'

'A miscalculation, I was to think later, for I did not realise that you knew Lindsay so well. Without him there, I might have succeeded. When he visited me in London the other day I knew by his questions that he suspected something.'

'Yet you still came to St Auburn?'

'To find out the lay of the land, Lady Lindsay.'

At that he moved forward and simply twisted her arm hard up behind her back. 'If you shout out, I will go straight up to your son's room and break his neck, do you understand? Like a chicken in a hen house. You or him. Make your choice.'

Fear ripped resistance into pieces. Cassie would wait till they were outside before trying to flee. Nodding, she went with him, past the first door and then the second, no servant in sight, the coast clear for his escape.

The third door was different. William Lindsay, the old Earl of St Auburn, was waiting in all readiness and with a shout he raised his cane and brought it down hard upon Hanley's head before falling.

The ungainly upending might have saved all their lives, she was to think later, for William took a sideboard full of bottles and glasses down with him and the noise was enough to wake up the dead. Blood dripped down into his closed eyes and Cassandra was certain that he had broken every bone in his body.

Hanley did not waver, finding an open window in the next salon and pushing her through it headfirst where she landed heavily onto an uneven brick wall and lost her breath.

'With you out of the way my secret will be safe and a quick escape to France will see to my own future.'

Shock had made him shake, and she felt his wrath course through her as he dragged her into the bushes surrounding the lake. Without hesitation, he pushed her into the water.

Icy coldness settled quickly.

Then his hands were about her throat, squeezing and squeezing. She tried to fight, she did, tried to stop him as the green of the water closed over her head, but already the world had begun to narrow into darkness. Sharp rocks dug into her back.

Floating. Peacefulness. The last release of bubbles as the warmth of death became brighter.

Then there was a noise, a hard punch and scream and a further whip of knuckles. The grip about her throat released and Cassie was lifted gently from the cold to be brought up into the arms of her husband where he cradled her against his warmth.

'It is all right, my love. You are safe.'

She was coughing, long, deep gasps of coughing, the air hard to find and the cold making it harder again. Her throat ached and her back had been bruised as Hanley had forced her down, but she was alive.

Alive.

Then she was crying, huge throaty sobs, her hands entwined in the fabric of his jacket.

'Your…gr-gr-grandfather tr-tried to s-save me.'

'I know, sweetheart. Don't try to talk just now. I will take you back to the house and a bath will be drawn.'

A bath. Warmth. She gritted her teeth together to try to stop the dreadful shaking and felt the heat from his skin beneath her cheek.

Nat lifted Cassie, making certain that he averted his gaze from the dark red bruises that were gouged into her throat and from the cut beneath her eye. If Han-

ley had not been unconscious, he would have hit him
yet again. Her hair was tangled with weed from the
lake, the mud at the bottom smeared across her face
and shoulders.

So damn close.

Another moment and they could not have saved her.
He looked over at his grandfather, worse for wear from
his upending, and saw the same thoughts in the opaque
eyes. With a smile, he bent his head. In homage and in
gratitude. Without William's quick-thinking actions...?

He shook away the horror.

Cassie was still crying, but her sobs were softer now.
Her breathing had eased a little, too, and the pale white
of her skin was rosier.

Her colour was returning and her fright receding.
He was glad Kenyon was there to help his grandfather
walk, the back of his head already showing signs of
a bruised swelling. Maureen had taken his other side
and she was speaking to him in the quiet and restful
tones of one who seldom panicked.

A family that would be there for each other when the
times got tough. A group of people joined by blood and
love. He kissed his wife's cold forehead as he strode
up the steps of St Auburn and the startled servants
came running.

He found his grandfather in the library an hour later,
sitting and looking out of the window with a heavy
bandage around his head.

'William.' Today the word did not sit upon his

tongue with the ease that it always had. 'Grandfather,' he amended and saw the old man turn.

'Is your wife recovered?'

'She is having a hot bath. The maids are with her and the warmth will stop the chills.'

'And Hanley?'

'Hawk has taken him back to London where he will be dealt with.'

'I would kill him if it were left to me.'

The sentiment made Nat smile. 'In that we are alike.'

'Are we?'

This time Nathaniel knew it was something else entirely of which William spoke. 'You never wanted my mother and father anywhere near you. You sent them from St Auburn and refused to ever see them again.'

'My Margaret had just died. I was not thinking straight and afterwards...' He hesitated. 'Afterwards it was too late. But now I see what I have missed.'

'You saved Cassandra. Without your bravery Hanley might have drowned her without a whisper.'

The earl shook his head. 'I hit him as hard as I could and it barely touched him.'

'But the noise when you fell alerted us. I owe you everything.'

His grandfather used his cane and came to stand next to Nat. 'We are both hard-headed and stubborn, Nathaniel, and we both love our wives with all our hearts.' The old eyes were watery as he placed his hand forward palm up. 'And our children.'

Pleading lay in the gesture. For family, it said, and for forgiveness, it asked.

Stepping forward, Nat brought his grandfather into his arms, tightly wrapped in an emotion that he had thought would be impossible.

'Thank you for saving her, Grandfather.'

'It was my pleasure, Nathaniel. And thank you, too, for saving me.'

Chapter Fourteen

She was wrapped in the warmth of wool and settled onto the generous blue sofa in the downstairs parlour.

Cassandra had had her hair washed and her body powdered and her feet were swathed in slippers of the finest lambswool, a present from William and one he had bought for his wife just before she had died.

She felt blessed. Jamie was cuddled into her side, and Nathaniel sat on a leather chair only a few feet away.

'If you had not been there, Grandfather, this could have all turned out far differently.' Her husband's words held a reverence and respect that was heartwarming.

'Which just goes to show that there is life in the old boy yet.' She saw William's hand rest lightly on Nathaniel's shoulder. They had spoken privately, she knew, before coming downstairs and the feud that had parted them seemed all but gone.

Reginald also had turned out to be a surprise. He had offered Cassandra a more than generous amount

to be put into the coffers of the Daughters of the Poor plus the free use of a property that he owned in Aldwych as a place to set up further employment. Compensation for his poor choice of friends, he had told everyone. He had also decided to leave the Venus Club.

When Cassie glanced over at Nathaniel she saw that he was watching her closely.

'Good things come out of bad,' he said and smiled, though when his eyes settled on the marks at her throat an edge of anger was still visible.

Protection. It was so very relaxing. She closed her eyes and slept.

Much later when she awoke she found that she was back in their own chamber, but Nathaniel was not in bed with her. He stood at the window, looking over the land of the Lindsays, a moon hanging in the sky. The calmness that was so much a part of him made her smile and she simply watched.

'You cannot sleep, Nathaniel?'

The effects of the toddy the housekeeper had made for her had almost worn off now, and Cassie felt as if the shadows and mirrors she had lived with all her life had been thrown away somehow, the strong lines of hope exposed by love instead.

'I could not live if you left me, Sandrine. I could not find a way to keep on going. Today when I thought...' His voice broke, and he turned away, but not before she saw the moisture on his cheeks and the terror in his eyes. 'I never slept with another woman after Perpignan. It has always been just you.'

Pushing back the covers, she joined him at the window, winding her arms about his coldness and infusing warmth.

'Love holds no barriers, my darling. Time. Distance. Space. They are just words against love. We will always be together because we will always love.'

'Do you promise?'

'Come to bed and I will show you how I know,' she whispered, the heat of ardour rising. 'Let me take you to a place that is only ours.'

'Like the memory of the high baths above Bagnères-de-Bigorre?'

She nodded and, taking his arm, led him back to the warm nest of their bed.

As often thro' the purple night,
Below the starry clusters bright,
Some bearded meteor trailing light,
Moves over still Shalott.

* * * * *

REQUEST YOUR FREE BOOKS!

 HARLEQUIN® HISTORICAL:
Where love is timeless

2 FREE NOVELS PLUS 2 FREE GIFTS!

Next month, follow A LADY OF NOTORIETY
by Diane Gaston and feel the heat rise as
Lady Daphne Faville and Hugh Westleigh find burning
passion in each other's touch...

The warmth of her body against his, the scent of roses that always clung to her, her low, brandy-soaked voice all intoxicated him as much as the brandy had intoxicated her. At this moment he did not wish friendship from her, but something more. Something between lovers.

He resisted the impulse, but he did not release her. "I will bid you a friendly good-night, then."

He placed his cane against the wall and searched for her face. Touching her cheek and cupping it in the palm of his hand, he leaned down until he felt her breath on his face. He lowered his face and touched his lips to hers, slightly off-kilter. He quickly made the correction and kissed her, as a man kisses a woman when desire surges within him.

"Mmm." She twined her hands around his neck and gave herself totally to the kiss.

He was acutely aware of her every curve touching his body. His hand could not resist sliding up her side and cupping her breast, her full, high breast. He rubbed his fingers against this treasure and she pressed herself against him, her fingers caressing the back of his neck.

He wanted to take her there in the hallway, plunge himself into her against the door to her bedchamber. She would be willing. Never had a woman seemed more willing.

"Daphne," he whispered.

Some rational part of him heard footsteps on the stairs.

"Someone is coming." He eased her away from him. "We had better say good-night before we do something two friends might regret."

"I wouldn't regret it, Hugh!" She tried to renew the embrace.

"Not now." He pushed her away gently.

The footsteps were coming closer, nearly at the top of the stairs, he guessed. He opened her door and picked up his cane.

"Oh, madame!" an accented voice said. "I—I have come to assist you. If—if I do not disturb you."

"You must be Monette," Hugh said. "I have walked Mrs. Asher to her room. She is a bit unsteady."

He heard Monette rush over to her. "Madame! Are you ill?"

"Not ill," Daphne said. "Feel wonderful. Am dizzy, though."

"She drank some brandy," Hugh explained. "Without realizing the effects."

"*Je comprends,* sir," Monette said. "I will take care of her."

He felt the two women move past him and walk through the doorway. The door closed behind them and Hugh was left to find his own way back to his bedchamber to await Carter's assistance to ready himself for bed.

Sleeping would be difficult this night, he feared.

*Don't miss
A LADY OF NOTORIETY,
available from Harlequin® Historical
July 2014.*

HARLEQUIN®

ℌISTORICAL

Where love is timeless

COMING IN JULY 2014

Rebel Outlaw
by Carol Arens

Looking for peace, finding...trouble

Colt Wesson Travers is headed for a life of tranquillity in Texas.
Here, he'll finally escape the obligations demanded by his
notorious outlaw family.

But when he meets his stubborn lodger Holly Jane Munroe, his
illusions of peace are shattered. Colt is thrown right into the
middle of two feuding families intent on winning Holly Jane's
hand...and her grandfather's land! He quickly realizes that life
with delicious Holly Jane is going to be anything but quiet....

Available wherever books and ebooks are sold.

HH29791

Love the Harlequin book you just read?

Your opinion matters.

Review this book on your favorite book site, review site, blog or your own social media properties and share your opinion with other readers!